'Warm, witty and wise'
Daily Mail

'Likeable, funny and relatable'
Heat

...is hilarious book will sweep you up in its sheer
brilliance'
Marie Claire

'Feisty and fabulous'
Milly Johnson

'Pure joy!'
Katie Fforde

'Laugh out loud'
Adele Parks

'Guaranteed to put a smile on your face'
Debbie Johnson

'Just the pick-me-up I needed!'
Jo Thomas

'Hilarious! A must-read for anyone who's ever been
on the wrong side of a relationship'
Coleen Nolan

'Warm, and extremely funny'
Reels and Reads

'Uplifting, life-affirming, and most of all funny'
Bee Reads

Readers' five-star love for Tracy Bloom

'So, so, so funny, I genuinely laughed out loud'

'No doubt about it . . . at least a 6 out of 5!'

'Peppered with fantastically humorous episodes . . . a joy'

'It wasn't long before I was so engrossed in it that I couldn't put it down'

'Funny, totally relatable and made me laugh out loud'

'Tracy Bloom has the lightest of touches with the deepest of understanding'

'Where has [Tracy Bloom] been all my life'

'I really loved this book, so funny and life-affirming'

'Hilarious, touching and really laugh out loud!!'

'A fab read which you don't want to put down'

'Just like catching up with a good friend'

'Utterly brilliant'

'Great story not least because it made me realize I'm not alone'

The
Weekend
Before the
Wedding

Tracy started writing when her cruel, heartless husband ripped her away from her dream job – shopping for rollercoasters for the UK's leading theme parks – to live in America with a brand new baby and no mates. In a cunning plan to avoid domestic duties and people who didn't understand her Derbyshire accent, she wrote *No One Ever Has Sex on a Tuesday*. It went on to become a No. 1 bestseller and publishing phenomenon. Since then, Tracy has written many more novels and been published successfully around the world. She now lives back home in Derbyshire with her husband and children.

To keep in touch with Tracy, visit her website and follow her on social media.

www.tracybloom.com
🐦 @TracyBBloom
f @tracybloomwrites

Also by Tracy Bloom

Single Woman Seeks Revenge
I Will Marry George Clooney (By Christmas)
Strictly My Husband
The Last Laugh
Dinner Party
The Wife Who Got a Life

No-one Ever Has Sex series
No-one Ever Has Sex on a Tuesday
No-one Ever Has Sex in the Suburbs
No-one Ever Has Sex on Christmas Day
No-one Ever Has Sex at a Wedding
No-one Ever Has Sex on Holiday

TRACY BLOOM

The Weekend Before the Wedding

HarperCollins*Publishers*

HarperCollins*Publishers* Ltd
1 London Bridge Street,
London SE1 9GF

www.harpercollins.co.uk

HarperCollins*Publishers*
1st Floor, Watermarque Building, Ringsend Road
Dublin 4, Ireland

First published by HarperCollins*Publishers* 2022
1

A catalogue record for this book is available from the British Library

ISBN: 978-0-00-843431-1

This novel is entirely a work of fiction.
The names, characters and incidents portrayed in it are
the work of the author's imagination. Any resemblance to
actual persons, living or dead, events or localities is
entirely coincidental.

Typeset in Sabon LT Std by
Palimpsest Book Production Ltd, Falkirk, Stirlingshire

Printed and bound in the UK using 100% Renewable Electricity by CPI
Group (UK) Ltd

This book is produced from independently certified FSC™ paper to ensure
responsible forest management.

For more information visit: www.harpercollins.co.uk/green

For my sister, Helen.
Thank you for being the best sister anyone could have.

And thank you for organizing my hen weekend nearly seventeen years ago.
I'm so sorry.
It really is the worst job.
Hopefully you will never have to do it again!

Chapter 1

Present day

Is there any more terrifying moment in a woman's life than when she looks in the mirror for the first time on her wedding day? Dress on, make-up done and hair primped.

It really could go either way, couldn't it? Elation that actually, yes, you look the best you ever have on the very day that you absolutely must look the best you ever have, or, total disappointment that the miracle didn't happen. The application of ivory satin and professional beauty-makers did not turn you into the swan that you wanted to be on the most important day of your life.

Shelley held her breath as she turned round to face the full-length mirror in her childhood bedroom. After all, she had waited a very long time for this moment. She looked herself up and down. She was very happy to see that the floor-length ivory dress did fit like a glove and that the pure white fake-fur stole draped flatteringly around her shoulders. So far so good. Looking up at her hair, she was pleased she had been convinced to have an up-do because, after all, even a bride who was nearly six foot tall needed to have a princess hairdo on her wedding day.

Yes, just for a moment she looked everything that she wanted to be. Bridal, feminine, and yes, maybe even beautiful. Finding someone to love and who genuinely loved her back had done wonders for how Shelley now viewed her crazy auburn curls, her long, gangly frame and her splattering of freckles. And of course she was wearing the one essential item that every bride must have on her wedding day in order to transform the total picture. Something so much more important than the traditional superstitions of something old, something new, something borrowed, something blue. She was wearing a beaming smile. In fact, she glowed with happiness, which shone from her eyes and lit up her whole being.

She'd take happy over standard beautiful any day of the week, she thought. Especially today. Her long-awaited wedding day.

'And who are you wearing?' she said into her bouquet, as if she were being interviewed on the red carpet.

'Today I'm wearing "happy",' she replied to the mirror. 'It's my favourite designer.'

'Well, it looks spectacular on you,' the pretend interviewer replied.

Shelley smiled wryly to herself. She wondered if she would have been wearing 'happy' if she'd got married when she was first supposed to have, nearly twenty years ago. She very much doubted it. The thought stopped her in her tracks and quickly brought a tear to her eye, which trickled down her perfectly blushed cheek. She automatically put her hand up to her face to brush it away, forgetting she was wearing pure white gloves.

She looked down. Pure white gloves now smeared with foundation and mascara. She looked back in the mirror. Mascara streaked down her cheek. She sighed. She'd looked pretty good for just a few minutes there. Not bad going.

'Come on then,' said her mother, Peggy, entering the room. She reached around her to pull out her veil then looked at her daughter. 'We need to get going if we're not going to be late. Oh, my goodness – you look . . . you look . . . lovely, but . . .'

'I know,' said Shelley, 'I need Becca to come in and touch up my make-up. I had a bit of a malfunction.'

Peggy peered at her closely then cocked her head to one side as a look of concern spread over her face.

'Have you been crying?' she asked.

'Not really,' she replied. 'I was just thinking that I would never have been this happy had I got married the first time around. Made me a bit emotional, that's all.'

Peggy smiled and shook her head, causing the feathery arrangement balancing in her hair to bobble about. Shelley took in Peggy's wedding-day look and sighed. At eighty-one, her petite mother somehow still managed to have a crazily good figure, which Shelley longed to have inherited, rather than her father's height and flat chest.

'You look gorgeous, Mum,' Shelley told her. This was a fact, but Shelley was also fishing for more compliments for herself if she was totally honest.

3

'You've never looked better,' said Peggy with a smile.

Shelley waited.

'If only your make-up wasn't halfway down your face.'

'Not bad,' grinned Shelley. 'But you really should have stopped at "you've never looked better".'

Peggy laughed and Shelley could have sworn she saw the faint glistening of a tear emerge at the corner of her mother's eye. 'I'm just delighted to finally see you in a wedding dress after all this time,' her mum told her.

'Well, I needed to be absolutely certain, didn't I?' replied Shelley. 'After all, it's only taken me nearly twenty years since we first met to make my mind up.'

'I've even forgotten how you did meet?' said Peggy, screwing her face up in deep thought. 'It's so long ago since this whole saga started.'

Her mum was not wrong. Shelley deciding to get married was indeed a saga. A saga that had lasted a very long time and had taken many twists and turns.

'We met at a wedding, of course! Don't you remember? What was her name? Claire, was it? My teaching assistant. Still don't really understand why she invited me. Never thought for one moment when I walked into that ridiculously posh mansion that I was about to meet my future husband. I totally expected to be the bridesmaid out of *Four Weddings and a Funeral* who moans about never having sex at a wedding. Apart from the fact that she did, of course, and I didn't.'

'Didn't you?' asked Peggy, raising her eyebrows.

'Of course not,' said Shelley. 'I would never have slept with someone at a wedding in my thirties. Such a cliché.'

4

'You did go to an awful lot of weddings back then,' stated Peggy.

Shelley shook her head. 'Even if I'd have wanted to, there was no way I had the confidence back then to chat someone up at a wedding.'

Peggy looked at her. 'As I recall you were desperate. To get married, I mean.'

'I was thirty-eight!' remarked Shelley. 'Of course I was desperate. *All* my friends were married *and* had kids. Don't you remember? To be honest, I nearly didn't go to that wedding. Couldn't face watching someone else walk down the aisle when I was nowhere near. God, I hated my thirties. Far, far too many weddings.'

Chapter 2

Priory Hall, Hampshire

May 1999

'Bloody hell,' whistled Shelley as she walked into the Grand Ballroom of Priory Hall to witness the wedding of Claire Elizabeth Grogan and Hugo William Gifford. Maybe she should have bought a new outfit? Her Dorothy Perkins lacy, lilac knee-length number which had stood her in good stead for at least three weddings might not be up to the high standard set by the opulent surroundings. Thank goodness she'd decided to battle with putting the tiny excuse for a hat, with its huge lilac feather, onto her mop of frizzy curls. It had made her swear – a lot – as her out of control hair repeatedly rejected the plastic comb which held it in place but she was glad she had persevered as this clearly was a hat-level wedding.

Claire must have hunted high and low for this location, she thought, given hardly anywhere had approval to hold civil ceremonies. The room was enormous, easily as much floor space as most churches, and its high ceiling did indeed give it an ecclesiastical air.

A red carpet ran down the middle of the room with chairs lined up on either side. Beautiful bouquets of white roses attached to the end of each row created a stunning aisle for the happy couple to walk down towards the registrar's lectern, which was situated at the bottom of a sweeping stairway. Shelley could hear a very familiar tune playing in the background and, looking up, she spotted a minstrels' gallery containing a string quartet playing their hearts out to – what was it? Oh yes, of course it was, 'Love Is All Around', the ubiquitous song from *Four Weddings and a Funeral* that had been constantly playing on the radio ever since 1994, reminding her cruelly that she really should have got married by now.

She looked round, half expecting to see Hugh Grant skulking somewhere, or even better James Fleet, who played Hugh's bumbling mate Tom. The one who was tall and lanky and trod in cow-shit. If she met someone like that at a wedding, she thought she stood half a chance maybe. At thirty-eight and still single, she'd take anything quite frankly. The feint whiff of cow-shit she could easily overlook. To paraphrase the words of the equally desperate Tom in the film, all she was hoping for was to meet some nice, friendly boy that she liked the look of, hoping that the look of her didn't make him physically sick. Not that meeting someone at a wedding ever seemed to work out for her. She reckoned she'd been to at least twenty weddings since she turned thirty, some with a boyfriend in tow, but at a fair few she'd been single. She'd spotted a few male options across a noisy hotel function room in her time but she wasn't the type to have the guts to approach them.

Weddings more recently had merely become a rather torturous process to get through, as she watched other people get on with their lives as hers stayed absolutely still. She'd actually thought about wimping out of this one that very morning. She couldn't think of anything worse than being single at a wedding at the age of thirty-eight. Even worse, a wedding to which she had no idea why she had been invited. Claire, her teaching assistant, had always been quite irritating. Always showing off about her amazing weekends with her 'loaded' boyfriend. Shelley just smiled and nodded politely – too politely as it turned out. Clearly, she hadn't sent the message out clearly enough that actually she wasn't that keen on Claire and her obsession with status and money. Perhaps if she had been less friendly, then she might not have been invited to the wedding and she could be home right now watching *SMTV Live* and trying to guess Wonkey Donkey. Instead, she was at the wedding of someone she barely knew, who wasn't even thirty yet, surrounded by strangers. Just wrong. All wrong.

At least she wasn't totally alone. Claire had also mysteriously invited the headmaster and his wife, Mr and Mrs Donaldson. They looked equally startled to be included, but happy to have a day out with two free meals and the chance to have a good gawp at the opulent surroundings of Priory Hall.

'Bride or groom?' a man in coat-tails asked whilst Shelley tried to not look like a fish out of water. She automatically stooped down to reply; the man couldn't have been more than five foot five and, at nearly six foot, Shelley towered above him.

'Bride,' she replied.

'Thought so,' he said, and pointed to the noisy, more colourful side of the room. Shelley realized there was some kind of class divide going on. Those on Claire's side were loudly chatting, chairs already askew, children playing in the aisle, whilst the groom's side were much more orderly and in some seriously expensive-looking gear. Shelley had no doubt there would be some killer sideways glances heading across the aisle during this wedding.

Shelley and Mr and Mrs Donaldson headed for the seats on the back row of the bride's side. They were well aware that they were very much on the fringes of this wedding; they knew their place. Shelley settled herself down, pushed the feather on her hat out of her eyes for the fiftieth time, thought about how long it would be before she could take her shoes off, and prepared herself to watch yet another bride live her happily ever after.

After the ceremony had finished and the three of them had hovered awkwardly in the 'Library' for a long time trying to catch the eye of the waiters floating around with trays of bubbly and orange juice, they decided they should go and check out the seating arrangements for the wedding breakfast. Shelley braced herself for sitting at a table full of random people, probably right at the back near the toilets, but nowhere near the top table. Thank goodness.

'I can't see my name,' she muttered when she survey-ed the framed seating plan resting on a large easel outside the dining room. She'd gone straight to the bottom of the large board and was scanning wildly. Her heart sank. What if she had been forgotten? What if she wasn't on the plan? What would she do? Hide in the toilets for five hours? Go and tell Claire and cause a major trauma on her most important day? Find a member of staff and try and prove that she was a bona fide guest and they had to squeeze her on somewhere? This was a wedding hell of epic proportions. She should just leave now.

'There you are, look,' said Mrs Donaldson pointing way too far up the sheet. 'Check you out. Right next to the top table.'

Couldn't be, thought Shelley, looking up. No way. I'm an add-on. An also-ran. Clearly someone had dropped out and she was just there as a filler to avoid a meal going to waste. She had to be. They hadn't even offered her the option of a plus one, which in her book meant she was only there to eat a meal destined for someone else. Either that, or Claire didn't think she was capable of finding a plus one to go with, which was a thought too depressing to even contemplate. There must be some mistake. But there she was amidst a sea of strangers. Nowhere near Mr and Mrs Donaldson, her only allies. This was just cruel. Heartless, if she was honest. When she got back to work, she would be making Claire do the twenty million small child toilet runs that typically filled a day in primary school.

She looked again at the list of people she would have to share the longest meal on earth with. There were two double-barrelleds. Jesus, she thought. What would she do with that? Christ, she hoped they weren't sitting next to her. She could draw no further conclusions from the other names. A random collection of surnames, so not all married, thank goodness. Probably all couples, though, in some form. This really was going to be absolute torture.

Shelley entered the dining room as though she were walking to the gallows. She ran through wedding etiquette in her head just to prepare herself for not making a fool of herself.

Don't sit down first – wait for the bride and groom to arrive and be seated. Despite the fact your shoes are crippling you and if they hadn't taken so long over the photos, you could be sitting down and on dessert by now.

Don't help yourself to the wine on the table – the waiters will pour it. Despite the fact you desperately need a drink because the waiters ignored you with the free buck's fizz, and you did not dare go to the bar because you didn't want to buy a round as it was bound to cost a fortune in this place.

Don't help yourself to the bread rolls – makes you look greedy in front of people you have never met before, even though you will more than likely never see them again. And even though you haven't eaten anything for eight hours because, well, it's a wedding day and that seems to always require the guests to starve themselves due to an awkwardly timed ceremony and a very late meal.

Keep your hat on – despite the fact it itches like hell and you are too hot and at every other meal you ever attend it is rude to wear a hat whilst eating but at a wedding it is seen as the height of politeness.

Be prepared to make dull polite conversation with someone you have never met before for several hours. Pray that people on either side of you are at the very least open to a two-sided conversation and don't want to sit there and tell you all about their last holiday/ their amazing wedding six months ago/their terrible divorce two years ago.

Shelley did the walk of doom past the tables at the back, weaving round lots of people who knew each other until she spotted table 3. It was indeed right next to the top table and totally empty, so she would have to loiter alone standing behind a chair looking like a lemon until she was joined by her other table dwellers, who would look her up and down and immediately want to ask why the hell she was alone at a wedding? What previous crime had she committed?

She sighed as she approached her fate. She circled the table until she found her place card, noting she had a double-barrelled on one side and a Colin on the other. This did not bode well. She immediately imagined Colin to be the gardener for the estate of Claire's wealthy fiancé. Or the dodgy uncle who talked to your chest rather than your face and who would probably end up passed out on her lap. She sighed again and looked up, preparing to smile politely to those giving her pitying looks, but was distracted by a tall man approaching at speed across the room. She watched as he nearly fell over a small child but managed to right himself. He was wearing tails, the trademark of the groom's side of the family. He was good looking in a fashionable floppy-haired, Hugh Grant kind of way and possibly a little older than her. All three of these facts wrote him off in her eyes. Decent looking and posh would mean he wouldn't be in the slightest bit interested in her, and in any case most probably married given his age and status in life. As he approached the table, he went straight for the bread rolls. He grabbed one, tore off a chunk and stuffed it in his mouth.

'Sorry,' he mumbled, catching sight of Shelley. 'But if I don't eat, I might faint. Running late this morning. No breakfast. Why on earth do we have to eat so late at weddings? Utterly famished. Sorry,' he said, wiping his hand on his jacket and offering it to Shelley. 'Colin. Groom's cousin. Would you like a roll?'

He picked up the basket and offered her one. She, of course, took one. She was also starving.

'And let's get this wine poured, shall we?' he said, grabbing a bottle of white out of an ice bucket and letting it drip all over the pristine white tablecloth. 'Didn't dare have a drink on an empty stomach. Might have fallen over. You happy with white?'

Shelley nodded and watched him slosh out two very large glasses.

'Do you mind if I sit down?' he said. 'They sent the wrong-sized shoes, would you believe, and my feet are killing me.'

'Mine too,' she said. 'I don't normally wear heels because . . . well, because I'm tall, you see – well, of course you can see. But if I don't sit down, I really do think I will fall down.'

'Well then,' he said. 'Let's sit down together, shall we? Take our shoes off, drink wine and eat bread. I reckon they will be at least another half-hour doing photos.'

And so they did. They sat down and ate the entire basket of rolls and drank an entire bottle of wine before there was any sign of the bride and groom arriving in the elaborate dining room to let the meal finally commence.

The conversation was fairly polite to begin with. Starting with the usual exchange of where they both stood in the hierarchy of this particular wedding.

Shelley admitted she worked with Claire at a school in Tottenham and had really no idea why she was there. Colin told her that he was an usher and that he worked with Hugo in the family construction firm.

Shelley also admitted that this was the poshest wedding she had ever been to.

Colin threw his head back and laughed heartily.

'Is it really? Well, we're not posh, I can assure you,' he said. 'I don't come across as posh, do I?'

'Well, a bit public school, maybe.'

'Damn it,' replied Colin, slamming his palm down on the table. 'I thought I was good at hiding all that. You've seen right through me. I did go to public school but only because Dad made a shed load of money and he thought that was the right thing to do with it. But don't call him posh whatever you do. He hates that. He came from pretty humble beginnings but even he'd admit that he's developed some pretty posh tastes over time.'

'So your dad is here then, is he?' asked Shelley.

'Oh yes, and Mum, and my brother and half the Gifford clan.'

'And your plus one?'

Colin looked down before he admitted there was no plus one accompanying him.

Shelley was gobsmacked. Colin struck her as the type of man who could have any woman he wanted and who would have a long line of women desperate to accompany him to a wedding. Good looking, well educated, very solvent. He was an A-list male if ever she saw one. So far out of her league that she decided she might as well relax; he was never in a million years going to be attracted to her so she may as well just be herself safe in the knowledge that she was never ever going to see him again after they had lived through this torturous meal together.

'What about you then?' he asked her. 'Where's your plus one?'

'Oh, I don't have one either,' said Shelley with a shrug. 'In fact, they didn't even give me the option of inviting one.'

'What a sad pair we are,' replied Colin, pouring her some more wine. 'Right then, why don't you tell me your story as to why on earth you have ended up invited to a wedding alone and then I'll tell you mine.'

Loosened by the wine and still a relatively empty stomach, Shelley found herself opening up to what appeared to be a willing listener who just kept filling her glass up.

'Well, my last boyfriend dumped me at a wedding,' she told Colin gravely.

'No way!' gasped Colin, his hand flying to his mouth in shock.

'Way,' nodded Shelley. 'Technically, it was in the car travelling between the church and the reception. He told me that he'd seen the way I looked at the bride and that I wasn't to get any ideas. That he was categorically never going to ask me to marry him and that he'd only invited me because his mum had told him he had to take a girlfriend because the rumour going round the family was that he was gay.'

Colin stared at her in astonishment. 'What did you do?' he asked.

'Dropped him off at the reception then drove straight home.'

Colin continued to stare at her. 'You were his girl-friend *and* his taxi and he said all that! I think I would have dumped him out of the car there and then.'

'Oh, it doesn't end there,' continued Shelley. 'He rang me around midnight begging forgiveness and asking if I'd go and pick him up.'

'You didn't, did you?' asked Colin.

'I didn't forgive him but I did go and pick him up.'

'Seriously – why?'

Shelley sighed. 'Because he was stranded and he couldn't get home, and because I'm too nice.'

'Way too nice,' agreed Colin.

'I also suspected he was gay but just couldn't come to terms with it. Or his parents couldn't come to terms with it. Either way, I kind of felt for him.'

'You are a very decent person,' said Colin, looking at her in awe. 'There is no way I could be that decent to someone who had been so horrible, whatever their circumstances.'

'Well, you know,' shrugged Shelley. 'None of us are perfect.

'How long ago was this then?' asked Colin.

'A couple of years ago now,' replied Shelley.

'And you've not met anyone since?' asked Colin.

Shelley shook her head. 'I've pretty much tried everything since then,' she continued, surprising herself. She was never normally this chatty with a man she had never met before. Must be the wine talking and the welcome opportunity to offload to a complete stranger.

'Speed-dating was the absolute worst,' she told him. 'It's my height, you see. Puts a lot of men off and they ask really rude questions.'

'Like what?' asked Colin.

Shelley felt herself blush. She must be a bit drunk already. She was being far too open.

'Like how do I have sex when I'm so tall?' she muttered.

'How rude!' gasped Colin. 'What did you say?'

'I told Ben from Dunstable that he would end up alone and rotting in a bedsit somewhere.'

'Good for you,' he said. 'Guys like that need to be told.'

'So then I tried online dating,' she continued. 'It's a legit thing now apparently. I thought I'd at least be able to firmly state *only* men over six foot, please. But these small men kept turning up. They just lie on the questionnaires, can you believe? That's the problem with online dating, you can say whatever you like. I don't think it will take off. '

'And hence no plus-one at a wedding,' concluded Colin.

'Exactly,' she said with a sigh. 'I currently spend my weekends watching *Sex in the City*, reading Bridget Jones or planning other people's hen parties and baby-showers. Everyone tells me there is a man out there who would be lucky to have me, but I don't seem to have the magic ingredients that men are looking for these days. And by that I mean a Wonderbra and a "Rachel" haircut,' she told him seriously. 'But anyway. Enough about me, come on, let's hear your story.'

Turned out that Colin had been engaged up until about six months ago. They'd had their engagement party at The Ivy. So posh that even Shelley had heard of it. Then she had dumped him. For Antony, who didn't have to work for a living. Who lived off a trust fund. Who could whisk her away to faraway places at the drop of a hat.

'Total wanker then,' said Shelley.

Colin laughed. Really laughed. Like he hadn't laughed in a while.

'Absolutely, total fucking wanker,' he agreed.

'Better off without her,' said Shelley.

Colin said nothing. He looked down at his glass,

lost in his own thoughts. For a moment she felt sorry for him. Going to a wedding so soon after getting dumped by one's fiancée had to hurt. However loaded you were.

'So this is where you are hiding,' said a man, suddenly appearing at their table, tailcoat flapping. 'I was about to send out a search party. Mum was stressing that you'd gone AWOL, given your feelings on weddings at the moment. Hello, I'm Neil,' he said to Shelley, holding his hand out. 'This idiot's brother and the black sheep farmer of the family.'

She could instantly tell they were brothers, though Neil was a rosier-cheeked, scruffier version. More Hugh Bonneville than Hugh Grant.

'Black sheep farmer?' questioned Shelley, shaking his hand.

'I've strayed from the flock and I'm not a fancy property developer like the rest of the clan you'll meet here today. I farm a few sheep on a small holding in Scotland.'

'And he's very proud of the fact as you can tell,' added Colin. 'We've been drowning our sorrows and bemoaning the fact we both hate weddings,' he told his brother. 'And she called Antony a total wanker.'

Neil grinned, looking her up and down. 'Very insightful lady then. Pleased to meet you.'

'We've eaten all the bread rolls,' she blurted.

'Blimey,' gasped Neil in mock horror. 'Before the bride and groom have even sat down?'

'Hoping to get barred from weddings for life,' said Shelley.

'Good plan,' grinned Neil.

'I'd better go and find Mum, had I?' said Colin, starting to get up. 'Tell her I'm not crying under a table somewhere.'

'No,' said Neil, putting his hand on Colin's shoulder and forcing him back down. 'I'll tell Mum you're in good hands. You've found a friend.' He winked at Shelley.

'Aww, thanks mate,' said Colin. 'Not sure I can cope with Mum's pity today.'

'I'll see you after the cheesecake course,' said Neil, walking away. 'Great to meet you, Shelley.'

'Better not be cheesecake,' mumbled Colin.

'It's always cheesecake,' said Shelley.

'We were going to have soufflé at our wedding,' he said mournfully.

'Look,' she said. 'At least you've got money. You'll get another girlfriend easily enough.'

'Oh thanks,' he said. 'You saying that's all I've got going for me?'

He wasn't smiling. He actually looked offended.

'I was trying to make a joke,' she said, thumping his arm. 'Cheer you up, that's all.'

She'd drunk way too much, she realized. Been rude to a complete stranger. She needed to slow down.

Colin continued to stare at her. He wasn't going to let her off the hook, she could tell.

'So, you wouldn't go out with me then?' he asked. 'You just think I'm shallow and lacking in personality; that my only asset is my money?'

'No!' she responded. 'I don't think that at all. I think . . . I think you seem great but . . . but . . .'

'You wouldn't touch me with a bargepole?'

'Of course, I would . . .'

'Only a very long pointy one . . .'

'No, quite a short stubby one actually.'

'Oh,' he said.

'I just,' she said. 'Well, you wouldn't look twice at me, would you? I mean, you must be able to have any girl you want, so why would you want to go out with me?'

'Because you are a breath of fresh air, Sheila.'

'Shelley.'

'Sorry, Shelley. I haven't met anyone like you in a long time.'

'Like what?'

'Well . . . well . . . just so relaxed and not treating me like I am loaded. Just like any other guy. And you aren't fussing with your hair or checking your make-up every five minutes.'

'You mean I don't care how I look?'

'No. I mean you seem comfortable with how you look, not fretting about it. It's not a big part of your life. How you look. I can tell.'

'Not sure that's a compliment.'

'Sarah looked at her hand mirror more than she looked at me.'

'Was she beautiful?' asked Shelley.

He nodded.

Shelley sighed. 'You see, you can't ask me out and be serious. You date pretty girls. I'm not a pretty girl.'

'I'm sick of pretty girls.'

21

'Wrong answer!' flared Shelley. 'You should have said, "But you are pretty, Shelley." See, we are doomed. You don't even fancy me. Of course you don't fancy me. We operate in separate universes.'

Shelley couldn't believe the conversation she was having. She wasn't normally so honest with men. Nor so blunt. Wine on an empty stomach must be affecting her.

'I do fancy you,' he said.

'You just said I wasn't pretty.'

'I didn't.'

'You did.'

Colin gave a deep sigh, looked at the floor and then looked up again.

'Shelley?' he said.

'Yes?'

'Would you do me the honour of letting me take you out one evening because I've enjoyed our chat and you have made me feel at ease and made me laugh for the first time in a very long time and I do fancy you, it's just that you're not my usual type. Shit, that didn't sound right, did it? I'm still screwing this up. For goodness' sake, please let me take you out on a date at some point in the near future and make amends for being an idiot.'

Shelley looked back at him and figured she had nothing to lose. She was certain he didn't fancy her and would change his mind, but she'd probably get a good meal out of it and a fun story to tell her mates.

She nodded.

'One date,' she said.

'Agreed,' he replied.

And that was how Shelley met Colin at a wedding.

Chapter 3

Present day

'Well, it just shows you that you should always say yes to things,' said Shelley as she took a cotton bud to her face and tried to wipe off the streaked mascara. 'If I hadn't have gone to that wedding, I never would have met my future husband.'

'You're still not married yet,' pointed out Peggy.

'I know.'

'And you are sure this time, are you?' asked Peggy.

Shelley turned to stare at her mother. 'How can you even ask me that?'

'Well, after last time.'

'Last time, when you were all so helpful, you mean?' asked Shelley, raising her eyebrows. 'Not!'

'Me?' replied Peggy. 'You can't just blame me. Others were there too. They all played their part. It wasn't all my fault.'

'Calm down, Mum,' said Shelley, smiling. 'I don't blame anyone. There's no one really to *blame*, is there? I mean, quite frankly, jilting my fiancé during my hen weekend was one of the best decisions I have ever made.'

Chapter 4

Colin's Parents' Posh House

Shortly after midnight, 1 January 2000

The dance floor was pretty much deserted now. Shelley had danced her feet off most of the night to the Spice Girls, Britney Spears, Steps, Oasis and Blur. She'd boogied mainly with Colin's sixteen-year-old cousin Delilah, as Colin was not a dancer, so she had been forced to find another, more willing partner. Despite the twenty-two-year age gap, she and Delilah had bonded over their love of Britpop and Nineties dance-floor fillers, harassing the DJ to play 'Wannabe' over and over again until they had perfected their 'Girl Power' poses. She'd had a much better night than she thought she would, given she hadn't expected to be celebrating the turn of the millennium with people she largely didn't know. She'd thought she'd be with her mates, downing After-Shocks and declaring their mutual love, but timing had been against her as usual. It always was. Turned out being in your late thirties at the turn of the millennium should be spent staying in with the hubby and listening for screams over the baby monitor. That was if you were lucky enough to have a hubby, of course.

Shelley didn't have a hubby, but she did have Colin. Her boyfriend of eight months now. And everyone thought she had finally met her Prince Charming, after all those years of kissing frogs.

Shelley had discovered, during the course of their first few dates, just what a catch Colin was. A partner in the family building and property development firm, Colin was a catch with a capital C. He had his own house, a flash BMW, a family villa in France, and a company flat in London. He was actually way too good to be true. And, almost certainly, way too good for Shelley.

'You *have* to marry him,' her best friend Becca had hissed when she first met him. 'He's such a catch.'

'If you think there is a cat in hell's chance of us getting married, you are mistaken. Me and Colin – never going to happen.'

'Why on earth not? You so deserve to have one of the good guys, and the fact he's rich – well, that's just a bonus. Speaking of which, can you imagine how fancy a wedding with Colin would be? A whole weekend in a country house, I reckon. At the *very* least. How amazing would that be?'

Shelley hadn't commented. She knew that there was no way that someone like Colin would be in it for the long term with her. No way. In actual fact she was pretty surprised every time he rang. And because she knew that there was absolutely no future in it whatsoever,

26

she continued to be just as she had been when they first met at Claire's wedding. Just herself. Saying what she thought rather than overthinking it. Not trying to impress him or be who she thought he wanted her to be in any way. Just herself. Her tall, gangly self with her hated halo of auburn curls, her green eyes which her mother had once helpfully told her gave of the look of a witch and her double-jointed elbows that were her weird party piece whenever she got a bit drunk. Despite all that, Colin seemed to enjoy her company. They got on surprisingly well given their opposite backgrounds and he was a great guy to pass time with, until the inevitable happened and someone else better slipped into his life. But so far it hadn't happened, which had kept them together for eight months and culminated in them being together on the eve of the new millennium.

New Year's Eve on steroids. A mind-bending time that caused you to reassess where you were in life and where you wanted to go.

She'd gladly accepted Colin's invite to celebrate in a massive marquee on his parents' massive lawn in deepest Berkshire, knowing all her friends would be babysitting their own kids. As for her own family – well, her mother would be doing a cracking impression of bah-humbug, whilst her brother would be dialling in from wherever he was in Australia.

It had actually been an okay night. Colin had caught up with some old school friends who were also there, but she had got bored of the regaling of tales of their childhood and so she had made her excuses and escaped to the dance floor as soon as a decent track

27

had come on, joining forces with Delilah to dance the night away. They'd just kicked up a storm to Prince's '1999' when she spotted Colin throw down a flaming Sambuca at the bar and then walk towards her as the DJ put on 'Angels' by Robbie Williams. Colin stumbled as he got near her. She laughed and he grinned back. Sometimes he reminded her a little of herself. There was a surprising self-doubting side to his personality, which was probably prompted by the huge expectation and pressure on his shoulders as the natural heir to his father's building empire. He'd confessed one night, after way too many drinks, that he often hadn't got a clue what he was doing when it came to the building business, but he didn't dare admit that to his father. Shelley had reassured him that in her job as a primary school teacher she also felt as if she was constantly making it up, and was continually concerned she would get found out. She winged it all the time, she admitted.

'Really?' he'd said in astonishment.

'Really,' she'd replied. 'I reckon most people haven't a clue what they are doing.'

Colin shook his head. 'I always think everyone around me knows exactly what they are doing, apart from me.'

'They don't,' said Shelley. 'They just don't admit it.'

'You're very easy to talk to,' he'd said, taking her hand across the table.

'Thank you,' she'd replied. They'd smiled at each other. Shelley had felt something warm in her tummy and dismissed it as being a bit pissed.

When Colin finally reached her in the middle of the dance floor, she fell into his arms, grateful for the support. Colin nuzzled into her ear making her giggle.

'We are going to get married, aren't we?' he whispered.

Shelley did a double take. Then she realized she must have misheard.

'I thought we were mullered already,' she stated. She'd felt wobbly for some time and had crashed into several other party-goers whilst on the dance floor. She really must not drink expensive champagne ever again.

Colin pulled away so she could see his face. He looked slightly dazed. Then again, he had just been downing Sambucas.

'Mullered?' he asked, squinting at her again. 'What do you mean, mullered? What is mullered? Is that some Derbyshire thing? Sometimes I don't understand a word you're saying.'

'You know, mullered,' Shelley replied. 'Like drunk. That's what mullered means. Anyway, you said it, so you must know what it means.'

'I didn't say it. I never said such a word.'

'So, what did you say?'

Colin blew his cheeks out and looked around him. Some of his relations were staggering about with their arms around each other, veering dangerously close to complete collapse.

'What did you say if you didn't say mullered?' she asked again.

He gripped her shoulders with both hands and looked her straight in the eye.

'I said married,' he said.

'Married?'

'Yes, married.'

'What do you mean, married?'

'What I said. We are going to get married, aren't we?'

Shelley felt her mouth drop.

'Well, I don't know. Are we?'

'Well, I think we should. I think it's about time.'

'Do you?'

'Yes. I do.'

Shelley could feel something bubbling up inside her. It felt a bit like excitement but she wasn't quite sure. There was a hint of confusion that was keeping it suppressed.

She waited, looking at him. But the words she wanted to come didn't, and she knew she had to hear them to be absolutely sure.

'Are you . . . are you asking me to marry you?' she asked finally.

He hesitated. Cast another look around the dance floor, and then nodded his head. 'Yes, I am,' he replied firmly. Then he suddenly dropped to his knees in front of her. Both knees, which gave it more the look of a confession than a proposal.

Shelley stared at him. Despite the presence of the millennium, she hadn't been expecting this at all. In fact, she had been expecting the opposite. The millennium was bound to spark the realization in Colin that he was with the wrong woman and that he should dump her. Go and find the truly delicate, pretty ladies again. Bound to. Sure, it had been going well. In

October they had even taken a vacation together and gone to his parents' villa in the south of France. It had been a great week and Colin had even told her he loved her. But she hadn't taken it seriously. She wasn't falling for that. He'd drunk at least two bottles of wine, so she'd laughed it off, putting it down to high spirits. She'd been his plus one to a few events in their inevitably plush surroundings, where she'd managed not to make a fool of herself, and he'd even attended Shelley's godmother's golden wedding anniversary in the local village hall, holding up okay to the scrutiny of her mother and her cronies. Not that it would have mattered if he hadn't. It wasn't long term, so who cared? The end of the road was imminent, she was sure, so much so that she'd upped her consumption of free champagne that night, in the assured knowledge that she might never drink champagne like this ever again. But no, the opposite appeared to be happening.

But this wasn't at all how she had imagined a proposal.

She was wearing Colin's uncle's velvet burgundy jacket for a start. He had gallantly lent it to her when they had stepped outside for the fireworks at midnight, and she had forgotten to give it back. When she'd popped to the toilet on her way back in and looked in the mirror, she thought she looked half drag act, half Bond villain. To make matters worse, Colin had discarded his jacket and bow tie, his shirt was untucked and he had drunk, sticky-up hair. Anyone looking at them, with Colin forced to his knees in front of Shelley, might have thought they were in an altercation at the end of a dodgy poker game, and *not* in the midst of a proposal.

Only one thing for it. She swiftly took off the jacket and ordered Colin to put it on, which he did in a sort of daze. She rubbed her lips together, hoping the last remnants of lipstick would be spread over her mouth, transforming her from mafia boss to sexy harlot. She attempted a smouldering gaze that Becca had told her never to use as it looked as though she was suppressing a fart, but it was all she had.

'Ask me again,' she said, looking down at Colin.

He looked confused, as though he had already forgotten he'd just asked her to marry him.

'Ask me to marry you again,' she urged.

He blinked and then cleared his throat. 'So will you . . . ?' he said. He took her hands and clasped them in his own. 'Will you marry me?' He stumbled left ever so slightly but righted himself again. Then grinned.

'I will,' she said. 'I will.'

Chapter 5

Present day

'Can I come in?' came a voice from behind Shelley's bedroom door. Thank goodness, she thought. Becca come to rescue her make-up. Although how they were going to cram the three of them into her childhood room, she had no idea. It was tiny. It still hurt that it was her younger brother Adam who got the bigger bedroom in the tiny cottage, despite the fact that she was taller than him. Hard to forgive parents such sexist discrimination, even after all this time.

'Come in, Becca,' shouted back Shelley. Her best friend had been applying her make-up in Peggy's tiny bathroom where the lighting was particularly poor. Peggy had stated, quite fairly, when Becca had complained, that bathroom lighting was the scourge of the elderly. Who wanted to see a well-lit reflection at over eighty?

'Well, will you look at you,' said Becca coming in. 'Finally in a wedding dress, after all these years. Never thought I'd see the day.'

'We were just saying that,' said Shelley. 'Actually, I think it should be mandatory to leave at least a

33

nineteen-year gap between your hen weekend and your wedding. Give everyone time to really think about it properly.'

'Still can't believe that you wouldn't let me throw you another hen party,' said Becca, sticking her bottom lip out. 'I could have just done with a weekend away.'

'Are you insane?' gasped Shelley. 'Do you really think any of us could go through what we went through that weekend again?'

'Worst hen weekend ever,' agreed Becca, nodding.

'Or perhaps the best, given the outcome,' added Peggy. She put her arm affectionately around Shelley and smiled. Shelley felt another tear spring to her eye. It still took some getting used to. Seeing her mum allow herself to occasionally display joy, look happy, be cheerful – occasionally even, dare she say it, be carefree. She'd been miserable for so long. Back then, Becca used to call her the black widow, such was her capacity for gloom. She still held onto her down-to-earth, no-nonsense attitude, particularly when it came to being a mother, but she had learned to let go. Show some positive emotion that had been gone for so long. The transformation from twenty years ago was still quite unbelievable.

Chapter 6

Derbyshire

3 January 2000

'I bought you some flowers to give Mum,' Shelley told Colin as they drew up outside her mum's terraced house on the outskirts of a small village in the Peak District.

'Oh, right, okay,' he said taking the modest posy of daisies and gypsophila out of her hands. She would have told Colin to buy some, but she knew he would go over the top and spend too much money and her mother would be completely unimpressed and would give the enormous bouquet the same look of disdain that she would his gleaming sporty car sitting outside her house.

'You look nervous,' she said.

'I'm not nervous,' he said. 'Well, I am a bit. Your mum scares me, if I'm honest. I don't think she likes me.'

'She loves you,' said Shelley firmly. 'She only locked you out of the house that time and refused to let you in because she thought you were the TV licensing man.'

'Will you tell her we are going to get married?' he asked. 'I think she'll take it better from you.'

Shelley shrugged. 'Of course.' After all, she had insisted that Colin tell his parents and she had been wracked with nerves just like he was now. They'd told them on New Year's Day, along with his brother, Neil. Colin's dad, John, was mildly terrifying, a huge, towering man with an exceptionally loud voice. She was worried she wouldn't be up to scratch and didn't deserve to be part of this hugely impressive family. Her profile didn't seem to fit. But John had headed straight for the wine fridge and come back with a huge bottle of champagne, which they had proceeded to drink despite their hangovers from the night before. John had asked her at one point what type of wedding she wanted, and she had replied that she would like it to be small, preferably, with only closest friends and family. She didn't like being the centre of attention.

John had laughed so loudly that Shelley had nearly spilt her champagne. He'd urged her to repeat her request to his wife, after which Joan had beamed and said, 'You really are a breath of fresh air.'

Shelley quite often heard this term related to her, particularly in London. She wasn't always sure it was meant as a compliment. Sometimes she was sure what someone was actually trying to say was, 'You are very different and weird.' But to be fair, Joan looked genuine.

'Oh really, why do you say that?' asked Shelley.

Joan looked a little awkward, but John stepped in

36

to spill the beans, encouraged by low-level drunkenness. 'Because the last one he got engaged to wanted the works. You name it – gold plated carriage and all,' he laughed.

Joan nodded in agreement. 'She was a nutcase, though. Stunning looking, but all the same, a nutcase. Psycho Sarah, we used to call her. We were so relieved when she called it off.'

'Right,' nodded Shelley. 'Colin did mention when we first met that he had been engaged before.' She tried to ignore the 'stunning looking' comment. It was no surprise. Colin had said so at the time, but still it stung. She still felt insecure about her looks in comparison to Colin and his circle. All his friends seemed to have partners who clearly had oodles of time for grooming whilst holding down high-flying jobs in law or finance. Without exception they always looked immaculate, whereas she looked exactly what she was: someone who had to hold down a full-time job corralling under-tens. She'd tried to keep up to their standards, but she just didn't have the time. If they were meeting in central London for a 7 p.m. dinner reservation, she didn't get back from work until 5.30 p.m., leaving her thirty-five minutes to transform herself from dowdy run-down teacher to glamour puss. Not happening. Colin reassured her that he loved her crazy curls and her time-saving 'au naturel' attitude to cosmetics. *And* he often pointed out that he was very happy not to spend half his life waiting for her to style her hair and make her face up. But still she couldn't help but fret that she didn't fit into the mould of partners that his friends seemed to have chosen.

'And at least you said yes,' announced John, letting out a booming laugh and slapping her on the back.

'What do you mean?' asked Shelley, feeling confused. 'Of course I said yes.'

'Oh, hush, John,' said Joan. 'No need to rake over all that business with Adriana.' She rolled her eyes at Shelley. 'He shouldn't have mentioned it,' she said, laying a heavily bejewelled hand on her arm. 'Just some girl he had a crush on in his twenties. It was nothing.'

If her name was Adriana, she was bound to be super posh and super beautiful, thought Shelley. Who on earth had a name like Adriana?

'He never mentioned an Adriana,' she said, trying to keep her voice even.

'Because it was nothing. It was a long-distance relationship. They'd barely been together a few weeks. Totally had his head in the clouds. He was young and reckless. Not any more though. You are good for him,' Colin's mother smiled, gripping her arm tight. 'Really good for him. You'll keep his feet on the ground. We are so glad he found you.'

Keep his feet on the ground? Joan made her sound like a lead weight. What about 'make him really happy'? So happy he has his head in the clouds?

Fortunately, Shelley was distracted as Neil bundled over and enveloped her in a huge bear hug.

'Congratulations. Colin is a very lucky man,' he said, holding her shoulders at arm's length, and beaming at her so hard, and with such a genuine smile, that she couldn't help but believe him. 'I knew the moment I saw you sitting together at Hugo's wedding that you were good together. Really good, and that you are exactly what Colin needs. Finally, my brother has shown some taste when it comes to women. He's picked a good 'un for a change. He really is a very lucky man.'

She laughed at his seemingly genuine joy at the match. His smile was infectious. But she dismissed his comment. What a ridiculous thing to say, she thought. She was the lucky one, not Colin.

She looked over at Colin, slightly cowering at her mum's front door as they stood together, clutching hands. She gave him a reassuring squeeze on the arm. She suspected that Colin very much saw her mother as similar to his father. High expectations and extremely judgemental. However, she was glad that her mother wasn't bowled over by his vastly higher status in life. Her mum was having none of that. She placed no value on money or wealth, just character, and she suspected that Colin understood that perfectly.

Peggy opened the door brandishing a broom.

'You're early,' she said. 'I hadn't quite finished tidying up yet.'

'You don't need to tidy up for us, Mum,' said Shelley, stepping in.

'No way, Peggy,' said Colin. 'No need to make any effort at all.'

'It's called having standards, Colin,' snapped Peggy. 'It's an important trait to have. You'll be glad of it when you marry my Shelley.'

39

'What!' exclaimed Shelley. 'How did you know? Mother!'

Shelley glanced over at Colin, who had visibly paled.

'Do you think I'm an idiot?' she said, holding her hands out to Colin who handed over the daisy posy. 'You go away to a fancy place for the millennium, then ring me the next day to say the pair of you need to see me as soon as possible and then you turn up with flowers. What's the saying? No shame, Sherlock!'

Shelley grinned at her mum. 'Nearly right, Mother,' she said, then waited. She grinned at Colin and waited longer.

Silence.

'I suppose we'd better have a cup of tea then, had we?' she finally said, turning around and heading into the kitchen.

'Mind your head,' said Shelley to Colin as they stepped over the threshold into the small cottage. Colin looked up as she spoke and immediately bumped his forehead on a low beam. He looked around him, dazed. He was too tall for this house, and he never seemed to get used to its small rooms. Shelley giggled.

Half an hour later, they were sitting in the lounge as Shelley patiently waited for Peggy to show some joy or excitement in her only daughter's forthcoming nuptials. Peggy sat on the edge of her seat, as if she was waiting for them to leave so she could get on with more productive activities.

'My father asked me to tell you that he would be deeply honoured if you would allow him to pay for the wedding,' said Colin. 'He doesn't want to push you out or anything, it's just that he really is—'

'Loaded?' interrupted Peggy.

'Mum!' exclaimed Shelley.

'Well yes,' said Colin. 'That does kind of sum it up, and he really doesn't want to put you under any unnecessary strain.'

Peggy turned slowly to face her future son-in-law. 'I can assure you that I would never allow your father to put me under any strain whatsoever.'

'Great,' said Shelley breezily. 'That's settled then. Any special requests, Mum? Anything you would really like to make sure happens at the wedding?'

'Yes,' said Colin. 'We need your input. You really need to be involved.'

Shelley looked at Colin. That was very sweet of him, she thought, but he clearly hadn't clocked what her mother was all about. Peggy wasn't your normal gushy mum. Oh no – gushy was not what she was about at all. Quite the opposite. However, Shelley did feel slightly disappointed that she hadn't shown more enthusiasm for her engagement; after all, Peggy had been dismayed at her single status for the last few years, coming out with some choice statements such as, 'By the time I was your age, I had two teenage children; by the time you have children, people will be asking if you are their proud granny, not proud mummy,' and, 'If you're not careful, you'll only have divorced men to choose from, and who wants someone else's cast-offs.' She made these comments as though Shelley could just rustle up a man like that. Like she hadn't been trying. Like she had ignored the massive pressure to get married.

41

She could at least say 'well done', thought Shelley miserably. She could at least show some pride in her achievement of finally hitting engaged status. Her mother's reaction appeared to be more along the lines of frustration that she had taken so long, and now could she just get on with it?

'Who's going to give you away?' Peggy asked Shelley.

Shelley had anticipated this. She cleared her throat and squared her shoulders.

'I'd like you to,' she said.

Peggy shook her head.

'That's not right,' she said. 'Your dad wouldn't have liked that.'

Shelley took a deep breath. 'He's not here, Mum. And I'd like it.'

Shelley's dad had been gone for nearly ten years. One day he'd gone out for a paper and never came back. Heart attack. Outside the cake shop, somewhat ironically. Shelley's mum had rung her at work. She had been very matter of fact. Still in shock. Actually, Shelley thought she might still be in shock. Somehow, it never seemed to quite have sunk in. Peggy talked about her husband all the time, but almost as if he was still there. Almost as though, if she kept talking about him, he would one day just sail through the back door again, put the paper on the kitchen table and shout out he was sorry he took so long but he got waylaid.

Peggy shook her head again. 'You know your dad was a stickler for tradition. He wouldn't be doing with me walking you down the aisle. It should be your brother.'

Wow, thought Shelley, she hadn't been expecting that. Her brother Adam was currently bumming his way round the southern hemisphere, pretending to be some kind of surfer dude, despite the fact he grew up in Derbyshire, the place the furthest away from the sea in the entire United Kingdom.

'Adam's not going to come back for my wedding,' said Shelley.

'Of course he will,' said Peggy. 'He's your brother.'

'Exactly. So if you won't do it, then the only other person I can think of is Uncle Thomas.'

'Uncle Thomas,' said Peggy, looking taken aback.

'Well, who else is there? He is my only living uncle, and actually he'd be great. It's right up his street, don't you think?' Shelley hadn't seen her uncle in about five years, since he moved out to Spain to retire with Auntie Nancy and a set of golf clubs. But she knew that – given his theatrical past – Uncle Thomas wouldn't be able to resist playing a major role at her wedding.

Peggy gave a big sigh. 'I suppose you're right. I'll ring your Auntie Nancy and Uncle Thomas later. They'll want to know anyway. Do you have a date in mind?'

Shelley looked over at Colin. 'Well,' she said, 'there doesn't seem much point in a long drawn-out engagement or anything . . .'

'Quite right, you are nearly forty,' added Peggy. 'You need to prioritize having a family at your age, so best to crack on with it.'

Shelley felt herself blush. 'Thanks, Mum,' she said, whilst Colin smirked.

43

'And you need to pull your boots up,' continued Peggy to Colin. 'What are you, forty-five?'

'Forty-one,' pointed out Colin, looking slightly aghast.

'Precisely,' said Peggy.

'Anyway, as I was saying, we both want to get on with it, so we were thinking of early July this year.'

'That doesn't sound like getting on with it,' said Peggy. 'That's months away. Me and your dad were engaged and married within three months.'

'I know, but you have no idea how hard it is to book stuff for weddings in the same year,' said Shelley. 'Especially this year, what with a glut of millennium engagements. You typically have to book stuff at least a year in advance.'

'We'll no doubt still have to pull a few strings to get what we want, ask a few favours,' explained Colin.

'Well, I suspect your family are expert at such things,' said Peggy.

Shelley was tempted to kick her mother. She was so good at the quiet put-downs. Shelley knew only too well from experience. Peggy had always been the type of parent determined to keep her children's feet firmly on the ground by subtly reminding them of their short-comings. Unfortunately, with Shelley this had the impact of making her overly aware of her faults which totally affected her self-confidence. She often wished that she could just tell her mother that she needed to hear encour-agement every so often rather than continually having her failings pointed out, but Shelley even lacked the self-confidence to do that.

'Right,' continued Peggy. 'Well, I'll ring Spain tonight and give your aunt and uncle a heads-up.'

'Is this your wedding day?' said Colin, suddenly pointing at a framed picture on the sideboard.

Peggy smiled for the first time.

'Yes. It was the thirteenth of March 1959. It snowed, and I nearly didn't make it to the church. We had thirty guests and my mother-in-law wept the entire time and could not look me in the eye. We had two nights in a B&B in Whitby for our honeymoon and the toilet didn't flush and it was so windy it blew my hat off and I never saw it again. We ate fish and chips out of newspaper on both nights because that was all we could afford. We couldn't even afford mushy peas. We sat in a bus shelter, freezing to death and sharing cold chips.'

Shelley rolled her eyes at Colin. She knew her father would have been mortified that he wasn't around to pay for his own daughter's wedding. She imagined her mum was too, but she'd struggled for money ever since Dad died so Shelley assumed she was probably secretly relieved, especially when Colin's family were clearly very wealthy.

'The actual wedding wasn't that important to me,' said Peggy. 'Not like these days when they seem to throw everything at it. Like it's proof of how much you love someone as to how much your wedding costs. I didn't need a fancy wedding to know I wanted to spend the rest of my life with Gordon.' She bit her lip.

'Neither do I, Mum,' said Shelley. 'I told Colin's mum and dad that we should keep it as simple as possible.'

45

'Good,' nodded Peggy. 'In any case, you are both too old to make a big fuss. You just need to get on with it. Get married, have a family, get on with your lives.'

'That's what we both want,' said Shelley, smiling at Colin.

'Good, good,' said Peggy. 'Well, congratulations,' she said raising her teacup finally in a toast. 'All the best to you.' She even managed a small smile.

Chapter 7

Peggy waved them off down the lane, standing at her garden gate. She watched as Shelley got into Colin's sleek sports car, parked on the village lane with no path, outside a row of terraced cottages with no garages. Can you imagine, no garages! Colin must have thought he'd landed on another planet, Peggy reflected.

Colin had accidentally parked the car with the passenger side a bit too close to the hedge, causing Shelley to have to squeeze herself between the hedge and the car. Her coat snagged on a bramble, and she had a brief altercation with said bramble until she managed to extract it from her coat, pulling several threads as she did so. Peggy noticed that Shelley didn't seem overly bothered about this; after all, it was a coat that she had owned for many years. She bent to open the door and managed to squeeze herself in through the narrow slit, lowering herself into the seat after bumping her head on the roof of the car. Peggy watched as she gave it a rub, then pulled the door shut and looked up to wave cheerily back at her mother. Colin crunched the gears into play and sped off.

Shelley was not built for fancy cars, reflected Peggy. Elegant movement did not come naturally to her daughter. She was tall and a bit ungainly and more suited to jumping in her dad's old Land Rover, which stank of cow muck and whatever chemicals they used to keep the dairy clean. She was worried that Colin's lifestyle demanded elegance and a certain self-belief brought about by status. Shelley was not elegant. And she had no airs and graces about her own status in life, despite the fact that she was – in many senses – way more successful than her future husband. A woman who had dealt with the untimely death of her father by embracing life and carrying on to become the successful and caring primary school teacher that she was. No mean feat. Peggy was very proud of her daughter. Not that she would ever tell her that, of course. Wouldn't want her getting too big for her boots. What had Colin ever done? Accepted all the handouts that his parents had given him, thought Peggy.

What would Gordon think of this union, she wondered. She wished she could ask him. Gordon would be kind to him, Peggy knew. Welcome him in. Treat him with respect. Gordon treated everyone with respect. He would respect his daughter's decision to marry him, but in private perhaps he would confess his concerns. Wish he was less rich, more down-to-earth – more like them, really. Isn't that every parent's dream, that their children marry someone exactly like them? Colin was not like Gordon. Gordon had been a dairyman at a farm on the other side of the village. He had got up every morning at 5 a.m., walked across the green, and milked over a hundred cows as if they were his own. No, Colin was nothing like Gordon. Still, beggars couldn't be choosers at Shelley's age. Shelley had made her choice, and just in time. Shelley could now get on with the important stuff, Peggy decided, like making a family. For that, Peggy was extremely relieved. Maybe he wouldn't have been her choice for her own daughter, but Shelley wanted to make it work and that was all that mattered. Shelley had left home twenty years ago, lived a life of her own choosing, then found the man she wanted to live the rest of her life with. That was all Peggy had ever wanted for Shelley. Not like how it had been for her. Still in the village she grew up in, due to circumstances beyond her control.

She watched as her neighbour's Corsa came trundling up the road. She stood steadfastly in the lane outside her house so that Ray couldn't park there.

'Hello Peggy,' he said as he got out of his car. 'Did you see that fancy car? Just about took me off the road it did. Did you see it?'

Peggy looked at Ray. Christ, he was a scruff bag. Ray's wife had left him for the man who ran the post office about five years ago, and Peggy reckoned he still hadn't worked out how to use the iron.

'That's my future son-in-law,' announced Peggy.

'What! You never said. Shelley getting married, is she?'

Peggy nodded.

'Well congratulations. That's amazing news. And to a rich feller as well, by the looks of it. You'll be buying a new hat then, Peggy. And getting those knitting needles out finally. Eh, she's not preggers, is she? Is it one of those weddings? A quick job.'

'No, she isn't pregnant.' Peggy felt a shiver run through her veins. 'Of course she isn't. They got engaged on New Year's Eve.'

'Nice,' nodded Ray. 'Good on her. Why don't you come in and have a cuppa to celebrate, eh? I've got a bag of reject biscuits from the factory that have got our name written all over them. I'll never eat them on my own. I'll end up giving them to the birds, no doubt.'

'No thank you,' said Peggy. She crossed her arms over her chest. She was starting to get cold, but the last thing she wanted to do was to step into Ray's chaotic house. A renowned hoarder, who couldn't resist a bargain, when she'd last ventured into his kitchen, she'd come away with a Cliff Richard LP that he'd bought from a car-boot sale three years ago. Ray had insisted that she have it, despite the fact she didn't have anything to play it on. Of course, he'd turned up a week later with a record player he'd found in a charity shop that was the ugliest thing she had ever seen.

'Sorry,' she said, backing away. 'I need to go in and . . . and . . .' she faltered. She had been about to say that she needed to go in and talk to Gordon and see what he thought of their daughter's engagement. But of course, that would sound very stupid to Ray. I mean who discussed their problems with their dead husband?

'I need to go and ring my sister in Spain and tell her the news,' she said, giving him a wave.

'Say hello from me,' he said as she disappeared through her front door into her empty house.

He always said that, she thought. Despite the fact he had never met her sister, Nancy. Ray really was a mystery to her.

Chapter 8

'Right,' said Becca as she finished touching up Shelley's mascara. 'All done. I think you have matching eyes again.'

Shelley peered into the mirror. It looked as if Becca had done a perfect job of patching her up. But then Becca usually did everything extremely well.

'Now,' said Becca. 'I do have to ask you an important question.'

'No, you are not my chief bridesmaid,' said Shelley firmly. 'I keep telling you. All my bridesmaids are made equal. I'm not doing the favouritism thing.'

'I would have been your chief bridesmaid last time,' said Becca, sticking her bottom lip out. 'You said I was.'

'That was last time and look how that ended.'

Becca cast her eyes down to the floor. 'Fair point,' she admitted. 'How many times do I have to say sorry?'

'I forgive you,' said Shelley. 'I always forgave you.'

Becca looked up brightly. 'I wasn't going to ask again to be your chief bridesmaid actually. I was going to ask what I should have asked last time and we might not have got ourselves in the mess that we did.'

'What's that?' asked Shelley.

Becca cleared her throat. 'Well, I'm thinking that it is really important that someone says it this time. Today. On this special day, which will no doubt be sure to become an amazing day, and we are all truly happy for you . . . but I think I couldn't live with myself if I didn't just ask you.'

'Ask me what?' urged Shelley. 'Come on, I'm due at church in fifteen minutes.'

Becca took a deep breath and pulled back her shoulders and looked Shelley in the eye.

'Are you really sure you want to go through with it this time?'

Chapter 9

Shelley's flat, Tottenham

4 January 2000

Shelley held her head away from her phone as Becca screamed.

'I knew it, I knew it,' she yelled. 'I am so pumped. I had the worst New Year's Eve of all time. Toby demanded feeding at precisely 11.45 p.m. I even missed the fireworks on the telly. But *this*, this, my friend, makes up for it all. This is the most amazing news. I am so happy for you. *And*, added bonus, I get to go to a wedding in some fancy country hotel, no doubt. I get nights away from home. I cannot wait.'

'You mean you're looking forward to your best friend in the whole wide world getting married.'

'My best friend, marrying the most eligible bachelor in the kingdom – it really is a fairy tale,' gasped Becca. 'What did I tell you? All this time. There is the most amazing man waiting for you, and boy have you found the most amazing man and might I add that Colin has of course bagged himself the most amazing woman. You are *the* fairy-tale couple.'

Shelley wasn't so sure that she was fairy-tale material.

'Just can you do it soon?' continued Becca. 'I'm begging you. If I don't get a night off from the twins from hell sometime in the near future, I might cut off my own ears.'

'Well, it's looking like this summer,' said Shelley. 'It's probably going to be a marquee on the lawn at his parents' house. But I'm with you. I want to get on with it. After all, I am getting on a bit.'

'You must be so excited . . . oh my God . . . you are going to have the best wedding ever. It's going to be amazing.'

'I can't believe it myself, Becca, seriously. He got down on both knees . . .'

'Both knees?'

'Yeah, too many Sambucas. Anyway, he got down on both knees and I thought he was going to dump me and I thought I'd misheard him. It wasn't how I thought it would be.'

'Does it matter? Honestly, Shelley. You are going to have a dream wedding and you are worried about how many knees he was on!'

'No, it's just, well,' hesitated Shelley. 'I guess it was all so quick and unexpected. I just didn't think when I finally got engaged that . . . that would be how it was.'

'Look, Jason took me to a really fancy restaurant and we had the most awful meal, do you remember? One of those meals with shavings of food rather than actual food and then he asked me and then we had to get a kebab on the way home because we were starving. It was not a dream proposal.'

'I'm still a little bit in shock, to be honest, Becca,' Shelley confessed. She paused. 'I am doing the right thing, aren't I?'

There was the tiniest pause. One minuscule moment of hesitation before Becca shrieked down the phone, 'Of course you are, you numpty. It's going to be brilliant. Now forget the proposal, you need to start planning the wedding of the century.'

'I guess,' said Shelley, feeling rather daunted.

'Oh my God, Shelley. You could have a Posh and Becks style wedding?' Becca gasped. 'You could have thrones, you could be in *Hello!* magazine; you could wear purple, just like Victoria did!'

'Me?' said Shelley. 'In purple? Colin would think he's marrying Barney the Dinosaur. No, it doesn't need to be really fancy or anything, does it? Colin's family has offered to pay, and thankfully Mum has accepted, but it doesn't mean we need to go over the top, does it? I don't need all the bells and whistles. You know me; I hate being the centre of attention. I don't quite know how to handle it to be honest, Becca. This all doesn't seem real. This kind of thing doesn't happen to me.'

'Well, it is happening to you, and so just enjoy it. Just say yes . . . yes . . . and yes again. To everything,' stressed Becca. 'This is going to be sooo epic. I bet you'll have a wedding planner. There *must* be a wedding planner. Let me be your wedding planner? Oh, please will you, per-lease? I would be such a good wedding planner, and it would get me out of the house and spending other people's money. It's like my dream job, I was born to be a wedding planner.'

'I thought that weird job you did was something to do with finance and numbers and stuff.'

'Exactly. Your future father-in-law could employ me to count all the money he's going to spend on his eldest son's wedding.'

'I'm not having a wedding planner.'

'What if the Gifford family insists? After all, this will be quite the society wedding. At least worthy of a mention in *Tatler*, I reckon.'

'No!' shrieked Shelley. 'No way. I'm not a magazine bride.'

'Surely you'd like to be in a glossy magazine?' asked Becca.

'Definitely not,' retorted Shelley. 'Don't be ridiculous, Becca. It's not a society wedding and I *won't* be having a wedding planner. We'll keep it simple. No fuss. I can't be the centre of all that attention. I'll just make a fool of myself. You know I will. I want it small. It's not about some massive party. It's about marrying Colin.'

There was a moment's silence.

'I think you are in for a shock if you think this is going to be a small affair,' said Becca. 'The family are in the *Sunday Times*' Rich List, for goodness' sake – they don't do small weddings.'

'Are they?' asked Shelley.

'Yes!' gasped Becca. 'How can you not *know* that? I mean they are very near the bottom. Not billionaires or anything. But still, they are there.'

'Well, that doesn't matter,' said Shelley. 'I don't care. Small wedding. That's what we are having.'

'If you say so,' sighed Becca. 'But promise me one thing.'

'It's a no to a Cinderella horse-drawn carriage,' said Shelley. 'I know you wanted one for your wedding but I'm not doing it. They'll all think it's the ugly sister arriving and there's been some huge mistake.'

'Oh Shel, that's absolute rubbish,' said Becca. 'You will be a stunning bride. 'You will look exactly how I imagine Nicole Kidman looked when she married Tom Cruise.'

'What, worried?' replied Shelley. 'I can't quite believe she's stuck with him so long.'

'Oh, I agree,' replied Becca enthusiastically. 'He has gone kind of weird, hasn't he? And *Eyes Wide Shut*? I mean what were they thinking? No, what I meant was you will look wonderfully tall and elegant with cascaded red curls billowing over a stunning strapless taffeta dress. Just like Nicole in a wedding dress.'

'I really don't think there is much chance of me looking anywhere near as beautiful as her,' said Shelley.

'You will,' said Becca. 'I know you will. But Shelley, promise me that that you will make the most of having the wedding of your dreams? Please don't think you don't deserve it because you absolutely do. And if you do happen to think of your best friend in the whole wide world whilst you are planning this party to end all parties then, could you please just think about having a vodka luge? It's the latest thing at weddings. Apparently, Alfie and Maria had one at their wedding, but I didn't get invited because . . . well, I'm too old for weddings apparently, or perhaps me not giving Alfie that promotion had something to do with it, but whatever, I've never experienced a vodka luge so you absolutely have to have one. For me. Please. My life has been one long sick-and-wee train since Toby and Miles arrived, and I really think this wedding might just save my sanity. Please ask for a vodka luge and I will be your best friend forever.'

'You already are my best friend forever. You said so in infants when I took the blame for the smashed paint pot that you dropped.'

'Will you ever let that go?'

'No.'

'Vodka luge . . . please, pretty please.'

'I'll consider it,' said Shelley. 'Just for you.'

'*Yesss*,' hissed Becca. 'I cannot wait for this wedding!'

Chapter 10

It was as though she wasn't getting married at all, thought Shelley as she arrived home to her minuscule flat in Tottenham and looked at her answer machine balancing on a stool in her minuscule hall. For two weeks she'd been coming home from school every night, hoping to see the light flashing on her answer phone to signal that her mother had left her a message to have some sort of conversation about the fact that her life was going through a seismic change. If she were totally honest with herself, Shelley would have loved to ask her mother out-right if she was happy for her. If she thought she was doing the right thing? Shelley was convinced she was, of course, but had niggling doubts that must be normal when, out of the blue, your Prince Charming turns up to rescue you from terminal spinsterhood.

Shelley jumped when the phone rang at eight thirty that night. She had completed all her school marking and was just tucking into a Weight Watchers ready-meal.

'Hello Shelley, it's your mum.'

Shelley heaved a sigh of relief.

'Oh, hi Mum. How are you?'

'Not bad, I suppose. Ray is driving me mad, parking his car outside my house all the time. I'm going to throw my food waste all over his Corsa if he does it again . . . And they've changed the hours at the Post Office. I went at nine yesterday and they were shut. Shut! At nine in the morning. Utterly ridiculous.'

'Right, well, that's a real shame.'

'I mean what if you have to be at work by nine-thirty like I do. What then?'

'How's work been since after Christmas?' asked Shelley.

'Oh, you know. Just mashed potato followed by more mashed potato. School dinners never change much. Anyway, I spoke to your Uncle Thomas the other night.'

'Oh, great, brilliant, wonderful news, Mum.'

Blimey, an acknowledgement that she was getting married. Shelley instantly felt her heart lifting.

'So, your Uncle Thomas is beside himself at the thought of giving you away. He really would be honoured, he said to tell you. I told him that he really needs to meet Colin before he makes any such claims, but there you go.'

'I'm sure they would get on like a house on fire,' said Shelley.

'Anyway, I had a quick chat with your Auntie Nancy and she's invited you over there for a weekend before the wedding – you know, for like a type of hen party. She said you would be very welcome to stay at their villa, if you wanted to. She said she'd even get rid of Uncle Thomas for the weekend.'

61

'Seriously?'

'I said you probably wouldn't be bothering with anything like that, but I promised I would pass the message on.'

'Seriously?'

'Why do you keep saying seriously?'

'Erm, various reasons. Auntie Nancy offering me the villa, which is amazing and so exciting, and why on earth would I not want a hen weekend in Spain?'

'Aren't you too old for all that now?'

'No! Most definitely not. I've helped to organize four other hen parties; there is no way I'm missing out on one of my own. Absolutely no way.'

'Right,' Peggy sighed. 'Well, I'll ring your Auntie Nancy back and tell her you've changed your mind. You would like to go out there.'

'You already told her I wouldn't want to?'

'Like I said. I assumed you were more grown-up than that. By the way, she invited me too.'

'Wow, Mum, you should go. What a brilliant idea. When did you last go? I keep telling you that you should go more often. The sunshine would do you so much good.'

'I just don't like travelling on my own since your dad died. You know that.'

'I know. But it will be worth it when you get there.'

'Well, if I come with you, I won't be on my own, will I?'

'What do you mean, come with me?'

'If I come with you on this weekend before your wedding.'

62

Shelley nearly dropped the phone. What was happening? Was her mum coming on her hen party, to Spain? This all seemed very unlikely.

'Nancy was very keen that I should come if you were coming,' said Peggy. 'No idea why. She doesn't normally make such a fuss of me. Normally she can go months without even bothering to call and see how I am. Oh, and she also mentioned that she would invite Rosalind and Chloe out as well,' said Peggy.

Shelley was speechless. This was all going topsy-turvy. Auntie Nancy, who had turned seventy last year, was suggesting she celebrate the end of her single days with her cousin, Rosalind, and her teenage daughter Chloe. Rosalind was seven years older than Shelley, and if she was totally honest, just a bit boring. She used to be fun when they were growing up. She would often stay with them in the summer holidays, and Shelley remembered many happy times roaming the countryside with her cousin. But then the older she got, the more serious she got, and then she met Robert and the young, fun Rosalind seemed to disappear into the sombre business of being Robert's wife. And when he became an MP – well, all fun was banned. She took her role as an MP's wife very seriously, hardly daring to be seen anywhere with a smile on her face. What on earth was Auntie Nancy thinking, gathering random family members for a hen party? That didn't sound like much fun at all. And if her friends came along, how would they get on with her relatives? *If* they came along of course. She couldn't imagine many of them being able to tear themselves away from their babies for a whole weekend. Apart from Becca. She would be up for it without a shadow of a doubt. There was no way she would turn down a chance to escape her motherly duties, even if it was with Shelley's weird combo of family members.

Perhaps if Becca came along, it would be okay. Fun even. And after all it was a chance to have a weekend in the sunshine before the wedding.

'Sounds good, Mum,' said Shelley. 'Just let me know when would suit Auntie Nancy. Now, do you want to come to London sometime and we'll go and look at dresses? I can send you a train ticket. You could come down and make a weekend of it?'

'We'll see. No rush, is there? When it's a bit warmer maybe.'

'Well, we'll have to get one soon or else it won't be ready in time.'

'What do you mean? You're not getting married until July, are you?'

'Yes, but you have to order them, and they can take a while, so I don't really want to risk it. And well, given my height, it might take a while to find the right one. I can't imagine it's going to be easy.'

Shelley could hear her mum sigh on the other end of the line. 'I suppose you will need a lot of fabric,' she said.

'Thanks, Mum.'

'Why don't you come and look in that lovely shop in Borrowash? Elizabeth Fleming got hers there and she looked remarkably thin in the photos. It really transformed her.'

'And thank you again, Mother.'

64

'I'm just telling you that, as you are well aware, Elizabeth was on the large side, and that Borrowash shop did wonders for her in terms of her wedding dress.'

'Thank you for putting me in the same category as someone who is morbidly obese.'

'And who managed to get married to someone five years before you did.'

'It's not a race,' replied Shelley.

'It sort of is, though, isn't it,' replied Peggy. 'A race against time.'

Shelley bit her tongue. This conversation wasn't going how she had planned. 'There's a wedding dress shop I walk past every weekend in Chalk Farm that I always thought I wanted to get my dress from. The ones in the window are amazing. They have a waiting list for appointments. Can I put our names down?'

'Why not?' said Peggy curtly. 'And if I can't make it, you'll just have to go without me. Why don't you take Becca? You don't need me telling you what dress to buy, do you?'

Why did her mother insist on not being involved? She didn't get it. It would be so nice if she showed just the slightest bit of interest in what was going on.

'How's Colin?' she heard her mum ask.

'Fine, great,' she replied. 'He's at some construction awards dinner thing tonight in the city in some fancy hotel. Said he was dreading it.'

'Didn't he ask you to go along?'

'God no. He said it was going to be full of blokes talking about planning laws and the price of steel girders. Said I would be bored to tears.'

65

Peggy left a judgemental silence. She didn't understand. Peggy had done everything and gone everywhere with Gordon. Shelley didn't think he'd gone for a night out without his wife for his whole married life. Things were different now. And Colin wasn't a dairyman who grew up in the village he lived in. Colin was an international businessman – his night out was work, not a social occasion to be shared with his fiancée.

Shelley said her goodbyes and put the phone down. Misery guts, she muttered at the phone. She didn't know why she expected anything else. Peggy had been miserable – well, for as long as she could remember. Certainly, ever since her dad had died. Well, she didn't care. She was going to enjoy getting married whether her mother liked it or not. She'd get an appointment at Pretty, Pretty and go on her own if she needed to.

Chapter 11

They had been sitting in a pub in Tottenham when Colin first mentioned his stag do. Colin had come to meet her after work. He claimed to like Tottenham and its 'real pubs', as he called them, but Shelley wasn't convinced. She'd ordered a pint of lager, longing for a long, cool drink after a hard day with the under-eights. He was nursing a red wine from a miniature bottle of the type you get on planes. He was attempting to look relaxed in his well-cut suit amidst the 'lads' strolling in in their bomber jackets and denim jeans, but he wasn't quite achieving it. But then the subject of hen and stag parties came up and he was suddenly completely animated.

'Oh, I forgot to tell you,' he said. 'Excellent news on that front. Jacob, you know Jacob, Jacob from Cheshire; well, he has offered me his loft apartment in Amsterdam for the whole weekend. I'm so excited about it. We thought about going further afield seeing as I am the last one of the crowd to get married. Like maybe Vegas, but Neil refused to leave his animals up in Scotland for a whole week. I tell you that small-holding will be the death of him. I've no idea why he doesn't just come back and work for the firm. Anyway, his devotion to his sheep means that Amsterdam it is. Apparently, you have to have your best man on your stag do.'

'Sounds great,' nodded Shelley, trying hard not to gulp down her pint, even though she was desperate to. 'Good news on that front for me too. I'm off to Spain – how cool is that?'

'Spain?' said Colin, nodding, clearly impressed. 'One of my favourite countries.'

'Yeah, so my auntie offered me her villa for the weekend – unbelievably I also have connections in a foreign country.'

He grinned. Why was he drinking his wine so slowly? She so wanted to get another pint!

'So, whereabouts in Spain?' he asked.

'It's not on the mainland. It's actually on the island of Majorca. A resort called Andelica. I've never been before,' she replied.

Colin paused just as he was about to take another gulp of wine. 'You are kidding me?'

'Do you know it?'

'Yeah, I do actually,' he said, nodding enthusiastically. 'We built some villas not far from there years ago in partnership with a Spanish firm. Dad sent me out there with his number two to try and help me learn the trade. Mick Johnson his name was. I think I turned his hair grey. He was supposed to be training me but I was way more interested in making the most of the

Spanish nightlife and learning to jet ski. Time of my life really.'

'Wow, that is so weird,' said Shelley. 'So, it's nice then?'

'Oh yeah,' replied Colin. 'You'll love it. There's a beautiful beach and a long line of bars and restaurants along the harbour. It was always buzzing. I wonder if the Flaming Flamingo is still there? I spent so much time in that place it was practically my second home.' He laughed. 'I would love to go back. How long have your auntie and uncle been there?'

'They moved out there about five years ago. Uncle Thomas is the one who is going to give me away. Says he wants to meet you before the wedding, actually, but I'm not sure how we can work that out. Perhaps you could call him sometime?'

Colin was looking at her, blinking. He put his drink down and leaned forward. Damn it, he was going to take all night to drink that wine.

'Why don't I come with you?' he said, clasping her hands. 'Come with you to meet him.'

'You want to come on my hen weekend?'

'Well no – that wouldn't be right, would it?' He paused for a moment. 'I've still got some business contacts out there. It would be great to catch up with them. I could go and see them and then maybe meet you and your auntie and uncle for a meal or something?'

Shelley stared back at him. 'Great,' she said. 'Perfect.' She couldn't believe he was making such a big effort to meet her family. Sounded like a brilliant plan, apart from the fact it was possibly going to be the weirdest collection of people at a hen weekend ever. Still, the hen weekend wasn't the main event, she reminded herself. It was the getting married that was important. The hen weekend was an added bonus.

She grinned at Colin. 'You're not enjoying that wine, are you?' she said.

He looked sheepish. 'It tastes like shit actually,' he admitted.

'Shall we pick up fish and chips on the way home and a decent bottle from the off licence?'

He grinned back.

'Now you're talking,' he said, giving her a hug. 'Practical solution for everything. No problem too big for you to get past. Let's go, Practical Pants!'

Chapter 12

Present day

'Can we come in?' came a voice from outside Shelley's childhood bedroom. 'It's only us. We've got the bouquets here.'

Peggy went over to the door and let in Shelley's cousin Rosalind and Rosalind's daughter Chloe. They were both dressed in the same forget-me-not blue full-length dresses as Becca.

'You look absolutely gorgeous, Shelley,' said Rosalind immediately.

'Thank you,' said Shelley grinning. 'I am so glad you are here.' She opened up her arms and pulled them all into a group hug. She felt a bit tearful having the whole gang together. Especially today, the day she was finally getting married.

'We wouldn't miss it for the world,' said Rosalind as they broke away. 'We've been waiting for this day for a very long time. After all, three of us have had their own weddings since your hen weekend, so it really is about time.'

'How crazy is that?' said Shelley, shaking her head. 'Who would have thought it?'

'Definitely not me,' replied Rosalind. 'Now here's your bouquet. I've put some Topaz gemstones in, which are your birthstone, as well as some Rose Quartz stones which bring happiness in relationships.'

'Really, Mum,' said Chloe, rolling her eyes.

'We ordered them from a temple in Spain. They have been blessed by Ohamaha.'

Chloe looked at Shelley. 'I apologize for my mother's insanity,' she said. 'You can take them out if you want to. Mum, you really are too old for all this. For goodness' sake, you seem to have really gone downhill since you turned sixty.'

'No!' cried Rosalind. 'That would be incredibly bad luck. And really, Chloe, do you have to be so sensible? Honestly, you need to learn to not take life so seriously. I would have thought you becoming a mum would have chilled you out a bit, but it really has made you very boring.'

'I don't think that doing stupid stuff like blessing crystals makes you "not boring",' retorted Chloe.

'Oh, look,' said Becca, thrusting her phone in Shelley's face to distract from the squabble. 'My son has sent a picture of your future husband waiting by the altar. He says he looks like the cat who is about to get the cream. Isn't that nice?'

Shelley looked at the picture. It was true. He did look a bit full of himself, and that gorgeous smile was lighting up his face. It was clear that he had no qualms at all about what was about to happen. She felt herself catch her breath.

Peggy cleared her throat. 'Well everyone,' she said, 'I think it's time don't you? There really is no reason to be late given that it has taken nearly twenty years to get here. Shall we?' she asked, stepping forward and taking Shelley's arm whilst grabbing her walking stick with the other hand.

'Let's do it,' said Shelley, nodding at her mother. 'And thank you for giving me away today, it means a lot.'

'Well, I should have offered to do it last time. I don't know what I was thinking.'

'I don't know what you were thinking either,' agreed Shelley.

'Or you,' stated Peggy.

'Or any of us,' added Becca. She shook her head. 'Christ, we were all in a right mess really, weren't we?' She looked round at everyone.

Rosalind nodded. 'Thank goodness for Shelley's hen weekend, hey? We might not be here today if that hadn't happened.'

'Goodness knows where we would have all ended up,' added Chloe.

'It really was the weekend that changed everything,' said Shelley. 'Now come on, let's finally get me married.'

Chapter 13

15 June 2000

Shelley and Becca caught the train up from London to stay with Peggy the night before they flew to Majorca. Becca had been so excited she was unbearable. She'd pulled a bottle of wine and two plastic cups out of her bag as soon as the train pulled out of St Pancras Station. She also pulled a plastic tiara out of her bag and demanded that Shelley wear it.

'But it's not my hen party yet,' she wailed.

'Yes it is. From the minute I closed the door behind me on the wailing banshees from outer space, then I was on your hen do. I do not plan to waste a single minute of it.'

'Look, it's not going to be your classic hen party, is it?' said Shelley. 'We're hardly out with party animals, are we?'

'You got me, sister,' said Becca, clinking her glass against Shelley's. 'We are going to make this the best, the most epic hen party of all time. I might never get away alone for the next eighteen years, so we are going to make this one count.'

'It's a shame none of the rest of the gang could make it,' said Shelley, gazing out of the window.

'You mean it's a shame no one else was willing to abandon their kids like me?' questioned Becca, her eyebrows flaring upwards.

'Well yes,' replied Shelley.

'Look on the bright side,' replied Becca. 'At least we haven't got Lisa droning on about the colour of Beatrice's poo and Clare swearing blind that Blake's first word was "millennium". I mean who would want to spend the weekend with a load of clucking hens on the phone back to base for constant updates. We *need* to party!'

Shelley had not been at all surprised that most of her friends had politely declined her invitation to accompany the random gathering abroad. She was the last one to marry by about two clear years, and so most were much happier downing a bottle of wine in front of the telly rather than dragging themselves out to a foreign country and undergoing the trauma of having to arrange childcare, or leave untrustworthy husbands to fend for themselves. No doubt they preferred not to spend all weekend worrying what they might come back to. But at least she had her best friend Becca. There was no way she was missing it. Previously life and soul of any party, she wore her new status as mother of twins as if she had been dealt the worst piece of bad luck on the planet. In fact, Shelley was slightly scared of what an unleashed Becca might be capable of. So desperate was she to relive her hedonistic days of freedom in the Nineties, Shelley wondered if they would ever get her back to her family.

'May I remind you that we will be spending the weekend with my mother,' Shelley said.

'The black widow,' hissed Becca.

'Quite. As well as seventy-year-old Auntie Nancy who is, let's say, larger than life in body and in soul. As well as my super-worrier, boring cousin Rosalind and Chloe, my rebel . . . I've no idea what she is – first cousin once removed? Sounds like one hell of a hen party, hey?'

'We'll make it work,' said Becca, snapping her fingers. 'You may be reliant on a desperate friend and an odd collection of relatives who have nothing better to do for your last weekend of freedom but that does not mean to say that we will *not* have a good time.'

Shelley clinked her plastic cup against Becca's. She was actually really excited about the next few days and couldn't quite believe she was finally on her hen weekend, which truly marked the countdown to getting married. It was all too good to be true. She'd hit the jackpot and was marrying a very decent man just a shade before her thirty-ninth birthday.

Having said that, having attended many hen parties over the last decade, she was all too aware that it paid to have low expectations. Hen weekends typically went the same way for her. Overhyped travel to the venue. Much excitement early evening, and too much drinking, despite many mutterings about pacing oneself. A cracking night on the Friday night where everyone is full of energy and joy, then the slow dawning realization on the Saturday that you had to do it all over again, when you wished with all your heart that you could go home and sleep off your hangover and not talk to another human being until Monday morning. The Saturday night of a hen do is unnecessary and unwanted. The term 'peaked too soon' is made for the Friday night of the hen party. In Shelley's opinion, hen parties should really stick with tradition and be for one night only – however, the invite to Spain had been too good an opportunity to miss.

Shelley wasn't the slightest bit surprised the next morning when their departure from Peggy's house turned out to be anything but smooth. Peggy had refused to book a taxi, saying it was an unnecessary expense, and somehow convinced Ray – yes Ray, who she constantly moaned about parking in front of her house – to give them a lift. When he failed to be at her door at 6 a.m., the agreed time of departure, she marched round to his house and loudly knocked on his door, no doubt waking up the whole street. He appeared almost instantly, sleepily rubbing his eyes and pulling a coat on over his pyjamas.

'You are not taking us to the airport looking like that!' exclaimed Peggy.

'Like what?'

'In your pyjamas. Go and put your clothes on.'

'But it's six in the morning, no one is going to see. In any case, these are my best pyjamas. Paisley look. Very smart, I thought.'

'Very smart for night time maybe but not for driving us to the airport. Go and get changed. We'll be waiting by the car,' instructed Peggy.

Shelley and Becca had been watching from the pavement, mouths agog.

'Potential there, I think, Mrs C,' said Becca.

'What are you talking about?'

'Single man next door, getting up to take you to the airport. I'd call that potential. In fact, in some cultures, they'd call that a proposal.'

Peggy gave Becca the most withering look, whilst Becca stifled an over-excited giggle.

'Sunglasses?' asked Peggy, taking in Becca's attire, which was totally suited to where she might be in six hours' time, but looked decidedly odd next to the backdrop of Ray's runner beans and a chilly start to the day. She was wearing a short summer dress, sunglasses, straw hat and platform gold strappy sandals. This contrasted heavily with Peggy's travelling wardrobe of elasticated linen trousers, a pale blue T-shirt, a cardigan and some flat canvas boat shoes.

'I'm getting in the mood, Peggy,' replied Becca. 'For all that sun, sea, sand and . . . and . . . sangria,' she replied, when Peggy gave her yet another sharp look.

'Now there are to be no shenanigans from you two on this break,' said Peggy, addressing Shelley and Becca like two naughty schoolgirls. 'Nancy has been very kind to let us go and stay, so no letting her down. Do you hear?'

'Yes, Mum,' grinned Shelley.

'Yes, sir, Mrs C, sir,' said Becca, giving her a salute.

'Well, what a fine group of young ladies I have the pleasure of transporting today,' said Ray, coming up behind them.

Becca swung round and beamed. 'Wow,' she exclaimed. 'You look super smart now. Not that the

78

paisley pyjamas weren't very tidy-looking but a shirt and tie? You really have gone beyond the call of duty. And you've brushed your hair! You look a million dollars.' She turned and winked at Peggy.

Ray had indeed pushed the boat out this time. His grey hair was carefully swept over his forehead, and he might even have had a quick shave. But it was the twinkle in his eye and the grin on his face that really made his appearance shine.

Ray blushed. 'I can't go letting you all down, can I,' he said, tucking his tie into the waistband of his trousers. 'I thought my best pyjamas might be acceptable but Peggy's right. Not for a trip to the airport, even at six in the morning. Right, let's get you in then. Not much room, I'm afraid. I hope Peggy told you I only had a small boot and you needed to be travelling light.'

He opened up the boot, only to find it full of all kinds of junk, including a butcher's meat slicer.

'That's where that went,' he exclaimed, wrestling it out of the car and dumping it over the hedge onto his lawn. 'I've been looking for that for ages.'

'Are you a butcher?' asked Shelley, trying to make conversation.

'No. But the butcher's in Apperly closed down and I happened to be in there and offered them forty quid to take it away. Thought it might come in useful sometime.'

Shelley and Becca exchanged glances.

Ray proceeded to pull various random items out of the boot and throw them on the ground, including a spanner, a saucepan, and a pile of coat hangers.

'There we go. Let's get them cases in then,' he said, grabbing Shelley's cabin case and throwing it in. He then picked up Becca's and pulled a face. 'What's in here?' he asked.

'Funnily enough, a butcher's slicer,' she said, helping him guide it in. 'You never know when you might need one.'

He looked at her and threw his head back and laughed the most wonderful bellow. 'Very funny,' he said. 'Very, very funny. Now, Lady Peggy, shall we have you in the front?'

'Don't call me Lady Peggy,' said Peggy.

'Oh, please do,' muttered Becca.

'Your car awaits,' said Ray, holding his arm out for Peggy to take, which she ignored and sighed, reaching for the door herself and letting herself in.

And so they were on their way.

Chapter 14

Rosalind hadn't seen her daughter since they stepped through the automatic doors at the entrance to the airport. She had been in the middle of telling her that she'd arranged to meet the others in the newsagents, when Chloe had stridden off in the direction of Boots the Chemist without a word. Rosalind was praying she was going in there to buy something as innocent as shampoo or insect repellent. That would be okay. Even better would be some hair dye, which might do something to cover the hideous homemade purple that her locks currently sported. Rosalind wasn't entirely convinced that taking her daughter to a Spanish island with an abundance of bars and clubs was a good idea. Chloe was currently keeping Rosalind up all night most weekends as she anxiously awaited her return from goodness knows where with goodness knows who. A string of men seemed to call for her. She couldn't keep track, and when Rosalind had asked if there was anyone special in her life, the sneer that Chloe had given her could have curdled cream. But her mum had insisted that she wanted to see her granddaughter. That it would be a good idea for them to all to spend some quality time together. Rosalind didn't think her mum realized that quality time with an eighteen-year-old basically consisted of a quick hello around midday when they got up, grabbed some toast and then disappeared.

'I'll be looking at the biographies,' Rosalind shouted after Chloe, but she didn't turn around.

Having browsed the shelves she settled on a book about Georgiana, Duchess of Devonshire, and had just paid at the counter when she heard someone say, 'Hi Rosalind.'

It was Shelley. The first thing she thought when she looked at her cousin was how old she felt. There was a mere seven years between them, but it might as well have been a century. It wasn't years that separated them. It was life experience. Rosalind had married Robert at twenty-three, straight out of university, and then promptly fallen pregnant with their son Oscar, quickly followed by Chloe. Her twenties and thirties had been awash with child rearing, whereas Shelley's life had followed an entirely different path. Shelley's twenties and thirties had been full of career and friends and travel, and being able to think only about herself. At family gatherings, whilst Rosalind shared stories of school reports and PTA meetings, Shelley was recounting tales of weekends away with uni friends, crazy nights out in bars and hungover days at work. Now Rosalind was rapidly approaching the end of her stint in 'child-rearing' mode, Shelley was possibly just starting to think about having children. They really couldn't be further apart.

They had actually been quite close as kids, with Rosalind often being shipped up to Derbyshire for the summer holidays. Her dad was the general manager of the local theatre in Bournemouth and her mum did whatever was needed to get the shows up and running. Both ex-performers, the theatre was their life and treated much like a favourite child with Rosalind often left feeling like a neglected sibling. So she'd loved staying with her cousins in the relative sanctuary and calm of Auntie Peggy and Uncle Gordon's household. Where meals ran on time every day and where routine reigned supreme. Not like in her chaotic homelife, where meals were grabbed on a whim, as and when there was time between theatre performances. If she was honest, she'd always been jealous of Shelley. Her little cousin had had exactly what she had wanted growing up. Was it any surprise, really, that Rosalind had married young, happily giving up all thoughts of a career to create the dream family life? One she thought she'd missed out on when growing up.

One look at Shelley and her friend made Rosalind's heart sink further. They were both wearing pretty summer dresses and had smooth shaved legs and wedge heels. Shelley's glorious auburn curls swayed free over her shoulders and made Rosalind feel even more self-conscious about the flecks of grey she had spotted in her close-cropped haircut. They both had cute fashion rucksacks slung over their shoulders, contrasting heavily with Rosalind's hiking rucksack, which contained supplies for all eventualities, including a mini first-aid kit, copious wet wipes, tissues and a large bottle of water. She was wearing the shorts she used for walking in, as they were the most comfortable thing she owned, and a polo T-shirt, along with some light walking shoes and socks made from a special fabric that wicked away moisture.

She'd not put any make-up on . . . well, because she never wore any make-up. She hadn't worn make-up during the day since 1994, when Robert had taken her and the children out to lunch for her fortieth birthday to the Hard Rock Café. Their choice not hers, of course. The only thing she put on her face was a bit of moisturizer now and then, if she'd been out for a walk in the bracing wind and her face felt a bit dry.

'This is my friend Becca,' Shelley announced, pushing Becca towards Rosalind.

'Very pleased to meet you,' Rosalind said, offering her hand to shake.

Becca stifled a giggle. 'Likewise,' she replied, offering her hand back.

'Becca has twin boys,' added Shelley and smiled.

'How wonderful,' said Rosalind. 'I have a son. Oscar. He's twenty now.'

Becca's eyes opened wide. 'And you're still standing. Impressive.'

'Sons are easy,' said Rosalind. 'Whereas girls. That's a whole other story.'

'Funny,' said Becca. 'That's what *my* mum always says. Apparently, I was a nightmare when I was growing up.'

'And now look at you,' said Shelley, grinning. 'A respectable mother of twins and a corner office in the city.'

'You're working?' asked Rosalind. 'What do you do?'

'Nothing much,' said Becca with a shrug. 'I just stare

at spread sheets all day long and make other people a lot of money.'

'She was Graduate Trainee of the Year in her company,' said Shelley proudly. 'Not bad for someone who once said they'd rather eat her own vomit than work in the city.'

'Well, you know,' replied Becca. 'People change. Anyway, all of that is just a pipe dream at the moment whilst I'm hanging off the every whim of the double threat that now exists in my home.'

'What's that?' asked Rosalind.

'My two sons, of course,' replied Becca.

'Well, it must be great to spend time with them,' said Rosalind. 'How old are they?'

'Ten months,' replied Becca. 'I'm hoping to go back to work full time as soon as,' she went on. 'But can you imagine trying to find full-time childcare for twins in London. And the expense – it's insane.'

'Perhaps it would be cheaper to give up work,' suggested Rosalind.

'Possibly, but then I would go insane,' grinned Becca cheerfully.

'I've never regretted not working when my kids were born,' said Rosalind. 'You can miss so much.'

'Well, that's just not me,' said Becca. 'The sooner we can get a live-in nanny, the better. Then all my prayers will be answered.'

Rosalind felt her eyebrows shoot up.

'I mean men go out to work and leave their babies at home all the time, don't they,' stated Becca. 'I don't see why I shouldn't.'

Rosalind was left somewhat open-mouthed. It was clear that Becca was not on her wavelength. The mere thought of leaving someone else to care for her children made her shiver. She really didn't know how she should respond, so it was lucky that Shelley stepped in.

'Where's Chloe?' she asked, looking round.

'The chemist, I think,' replied Rosalind.

'Shall we all go and find her?' said Shelley. 'Mum should be in there too.'

'Do you need to buy a book or anything whilst you are here?' asked Rosalind. 'I've just bought this one on the Duchess of Devonshire. Have you read it?' she said, showing it to them.

'Err no,' said Shelley. 'I brought *Bridget Jones* to read again.'

'Oh,' said Rosalind. 'I tried to read that but, well, I didn't really get it.'

Shelley and Becca blinked back at her.

'Are we going to check in then, or what?' came a voice from behind them. They turned to see Chloe, standing there looking expectant. Rosalind wondered what Shelley and Becca must think of her daughter, with her hair dyed purple, multiple rings trailing right up her ears and her eyes rimmed in very heavy black eyeliner. She wasn't wearing pretty dresses like them, but sported a crop top and combat pants. Rosalind watched Shelley and Becca take in Chloe before Shelley began with the introductions.

'Er, hello Chloe,' she said. 'This is my friend Becca.'

Becca said hello. Chloe nodded.

There was an awkward silence.

'Did you get what you wanted from the chemist?' asked Rosalind.

Chloe shook her head. 'I can get them cheaper in duty free,' she announced.

'Oh,' replied Rosalind, forcing a smile. 'Can I get you a book to read? I'll treat you?'

Chloe looked at her mum like she had grown two heads. 'No,' she said, shaking her head.

'Well, shall we go then?' said Shelley. 'Get ourselves checked in.'

'There's an idea,' said Chloe sarcastically.

'Come on then,' said Rosalind, leading the way. 'Let's go.'

'We are going clubbing, aren't we?' Rosalind heard Chloe ask Shelley as they made their way towards the check-in desks. 'We are not just doing boring shit like cocktails and restaurants?'

'Well err . . .' faltered Shelley. 'Well, I think we'll just go with the flow, eh. I've never been before so we'll just have to see what there is.'

'Just let's not do any cultural rubbish though, hey,' said Chloe. 'Please. Mum's already got ideas about us going to a museum or something. So be warned. When she mentions the museum, you have to promise to say that there is no way on this planet that you are going to go to a museum. Okay?'

'Absolutely,' Rosalind heard Shelley reply. 'There is no way I am going to a museum.'

Chapter 15

Shelley sighed with relief when she heard her mobile phone ring in her bag when they were all finally standing in the queue waiting to check in. She had been waiting to hear from Colin who'd ended up flying to Majorca the day before with Neil. The plan was that they would all meet up on Sunday night for a meal, with Uncle Thomas and Auntie Nancy as well. Shelley had been surprised that Colin was going to so much effort to meet her relations before they got married, until it transpired that he saw it as a way of having an extra stag do. There had been lots of talk of clubbing and visiting bars that he and his brother knew. She was fine with that, but Colin had promised to ring her last night when he arrived.

He hadn't.

Which was also fine.

He was in an exciting place. It was his first night. So, he'd gone for a meal with his brother and some business contacts and clean forgotten – no big deal. But she was mighty relieved to hear her phone ring now, knowing it must be her fiancé calling to apologize and to say he had arrived safely and tell her about the great evening he'd had out with Neil.

She grabbed at her phone and pushed it to her ear. 'Hello!' she gasped. 'How are you? Is everything okay?'

Silence at the other end.

'Hello, Colin . . . hello, are you there?'

The line went dead.

'Oh,' she said staring at her phone. 'That was weird.'

'What's wrong?' said Becca, turning in the queue to look back at her.

'Nothing,' said Shelley, shaking her head. 'I'd been waiting to hear from Colin in Majorca and he just tried to ring me and the line went dead.'

Inexplicably, she felt tears prickle her eyes. She was mortified. Why was this upsetting her so much? He'd forgotten to ring her, that's all. No big deal, right? What was wrong with her? Must be pre-wedding nerves. This weekend did signify the final countdown into getting married and if she was honest, she was finding it slightly unsettling for some reason. She just needed to get a grip. She looked away. Next thing she knew, Becca had her arms around her.

'I'm fine, I'm fine,' she said. 'I just . . . I just . . .'

'When did he say he would ring?' asked Becca, putting her hands on her shoulders.

'Last night, before they went out.'

'And he didn't.'

'No.'

'Why are men utterly incapable of making a phone call at a specified time? It's ridiculous, right? They just can't do it. They can remember exactly what time a football match starts, or what time the pub opens, but ask them to make a call at a specified time. No! No chance.'

'Becca, it's nothing really. I don't know why I got upset. Stupid. Just ignore me.'

Becca paused, looking at her.

'Why shouldn't you be upset?' she said. 'He said he'd call and he didn't. You want to know he's okay, that's all. Is it too much to ask?'

'What's wrong?' Peggy asked, turning round as they shuffled forward.

'Men!' exclaimed Becca. 'That's what.'

Peggy looked back at her, alarmed.

'Colin hasn't rung,' stated Becca.

'It's nothing, Mum,' said Shelley. 'Colin said he'd call me last night to say he had arrived safely and he didn't, that's all.'

'He didn't call you after a journey to say he had arrived safely? Well, that's just common courtesy,' said Peggy.

'Exactly,' said Becca.

'It's nothing,' said Shelley, starting to wish she'd never mentioned it. 'He probably just forgot. He was going out with his brother last night, so he'll have just got distracted. No biggie. Seriously. Just forget I said anything.'

'What's Colin done?' interjected Rosalind, turning round, and catching sight of three serious faces. 'What's happened? He's not called it off, has he? Oh Shelley, what has happened?'

90

'Nothing!' exclaimed Shelley. This was exactly why she mostly kept her emotions in check. This was what happened. People totally overreacted. 'He's done nothing. All that's happened is that he forgot to call me yesterday to say he had arrived safely.'

Rosalind stared at her, blinking.

'Colin didn't call you,' she stated.

'Yes,' replied Shelley.

'That's a shame,' said Rosalind.

'He just forgot!' said Shelley. 'It's fine. It's really not a big deal.'

'Gordon never called me,' added Peggy. 'Never needed to. We were never apart, except for work. I don't know what he would have made of these mobile phones. This constant need to be in touch. Just ridiculous, if you ask me.'

'I *love* my mobile phone,' gasped Becca. 'I have no idea what I did before texts. Saves so much time making plans. And using letters as short cuts to words. *Love* it.'

'What is going to happen to our children's education if they are encouraged to just use letters rather than words,' stated Rosalind. 'Your poor twins could grow up illiterate.'

Becca stared at Rosalind for a moment. Shelley held her breath. She knew that look on Becca's face. She was formulating a scathing response. 'Look,' she said, brushing past them both and heading towards the empty check-in desk, hoping to throw them off topic. 'We're next.'

'Do we get an upgrade – we're on a hen weekend?' Chloe asked the man standing behind the desk.

'Shhh,' said Rosalind. 'You're making his job much harder. Anyway, don't go shouting it about that we are on a hen weekend.'

'Why not?' asked Chloe, turning to look round at everyone and catching sight of their glum faces. 'What's happened? Why does everyone look so miserable?' You all look like someone died.' She paused.

Nobody smiled.

'It's not the groom, is it?' she asked, wide eyed. 'It's not, is it? If it is, we will still go, won't we? There's no need to call off a hen weekend just because the groom is dead?'

'Chloe!' hissed Rosalind.

'Colin hasn't died,' said Shelley. 'He's fine. He just didn't call when he said he would. That's all.'

Chloe's eyes opened wider still.

'He didn't call?'

'No. So no biggie, right? It's all fine.'

'Auntie,' said Chloe, putting her hand on her arm. 'They never call. Believe me. I shouldn't have to tell you that.'

'I am *not* your auntie,' snapped Shelley. 'We're third cousins, aren't we?'

'I don't think you're third cousins,' interjected Rosalind. 'I think you'll find that you are—'

'For goodness' sake, Mum!' said Chloe, turning on her mother. 'Does it really matter?'

'So here are your boarding cards,' said the man behind the desk, leaning forward to intervene. 'I've put you all in a row, three on one side of the aisle and two on the other. Have a good trip.'

'Bagsy window seat,' said Chloe, grasping the boarding cards and walking off.

'Now, does anyone need the toilet before we go through security?' asked Rosalind.

Shelley watched as Becca stopped in her tracks. 'Do you know what, I'm really glad you asked me that because, now I think about it, I *do* actually need the toilet, and if you hadn't asked me then who knows? I might have wet my pants, which quite often happens if I'm honest, as I've not quite mastered the art of deciding independently whether I need to go to the bathroom.'

Rosalind grimaced at Becca. 'I just thought that this would be a convenient time for us all to go whilst we are together, so we don't lose each other because we have to wander off at an inconvenient time to use the toilet.'

Becca stared at Rosalind as though she was from a different planet.

'I need the loo,' said Shelley, seeing that Becca and Rosalind had made a rocky start in their relationship, which did not bode well for the weekend. 'Let's all just go, eh?'

They all followed each other and stood in line waiting to use the toilet. The queue was bubbling with all shapes and sizes and ages. There were pensioners in their nylon clothes and harassed mothers trying to change nappies whilst toddlers wreaked havoc. A girl hogged a mirror, applying false eyelashes, whilst another girl with a near shaved head pushed her out of the way and grabbed a can out of her bag. She sprayed a red cross on her very short blonde hair and shouted, 'Come on England' before she stalked back out.

Peggy raised her eyebrows.

'By the way, I've booked tickets for us all to go to a ceramics museum,' announced Rosalind. 'Hope that's ok? It's supposed to have some fantastic items on display.'

'Shelley?' said Chloe, turning to face her.

Shelley looked at Chloe, startled, then turned to Rosalind. 'I guess,' she said with a shrug.

'*No*, Mum, no way,' said Chloe. 'Shelley doesn't want to go to a poxy museum, do you?' she demanded. '*No* museums.'

'But it could be really interesting. These are examples of some of the best contemporary ceramics in the whole world,' said Rosalind.

'Teacups and teapots,' muttered Becca. 'I thought this was a hen weekend, not an OAP coach trip.'

'There is nothing wrong with OAP coach trips,' said Peggy, turning round to Becca. 'I'll have you know that Tenby in October is very pleasant. I've been every year for five years.'

'But we are going to Majorca in June,' said Chloe. 'No one goes to Majorca in June for the museums!'

'It's your turn,' said a woman, frowning at Rosalind and pointing at an empty cubicle.

'So sorry,' she said, walking forward and locking the door behind her.

'I've paid for the tickets,' she shouted through the locked door. 'I had to book a time and they only had three-thirty in the afternoon or eight o'clock left.'

'Tell me you didn't book eight o'clock?' Chloe shouted back.

'Of course I did – it'll be too hot at three thirty.'

'Mother, what were you thinking?' continued Chloe. 'There is *no way* Shelley wants to be in a museum at all on her hen weekend, never mind at eight in the evening!'

'Please don't swear, darling,' replied Rosalind, still behind the locked door whilst those in the queue looked on, bemused.

'I'm not ten!' shouted back Chloe. 'Why are you trying to ruin Shelley's weekend, not to mention Auntie Peggy's and Shelley's friend's?'

'Becca,' said Becca. 'The name's Becca.'

'Yeah, whatever,' said Chloe.

'Erm, can someone pass me some toilet roll,' said Rosalind from the other side of the toilet door.

'Chloe, pass your mum some toilet roll under the door,' said Peggy.

'Only if we don't have to do the museum,' replied Chloe.

'Come on Chloe,' said Rosalind. 'Please.'

'Not unless you ditch this stupid museum idea,' said Chloe.

'Can you please just pass her the toilet roll,' a lady requested. 'There is quite a line forming here.'

'Do you hear that, Mother?' shouted Chloe. 'You are causing a queue. Now drop the museum idea and these nice ladies can use the toilet.'

No answer came from behind the cubicle door.

Peggy sighed.

Shelley held her breath.

'Look lady,' said the girl, still attaching her eyelashes. 'Enough on the museum already.'

Again, silence, followed by a murmur of, 'Okay.'

'Louder,' demanded Chloe.

'Okay, no museum. Now will you please pass me the loo roll?'

Chloe stalked out, triumphant, leaving Shelley to tug toilet paper out of a reluctant holder and crouch down uncomfortably and wave her hand under Rosalind's cubicle until she took it from her. All-in-all, not what she would call a team-building exercise.

Emerging from the toilets, Shelley decided to head to Boots the Chemist, hoping for a few minutes' peace to gather herself.

Having perused the aisles for toiletries she didn't know she needed, and having stared at the lipsticks, hoping the perfect shade would leap out at her, she found herself in the queue wondering how she was going to fit the box of tampons and can of mosquito spray into her already bulging carry-on case. Why was it necessary, she thought, whenever you flew somewhere, to empty your bank account into the chemist at the airport before you left? There was always something you had forgotten that suddenly seemed essential. And it seemed to cost you at least twenty quid. Chemists in airports were the devil's work. She looked up and caught a very attractive man behind her looking into her basket, and hastily shoved her cardigan over its contents, feeling herself embarrassingly start to blush.

Why was this queue taking so long, she thought, looking up to see what the delay was.

'I don't have my boarding card with me,' the girl at the till was saying to the cashier.

'I'm sorry, but you need your boarding card to be able to purchase.'

'Are you serious? I'm buying condoms. Like protection,' the girl replied. 'You can get them free in loads of places. We always have people coming into college telling us where to get free condoms. You cannot move for free condoms as a teenager. And you are telling me I need some stupid piece of paper to be able to give you money in exchange for condoms. What if I get pregnant whilst I'm on holiday? I'm going to write a letter to your head office and tell them I'm pregnant because I didn't have a boarding pass? Really? Are you going to let that happen?'

Shelley thought she had better step in and prevent Chloe from getting banned from an airport chemist.

'Hi Chloe,' she said, sidling up to her relation. 'Everything okay?'

'Hey Auntie,' said Chloe, surprisingly throwing her arms around Shelley.

'I'm not your auntie,' said Shelley sternly.

'Second auntie?'

'Maybe second cousin? Or, I think actually it's first cousin once removed.'

'No way, you must be older than that. At least third cousin.'

'Shall we agree at third cousin and pretend we know what that means?'

'Deal. You got a boarding card?'

'I have, as it happens.'

Chloe turned to face the lady behind the counter. 'So, my third cousin is going to stop me getting pregnant. Satisfied?'

'Err, I never said that I would help you buy contraception,' said Shelley, starting to panic. 'What would your mum say if she caught me buying condoms for you? Are you sure you're going to need those?'

'It's a hen party. We are going to a holiday resort,' said Chloe, nodding determinedly. 'Of course we need condoms.'

'You are eighteen, you are with your mother and your auntie, and your third cousin,' replied Shelley.

'Just in case,' said Chloe. 'Just in case.'

'Look, do you want to buy these condoms or what?' said the cashier, getting impatient. 'I have a long line of customers forming behind you.'

Chloe looked at Shelley and Shelley reached into her bag to pull out her boarding card. She also unloaded her tampons and mosquito spray to add to the purchase.

'Hang on a minute, Shelley,' said Peggy, rushing up behind them. 'Get me this, will you, and I'll pay you back.' Peggy placed a box of anti-diarrhoea tablets on the counter. Shelley stared down at it.

'People get bad tummies in foreign countries,' said Peggy. 'It's all that foreign food.'

'Not in Spain they don't, Mum.'

'You never know. And they might not have anything for it over there. You don't want me sat on the toilet all weekend, do you?'

'Can I ring these through now?' asked the cashier, raising her eyebrows.

'Yes, yes, of course,' said Shelley, wanting to escape the hell of the airport chemist as soon as possible.

'Wait!' came a cry. 'Wait a minute,' gasped Rosalind, puffing up. 'We might want to take some of this. Last time I went to see Mum, her villa was a hotbed of bugs and goodness knows what. You know her, she never was one for housework.' Rosalind thrust two cans of bed-bug spray into Shelley's hands. Shelley felt an instant need to scratch her head and her armpit.

'I can tell that the first thing I'll need to do when I get there is to get the mop bucket out,' said Peggy, tutting. 'My sister wouldn't know a mop if it slapped her in the face.'

'Do you need a bag?' asked the cashier, scanning all the items rapidly.

Yes, to put over my head, thought Shelley, going crimson. The good-looking man behind her in the queue was trying not to laugh at them, she could tell. And he was the one standing there openly with a packet of laxatives in his hand.

'Who's buying condoms?' exclaimed Rosalind, pointing at the incriminating package.

'Aaah . . . aaah,' stuttered Shelley, looking at Chloe, who was now studying something on the floor.

'Me actually,' said Becca, coming up from behind.

Peggy turned to stare at her. 'You are *married*, young lady,' she exclaimed. 'I told you this morning, I will not stand for any shenanigans on this holiday.'

'They're not for me, they're for Shelley,' Becca told her.

'Shelley! Why does Shelley need condoms?' asked Peggy. 'Why does anyone need condoms on this trip?'

'For some party games,' said Becca. 'We are on a hen party, are we not?' she asked the crowd.

'Yeah, that's right,' said Chloe, looking gratefully at Becca. 'Every hen party needs condoms.'

Peggy stared at Shelley, as though it was all her fault that Becca was pretending to buy condoms to play games with at her hen party.

'I . . . I . . . don't look at me like that,' stuttered Shelley. 'I'm just the bride-to-be.'

'I've no idea what your Auntie Nancy is going to say,' said Peggy, still looking utterly disappointed at Shelley. 'Come on, Rosalind, let's wait outside. I'm not sure I want to be a part of this.'

Shelley paid and hustled Chloe and Becca out of the shop. 'Thanks Becca,' she said. 'I think.'

'I assume they are yours,' said Becca, looking at Chloe.

'Thanks,' she muttered, taking the offending items and stuffing them in her silver rucksack. 'Now, are we going to the pub then, or what?'

Chapter 16

'I cannot believe I'm in a pub at eight in the morning!' exclaimed Peggy, as she dropped herself into a battered red leather seat in front of a table already littered with empty lager glasses. 'Who drinks at this time in the morning?'

'We do,' announced Becca, putting five gin and tonics on the table. 'Get that down you, everyone, and then we will consider our battle plan for the weekend, now that we have managed to set some boundaries.' She raised her eyebrows at Rosalind.

Chloe sat down with a sigh of relief. It looked as if Shelley's mate was actually going to be all right, despite the fact that her mother had already made a point of telling her Becca's entire CV which had of course included the obligatory stint at university.

'Why are you telling me all this?' Chloe had demanded.

'I just thought,' said Rosalind, 'that you'd be interested.'

'Why?' Although she didn't need to ask why.

'Well because—'

'Because you thought that Becca might convince

me to get my arse into gear and go to university. Is that why? Don't patronize me, Mum.'

Her mum had given her that mortally wounded look, as though she'd kicked her. God, she hated that look.

But Becca seemed like fun. Becca seemed like she wanted to have a good time somehow on this weekend, so Chloe was willing to give Becca a chance as long as she didn't try and lecture her on the merits of going to university at any point.

A loud ring interrupted the silence.

'I bet that's Colin,' said Peggy, nodding at Shelley. Chloe watched as Shelley frantically grabbed her bag to find her phone.

'No,' said Shelley, looking up, disappointed. 'Not my phone. I think it's coming from your bag, Becca.'

Becca reached into her bag and pulled out her phone. She glanced at it then put it back without answering. 'I've only been gone five minutes,' she muttered, taking a gulp from her drink.

'Jason?' asked Shelley.

'Yes,' said Becca. 'I'll adjust my earlier statement. Men do call. They always call when they want something, when they need help. You can guarantee that.'

Becca's phone started to ring again from the depths of her bag.

She ignored it.

'Perhaps it's an emergency?' questioned Rosalind. Becca gave her a cold stare.

'Even if it is, what am I expected to do from here?' said Becca. 'He's there. I'm not. In any case, he's much better with them than me.'

102

The phone rang off. They all stared at it. It didn't start again.

'See,' said Becca. 'He's worked it out. I knew he would.'

'Perhaps I should ring Colin,' said Shelley, looking as if she was in another world.

'Yes,' said Peggy and Rosalind.

'No,' said Becca and Chloe.

'You don't want to appear too desperate,' said Becca.

'They're getting married!' exclaimed Rosalind. 'There's nothing desperate about wanting to talk to your fiancé, is there?'

'You should just phone him,' said Peggy. 'Put your mind at rest.'

'Bollocks,' said Chloe. 'She'll just sound pathetic.'

Peggy looked at Rosalind.

'Do not swear at your great-aunt,' said Rosalind.

Chloe had always thought that Great-Auntie Peggy disliked her. Then again, Chloe thought perhaps that Auntie Peggy disliked everyone.

'Just ring him,' sighed Becca, 'and then perhaps we can start enjoying ourselves.'

Chloe shook her head as Shelley got her Nokia phone out of her bag and found Colin's number. Chloe replaced her headphones on her head. She'd had enough of this ridiculous conversation, although she didn't switch on her music. She had to make sure they didn't end up deciding on anything stupid, like actually going to the museum. Chloe watched Shelley wait for Colin to pick up. She really hoped that whoever this Colin was that he wasn't a total shit.

Shelley deserved better than that if she really wanted to pursue this ridiculous dream of getting married. Chloe couldn't understand why any woman would want to shackle themselves in such a way these days. Most men seemed to be total bastards. Take Guy Bostock for example. Biggest bastard in the history of the universe. Fact. Guy Bostock who had sworn his undying love on her sixteenth birthday, and not long after that they had slept together. He'd promised it was his first time too. Then Archie Fisher had told her he'd been shagging Vicki Cartwright all along. Everyone knew, apparently. He'd just wanted to knock the girly swot that Chloe was off her perch.

Utter bastard.

Was it any wonder she'd decided not to carry on to sixth form and enrolled in college instead, where she could redefine herself. And she had. Girly swot no more. No one was ever going to mess with her again.

'No answer,' said Shelley, switching her phone off.

Really. What a surprise, thought Chloe. She wanted to scream at her: *What the hell are you doing? Why are you getting married? You must be insane . . .* She knew she was never going to give up her freedom for the sake of a man. No way. She didn't want to become a housewife and a mother. Not like her own miserable mother. Because that's what happened. Young women with dreams and ideas and plans just ended up cooking and cleaning up after other people. When her mum had been trying to think of a wedding present to buy Shelley, Chloe had suggested a mop and bucket. Because that was what marriage led to – every single time. Shelley was an idiot, if you asked Chloe. She'd got away without getting married until now – why did she want to ruin it?

Still, looking on the bright side, at least the impending nuptials got Chloe a weekend on a sunny Spanish island. So she might as well make the most of it.

'Shit, I nearly forgot,' said Chloe, pulling her headphones off and rummaging in her bag. 'I grabbed this off the car before we left and put some ribbon on it. You have to have one of these, Shelley. Just to make it all official. Just so everyone knows we are on a hen party.'

Chloe pulled an L-plate out of her bag. She'd painstakingly attached pink ribbon to it so that Shelley could hang it around her neck. 'There you go, put it on,' urged Chloe.

'Really?' said Rosalind. 'Surely no one does that any more? And an L-plate – hardly appropriate.'

Chloe stared back at her mother and shrugged. 'So, she's been with other men. Who cares?'

'Not many, to be fair,' said Becca.

'Thanks a bunch,' said Shelley, punching her friend.

'Well, not as many as me,' said Becca.

'That's because you were a slut at college,' said Shelley.

'Aah, those were the days,' said Becca wistfully. 'And look at me now, being harassed on the phone by my husband because he can't remember how to look after our babies,' Becca's shoulders sagged. 'I'm sorry. Ignore me. All I want this weekend is to stop worrying about being a mum, just for five minutes. That's not too much to ask, is it?'

'Once you become a mum, you never stop worrying,' pointed out Rosalind. 'Comes with the job.'

'Oh please,' said Chloe. 'You could worry about me getting pregnant in amongst a herd of nuns. You thrive on worry. You love it.'

'Well, you certainly keep me busy with it,' said Rosalind. 'That's for sure.'

'Oh my God! Is it your hen weekend too?' screamed a woman in her mid-twenties wearing a sparkly pink Stetson and pointing at the L-plate sitting in Shelley's hands. She leaned towards Shelley, almost spilling out of her low-cut top and Daisy Duke shorts.

'Err yes,' said Shelley, looking half terrified.

'How excited are you?' the woman continued to shout. 'We have been planning this for *weeks*. I cannot tell you how excited I am. We're staying in Palma, Majorca – are you? Please tell me you are. How much fun would that be? We should meet up, that would be so cool.'

'Actually, we are staying with my auntie in her villa in Andelica, about thirty minutes from Palma,' said Shelley.

'You're staying with your auntie? For your hen weekend?' She looked around the rest of the crowd, pausing to stare at Peggy, holding her handbag primly on her knee and looking black as thunder, and Rosalind in her walking coat and trekking shoes.

106

'Oh,' replied the woman, already starting to back away. 'Well, have a great time. Maybe see you in a bar someplace. Good luck.' She waved and then ran.

'Can I join that hen weekend?' asked Chloe, moodily gazing after the woman who was running away.

Chapter 17

By the time they landed at Palma airport on Majorca, everyone was as low as a group of women going on a weekend to somewhere sunny could be. They'd barely spoken for the entire flight as they tried to ignore the squeals of laughter coming from the back of the plane from the other hen party, who sounded as if they were having the best time ever. Shelley's group filed through security in silence, and came out blinking into the bright daylight of the arrivals hall with heavy hearts.

Nancy had said she would meet them at the airport. Shelley looked around the hall as most people headed towards tourist reps holding clipboards, to be sent on their way via coaches to all corners of the island. Shelley couldn't see Nancy anywhere but, having said that, she hadn't seen her in probably five years since she'd moved out to Andelica, so she might struggle to recognize her anyway.

'There they are,' she heard a shout coming from her left. 'I'm here, look here, over here.'

Shelley swivelled round and immediately recognized

her Auntie Nancy holding up a massive sign saying 'Majorca Welcomes Bride-to-Be Shelley' painted in pink. She couldn't mistake her enormous smile, despite the fact she looked somewhat browner since the last time Shelley had seen her, as well as somewhat rounder. Clearly Nancy was enjoying being on holiday 365 days of the year.

'Here she is,' said Nancy, walking towards Shelley. 'The lady of the moment. The blushing bride-to-be. You look well on it, my dear,' she said, engulfing Shelley in her arms and a cloud of lavender perfume. 'Very well indeed.'

'And you look well,' said Peggy to her sister. 'And I mean well. I mean not in a good way.'

'And it's always a pleasure to see my little sister,' declared Nancy, releasing Shelley and rolling the super-skinny Peggy into her bulging arms. 'Now, you look – and feel – like you need some meat on those bones, sis. And here's my little Chloe. Oh, my Chloe, what a character you have become. Just look at you. Stand right out as something – not quite sure what yet, but I'm sure you'll figure it out.'

'Hi Nan.' Chloe grinned and ran into her now empty arms. 'Will you teach me how to make sangria again? And can you tell Mum that it's okay for me to go out on my own because she doesn't believe me that it's safe and that I can look after myself and – well – she's being Mum, you know what she's like.'

'I know what's she's like,' said Nancy, turning to her daughter and walking forward and embracing her. Rosalind remained stiff and awkward, as if she was being hugged by someone she didn't know, not by her mother.

Nancy put her at arm's length and shook her gently, looking her right in the eye. Rosalind grimaced back.

'Hi Mum,' she said. She looked her up and down. 'Have you been going to that yoga class I told you to go to?' she asked.

'No time, darling. Like I said on the phone. No time for things like that. Too busy looking after your dad. Anyway, yoga's not me, is it? I don't have the body for yoga.'

'You might do if you just tried it,' said Rosalind. 'Then maybe you wouldn't need that mobility scooter.'

'You have a mobility scooter?' exclaimed Peggy. 'Nancy!'

'Just for going to the shops,' said Nancy. 'We live at the top of a hill, don't forget. That's no good at my age. Now, we haven't been introduced?' she said, turning to Becca and holding her arms out towards her.

'I'm Becca,' she said, stepping forwards. 'Long-term best friend. Thank you so much for allowing me to stay. Really. I have ten-month-old twin boys and I cannot tell you what a lifesaver this weekend is. Seriously, I think I might have collapsed with exhaustion and desperation, had this weekend not happened.'

Nancy smiled sympathetically then said briskly, 'You'll cope. We all do. Now ladies, let's get you back to the house and settled in and then I want to hear all about Colin and this amazing wedding you're going to have, Shelley. Your Uncle Thomas is as proud as punch to be giving you away. He wants to show you the suit he's bought to check you are happy with it, and talk to you about what you need him to do on the day, and he wants to ask you if you want him to do a speech but you know, no pressure . . . you don't have to let him.'

'*Don't* let him,' said Rosalind. 'He insulted the vicar on my wedding day. Asked her if female vicars had to be celibate like men do, or if they are allowed to have sex but only to make babies. I was mortified. Mortified!'

'Let your dad have his fun,' said Nancy. 'Now, shall we go? You must be starving. I've got drinks and snacks ready back at the villa.'

Shelley eagerly offered to get a cab with Becca when Nancy announced that they couldn't all get in her car. Nancy delivered them to the taxi queue, then spoke in fluent Spanish to the driver before they sped off ahead of the rest of the party, windows wide open in an effort to get some breeze in the blistering heat.

They had only just pulled out of the airport when Becca's phone started to ring. Shelley watched as she pulled it out of her bag, sighed and then tapped a button to answer it.

'Hello,' she said. 'Yes, we've just got here. We are in a taxi.'

There was a pause as Becca listened to whatever Jason was telling her.

Eventually she said, 'It's two parts water, one part formula. The instructions are on the box as well as on the list I left you.'

Becca followed this up with a series of terse mm's until she said goodbye in a tone usually reserved for cold callers.

'Everything okay?' Shelley asked.

'He couldn't remember how to mix the formula,' said Becca through gritted teeth. 'I've shown him, it's written on the box and I typed it out, for crying out loud. They're his babies too! Do you know, as I left, I said to him that he knew as much about looking after those boys as I did, but he looked like I'd pushed him out of the lifeboat of the *Titanic* or something,' she said, shaking her head. 'This is what it's like once you have kids, Shelley. You think you are on this ship together and you are having a great old time, partying every night, and then you have kids and it's like that scene from *Titanic* where Kate Winslet just lets Leonardo slip away off the piece of wood. Doesn't even hold out a hand. That's it, cast away into motherhood without even a lifejacket.'

'Jason does help you, doesn't he?' asked Shelley.

'He does, but you always know *you* are the lifeboat. You sink, the rest of them do. I *hate* being the lifeboat,' said Becca, looking quite stricken. 'I'm rubbish at being the lifeboat. I can't stop those damn rugrats from jumping out of the lifeboat. And what if one of them does? Then what?' Becca shook her head. 'I didn't think that marriage meant I had to become the lifeboat.'

'What do you want to be then?'

'I want to be the captain,' said Becca, turning to look at Shelley. 'Promise me you'll be the captain in your marriage, Shelley. Please. Start as you mean to go on. Be the captain and let Colin be the lifeboat.'

'But I don't think I want to be the captain,' said Shelley. 'I think I'd quite like to be the lifeboat, actually. I quite like the idea of looking after Colin and maybe, you know, if we are lucky enough . . . maybe some kids as well.'

'Well, just promise me you won't give up work,' said Becca. 'You don't have to, you know. You keep your own identity. You can have it all nowadays. You can have kids and a career. Or so they say.'

Shelley didn't reply. Sometimes she felt like Becca had no idea what it was like to be her. Becca had gone through life, expecting to have choices about everything. Men flocked to her, so she could take her pick. She was in control. She'd never been like Shelley, mostly waiting to be picked, given her lack of self-confidence to even dream of doing the picking.

Would she put herself first in her marriage to Colin? She very much hoped it would be a true partnership. That they would put each other first. But she also believed that marriage was all about compromise. That they would both have to make concessions in their life in order to make it work. What those would be she had no idea of yet, but she believed that when those moments came, they would work it out.

'Have you talked to Jason about hating being the lifeboat?' she asked Becca. 'Perhaps you could have a job share on the lifeboat?' she suggested.

Becca turned to look at her and smiled sadly. 'You are the queen of mediators, Shelley, but I think even you would struggle to make my husband realize that the lifeboat even exists.' She turned to gaze out of the window and they fell into silence as they watched the dusty roads whizz by. It felt as if they had been awake for hours, but the day was just beginning, and who knew where it might end?

Becca leaned her head out of the window.

'Can you smell it?' she said, coming back inside.

'Smell what?'

'Freedom,' she said. 'Pure freedom.'

Chapter 18

'So, what's with the miserable face?' Nancy asked Peggy, as they pulled out of the airport in Nancy's tiny little Renault. Chloe was in the back with her headphones on, and Rosalind was leaning on the headrest with her eyes closed, fast asleep.

'It's not a miserable face,' said Peggy.

'Oh yeah, I forget, you have a resting miserable face,' replied Nancy with a grin.

'I do not!'

'You are so easy to wind up.'

'Watch that moped! Nancy, can you slow down a bit?' Peggy put her hands around the handle above the window and held on tight. She fought the urge to close her eyes. She was the much younger sister. By eight years. Although it felt more. Nancy was seventy now for goodness' sake. Seventy! Peggy was nowhere near her seventies. But being the eldest, Nancy was supposed to look after her, wasn't she? No, that had never happened. Nancy had always been the free spirit, shy of any responsibility for anything. Always trying to get Peggy into trouble for something or other, even when they were really young. Blaming little Peggy for all her misdemeanours. Like the time when Nancy was twelve and had crashed her bike, causing the wheel to buckle because she'd been trying to do stunts on it. She'd claimed that Peggy had sleepwalked in the night and ridden it and then left it in the middle of the garden. Even though she was only four years old! It had taken Nancy a week to admit that it was a lie.

And, of course, there was always an elephant in the room whenever they were together.

Dorothy.

Poor dead Dorothy.

The sister who had got between them ever since she had died at the age of fourteen of scarlet fever. The sister whose death had immediately driven eighteen-year-old Nancy to leave home to escape the grief, leaving Peggy – at the tender age of ten – to deal with the aftermath with their parents.

Peggy had begrudged her eldest sister leaving her for more than fifty years.

'You've put on weight,' said Peggy. 'You need to watch that. Not good for you at your age.'

'Not good for me?' replied Nancy. 'I think I'm old enough to decide what's good for me. I know exactly what's good for me. Having a good time. That's what's good for me at seventy. I'm not wasting the rest of my days eating rabbit food and water and being miserable.'

'Each to their own,' replied Peggy. She waited. She knew what was coming.

'You could do with a bit of enjoying yourself, you know, have some fun. Do you good.'

'I'm perfectly fine, thank you,' clipped Peggy. They swerved round a cyclist and Peggy hung on for dear life. They didn't speak for a few minutes. Peggy tried to form the words of gratitude for inviting them all, but they wouldn't come.

'How's Thomas?' she asked out of politeness and something to say. Nancy didn't speak straight away. Peggy perceived a small sigh.

'He's fine. I think.' She laughed a little too hard. 'You know, still out on the golf course all hours. He's very excited and honoured to be asked to give Shelley away. We were both a bit surprised, actually. We just assumed, when the day came, that you would do it.'

'Gordon wouldn't have wanted that,' replied Peggy, shaking her head. 'You know how he was for tradition. I think he would have wanted a male member of the family to do it.'

'I know, but what do *you* want? Wouldn't you like to give your only daughter away?' asked Nancy.

Peggy said nothing. She swallowed. Of course, she would love to give Shelley away. She just didn't think she could. She couldn't step into her dead husband's shoes. Not without falling apart. It was bad enough that this important occasion was happening without him, without her taking his place and feeling every emotion he should have been alive to feel. She couldn't do it. She knew she would not be able to bear the tsunami of feelings that it would invoke.

'No, I think Thomas should do it. He's such a born showman anyway, isn't he? He'll do a really good job.

Take the lead; keep up our side of the family. I couldn't do that.'

'Well, he likes to give a good performance, I'll give him that. He's already working on his speech. You know how he loves an audience, and he doesn't get in front of one much these days.'

Peggy knew only too well that both Thomas and her sister loved an audience, stemming from their days treading the boards in London whist she was at home coping with grieving parents.

'So, what's he like then?' asked Nancy, suddenly.

'Who?'

'Colin, of course. We can't wait to meet him. So glad he could join us this weekend. Would be very weird meeting at the wedding. But do spill. What do you make of him?'

Peggy thought for a moment. What did she make of her future son-in-law? She sighed, wondering how to describe him to her sister.

'He's okay,' she shrugged. 'Had life a bit too easy, if you ask me. Lacks a bit of *oomph*, if you know what I mean, but he will look after her. He'll do.'

'He'll *do*?' asked Nancy, scrunching her face up. 'He'll *do*? Is that enough?'

Peggy turned to stare at her sharply. 'Of course it is. Quite frankly, I think Shelley's been very fortunate. At her age she's lucky to get anyone. She just needs to get on with it now.'

'Right,' said Nancy. She said nothing for a moment. 'You know, I never really took to Robert if I'm honest,' she announced. 'I mean, when Rosalind first brought him home, I thought she'd lost her mind. He turned up in a suit and tie for Sunday tea? I just hoped that Rosalind saw something in him. Because that's all that matters, isn't it?'

'Exactly,' said Peggy. 'I'm just so relieved that she has finally found someone. That she's not alone.'

'Because there is nothing worse than being alone, is there,' said Nancy.

'No, there certainly isn't,' agreed Peggy.

Chapter 19

Becca and Shelley were sharing a room in Nancy's ground-floor three-bedroom villa that was part of a four-storey complex. Rosalind and Chloe were in another, and Peggy was bunking up with Nancy. The complex was slightly faded but comfortable, and Nancy had the benefit of a large patio overlooking the pool area, where they were all now sitting, sipping sangria and eating fresh bread, cheese and ham. Shelley felt herself start to relax. A true Brit could never fail to be seduced by a kidney-shaped pool, filled with crystal-clear water with the sun beating down on it. There were plenty of sunloungers scattered around which Shelley hoped to be taking full advantage of in the not-too-distant future. She couldn't wait to drape her Teenage Mutant Ninja Turtle beach towel over a white plastic chair, slather her highly burnable fair-skinned body in sun lotion and then lie down, close her eyes and feel those sun rays work their magic.

She could already feel a sense of calm flow over her as she munched on salami and warm ripe tomatoes. Until Nancy spoke.

'So has Colin arrived on the island okay?' she asked.

'Don't ask,' muttered Chloe.

Shelley felt herself blush. She'd just about stopped checking her phone every five minutes, but she had to admit that it was still bothering her that he hadn't called.

'I believe so,' she replied, trying to smile at her auntie.

'It's very fancy where they are staying,' said Nancy. 'It's at the more exclusive end of the resort on the other side of the harbour. Where it's a bit quieter. It looks really beautiful. We often get celebrities staying there.'

'Really,' piped up Chloe. 'Like who?'

'Well, last year Judi Dench stayed there.'

'Oh, right, old celebrities,' said Chloe.

'Have you ever been in the hotel, Auntie Nancy?' asked Shelley.

'No, no, they wouldn't want someone like me making the place look untidy.'

'So, he's rich then, this Colin?' asked Chloe.

'Chloe!' said Rosalind.

'Minted,' said Becca, before Shelley could answer.

'Like a millionaire?'

Becca nodded.

'Wow, Auntie Shelley—'

'Third cousin, remember,' interrupted Shelley.

Chloe shook her head. 'I will be whoever you want me to be, cousin, if you invite me to stay in your swanky pad every so often.' She paused. 'So how did that happen? I mean, no offence, but you aren't the type I would have expected to marry a millionaire.'

Shelley knew exactly what she meant. She didn't think she was the type either, until it happened.

'You mean she's no gold-digger, don't you,' said Becca. 'Exactly right. Shelley bagged herself a millionaire because she's a brilliant person and Colin must have seen that straight away. He's totally the one who struck gold if you ask me.'

'Aw, thanks,' said Shelley looking gratefully at her friend. She felt the tears well up in her eyes. It was exactly what she needed to hear someone say. The feeling of not being worthy of Colin and his money was something she was finding difficult to manage. There was a voice inside her telling her that this was all too good to be true and that she was ridiculous to think that this could actually happen to someone like her.

'To be very clear, I'm not marrying Colin for his money,' Shelley told Chloe. The mere thought of it made her shiver. The only thing that gave her reassurance that people didn't think she was a gold-digger was the fact that she looked nothing like a gold-digger. Labelling her a gold-digger would be like accusing Dame Maggie Smith of being a slut – just ridiculous.

'I would,' replied Chloe, flicking a crumb off her bikini.

'Would what?' asked her mother.

'Marry for money.'

'No you wouldn't!' exclaimed Rosalind. 'Why would you do that? You should *never* marry for money.'

'Why not?' shrugged Chloe. 'Most marriages end in divorce anyway, so you might as well get something out of it.'

'Chloe!' said Rosalind.

'What do you get out of your marriage, Mother?' asked Chloe.

'Chloe!' It was Nancy's turn this time to scold her granddaughter for her outspokenness.

'I will not dignify that with an answer,' said Rosalind.

Shelley felt sick. Why was her hen party starting out so traumatically?

'I just want everyone to know I'm having a really great time,' said Becca, giving a cheesy thumbs up. 'This is all going exactly as planned.'

Everyone looked down.

'So Shelley,' said Becca, clearing her throat and turning to her. 'We do have some surprises planned for this evening.'

'Do you?' asked Shelley, smiling. That sounded more like it.

'Of course,' replied Becca. 'Myself and Nancy have managed to collude to make sure this send-off is truly memorable.'

'You've been speaking to Nancy?' exclaimed Peggy.

'We've been emailing actually,' replied Becca.

Peggy looked blank.

'Sending letters but via the computer, Mum,' added Shelley.

Peggy turned to her sister. 'How on earth do you know how to do that?'

'Oh get with it, Peggy,' replied Nancy. 'Andy, who runs the bar down the road, showed me how to do it. He lets me use his computer sometimes when I need to.'

Peggy shook her head in sadness, as though Nancy had committed a major crime by agreeing to bring her communication channels into the twenty-first century.

'Anyway,' said Becca, 'as I said, we have plans for later, but can I suggest that we fully launch Shelley's hen party weekend by getting ourselves to the bar.'

She stood up and pointed into the distance.

'That's actually towards the mountains,' pointed out Nancy.

'To the bar,' said Becca, turning one hundred and eighty degrees and pointing in the opposite direction.

'That's inland towards the airport,' added Nancy. 'Try that way.'

'To the bar,' said Becca for the third time, pointing where Nancy had indicated. 'Let's go.'

'I need to change,' said Chloe.

'I think I'll just clean the bathroom first,' said Rosalind.

'And I could do with a sit-down for a bit and a nice cup of tea,' said Peggy.

'Said no one at a hen party ever,' said Becca.

'I bet I've said that,' admitted Shelley. 'In fact, I know I have, at Vanessa's, after we'd been out all night and finally got in at four in the morning and you suggested we head down to the hotel bar.'

'You did, I remember. Killjoy,' answered Becca. 'Mind you, I remember that was a bit of a dull weekend. I didn't even throw up.'

'Why don't you two go off and have a good time and I'll bring the rest of them down when they are ready,' said Nancy. 'Sound good?'

'Perfect,' said Becca, smiling gratefully at her.

'Do check out Andy's at the bottom of the hill,' Nancy told her. 'Look out for him behind the bar and tell him who you are. He'll look after you. Sit you next to the karaoke if you want.'

'I want,' said Becca, nodding furiously. 'I want very much. Let's go,' she said, pulling at Shelley's arm.

'Are you sure, everyone?' said Shelley, looking around the table with a concerned expression on her face.

'They're sure,' said Becca, grinning at them behind Shelley's back. '*You* are coming with me.'

Twenty minutes later, Becca sighed and looked around her. Andy's bar was located at the bottom of the hill below Nancy's villa and was the first of a long line of bars and restaurants overlooking the harbour. All Becca could hear was the gentle lapping of the tide and the tinkling of bells strapped to the top of yacht masts.

She listened harder.

No, there was no interruption of a baby crying to be heard. This was absolute bliss.

Andy's was by no means the most fashionable-looking place on the strip, with its moulded plastic seats and sports screens on the wall, but they served very large cocktails, one of which was now in front of Becca, provided by the very accommodating Andy.

'I'm Nancy's niece,' Shelley pointed out when they ordered their drinks.

'I thought so,' said Andy, grinning at them.

'How come?' asked Shelley.

'Err well, she said you were tall.'

Shelley turned pink.

'She's a lovely lady, your aunt,' added Andy. 'Proper character. Always down here on the big karaoke nights. And her husband.'

Christ, thought Becca. That could spell trouble. A singing granny in their midst.

'So, can you sing?' he asked them.

'Like a strangled hamster,' snorted Shelley. 'I'd have to be really drunk. Like hideously.'

'That's what these are for,' interrupted Becca, grabbing her drink. 'We will be singing later,' she told Andy. 'After a few of these.'

'No way,' said Shelley.

'Yes way,' replied Becca.

'Well, I will look forward to it. Just you give me the nod whenever you are ready,' said Andy.

They moved to find a seat with a view of the walkway running along the harbour. A bundle of middle-aged men were sitting up at the bar, staring at football screens and ignoring each other, mechanically raising pint glasses to their lips like pre-programmed robots. They only looked up when a hot young twenty-something walked by in a bikini and flip-flops. Becca looked at her body longingly. She used to look like that, she thought. Not now. Being pregnant with twins gave you stretchmarks that made you look like you were living with a fault line. She would never wear a bikini again. It made her want to cry watching this beauty walk past her. It reminded her of her honeymoon nearly two years ago in Bali. She'd brought four bikinis and, thanks to her pre-wedding fitness regime, she probably looked the best she ever had. Jason had certainly thought so. He couldn't keep his hands off her. Literally. Occasionally she had to beg to leave the room so they could at least go and enjoy the luxurious amenities.

It was probably the last time she had felt like her.

I mean, who gets pregnant on their honeymoon?

I mean, really.

They'd planned to start trying pretty quickly – after all, she was getting on a bit – but she'd figured it wouldn't happen straight away. And really, she hadn't quite prepared herself. She had just been promoted at work to head of department, and she'd wanted to get her teeth into that before any kind of maternity leave. Before someone younger covered her position and she was put on the 'no longer at full capacity' pile.

Married. It's okay, she thought. It won't change me. It's just a piece of paper.

Pregnant. It's okay, she thought, lots of women do it and dive back into their career unscathed. There are plenty of good nurseries around here.

And then the shock of twins. Shit! Twins – a totally different league.

She first suspected that her life was never going to be the same again whenever she told anyone she was pregnant . . . with twins. With no exceptions, people's expressions turned from delight to horror then back to fake delight. Not one person told her that everything was going to be okay. It was fine. Two was just as easy as one baby to handle. People were more likely to back away rapidly and never contact her again.

And then her belly grew and grew and grew and grew, like something out of a pantomime. It didn't stop. She became a mountain, and the remnants of the explosion of that mountain were still there, scarring her for life.

She felt her phone buzz in her pocket and took it out.

Help – it's chaos! But Toby just said tractor! Jx

It was from Jason. She didn't want to know what was going on back at base. Texts and updates from Jason were all well and good, but she didn't want them. She didn't want to be reminded of her other life, where she was barricaded in the house by a mountain of nappies and bottles and push toys and nursery rhymes. If she heard another nursery rhyme she would scream. In fact, she'd just resigned the three of them from Music with Mummy because she feared for the life of the leader. She thought she would actually strangle her if she suggested another round of 'Old MacDonald's Farm'. She'd had a lot of murderous thoughts, in fact, since having the twins. She'd wanted to kill Jason during labour for putting her through this hideous nightmare, then she'd wanted to kill the health visitor for pushing her into breast feeding, and then she'd wanted to kill her mum for telling her that she really should have them both sleeping through by four months old, and then of course she'd really wanted to kill *all* the mums she met who appeared to have totally nailed everything, and who glided into Music and Mummy with clean clothes on and blow-dried hair and clean babies who gurgled and giggled and never threw the instruments around like Toby and Miles did. Or hit each other like Toby and Miles did, or decided to have simultaneous poos like Toby and Miles did. She hated those mums who seemed to make it all look easy; in fact she hated all those mums who had managed to have just one baby!

She put her phone back down again. She didn't reply. She would call later. Just to say she was missing them all. Although, if she was perfectly honest with herself, she wasn't. She kept waiting for the pang, the longing to see her babies, but it didn't come. She wished it would. Then perhaps she would finally feel like a proper mother, not this poor impersonation of one that she seemed to be so far presenting. She had no maternal instincts whatsoever. That wasn't normal, right? Nothing. Zilch. She was failing spectacularly, and Becca never failed. Success was her middle name. Failure was something she had no idea what to do with.

But for now, all she wanted to do was to forget about it and sit here on her seat in a bar overlooking the sea, sip a cocktail and watch the world go by.

She watched a couple walk along the harbourfront in front of them. They were clearly doing the walk of shame. Well one of them was anyway. Either he was escorting her back to her hotel after a night of debauchery or she was walking him back. They held hands, but there the connection finished. She was wearing a crumpled white dress and high shoes unsuitable for a lunchtime stroll. Her hair was untidily pulled back in a ponytail and there were smudges of mascara around her eyes. His 'best shirt' looked as if it had been thrown on the floor and stamped on, and his white shorts, presumably pristine fourteen hours ago, had what looked like beer stains down them. They both squinted in the sunlight, neither wearing sunglasses. They hadn't needed them the night before when they had headed out in the darkness. They looked firmly ahead, not chatting, silent, awkward, both contemplating the regret running through their heads.

Becca nudged Shelley.

'Look at those two,' she said. 'They so had a one-night stand last night, and now they are both wondering how they agree never to see each other again.'

They both gazed after them as they passed. She had grass stains on the back of her white dress.

'How has she got grass stains on the back of her dress?' asked Shelley.

Becca shook her head. Sometimes her friend could be so naive. It was a wonder she had ever had a boyfriend at all, never mind bagged the most eligible fiancé around. But, of course Becca could see exactly what Colin saw in Shelley. She really was the greatest person anyone could have by their side. Loyal, genuine and beautiful inside and out, although you could never convince Shelley of that. Colin clearly saw it though. They'd double-dated a few times. Her and Jason and Shelley and Colin. They'd been out for meals, the four of them. Colin was eager to please. She'd give him that. He certainly didn't look down on anyone due to his status, but something had niggled at her the entire time during that first dinner. He did everything right. He was polite and appeared interested in her and Jason. He had talked quite knowledgeably about the family construction company when asked, and clearly had a valid place in the firm beyond his family connections. But still, something niggled.

In the end, it was Jason who worked it out.

When she asked him in bed later that night what he thought of Shelley's new, highly successful boyfriend he said, 'Bit needy. Desperate to show that he isn't just a trust-fund baby. Insecure, I guess. Not what I was expecting at all.'

'Mmm,' agreed Becca. 'I think you're right. Bit hungry for compliments, wasn't he? Not sure that's what Shelley needs. She can be insecure enough as it is. She needs a man who can big her up, not someone who needs bigging up himself.'

'If I were her,' Jason added, 'I'd have a damn good time on his money then dump him. She deserves some fun. She's never had much luck with guys, has she?'

Except Shelley hadn't moved on. The music had stopped and they'd landed in the same seat together. Damn millennium. Becca secretly worried that her greatest friend in the whole world had succumbed to the dangerous combination of female, late thirties, clock ticking, last one single, limited options . . . all roads led to the next man standing.

Becca had told herself when Shelley rang with the engagement news that it would all be fine. She was so excited and thrilled that it had to be okay. There was no way she was going to be the one to cast any doubt on their match. Shelley had said yes, and so she must be sure, and so Becca had buried any of her reservations deep in the back of her mind. The time had passed for doubts. She should have shared them long ago. And Shelley was finally getting married. The thing she had dreamed of. It was what she wanted, so best leave alone.

'Good to be here, right?' said Becca. 'Finally, on your hen weekend.'

Shelley grinned and took a sip of her drink. 'Who would have thought it, hey?' she said, leaning back. 'You know, I never thought I would actually get married.'

'Why on earth not?' asked Becca.

Shelley frowned. 'I guess I just didn't think there was anyone who would have me. I'm just not obvious marriage material, am I? You don't see anyone who looks like me in the bridal mags. No one. Clearly the only women who get married are the skinny, blonde ones with milky skin and dewy eyes. That's what a bride looks like. Not like me. Crazy hair that looks like I permanently have my finger in a plug socket, witch green eyes, or so my mother calls them, and freckles! I'm more bride of Frankenstein than bride of the year.'

'You are looking in the wrong mirror and you pay too much attention to what your mother says. Look at you sat there with those super-long legs stretched out, and those sexy freckles coming out to play. Stop pulling yourself down. In any case you're Colin's bride of the year and that is all that matters,' reassured Becca.

They both looked up sharply when they heard a loud tooting coming from somewhere behind them. Becca couldn't believe her eyes. Nancy was on her mobility scooter, driving down the pathway that ran alongside the bar. Chloe was riding shotgun on the back, shades on, and hair streaming out behind her.

She looked as amazing as one could look riding shotgun on the back of a mobility scooter. Nancy was tooting her horn and shouting at people to clear out of her way as she turned left onto the harbourfront, Chloe nodded her head rhythmically, headphones as ever wrapped around her head.

'Over here,' shouted Becca, getting up and waving manically at them.

Nancy came to a screeching halt – well, as near to a screeching halt as you could when only travelling at twenty miles an hour. She glanced behind her and, on seeing a suitable parking spot, turned the handles and began to accelerate backwards, causing Chloe to nearly fall off and a gentleman – whose beer belly was hanging out of the bottom of his T-shirt – to leap quickly to one side.

'You are lethal with that thing,' said Becca as they approached their table.

'I rode a Harley once,' replied Nancy nonchalantly. 'Back in the day.'

Becca noticed that Nancy was breathing heavily, despite the fact she had driven down, so quickly found her a chair to sit on, which she took gratefully.

'Your mother and Rosalind are walking down. They said to order them a goldfish bowl each,' she said.

'Did they?' gasped Shelley.

'Of course they didn't, but that is exactly what we are going to get them.' Nancy raised her hand in the air and gestured to the man behind the bar.

'Hey, Andy,' she shouted. 'We'll have three of your best over here.'

'Coming right up,' responded Andy.

'Contacts everywhere, eh Nancy?' said Becca.

'Always wise to be on the right side of the bar staff round here,' replied Nancy. 'In any case he's from Derbyshire, would you believe, and I regularly ring his nan for him to tell her he's okay. Here are the other two, look. Go and get them, will you Chloe?'

Chloe hadn't said a word, just sat down, still bobbing her head. Nancy reached over and lifted a headphone from her ear.

'Oi, Chloe – go and get your mother and Peggy from over there, look.'

Chloe looked up and trundled off. She was soon back with the rest of the party, just as Andy settled three enormous goblets of cocktail on the table.

'What are those?' said Peggy, curling her lip.

'Just drink it,' said Nancy. 'I like to call it "happy juice".'

'No need to drink it so fast,' Rosalind scolded.

Chloe glanced over at her. 'I'm eighteen, Mum. I can drink as fast as I like.'

'I remember going to Faliraki after my A-levels,' said Becca. 'Wow, I could drink fast then.'

Rosalind glared at Chloe.

'I dropped out just before my exams,' said Chloe, 'if anyone wants an explanation as to why Mum is looking at me like that. Cheers everyone.'

Everyone turned to stare at Chloe.

'What did you want to go and do that for?' asked Nancy. 'Clever child like you?'

'Exactly,' said Rosalind.

134

'All seemed a bit pointless,' said Chloe. 'I was just learning boring rubbish.'

'Boring rubbish that could have got you into university to do something you *would* be interested in,' continued Rosalind. 'I can't understand why someone can be so smart and yet so stupid.'

Chloe put her straw back in the glass and took a long draught, staring deep into the lurid green liquid.

Becca studied Chloe. In many ways she reminded her of herself at that age. Kind of angry all the time and out to prove that she knew best. Only fortunately, as it turned out, Becca had been motivated to prove she wasn't stupid to all the people who seemed to think she was. It was an act of rebellion for her to get into university, against all the teachers who wrote her off as a good-time girl. Chloe will work it out, she thought. Smart girls always do.

'Come on then, Nancy,' said Andy, approaching the table. 'You going to give us a blast on the karaoke?'

'It's far too early for that!' exclaimed Peggy.

'No, Mum,' said Rosalind, shaking her head. 'Please no.'

'Yes, Nan,' said Chloe, squealing and clapping.

Becca raised her eyebrows at Shelley. This could all be a bit cringey, she thought. A geriatric granny singing badly in the early afternoon sun. She watched as Nancy heaved herself up from her chair. She can't actually be aiming to sing, she thought. She'd barely touched her cocktail. No one sang karaoke on holiday, in the daylight, totally sober! That was like eating a kebab sober. Just not wise.

'Seriously?' said Peggy to her sister, shaking her head. Rosalind merely buried her head in her hands.

This was going to be terrible, thought Becca. Like excruciating. Like they might not be able to show their faces in this place again.

Andy offered his arm to Nancy, and she ambled over to the makeshift stage at the far side of the bar. Becca watched as the men at the bar glanced over and collectively shook their heads. Becca wondered if she should just make a run for it.

'Your usual?' asked Andy, as he handed her the microphone.

Nancy nodded as she also accepted a shot glass and downed whatever was in it.

'For the love of God,' muttered Rosalind.

Moments later, Becca was left with her mouth wide open.

She recognized the intro but it seemed so unlikely. She had been expecting some out-of-date twaddle from the Sixties perhaps. Some excruciating rubbish that she would have to clap to. But no, this was totally not what she had been anticipating. When Nancy started to sing, an enormous grin spread across her face. What a great choice of song. And soooo appropriate.

Nancy could really carry a tune. Like in a big way. Like sit up and prick up your ears kind of way.

Especially when it was as epic as the one-and-only Cyndi Lauper song 'Girls Just Wanna Have Fun'.

'It's definitely all I really want!' declared Becca, leaping to her feet and shouting at the top of her voice.

Wow. It felt like Nancy understood her very soul.

Yes. That was it. All Becca wanted to do was have some fun, and she absolutely could not remember the last time she had had some fun. Was it too much to ask? Why couldn't a married woman in her late thirties with baby twins just have some fun? What happened to her? When did it happen to her? When did she stop having fun? When did she stop *being* fun?

She felt like screaming.

At the top of her voice.

That she *just* wanted to have some fun.

Nancy was beckoning her over to the small stage now as she embarked on singing about a phone ringing in the middle of the night. Could this granny be any cooler, thought Becca, as she blindly gravitated towards Nancy, wanting to get more involved in the action.

Nancy gladly shared the microphone with her and they both belted out the tune, with Becca singing it from the very bottom of her heart. She had never sung with such passion ever before in her life, as she noticed Peggy and Rosalind looking on in slight horror and embarrassment. Becca was delighted, however, to see Chloe making her way towards them across the bar with a big grin on her face. Dressed effortlessly in a bikini top and a wrap draped around her waist, she looked amazing in the way only the young can. Becca felt a pang. She used to look like that. Just a dash of lip gloss and she was good to go. Not now. Now there was careful organization of belly-crushing pants and the draping of chiffon over dimpled upper arms. Looking good was no longer effortless. Looking good took careful planning and

137

thought and time. *Time*, for goodness' sake. The one thing she didn't have.

Still, she warmly greeted Chloe onto the stage and she and Nancy nudged themselves to the side so that Chloe could let her voice be heard. Becca tried not to mind making way for the younger model. But it stung just a bit. Just for a moment, there she was front and centre, and now she wasn't as she realized, she wasn't the only girl to want some fun.

Becca closed her eyes as she sang the last line, feeling it deep in her heart. She hoped that this wasn't going to be her only moment of fun this weekend. She needed to stock up on fun, or else she was never going to face up to the total and utter lack of fun that was waiting for her at home.

'Take a bow, ladies,' said Nancy, taking Becca and Chloe's hands.

They dipped forward. The men at the bar who had taken some interest in the three lively women had returned to supping their pints, saying nothing. Peggy and Rosalind were deep in conversation with each other, clearly deciding to ignore the troublesome members of their group. Shelley was enthusiastically clapping. In fact, she was standing up and giving them a one-woman ovation.

'You were amazing,' said Shelley as they got back to the table. 'You should be in a band, seriously. Form a group or something. That was so cool. Did you know that Auntie Nancy used to be a professional singer, Becca?'

'No way,' said Becca, feeling a bit giddy. 'What, like you got paid to sing?'

'Absolutely,' said Nancy, raising her glass to her lips.

'Nana was in the West End, weren't you Nan?' said Chloe.

'*Really?*' exclaimed Becca.

'Well, for a short while,' said Nancy modestly. 'After the war. When people were crying out for entertainment.'

'What kind of thing were you in?' asked Becca.

'Mostly review-type shows. Mostly chorus, but occasionally I'd get to stand in.' Becca noticed that she had gone all glassy eyed. 'There is not a feeling like it in the whole world, you know. Standing there giving it everything and then – well, getting the reaction you've always dreamed of since you were a tiny little girl. People clapping, smiling, some even standing. I can remember it as if it were yesterday.'

'Wow,' said Becca. 'I had no idea you had such a superstar in the family, Shelley.'

Peggy harrumphed and crossed her arms.

'What happened?' asked Becca.

'I met Thomas and fell in love,' Nancy said simply. 'We toured for a while across America with a theatre company. Now that was an experience. America in the Fifties was an amazing place to be. The stories I could tell you.'

'I'm so jealous, Nan,' said Chloe. 'Sounds so cool.'

'So why did you come back?' asked Becca.

'Why do you think?' said Nancy with a grin. 'I only got pregnant, didn't I, so me and Thomas thought we had had our fun and should go back to the UK and settle down. Thomas got the promise of a job in a theatre in Bournemouth, and so we got on a boat and went home. Rosalind was born six months later.'

'So sorry to ruin your budding thespian career,' said Rosalind bitterly.

'I never said that,' said Nancy. 'I wouldn't change a thing.' She winked at Becca. Becca wondered if she really meant that. Had having a baby ruined Nancy's life, she wondered? Does she ever wonder what might have been if she hadn't got pregnant? Could she have been another Doris Day? She certainly seemed to have the voice, if her most recent rendition was anything to go by. How do you even begin to get over that? The sneaking suspicion that having children may just have ruined your life.

Chapter 20

Rosalind looked at her watch. It was a very functional Casio digital. She liked it because it had a stopwatch. Useful when she was training for hockey or just challenging herself as to how quickly she could get up a hill.

If they left now, they could still make it to the ceramics museum for three-thirty. Dare she suggest it? She was worried that she was going to be shot down, but really what else were they going to do? They were just sitting around drinking at the moment. She really didn't want to spend all afternoon doing that. Didn't see the point in it. Surely there was a plan. There had to be a plan. They weren't just going to sit here, were they? Somebody must have planned some afternoon activities. Thought about how to fill their time whilst they were here. She didn't want to sit and do nothing. She never sat and did nothing.

'So,' she said, slapping her hands down on her knees. 'What's the plan then?' She looked up expectantly.

'Few more of these, I reckon,' said Becca, nodding at her empty glass. 'Maybe a quick nap, get changed, then we'll hit the town. Me and Nancy have it all organized for this evening.'

Now Rosalind felt really depressed. What a waste of an afternoon. There were sights to see, walks they could go on, and museums they could visit. The last thing she wanted to do was just sit.

She had to say it, she just couldn't stop herself. 'If we go now, we could still make the 3.30 p.m. slot at the ceramics museum?'

'Mum!' complained Chloe. 'You promised. Nobody wants to go to the museum.'

Rosalind looked around her. Everyone looked away, apart from Shelley.

'I'd quite like to go,' she muttered.

'Oh Shelley,' said Becca. 'A pottery museum? You cannot possibly go to a museum on your hen weekend.'

'Why can't she?' asked Rosalind. 'If she wants to go to a ceramics museum then she should. Why not?'

Becca shook her head at Shelley.

'You know I collect teapots,' said Shelley. 'Just thought there might be some interesting ones there. Maybe even a gift shop. I do love a museum gift shop, and they might have some amazing teapot that I could buy for Colin's parents as a thank you for paying for the wedding.'

'I love a museum gift shop?' repeated Becca in amazement. 'Did you really just say that? How actually old are you, Shelley? If I hadn't been at school with you, then I would have sworn you were a pensioner with that previous statement.'

'Oi,' said Nancy, offended.

'Sorry,' muttered Becca. 'Present company excepted, of course.'

Rosalind was really starting to dislike Becca. Why did it all have to be about what *she* wanted to do? Everyone kept saying it was Shelley's weekend, and she had just said she'd like to go to the museum, so why shouldn't they do that?

'Perhaps we should all have some free time?' suggested Rosalind, trying a different tack. 'Perhaps we could all go off and do our own thing for a couple of hours, then meet back at the villa later?'

'Yess,' hissed Chloe. 'You go to the museum, and those who are in the slightest bit interested in having a good time, stay here. Take your pick. Shall I get another round in? Who wants another drink?' Chloe stood up, looking round expectantly.

'Me,' said Becca. 'What about you, Shelley?'

Rosalind stood up. The group was clearly about to splinter, but no one was quite sure how. Rosalind picked up her bag, digging round in it for her sunglasses.

'You coming, Shelley?' she said.

Rosalind watched as Shelley glanced over at Becca. This was so unfair on Shelley, she thought. She clearly wanted to go to the museum and her best friend was making her feel bad about it.

Shelley appeared to be rooted to the spot.

'I think I'll stay here,' announced Nancy. 'It's quite a way to the museum and my battery is nearly flat. I'll have a wine spritzer, Chloe love. When you are ready. Get me the karaoke song book whilst you are up there, will you? It's about time I updated my repertoire.'

Peggy instantly got up. 'I'll come with you, Rosalind,' she said. 'One song is enough for me.'

Rosalind wanted to agree wholeheartedly. She felt as though she had spent her whole life with her parents in the spotlight, whilst she stood firmly in the wings. *Nancy and Thomas, life and soul of the party, what a fun couple; oh, and have you heard them sing – wow – just incredible. Shame Rosalind didn't inherit their talent.*

'Shelley? You coming?' she asked again.

Shelley visibly paled.

'Auntie!' declared Chloe.

'Third cousin,' corrected Shelley.

'Whatever. Don't be a loser. This is your one-and-only hen weekend. Don't spend it in some tin-pot, teapot factory.'

'It's a ceramics museum,' pleaded Rosalind.

'I rest my case,' said Chloe.

'Oh, for goodness' sake,' said Peggy. 'I'll look out for a teapot for you, and if there are any I think you might like, you can go and have a look tomorrow.'

Shelley grinned. 'Thanks, Mum,' she said. 'Great idea.'

'Let's go, Rosalind,' said Peggy, bustling off. 'We might even find a decent cup of tea on the way there.'

Rosalind looked round at the rest of them in dismay. 'Well, we'll see you later,' she said primly. 'Just behave yourselves, won't you.'

'Yes, Mum,' said Chloe and Becca in a singsong voice.

Rosalind turned to leave, extremely worried at what she would return to find. Little did she know it would be nothing like what she expected. It would be a hell of a lot worse.

Chapter 21

Shelley gulped as she looked down at her phone screen for the second time. They'd spent the last hour sitting, supping and singing. Actually, it had been heaven, and she was so glad she hadn't gone to the museum. All the tension had gone out of the group the minute Rosalind and Peggy left. She had actually started to feel like she was on her hen weekend. Yes, her hen weekend. She, Shelley, was on her hen weekend, an event that she had never thought would happen in a million years. She had even forgotten that Colin hadn't rung when he said he would, but then her phone had pinged and she'd made the fatal mistake of reaching in her bag and reading the text. She thought it would be a text from him but it wasn't. It was from an unknown number.

Had a wonderful time with your fiancé on the dance floor last night – just so you know.

Suddenly she wished she were in a museum. A museum sounded calm and serene and the total opposite of the turmoil she was feeling right now. She wanted to go and hide in a corner, to curl up into a ball as she tried to process what the text said. She quickly made her excuses and took herself off to the toilet, where she sat with her head in her hands.

It wasn't long before she had the absolutely crashing realization that somehow she wasn't surprised this was happening. She had been waiting for this moment the entire time she had been seeing Colin. Of course this was happening. It was all going too well for Shelley – things never went this well for her. Her dad had gone out one day to fetch the paper and never came back. The first school she worked for fell down. Yes, actually fell down. Every time she covered maternity leave, for a job higher than her grade, they always came back! All of her previous relationships had ended pretty badly. Her last boyfriend had ditched her at a wedding, for goodness' sake. Shelley was unlucky – fact. Meeting a man taller than her, and successful, and who wanted to marry her was a ridiculous idea. How on earth had she ever thought she was going to pull this off?

She splashed her flushed face with cold water and made her way back to the table slowly, thinking she would hide what had happened. She couldn't deal with everyone else's feelings on the matter. She'd have to pretend everything was fine for now, and then find some quiet time to work out what to do about it.

But she might have known that she couldn't hide her distress from Becca. She stopped mid-cackle at something Chloe was saying and stared. Shelley knew she would root it out of her like the Rottweiler that she was, so she silently handed her phone over to Becca.

Becca read the text then looked up at her, her mouth hanging open.

'Is this for real?' she asked.

Shelley shrugged, feeling tears prickle her eyes. She looked away. Next thing she knew, Becca had her arms round her. And then she couldn't help herself. The tears started to flow.

'What on earth has happened?' asked Nancy.

Shelley lifted her head off Becca's shoulder and looked at her auntie. 'I've just had a weird text,' she told her.

Becca handed the phone over to Nancy, who couldn't read it without her glasses so handed it over to Chloe.

'It says and I quote – "Had a wonderful time with your fiancé on the dance floor last night – just so you know, kiss, kiss",' read out Chloe.

'What on earth does that mean?' asked Nancy.

'It means that the wedding is off,' announced Chloe instantly.

Shelley gasped to hear the words said out loud. No, it could not mean that, she thought. It had to be a big mistake. It couldn't mean that. 'Maybe not,' she said. 'I mean, we don't even know who sent the text. It could be a hoax.'

'You don't know who sent the text?' asked Nancy.

'It says it's an unknown number,' said Chloe.

'Have you any idea who it might be?' Becca said, turning to Shelley.

Shelley shook her head and bit her lip to try and stop the tears.

'Why would anyone do that?' stated Nancy. 'What are they, cowards? You don't text a message like that.

At the very least, you pick up the phone and say who you are.'

'It must be someone who has managed to get your number, Shelley,' said Chloe. 'Which they must have got from Colin?'

Shelley felt confused and disorientated. 'I guess,' she said. 'What am I going to do?'

'Well, it's obvious, isn't it, the first thing you should do?' said Chloe, helping herself to her drink and taking a big gulp.

'What's that?' said Shelley. It so wasn't obvious to her.

'We call the number,' said Chloe. 'Speak to the idiot who sent it. Find out what's going on.'

'Genius,' said Becca. She gave Chloe a thumbs up.

'Why don't I ring it,' Becca said, holding her hand out to Shelley. Shelley gingerly passed her the phone. Becca pressed the dial button and put it to her ear whilst everyone held their breath.

'Straight to answer phone,' she said. Clicking the phone off.

'Why didn't you leave a message?' asked Chloe.

'Because . . .' faltered Becca.

'Give it here.' Nancy offered her hand to Becca to get the phone.

'No, Auntie Nancy!' exclaimed Shelley, lunging forward. 'Don't!'

'Look, you need to know,' said Nancy, staring down at the phone like it was an alien object. 'This can all be sorted out by just talking to each other. Now Becca – could you dial the number for me?'

Shelley closed her eyes. This was so going to end badly.

Becca looked nervously at Shelley, then took the phone and pressed the relevant numbers before giving it back to Nancy. Nancy cleared her throat.

'Hello there,' she said. 'Whoever you are, I would like you to call us back and explain yourself. Pronto.' She handed the phone back to Becca who turned it off.

'Oh God,' moaned Shelley.

'They'll call back as soon as they get that,' said Nancy, smiling confidently.

'Yeah, I bet they are quaking in their boots,' muttered Chloe.

'Shouldn't you call Colin, Shelley?' asked Becca. 'Ask him outright.'

'What would she want to do that for?' said Chloe. 'That's a stupid idea.'

All eyes turned to Chloe.

'Why is it stupid?' asked Becca.

'Because he's just going to deny it, isn't he?' she answered with a shrug. 'Of course he is. If you say you've got a text from a stranger implying that he has gone astray, he's just going to say it's a lie and why are you taking any notice of an anonymous text. And then it will all blow up in your face and he'll say this is just an excuse to call off the wedding and you don't really love me and then you can wave bye to your fancy schmanzy wedding.'

'How old are you again?' asked Becca.

'She's eighteen,' said Nancy proudly. 'Don't chew your nails, darling,' she added, slapping Chloe's hands down.

'I think Chloe has a point,' said Becca, nodding

149

slowly. 'That is exactly what he is going to do. I mean, what else would he do, and then you are no further forward. Don't you think? He will just deny it.'

There was silence for a few moments.

'It shouldn't stop us having a hen party, should it? The fact that the groom might be playing away?' asked Chloe.

'Now let's just hang on a minute,' said Nancy, holding her hands up. 'It doesn't actually say he is playing away, does it? It only mentions dancing. Perhaps we are all overreacting a little bit. Maybe Shelley just needs a casual chat with Colin to find out exactly what has happened before we get ahead of ourselves.'

Shelley nodded. 'You're right,' she said. 'I should just talk to him. I'm sure there is a perfectly good explanation.'

'He'll just deny it all, Auntie,' said Chloe, giving her a knowing look of a woman twice her age and experience.

'How many times? We agreed *third cousin* for the purposes of this weekend,' snapped Shelley, getting out of her chair suddenly. 'I'll go and see him,' she declared. 'Ask him to his face. See what he says. Clear it all up. I'm sure there is a completely logical explanation. I'll just go to his hotel and ask him what it's all about.'

'I think that's a good plan. Do you want to take the mobility scooter?' asked Nancy. 'The hotel is all the way over there, look.'

Everyone turned to where she was pointing. The hotel stood proud on a small peninsula on the other side of the harbour. It really was quite breath-taking. Its grand

150

old architecture rose to six floors with rows of iron-railed balconies that overlooked the glittering sea. There was a terrace out front, which bordered a perfectly manicured, highly irrigated, lush, green lawn containing an abundance of flowering bougainvillea that stretched down to the edge of the cliff. The impression was of an exclusive club reserved for the rich and famous.

'Bloody hell,' breathed Chloe. 'He really is loaded, isn't he?'

Shelley wasn't in the least bit surprised that this was the type of hotel that Colin would be staying in.

She swallowed.

'I think I'll walk,' she replied, declining her aunt's kind offer of wheels.

'I'll come with you,' said Becca, quickly getting up. 'I really need to see inside that place.'

Chapter 22

Shelley's heart was hammering in her chest by the time she knocked on the door to Colin's hotel room. She'd marched along the harbour front with Becca, barely saying a word. She wanted to get this all behind her. Hear Colin's perfectly reasonable explanation and start looking forward again to her wedding day.

Becca had whistled when they finally approached the entrance to the hotel. A sweeping drive curled around an enormous fountain which provided the calming soundtrack of continual falling water. A doorman was waiting to greet them in full livery. Shelley was surprised that he deigned to let them in given their very casual attire. Inside the double-height reception area they were greeted by shiny marble floors and the smell of fresh flowers which oozed from at least fifty stems in a vase on a central, highly polished, table. This was no package holiday hotel. This was, well, to be honest, it looked like a honeymoon hotel.

The receptionist had been remarkably relaxed about

giving a stranger someone's room number and a key. Shelley had made up some story about forgetting her room key and wanting to go and freshen up before her fiancé got back from playing golf, and how she was so stupid she couldn't even remember her room number. She'd done this whilst making a massive show of her enormous diamond engagement ring to illustrate that she was definitely the type of person who stayed in such a fancy hotel, and why would the receptionist have any cause to disbelieve her? She was grateful that the receptionist couldn't see her flip-flops that had broken at the top of the hotel driveway, so that now she was accompanied by a curious clapping sound everywhere she went, and had to do a silly walk to just try and keep the shoe from falling off her foot.

Shelley wanted to surprise Colin. See his face when she asked him out of the blue about the text. Then she'd know. She'd know if there was anything she needed to worry about. She left Becca to go and find the pool bar as she made her way upstairs.

Shelley had to knock twice before he opened the door. She decided not to just let herself in. That would have raised too many questions as to why she had a room key.

'I told you I'm on my way,' he said as he pulled open the door, dressed only in a towel round his waist.

'What are you doing here?' he said, looking surprised. 'I thought it was Neil. I was supposed to be meeting him by the pool half an hour ago.'

'Thought I'd surprise you. Can I come in?' asked Shelley.

'Err, sure,' he said, looking back around him into the room. It was a shambles despite its obvious luxury. That was probably why he looked a little unwelcoming, thought Shelley. He was embarrassed. His clothes, presumably from the night before, were lying on the plush deep pile carpet. On the solid wood dressing table was a clutter of keys and receipts and toiletries. The hairdryer was still out, casually resting against a *Times* newspaper that Colin must have read on the plane. There was a used coffee cup, stains dribbling down the outside, and some empty plastic packaging, maybe from some biscuits that had been eaten to soak up the alcohol the night before. Colin stood to one side to let Shelley into the room. He'd not bent to kiss her as she shuffled past.

Now what?

She stood next to the enormous unmade bed, not knowing how to start the conversation. She noticed the stunning view out of the window. He had a sea view. Of course he had a sea view. She wondered fleetingly if Colin even realized that hotel rooms existed that didn't have a view. Had he ever stayed in a scruffy bed and breakfast in Blackpool? Those were the type of hotels she had grown up with. Had he ever had the joy of opening the curtain and seeing a brick wall? Something for their first anniversary maybe?

'I err, just err . . .' she began, then her eyes settled on an empty bottle of wine on a table near the vast French window at the end of the room. Next to it stood two used wine glasses.

Colin was breathing very deeply, his chest rising and falling at a dramatic rate. She glanced back to him and then back to the two wine glasses. His gaze followed hers. She could feel herself holding her breath.

'Christ, you must think I'm an animal,' he said, lunging forward and grabbing the wine bottle and placing it in the bin before putting the two glasses on the tray with the kettle and the hot drink sachets. 'Neil and I kicked off the night with drinks in here before we went out. Neil's idea. I told him we needed to pace ourselves but you know what he's like.'

She knew something of Neil, but she didn't put him in the 'leading Colin astray' category.

'You mean you invited Neil to your room, then plied him with drinks before you headed out?' asked Shelley.

Colin paused for a moment. Then nodded vigorously. 'Yeah, that's it. You got me. That's exactly what happened. And then we ended up in the Flaming Flamingo until gone two. I cannot believe it's still open. And it's exactly the same as I remember it. Unbelievable. It was all a bit messy, to be honest. Sorry I haven't phoned but I literally only got out of bed half an hour ago. Anyway, you were saying . . .'

'Well,' she said, feeling a bit trembly, 'it's just that I got this weird text from someone, talking about you, and it's freaked me out a little bit, so I thought I'd come and ask you if you knew anything about it.'

'What do you mean you got a text?' he asked, his hands flying up to rake through his hair.

'Look,' she said, getting her phone out to show him. 'I don't know who sent it, it just appeared.' Her fingers stumbled to put her passcode into the phone and to find the offending text. All the time she could feel Colin

155

breathing over her shoulder, saying nothing. He smelt slightly of beer. She handed him the phone and swept the hair out of her eyes as she watched his face whilst he read the message.

The shaking of the head started and lasted a few seconds. He didn't look at her, just stared at the phone for a lot longer than it would take to read the simple sentences. A lot longer.

'Weird!' he said, suddenly rearing his head up. 'Like really weird. Do you think someone is trying to break us up? I mean, who would do this? Is it an ex-boyfriend, do you think? Can you think of anyone?'

Oh, thought Shelley. She hadn't considered that. She thought about her most recent relationships and quickly concluded that none of them would go to these kinds of lengths to try and get her back, if that was their motive.

'No one,' she said firmly. 'I don't know anyone who might have sent this.'

He swallowed as they locked eyes. Then he looked up to the ceiling, as if trying to wrack his brains, still ever so slightly shaking his head. Shelley was aware she was holding her breath.

'So who were you with last night?' she asked tentatively. She hated the feeling of questioning him.

'Oh, some ex-business contacts, that's all. No one exciting.'

'You said you were going to call,' she said.

'God, I know. I'm sorry. But it ended up being a late one. It was such a trip down memory lane being back here so we didn't get in until really late and then, as

156

you can see, I have only just got up. I was just about to phone you.'

Shelley nodded, at a loss for what to think.

Colin looked down at her phone again, which was still in his hand. 'I know what this is . . .' a look of relief flooding his face. 'It'll be from one of the lads. Of course it will. You know, like a practical joke. I bet it's Callum. He was cross I didn't invite him on this trip. Said it was practically another stag do and he should be here. He's got a really weird sense of humour.' He looked down at Shelley's phone again and pressed some buttons. 'The best thing we can do is delete this. It's someone who's playing a stupid trick. Probably Callum. Thinking it's funny. There, it's gone.' He held the phone up to show her.

Shelley gasped at the blank screen. 'Don't you want to be sure who it is?' she said.

'Not really. Let's not give them the satisfaction. Callum would think it was hilarious if he thought you actually believed it.'

He paused, looking at her, then held out his arms and drew her in.

'Come on,' he said into her hair. 'Sorry to have idiots for friends.'

They stood there for a few moments in silence, until Shelley could feel the damp of his towel soaking through her shorts.

He pulled away.

'Now I really am late to meet Neil down at the pool,' he said. 'Everyone all set to meet for dinner here Sunday night?'

'Yeah,' said Shelley. 'Everyone is really looking forward to it.'

'Oh, and some really great news. Mum and Dad are flying out tomorrow so they can join us. Dad said he'd like to meet your uncle too. He really loves staying here as well. He was really jealous of Neil and me coming out.'

'Oh wow,' said Shelley. 'That's great.' She tried to imagine all her crowd seated round a table with Colin's mum and dad. Nancy might need to buy a new kaftan. She wondered if they valet-parked mobility scooters here.

'So, we'll see you here at seven on Sunday then,' said Colin, putting his hand on her shoulder. 'Now I really should get ready to meet Neil. Forget all about that stupid text, hey,' he said. 'Don't let it spoil your weekend. Callum would love that. Now, what are you doing tonight?'

'I don't really know. Becca and Auntie Nancy have been cooking something up. You?'

Colin shrugged. 'Quiet night, I reckon. Just a couple of beers down at the Flaming Flamingo maybe. Now, just you make sure you enjoy the next couple of days. Don't do anything I wouldn't do, will you?' He gave her a cheeky smile and went for a lame high-five. She tapped his hand and turned to leave. He followed her to the door where they kissed and she left. More confused than when she'd arrived.

Chapter 23

When Peggy and Rosalind returned from the ceramics museum to the villa, Nancy was waiting for them at the kitchen table. Peggy didn't have a chance to wax lyrical about the beautiful things they had seen as Nancy was clearly bursting to tell them something. She quickly shushed them both and told them that the three youngest of the party had all gone to bed for a siesta as it had been quite an eventful afternoon. She shared with them in hushed tones the story of the text and Shelley's departure to Colin's hotel.

'So what did she say when she got back?' asked Peggy.

'That he reckoned it was one of his mates winding them up, playing some kind of trick. She seemed okay with that explanation, but I think it's thrown her a bit.'

Peggy didn't say anything. She supposed she should go and talk to Shelley and see if she was all right, but she wasn't quite sure what she was supposed to say. She'd never been much good with heart-to-hearts with her daughter. Her own mother had never discussed emotions or feelings with her. The death of her sister Dorothy had consumed her during those years when Peggy could have done with her advice or comfort. Peggy had never felt as though her problems were big enough to warrant troubling her mother in her grief, and so she had just coped on her own. And so asking her own daughter how she was feeling was alien to her. She just didn't know how to do it.

'You should go and talk to her,' said Nancy.

Now that just made her cross. What right did Nancy have to give her parenting advice? She had never won any prizes for being the best mother in the world, often offloading Rosalind on them in the summer when they were busy with the theatre. She had always put the theatre ahead of being a mother, in Peggy's opinion.

'Or shall I go and talk to her?' asked Nancy.

Peggy would be damned if that was happening.

Despite not wanting to, she got up without a word and headed for the bedroom that Becca and Shelley were sharing. She pushed the door open and tiptoed in. She could tell the bed that Shelley was sleeping in as the hump was long and sprawling, unlike Becca's more petite bulge on the other bed.

'Mum?' said Shelley, rolling over and squinting through the darkness. 'Are you okay? What's the matter?'

Peggy sat down on the edge of the bed. 'Nancy said I should come and talk to you.'

'Okay,' said Shelley slowly. 'About what exactly?'

'About the text you got,' answered Peggy.

'Okay,' repeated Shelley.

There was an awkward silence.

'Did Nancy tell you what the text was about?' asked Shelley.

'I understand that Colin has some ridiculous friends who like cruel jokes.'

'Do you think? Do you think that it was one of his friends?'

'Well, that's what you think, isn't it?'

'I think so. It's what Colin told me.'

'Well then.'

Was she done? thought Peggy. She had no idea what else she should be saying. Could she go now?

'Mum?'

'Yes.'

'What do you really think of Colin?'

'It doesn't matter what I think.'

'Yes, it does.'

Peggy paused. What to say?

'I think he's a fine, youngish man.'

Shelley didn't speak for a moment. But then she took a deep breath and said, 'What would Dad have thought of him, do you think?'

Peggy swallowed.

'Your dad would have been as proud as anything to see you walk down the aisle,' she said. 'Now I'm off to get some sleep. Goodness knows what your Auntie Nancy and Becca have planned for this evening. I think I'll need all my strength.'

She stood up, knees creaking slightly, and walked towards the door.

'Sleep well,' said Becca, just as Peggy closed the door behind her. 'You will definitely need it.'

Chapter 24

Shelley opened one eye. She forgot where she was for a moment. Forgot who she was. Why was she in bed at five-thirty in the afternoon with her clothes on, her bra wire digging into her side? Oh yes. She was on her hen weekend. In Spain. Hopefully her hen weekend. If she actually ended up getting married. No, she wasn't going to think like that. She was getting married. She definitely was. She couldn't let a stupid text from one of Colin's mates throw her off. The thought of not getting married made her feel so terrible she couldn't even think about it. No, she was getting married and that was that. Colin wanted to marry her. She wanted to marry Colin. And the more she thought about it, the more she thought the text had given Colin the perfect get-out if he had wanted it. If he didn't want to marry her, all he had to do was say – yep – hands up – sorry – caught red-handed. I was with another woman last night so let's not get married. He had been given a free pass and he'd not used it, so he definitely wanted to marry her.

No question.

What a relief.

Yep, that was it.

It was all going to be fine.

As she stirred herself, she heard raised voices coming from the kitchen. It sounded like Becca and Nancy having a bit of an argument. What on earth could they have fallen out about? She rubbed her eyes and raised herself up slowly just as she heard Becca say, 'We can't go out dressed the same. It will just look really weird, especially when we only have one of the rest of them.'

Shelley thought she'd better go and investigate what was going on before there was another fallout on this merry little hen weekend.

Nothing could have prepared her for the sight that met her as she walked into the kitchen. It really was the most hilarious and the most peculiar thing she had ever seen. She stood with her mouth open for some time before Becca and Nancy even spotted that she was there. It was Becca who glanced her way first. She turned to face Shelley and put her hands on her hips, looking as defiant as the Spice Girl she was dressed as in her signature Union Jack skimpy minidress.

'Tell your Auntie Nancy that we can't possibly both go out dressed as Ginger Spice,' she demanded.

Shelley was speechless. Nancy was also wearing the iconic Union Jack dress that Geri Halliwell famously wore for the Brit Awards in 1997, but whereas Becca's version was tight and short just as Geri's had been, Nancy's was more kaftan than minidress. In fact it looked as though she had actually sewn two enormous

Union Jack flags together as it flapped around her ankles. They both also sported striking ginger wigs, but whilst Becca was wearing eye-wateringly high, platform-heeled, bright red boots, Nancy was looking cosy in red booty slippers.

Seeing them standing next to each other was an extremely weird experience. Nancy looked like a Ginger Spice of the future. This was how Geri Halliwell would look if she let it all go in her old age. This was Geri Halliwell gone to seed.

'You both look epic,' was all Shelley could say, trying not to laugh. 'But why?'

'Because, my dearest friend Shelley,' said Becca, a grin suddenly spreading across her face, 'in true, *Stars in Their Eyes* style: tonight, Matthew, we are going to be the Spice Girls.' She jumped up and down in excitement. 'Your favourite girl power band. I know how much you love the Spice Girls, so Nancy and I have organized for us all to dress up as them to make your hen night truly memorable.'

Shelley swallowed. She couldn't work out if she was delighted or horrified. She'd had a really bad experience last time she'd dressed up. It was for Halloween at the school and all the teachers had agreed that they would go for it. She'd had gone as a toweringly tall Frankenstein's monster. Three infant girls fainted. She'd had to ring their parents and tell them she had half scared them to death.

But dressing as the Spice Girls could be fun though, couldn't it? Especially on her hen night. Depends which one, though, she thought. Then it struck her that they might dress her as Sporty Spice. They'd all be glam in little short dresses and she'd be in a footie kit.

'I'm not Sporty Spice, am I?' she demanded.

'God no, of course not,' said Becca. 'You're going to be the most glamorous out of all of us. You wait and see.'

Shelley felt herself sigh with relief. 'But clearly not Ginger Spice,' she said. 'You two are much more suited to that role. I mean, you both have all the credentials. Colourful characters, not afraid to voice an opinion, like to be the centre of attention . . .'

'No we do not,' said Nancy and Becca in unison.

'You both want to go out in public dressed like that,' said Shelley, pointing at their attention-grabbing costumes.

Becca and Nancy turned to look at each other and laughed.

'I guess you have a point,' said Becca.

'I know,' said Nancy. 'I'm Ginger *after* she left the Spice Girls. You know, after she stopped working and had a few holidays in the Caribbean.'

'Oh that's genius,' agreed Becca. 'That's it. We are Geri Halliwell before and after the Spice Girls. We have taken it to a completely different level.'

'Brilliant. So that's settled then,' said Nancy. 'Now shall we get everyone else up so they can get into costume. We'll be leaving after midnight at this rate.'

'But who *am* I going to be?' asked Shelley.

'You just wait and see,' said Becca with a wink. 'Now, do you think if I play "Who Do You Think You Are?" at full blast then everyone will wake up?'

The answer was yes. It only took a few bars of the epic Spice Girls track to rouse Rosalind, Chloe and Peggy from the depths of their beds, to emerge blinking into the kitchen and wondering what on earth had hit them.

'You look ridiculous,' Peggy told her sister.

'Cheers, sis,' said Nancy, handing her a cup of tea.

'What's happening?' asked Rosalind.

'I'm not sure if I'm going to like this,' admitted Chloe.

'So,' said Becca, clapping her hands together to get everyone's attention. 'Hang on a minute, I'll have to sit down – these boots are killing me. That's better. So, ladies, to create some special unique memories for Shelley's first and hopefully last-ever hen night, tonight we will be hitting the town dressed as Shelley's favourite band . . . the Spice Girls.'

'Oh God,' said Chloe, covering her hands with her eyes.

'No, I don't think so,' said Rosalind.

'How ridiculous,' said Peggy.

'Great,' grinned Becca. 'So glad you are all so up for it.'

'I assume you haven't included me in this nonsense,' added Peggy.

'Of course we have,' said Becca. 'We couldn't leave you out, Mrs C. You will be dressing up as our very own Scary Spice!'

'Shit. That's who I wanted to be,' said Chloe. 'Can't believe you picked Great-Auntie Peggy over me.'

Peggy looked astonished. 'Why Scary? Oh this is so stupid.'

'Because you are scary, Mrs C,' said Becca.

'No I am not!'

'My dad wouldn't come and pick me up from your house when I was little. He was too scared of you. He'd make Mum come.'

'That's ridiculous,' huffed Peggy. 'He must be very easily scared.'

'He's a solicitor and prosecutes murderers,' responded Becca.

Peggy stared back at Becca.

'Come on,' said Becca. 'It's for Shelley. All you have to do is wear Scary's signature look. A leopard-print jumpsuit.'

'Oh jeez,' exclaimed Chloe. 'I would look so good in that.'

'Are you implying that I won't?' Peggy asked.

'No,' replied Chloe. 'I just think it's suited to someone younger, that's all.'

'Hand me that suit,' said Peggy, holding her hand out. 'We'll see about that.' She strutted off into a bedroom.

'Now, we've found you a lovely dress to wear as Baby Spice.' Nancy smiled, turning to her granddaughter.

'You have got to be kidding me,' replied Chloe. 'Why Baby? Seriously?'

'Because you are the baby of course, darling,' said Nancy.

'I'm *not* the baby,' said Chloe firmly. 'What colour is it?'

'Pink,' said Nancy, a mischievous grin on her face.

Rosalind bellowed with laughter. 'You'll never get her to wear pink; not since she was six has she touched pink.'

Chloe turned on her mother. 'I can wear pink if I want to wear pink. Don't tell me which colour I can and can't wear. Here, give it to me,' she said, holding her arm out to grab the shimmering pink minidress. 'Who's Mum gonna be?' she asked. 'Grumpy Spice?'

'We thought Sporty Spice might suit your mum down to the ground,' said Nancy.

'Sporty Spice?' asked Rosalind. 'Can I wear my running gear? And trainers?'

'If you want,' said Becca. 'As long as you put your hair in a ponytail and wear a sweat band then you are all set.'

'I'm okay with that,' said Rosalind, looking extremely relieved that she wasn't being asked to squeeze into some kind of revealing dress.

Meanwhile Shelley was mentally calculating who that left for her to dress up as. Which Spice Girl remained? Slowly it dawned on her that she had been left with the least appropriate of all.

'I can't be Posh Spice!' she gasped. 'There is nothing whatsoever about me that says Posh Spice.'

'Aha – well, that's where you are wrong,' said Becca. 'Posh Spice is supremely appropriate, since with your marriage you are entering the realm of being permanently posh. What with marrying into money and all that. You are the new Posh Spice. It is so you.'

Shelley was horrified. She wasn't posh! She couldn't see herself as ever being posh, no matter how rich a family she was marrying in to. It just wasn't her. She was just Shelley. Gangly, awkward, unposh Shelley.

'We've got you a fabulous LBD that is going to suit you down to the ground,' Becca told her. 'And I thought you could wear those black stilettos you always wear when you dress up, and we've even got you a short black bobbed wig to cover your curls,' said Becca, laying everything out for Shelley to see. 'But of course we can't let you go out dressed just like that. You are a bride-to-be, after all, so we have a veil and a tiara and Chloe's L-plate and a bride-to-be sash. Because you, Shelley, deserve to have all the bells and whistles that every bride-to-be gets on their hen night.' Becca looked very pleased with herself.

Shelley ran the cheap netting of the veil through her fingers and stared at the pink sash that bore the words 'bride-to-be' in curly swirly writing. She suddenly felt quite emotional. This *was* her hen weekend. It had finally happened, after all those years of waiting and attending all her friends' hen weekends. Here she was, finally, on hers, with her own cheap veil, plastic tiara and lurid pink sash. She looked up at everyone with tears in her eyes.

'Let's do this,' she said, getting up out of her seat, a determined look on her face. She hopefully was never going to have another hen party in her life, so she might as well go for it and make the most of this one. Even if it did mean she had to dress up as Posh Spice.

'Just promise me one thing,' she said. 'We can't go anywhere near the Flaming Flamingo. Colin's going there tonight and I really don't think he needs to see me pretending to be posh.'

'You got it,' replied Becca. 'The last thing any self-respecting hen wants to see on her hen night is the groom. Tonight is all about you. Now off you go and get that veil on.'

Chapter 25

Becca couldn't remember the last time she had felt this excited as she waited for the rest of the crew to get ready. This was like a dream night for her. She got to dress up. Tick. Pretend she was somebody she wasn't. Tick. Be absolutely ridiculous. Tick. Know absolutely that by the end of this evening there would be a tale to tell that would be passed on for generations to come. Tick, tick, tick. This evening was going to be fun with a capital F. Oh, how she had missed nights like this since she had got married and become a mother. She reached for the wine bottle open on the table and topped up her glass.

Becca couldn't quite believe her eyes when Chloe walked in. She had taken all her piercings out and scraped her purple hair into two high pigtails. Still sporting her trademark heavy black eyeliner, she looked like Baby Spice's cooler older sister with the shimmering pink short baby-doll dress and knee-high shiny black boots.

'I really like what you have done with that,' said Becca. 'You look great.'

'Thanks,' said Chloe. 'Mum said I should ditch the black boots but I wanted to do my own take.'

'Quite right,' said Becca. 'You still look like you.'

Chloe nodded and grabbed a glass and poured herself some wine.

Unsurprisingly, Rosalind looked very at home in her Lycra shorts and sports vest. She looked as if she was about to go for a run rather than go out on the town, but at least she had joined in. Nancy had been right about giving Rosalind the Sporty Spice look.

Peggy arrived, absolutely rocking the leopard-print jumpsuit. Her frugal lifestyle meant she had an admirable figure for a lady of her age, and so the jumpsuit fitted her perfectly with not a ripple of fat exposed . . . because she didn't have a ripple of fat to expose.

'I think Peggy needs some of your make-up skills,' Becca whispered to Chloe. 'How about giving her some bright red lipstick and a brush of mascara?'

'Of course,' nodded Chloe. 'Consider it done.' She bustled off to rummage through her considerable make-up bag.

A hush fell over the kitchen when Shelley walked in. Becca noticed that Shelley already had the plastic tiara firmly in place, and the veil was over the front of her face rather than behind her head, in true bridal style. She walked in at a stately pace, as though she were gliding down the aisle. Becca could quite believe she was imagining that very moment.

'You look amazing,' said Becca, walking up to her friend and giving her a big hug.

'Do I?' asked Shelley nervously.

'Of course you do,' replied Becca. 'And look at those legs in that short dress. Jesus, Shelley, I'd kill for those legs.'

'I was thinking they looked very pasty,' said Shelley, glancing down concerned.

'No, not at all,' said Becca. 'You look like an English rose. And the veil . . . well, looking bridal really suits you is all I can say.'

Becca could see Shelley's eyes welling up through the thin veil. She knew how much this all meant to her. Thank goodness that text had proved to be something and nothing. Becca didn't know what she would do with Shelley if it turned out that Colin was not who she thought he was. She was so relieved that Shelley had been satisfied with Colin's explanation. Personally Becca still felt a bit suspicious, but thought they had no choice but to give Colin the benefit of the doubt. And with that in mind, it fell to Becca to make sure Shelley had the time of her life this evening. After all, her friend really did deserve the very best.

'Right – listen up everyone,' said Becca, tapping the side of her glass. 'We need a photo of all of us whilst we are still sober.'

'Good idea,' said Nancy. 'Let's take one with the mobility scooter. Don't forget that's had a Spice Girls makeover too.'

'You are not going round on your mobility scooter,' said Peggy, pointing her finger at Nancy and looking possibly the scariest Scary Spice has ever looked.

Nancy pulled a face. 'I most certainly am. My legs aren't feeling so good. I'm not sure I'd make it if I had to walk.'

Peggy shook her head. 'You need to do something about those legs of yours,' she said. 'It's not right at your age, not walking. Have you been to the doctor's about it?'

'Yes, Mum,' chipped in Rosalind. 'When was the last time you got checked out?'

'Oh, I'm in and out of there all the time. They practically have a seat with my name on it.'

'And?' asked Rosalind.

'Nothing to worry about,' she replied briskly. 'Bit of high blood pressure, that's all, and some threats about losing weight. Which you know I'll get round to at some point.'

'I'm going to clear out your cupboards before I go,' said Rosalind. 'It's all processed rubbish. Are you eating your five a day?'

'Yes, typically I have about five meals a day,' said Nancy with a grin. 'If you count elevenses and afternoon tea. Oh, and snacks with pre-dinner drinks, of course.'

'You need to eat more fruit and veg, Mum, it's good for you.'

'Yes, yes, whatever,' said Nancy. 'I'll do all that. Now, enough about me, are we going outside for a photo op or what? You are all sounding more like the Golden Girls than the Spice Girls.'

It took a while to get everyone positioned around the mobility scooter, which was bedecked with fairy lights and tinsel and had a large Union Jack flying from a six-foot-high pole attached to the back of Nancy's seat. Rosalind was in charge of working the timer on the camera, because she reckoned she had done it a million times for family shots, but somehow she was never satisfied with the result. She kept shouting at Shelley to look more posh, for Peggy to look more scary, and for Chloe to look more babyish, which wasn't going down well.

'I think you actually might be taking the roles too seriously? It's not a competition we are entering,' said Becca after the fifth try to get the shot right.

'Everything is a competition to Mum,' sighed Chloe. 'I gave up hockey because it was so embarrassing having her shout from the sidelines all the time.'

'You got dropped from the team because you never showed up for practice,' pointed out Rosalind.

'I never showed up to practice because I wanted to get dropped from the team,' said Chloe. 'So I wouldn't be embarrassed by you shouting from the sidelines.'

Rosalind was behind the camera, fiddling with the timer again. She looked up at Chloe, stunned.

'Is that true?' she demanded.

'Of course it's true,' said Chloe. 'You were an utter nightmare.'

'Why on earth didn't you say something?'

'I did!'

'No you didn't.'

'I did. You just didn't listen. You ignored me and shouted at the goalie for coming off her line.'

Becca watched Rosalind as she registered this information. She feared Rosalind and Chloe's mother/daughter bickering was in danger of ruining the entire night.

'I was just sharing my experience,' said Rosalind. 'What's wrong with that? I was trying to help—'

'No one wants to listen to their own mum's experience,' interjected Becca. 'My mum is trying to show me how to be a mum. She's driving me mad. If she tells me one more time how to puree carrot, I may kill her. Advice from your mum always comes across as criticism.'

'What she said,' agreed Chloe.

'But all mums ever want to do is to help,' said Rosalind. 'All mums ever want to do is to make their children's lives better.'

Becca shrugged. 'Just telling it how it is, Ros.'

'Yeah, what's she's saying,' Chloe agreed.

'Who made you the expert?' asked Rosalind, pointing her finger at Becca. 'How old are your boys again? Ten months? I don't call abandoning them for the weekend to get drunk "being a good mum", do you? And it's Rosalind *not* Ros.'

Becca gulped. What had brought that on?

'Ladies, ladies,' interrupted Shelley. 'I think it's this kind of thing that could lead to the rest of the Spice Girls splitting up. So shall we put our differences aside just for now and make this a harmonious reunion?'

Thank goodness for Shelley, thought Becca. She was always so good at smoothing the waters. 'You're right, Shelley,' she said, swallowing the retort she was about to give Rosalind. 'We need to get in the party spirit, because I tell you what I want, what I really, really want . . .'

'Is it a zigazig, ah?' asked Chloe.

'No actually. It's a very large vodka and Coke. Now let's take this photo and get on the road, shall we?'

Chapter 26

Shelley wasn't entirely sure about Becca insisting that Colin should join them on this special night, even if it was in the form of a four-foot-high helium-filled balloon in the shape of Bob the Builder.

'Do you get it?' she asked proudly. 'I always call Colin "Bob the Builder",' she said.

'I know, because it's hilarious because he isn't a builder, he's a rich property developer,' added Shelley sarcastically; however, Becca didn't seem to hear the sarcasm.

'Of course it's hilarious,' said Becca. 'Now, I need a photo of Posh Spice and Bob. Put your arm around him,' she said, waving at her from behind her Sony camera. 'Give him a kiss. That's more like it.'

After a few more photos with Bob Balloon, they were finally on their way into town, Nancy leading on her trusty mobility scooter, her Union Jack kaftan billowing around her legs. Peggy walked by her side looking scary, or was it angry? Rosalind looked pretty chilled, clearly delighted to be going out in sporty attire, and Becca and Chloe were merely enjoying the admiring glances from passers-by.

After only a few yards, all Shelley wanted to do was sit down. Her standard black stilettos did go really well with the little black dress she was wearing, but they were killing her feet. By the time they got down to the harbour front, she was ready to collapse. An array of fairy lights now lit up the bars and restaurants as the sun slowly slipped over the horizon. Couples and families paraded up and down trying to pick where to enjoy their paella and sangria, or perhaps their plaice and chips depending on their culinary tastes or who in the group shouted loudest. Nancy however took them straight to a traditional Spanish-looking eaterie where tables covered in crisp white cloths lined up under underneath a huge burgundy red awning which proudly welcomed them to 'Julio's.' Yet another friend of Nancy's.

'Wow,' Julio said, holding his arms out wide as they approached. 'Is that really you, Nancy? I have never seen anything like it in my entire life. I thought this was a celebration for a new bride? Not some British patriotic nonsense?'

Nancy laughed. 'Well, if you don't like it, we can always go elsewhere, Julio.'

'No, no. Nancy is always welcome here you know that. Now where is my bride-to-be? I have reserved a table for you girls right here at the front where everyone can see you. I was expecting that the sight of you will bring the boys swarming in, but . . . well, maybe not. Now, where is the blushing bride? I need her here in pride of place.'

Shelley raised her hand. How could he not tell it was her? She was wearing a veil, for Christ's sake.

'Really – are you a supermodel?' he asked.

Shelley felt herself blush as she took off her veil to reveal her face beneath the classic Victoria Beckham bob-cut wig.

'Please, please, you must sit,' gushed Julio indicating a space right at the front. Please sit here. Pride of place. You can see everyone around you.'

Shelley plonked herself down on the seat indicated by Julio. She hastily put the veil on the back of her head this time, so the material did not cover her face. She needed a drink, and fast, after all.

'Where is Nadia?' Nancy asked Julio as he handed them all menus.

'Cooking, of course,' replied Julio. 'She'll come out later to say hello.'

'Always in the kitchen, Julio,' replied Nancy, shaking her head. 'It's about time you let her out into the lime-light, isn't it?'

'Aah, she loves it in there,' said Julio dismissively. 'Now I shall go and get some bread for my hungry pop princesses.'

'He's a lucky man that Julio,' said Nancy to them all when he had disappeared. 'Nadia works like a trojan. It's Julio's family restaurant but it's Nadia who keeps it afloat. He has no idea how lucky he is that he married her.'

'Behind every successful man . . .' said Rosalind.

'There's a woman doing all the shit jobs,' said Becca. She was already pouring herself her second glass of wine and they had literally just arrived. She looked like a woman on a mission.

'And what shit jobs do you do for Jason?' asked Shelley.

'I gave birth to his children via my vagina. Now if that isn't a shit job, I don't know what is.' She raised her glass and took a massive gulp.

'Childbirth is a privilege, if you ask me,' said Rosalind.

Oh no, thought Shelley. Were Becca and Rosalind close to having cross words yet again?

'I don't call tearing your cervix and having someone stick a needle where a needle should never be stuck, a privilege,' said Becca.

Shelley gave Becca a kick under the table and a hard stare. She watched her friend's expression soften as she noticed Shelley's look of concern.

'Anyway, enough of this type of talk,' she said brusquely. 'Time to concentrate on Shelley's upcoming nuptials. Tonight we are all here to support Shelley on her journey to becoming a married woman. And with that in mind, I have prepared a little quiz, to find out just how ready our Shelley is.' She raised her glass again and grinned.

Shelley groaned. Bob the Builder – who had been attached to the back of her chair – drifted in front of her eyeline, so she punched him out of the way.

'Oh, I love a quiz,' said Nancy.

'It's not a test, is it?' said Chloe. 'Jesus, I might as well be back at school.'

'Well sort of,' said Becca. 'But for Shelley. Not for you, Chloe. I've got a list of questions about Colin to ask Shelley so we can find out exactly what she knows about him. I've already got the answers from Colin, as I secretly sent them to him last week.'

'He never said,' said Shelley, feeling shocked.

'He doesn't have to tell you everything,' said Becca, raising her eyebrows. Shelley stared back at her. Not a very appropriate thing to say given the day's events, she thought.

'What sort of questions?' asked Peggy, looking very confused.

'How many zeros does your bank account have?' asked Chloe. 'Tell me you asked him that. I so want to know exactly how loaded he is.'

'Oh God,' said Shelley. 'You didn't ask him that, did you? Tell me you didn't ask him that. How would that make me look if my best friend asked him that?'

'Of course I didn't ask him that,' said Becca. 'Who do you think I am?'

'So what did you ask him then?' questioned Shelley.

'You'll just have to wait and see,' said Becca. 'Now, who do we have to shag to get another bottle of wine on the table? This is a hen party, not a funeral.'

Julio appeared, as if by magic, wielding large carafes of wine, accompanied by two waitresses who laid down endless delicious tapas dishes of smoky chorizo, gambas and patatas bravas. Spotting a woman in need when he saw one, Julio kept Becca's wine glass fully topped up throughout the meal, which resulted in her having a slight wobble after dessert when she rose from her chair and hit her spoon against a wine glass causing it to smash.

'Oh, shit,' she said. 'I just wanted to get your attention, that's all.'

'For goodness' sake, Becca,' said Peggy, carefully putting the broken glass into a napkin. 'Do you think you'd better slow down?'

183

'No way,' replied Becca, grabbing another glass and pouring herself some more wine. 'We are here to celebrate Shelley getting married and celebrate we shall. Now, what are we going to do first? Oh yes, first of all a quick toast. Now Shelley,' said Becca, swinging round to face the bride-to-be. Shelley braced herself. Becca was clearly a bit drunk and heaven knows what she might come out with.

'You have been my bestest friend for a very long time and I'm sure no one will disagree with me when I say that there were times when I thought this day would never come.'

Shelley noticed her mother nod enthusiastically.

'I do so love you, Shelley, and you deserve more than anyone I know to have the best, most happiest of lives. So let's all raise our glasses and wish Shelley all the best.'

'All the best, Shelley,' said everyone, raising their glasses.

'Good. Now, shall we do the quiz?' said Becca, clapping her hands together in glee.

'Yes,' everyone cried, apart from Shelley and Peggy. The quiz was making Shelley feel a bit nervous, if she was honest. She wasn't sure she was going to do very well at it.

'I still don't understand the nature of this quiz,' said Peggy. 'What sort of questions are they?

'You know,' replied Becca. 'Along the lines of "what is your favourite part of your partner's body?"'

'No you didn't!' exclaimed Shelley, her hands leaping up to her face in horror. 'Tell me you didn't.'

Shelley could feel herself going bright red just thinking about it.

'I did.'

'But he won't have a favourite part of my body.'

'Of course he has.'

'Well, what is it then?'

'You want to know now. I've got a load more questions before that one.'

'Yes! Tell me now.' Shelley's heart was pounding. She really needed to know.

Becca started to rummage around in the shiny silver backpack she had slung over her shoulder before they left the villa. 'I'll need to find the list of questions then,' she said. 'Hang on.' She hiccupped and then giggled.

Shelley thought she was going to reach over and throttle Becca. She needed to know *now* what part of her body was Colin's favourite. It felt like vital information that was going to make her feel so much better about everything.

'Right, here we go,' said Becca eventually, folding a piece of paper out in front of her on the table. 'Let's see, I think it was about halfway down.'

Goodness me, thought Shelley. How many questions did she ask him? They could be here all night and her nerves would be shot to shreds.

'Right, so Colin's favourite part of Shelley's body is . . .'

'Her heart,' said Nancy immediately. 'As well as her lovely round bottom,' she continued with a wink.

'Her mind,' said Rosalind. 'As well as her beautiful hair of course. If it really has to be a physical attribute.'

185

'Her tits,' shrugged Chloe. 'It's always the tits.'

'Her neck,' said Peggy.

Shelley looked at her mother, bewildered. Her neck? What on earth was her mother thinking? Her mother thought her greatest physical feature was her neck! Was it any wonder that her self-confidence was lacking with a mother who said things like that.

'No, none of those,' said Becca looking up. She paused.

'For goodness' sake just put me out of my misery,' said Shelley.

'Your eyelashes,' announced Becca.

There was silence around the table.

'My eyelashes,' she said.

'I know,' replied Becca. 'How cute is that?'

'Cute? Do you know the only thing renowned for its eyelashes?'

'Err . . .' began Becca, looking slightly taken aback.

'Cows,' blasted back Shelley. 'Jersey cows! He thinks I look like a cow! Oh my God. My fiancé thinks I look like a cow.'

Everyone looked at her aghast.

'He doesn't think you look like a cow,' said Nancy. 'It's just you have got very impressive eyelashes.'

'I haven't,' replied Shelley, shaking her head vigorously. 'No one has ever commented on my eyelashes ever before in my life *ever*. There is *nothing* remarkable about my eyelashes.'

Again there was silence.

'And if there is nothing remarkable about my eyelashes, then that means that Colin's favourite thing about my body is something completely unremarkable,' said Shelley, feeling close to hysterical.

'I think you are making far too much of this,' said Peggy brusquely. 'It's these stupid games you play. I don't know why all this is necessary. What good is it doing anyone?'

'It's supposed to be fun, Peggy,' said Becca.

'Doesn't seem much like fun to me,' replied Peggy.

'Shots anyone?' asked Becca feebly, looking round the table.

Shelley had to agree with her mother. She wasn't having fun at all. She was trying to be posh and bridal and just a bit glamorous in her little black dress and heels whilst being told that her fiancé's favourite part of her body was her mediocre eyelashes. This really was a low moment.

'Your dad was a fan of eyelashes,' piped up Peggy. 'It's why he loved those Jersey cows so much.'

'Not helpful, Mum,' snapped Shelley. 'Is it too much to ask that my fiancé admires something more significant about me than my eyelashes?'

Oh no, I've done it now, thought Shelley. She looked over at her mother. She knew only too well that Peggy did not respond well to being shouted at. Shelley watched fearful as Peggy folded her arms across her leopard-print jumpsuit. She knew what was coming. It was a mini-lecture according to the world of Peggy. Not at all what she needed right now.

'I think the problem with your generation is that you just expect too much,' announced Peggy through pursed lips. 'You want everything in a husband. You want him to be masculine and sexy and yet you also expect him to cook and clean and do his fair share of domestic duties. You want him to have drive and ambition but still be sensitive and willing to show his emotions. You expect equality and yet want to be cared for and protected. You want dependability and trustworthiness and yet you also want excitement and spontaneity. You expect men to deliver on so many levels, is it any wonder everyone is getting divorced? What you expect from men and marriage has gone through the roof.'

Shelley chewed her lip, praying Peggy had finished with her mini-lecture.

There was silence around the table.

Becca picked up her wine glass and took another gulp. 'Bullshit,' she muttered.

Peggy turned slowly to look at her. 'Please don't use that language around me, Rebecca Ramsbottom,' she said.

'Your surname is Ramsbottom?' said Chloe, pointing at Becca and laughing.

'Yes,' said Becca through gritted teeth, not taking her eyes off Peggy. 'My married name. What a wedding gift that was!' She paused, taking several deep breaths before she addressed Peggy. 'Don't tell me we expect too much of our husbands, Peggy. That is total bullshit. It's the expectations on wives that are far too high. Men don't get married, have kids, and then be expected to make their entire lives pivot seamlessly, without difficulty or complaint. Husbands have it pretty easy if you ask me. In fact, it must have been a man who invented marriage. Tell you what, let's set up a binding contract that means every man can secure a woman for life who cooks, cleans, gives birth, raises children and has sex with them. I tell you what: that sounds like a pretty good deal to me, if I was a man.'

Becca looked close to tears now. There was clearly a lot of marital angst coming out. Shelley had never seen a happier bride on her wedding day than Becca. She clearly was totally in love with Jason. Shelley felt a sick feeling well up in her stomach. Christ, if Becca wasn't dealing well with the pressures of marriage and motherhood, then that didn't bode well for Shelley.

'Wow,' piped up Chloe. 'You are doing a great job of selling marriage to Shelley. Best not ask Mum how she feels about marriage, or else there will be no wedding at all.'

All eyes turned to Rosalind.

'When I got married, I felt like the luckiest girl in the world,' declared Rosalind.

Shelley watched Chloe roll her eyes.

'And do you still feel like that?' Shelley couldn't help but ask.

Rosalind paused for a moment, clearly contemplating her answer. Perhaps she was wondering how honest she should be with her cousin who was about to take the plunge. Someone who was starting on the journey that she had travelled for a long while.

'Of course,' she said eventually. 'Of course I do, it's just that . . . well, the thing is that you just have to recognize that things will change. You will change, your husband will change, your circumstances will change.

You just have to expect that. I think the secret to a good marriage is learning to adapt to each other's needs over time. What you need at twenty-three might be different to what you need at thirty-three and then completely different to what you need at fifty-three. When you are young, all that matters is love and then, as you get older, quite frankly all you really want is someone who asks how you are and helps with the dishes and takes the bin out.'

'And has Robert adapted to your needs?' asked Nancy, looking intently at her daughter.

'He said he'd get me an ironing lady,' replied Rosalind.

'And that, my friends, is marriage,' said Becca, slamming her hand on the table.

'Oh Becca,' said Shelley. 'You don't mean that. You and Jase are happy, aren't you? You love being married to Jason.'

Becca looked at her bleary-eyed. She shrugged.

'Yes you do,' implored Shelley. 'You're drunk. You love Jason.'

'Of course I love Jason,' said Becca. 'I'm just not that keen on marriage at the moment, that's all.'

'Yes you are,' protested Shelley. 'You loved your wedding, you told me you did. You said it was the happiest day of your life.'

'It was. Then it all went a bit shit, really. I had babies and it all went downhill.'

Shelley stared back at her. 'You are supposed to be telling me how great marriage is. That's what I need to hear. I mean, I'm feeling insecure enough about it as it is. I've got a fiancé who loves me for my eyelashes, not to mention a random text telling me they enjoyed my fiancé's company on the dancefloor last night, which is allegedly from one of his mates but still . . . Who else but me would get a text at their hen party saying that their fiancé might be up to no good and have their hens tell them how shit marriage is?'

Shelley collapsed in a heap on the table.

'You lot are rubbish,' announced Chloe. 'Can't you see Shelley doesn't need your stories of failed attempts at marriage?'

'I did not say my marriage was failed,' said Becca indignantly.

'Neither did I,' said Rosalind.

'Well, you don't half moan about it then for saying it's been such a wild success,' replied Chloe. 'Strikes me that's what marriage always ends up as. One long list of moans to the wrong people.'

Becca stared for a moment at Chloe before she put her hand on Shelley's shoulder.

'Oh Shelley, I'm so sorry,' she said, shaking her head. 'Not the time or the place. We're just going through a bit of a bad patch, that's all, what with the twins and everything. I shouldn't have said anything. And Chloe's absolutely right. I should moan at Jason, not at anyone else. And especially not you.'

Shelley kept her head buried in her arms.

'I'm sure he loves your whole body and mind,' said Rosalind, looking distressed. 'Not just your eyelashes.'

Shelley couldn't bear to raise her head and look at anybody.

191

'I thought you believed him about the text,' said Nancy gently. 'I thought you'd got past it?'

Shelley shrugged her shoulders, desperately wanting to cry.

'Shelley?' said Chloe, tapping her shoulder.

'Leave me alone,' said Shelley.

'Don't moan to us about the text and the screw-up with the eyelashes thing,' said Chloe. 'Go and give him shit about it.'

Shelley didn't know what to say. Her head was a mess.

'Do you know what,' said Nancy gently. 'I think that is the wisest thing anyone has said around this table, this evening.'

'But I have already tackled him about it,' said Shelley, raising her head from her arms and slumping in her chair.

'Were you totally convinced?' said Chloe.

Shelley looked over to her.

'Were you?' Chloe asked again.

She shook her head sadly.

'You think there may be some truth in it?'

She looked around the table. Everyone was staring at her solemnly.

Shelley nodded.

'I don't think Colin is a cheater,' announced Peggy. Shelley looked up hopefully.

'He hasn't got it in him. He might look, but he's not brave enough to touch.'

'Gee, thanks Mum,' sighed Shelley. 'Nothing to do with loving me and being loyal then.'

'I'm just saying that I just don't think he's that type,' said Peggy.

192

'Well, let's go find out, shall we?' said Chloe. 'Why are we wasting time sitting around here? Let's go and find out exactly what type of man he is.'

'What do you mean?' asked Shelley.

'You said he was going to the Flaming Flamingo tonight, right? Well let's go find him. See what he's up to.'

'Spy on him?' exclaimed Shelley. 'I can't do that.'

'All right then, you stay here and moan about him. See how that works out for you,' replied Chloe.

'I don't think it's a bad idea,' said Nancy. 'If it settles your mind. In fact, I think it's a good idea, Shelley.'

'It's ridiculous idea,' said Peggy.

'But there is nothing to lose, is there?' asked Nancy.

'Her dignity, that's what,' said Peggy.

'Her dignity will be worth nothing when she's stood at the top of that aisle still wondering whether she believes that text or not,' replied Nancy.

Shelley looked at Nancy, shocked at her firmness.

'I'll come with you, Shelley,' said Chloe. 'You don't need to go on your own.'

'We'll all come,' said Becca. 'After all, we Spice Girls need to stick together.'

'Oh no,' said Shelley, her hand flying up to her wig. 'What if Colin sees me dressed like this? No, it's far too embarrassing.'

'You've got nothing to be embarrassed about, you look great,' said Becca. 'Anyway, I bet it's a huge place. With a bit of luck we can slide in, observe from afar and leave. He'll be none the wiser, if that makes you feel any better. If you don't want to talk to him, then it doesn't matter. At the very least, let's just go and see what he's up to, like Chloe says.'

'You really think that us lot dressed up like this is going to go unseen?' said Shelley, aghast. 'Have you seen us?'

They looked around at each other. They really were quite a sight.

'Well, who cares,' said Nancy. 'Let's go for it. What do they say, Girl Power, is it?'

'Yeah, Girl Power,' said Becca. 'Come on, Shell. Posh wouldn't sit around moping, wondering what David was up to. She'd go and find out for herself, wouldn't she?'

Shelley looked at Becca wearily.

'Wouldn't she?' pressed Becca.

Shelley nodded slowly.

'That's the spirit,' said Becca. She glanced around the rest of the table. 'Come on, ladies. Flaming Flamingo, here we come. We are on a mission.'

They paid up, and with much muttering and scraping of chairs, stood up and started gathering their things. The two men on the next table looked up, watching their every move until one of them tapped Chloe on her shoulder.

'Just wanted to say we love your outfits,' he said to Chloe.

'Really,' said Chloe, instantly touching her hair and smoothing down her dress. They were maybe in their early twenties and were wearing black ripped jeans and white T-shirts, and one of them had a tattoo of a sword through a heart on his left arm, a left arm that was bulging with muscle. The other one was a skinny rake and had several piercings in one ear and was wearing a Sex Pistols T-shirt. Their uniform was somewhat different to the usual type found in the bars and restaurants of Andelica, where most men could be found in pastel shorts and shirts and espadrilles.

'I'm Jay,' said the one with the tattoo, sticking his hand out to shake Chloe's.

'Hi,' said Mr Piercings. 'I'm Tommy. You are making me feel very underdressed.'

'No, I love what you are wearing. Much more my style really,' giggled Chloe. 'I'm Chloe by the way.'

'Chloe,' said Tommy, grinning from ear to ear. 'Nice name. Really nice name.'

'I know,' said Rosalind, leaning forward and somehow managing to get in between them. 'I picked it. I'm Rosalind. Chloe's mum.'

'Muum,' moaned Chloe, covering her eyes.

'Seriously,' said Tommy. 'Her mum?'

'Seriously,' said Rosalind. 'I'm her mum and she's only eighteen. Just so you know.'

'Jesus, Mum,' Chloe said again. 'Sorry,' she said to the two men. 'So this is my mum and there is Shelley, my auntie . . .'

'Third cousin,' Shelley reminded her through her veil, which she had placed back on her head.

'Oh yeah, third cousin,' said Chloe. 'And that's her best mate Becca, and over there is my Great-Auntie Peggy a.k.a. Scary Spice, and on the mobility scooter is my nan who is . . .'

'Old Spice,' whispered Tommy, with a massive grin.

Chloe laughed. 'Well, you could say that.'

'So you are all on a hen night then, I take it?' asked Jay.

'Correct,' said Becca. 'My idea, all this,' she added. 'But we've gotta go, guys, I'm afraid. We're on a mission.'

'Oh, sounds fun. Can we . . . I mean . . . I don't know about you, Jay . . .' stumbled Tommy. 'But can we join your mission?'

'No,' said everyone apart from Chloe who said, 'Of course you can.'

Chloe spun round, away from Tommy and Jay. 'But why not? They could be real assets.'

Becca burst out laughing. Chloe glared at her. 'What?' she said.

'I think we need a team talk,' said Becca.

'Okay,' said Chloe defiantly. 'If you insist.' She turned back to Tommy and Jay. 'A team talk has been requested. May I get back to you?'

'Sure,' said Tommy with a smile. 'We were just going to the bar next door, okay?'

'Okay,' nodded Chloe feverishly. 'Don't go anywhere else, will you?'

'No,' Tommy agreed. 'We'll be right there.'

'What was that all about?' she raged as soon as they were out of earshot. 'They could help us blend in a bit more. Be really helpful.'

'Rubbish,' scoffed Becca. 'You fancy them. End of.'

'No!' said Chloe, blushing bright red. 'I just thought a couple of men on the team would be useful additions on our mission.'

'If you say so,' replied Becca.

'He had a tattoo!' said Rosalind. 'And he was at least twenty. No Chloe. No way.'

'So you've got a thing against tattoos now, have you?' Chloe said to her mum. 'Anything you don't have a problem with? Christ, you threw my last boyfriend out of the house because he'd never had pesto.'

'But you can do so much better than this,' said Rosalind. 'Why do you always set your sights so low?'

'Why are you so judgemental?' declared Chloe.

'Not much of a team discussion, is it?' said Nancy.

'Mum never wants to discuss, she always wants to dictate,' said Chloe. 'She is a one-woman dictatorship.'

'How about we have a vote?' said Nancy.

'Really?' said Shelley, thinking that was way too diplomatic. The last thing she needed was for two young men to be observing their weird mission to stalk her fiancé.

'Everyone who wants Tommy and Jay to join the team, raise your hand,' said Nancy.

Only Chloe raised her hand.

'Carried,' said Nancy cheerfully. 'Sorry, Chloe. But we are a tight unit. Two outsiders could really affect team morale and prove to be a major distraction to the success of our mission. You understand, don't you?'

Chloe looked at her sulkily and cast an evil stare round the rest of the group. She turned away and walked towards the next-door bar.

'Where are you going now?' shouted Rosalind after her.

'To find out where they will be later,' she shouted back over her shoulder.

'Brilliant,' said Rosalind, 'just brilliant.'

'Come on,' said Nancy. 'Give her some space. She is out with a load of geriatrics, after all.'

'Thanks,' said Becca and Shelley in unison.

'You know what I mean. It's hardly the holiday of the century for her, is it?'

'But all she does is make bad decisions at the moment,' said Rosalind.

'Don't we all at that age?' said Nancy.

'I didn't,' said Rosalind. 'I did my exams and went to university.'

'And got your degree that you never did anything with,' pointed out Nancy.

Rosalind opened her mouth and shut it again.

'Look, we don't have time for this right now. Shall we get moving?' said Nancy. 'You ready, Peggy?'

Peggy shook her head. 'Ray told me I needed to relax and have a good time. I'm not sure that he had this in mind.'

'You spoke to Ray?' asked Shelley, aghast.

'He told me to call to let him know we had safely arrived.'

'So you called him?'

Peggy nodded. 'He said to say he wished he'd known we were all dressing up, because he has the entire wardrobe of the old Derby Theatre in his shed.' She shook her head in exasperation.

'You told him we were dressing up?'

Peggy nodded.

'You had quite a chat with him then?'

'Well, he started telling me about Pippa and Mike next door getting a new kitten and it getting into his shed and him having to get it out for them and being able to give them a litter tray that he'd picked up at a house clearance. So, you know, I had to make conversation. Tell him what was going on here. Oh, he told me to buy you a drink from him,' she told Shelley. 'He gave me some euros to spend on you. Said he found them in a suit pocket that he bought at a jumble sale.'

Shelley stared at her mother. 'That's kind of him. He seems like a nice man, Mum.'

Peggy nodded and pursed her lips. 'Let's go,' she said, stepping into the road. 'The sooner we get going, the sooner this ridiculous pantomime will be over.'

Chapter 27

All too quickly they were outside the Flaming Flamingo, a huge monolith of a bar on the main road leading from the harbour towards the town square. Clearly at the centre of the Andelica nightlife scene, teenagers and flyers littered the outside as they touted for business, trying to cajole holiday-makers inside rather than into any of the other bars and clubs on the strip. Curiously everyone seemed to part ways as Shelley and her group approached, led by the old lady in a Union Jack kaftan. As they arrived at the doorway, Nancy spun round and faced her entourage.

'Team talk time, guys,' she said. 'Gather round.'

The rest of the Spice Girls shuffled to surround her.

'Act natural. We go in there. Find our target. Gather the necessary information and then leave. Do you all understand?'

They all nodded.

Shelley felt sick. She could already feel this getting out of hand.

Rosalind put her hand up.

'Yes, Rosalind,' said Nancy.

'Can I just clarify exactly what the necessary information is?' she asked.

'Whether or not Colin is acting in a dubious manner whilst here on holiday.'

'And can I ask how we will determine this?' asked Rosalind.

'I think we'll know,' said Nancy, looking Shelley straight in the eye. 'I think we'll know.'

Shelley nodded. Christ, she hoped so.

'Onward,' Nancy cried, doing a three-point turn.

'You can't bring that in here,' said a man in a suit, immediately stepping forward into Nancy's path.

'Really,' said Nancy. 'Watch me.'

She nudged her scooter forward, bumping into the man blocking her path.

'Oi,' he shouted at her, putting his hand in her face. 'I said you can't bring that in here.'

'I think you'll find,' said Becca, stepping forward, 'that you would be in breach of disability law to not let this lady enter the premises with her mobility aid.'

'Says who?' he asked angrily. 'I'm going to have to ask you all to leave. You are causing an obstruction, wanting to bring a vehicle onto the premises, and you are too old,' he said, glaring at Nancy.

Nancy gasped. 'I have been made welcome in every establishment in this town until this one,' she said.

'Leave it with me,' said Becca, placing a hand on her Spice sister's shoulder. 'Listen up,' she said. 'I'm a lawyer. In London. Dealing in licensing law,' she blagged. 'I'm guessing that you are probably breaching several codes

201

of practice as we speak, from fire door regulations to maximum capacity allowances. Not to mention you are most definitely in breach of the disabilities act of 1984, which requires all establishments to meet minimum requirements on allowing safe access for those with disabilities. Those guilty of restricting access can be slapped with a minimum fine of twenty thousand euros. This is the Spanish law as regulated by the European Council. Now it would only take one phone call and . . .'

The suit sighed. 'Come in, ladies,' he said, stepping aside. 'But you keep that thing on a low gear,' he said to Nancy. 'Understood? No driving into the other customers.'

'This machine is totally under my control,' said Nancy. 'I can assure you that the safety of the other guests is my utmost priority.'

'Ow Nan,' shrieked Chloe, hopping up and down. 'You just rode over my foot!'

'You were in my way,' declared Nancy, putting her hazard lights on and gliding in through the doors before the bouncer could change his mind.

It was still relatively early in the evening, so the place was barely half full. There was a pleasant bustle around the enormous bar area, but in the main section youngsters were hanging out around sofas and low tables. A DJ was blasting out tunes to a largely empty dance floor. Two young women staggered around in the middle, clearly having made an early start on the alcohol. They looked unlikely to make it to a late finish.

Shelley was getting her bearings, casting her eyes around the room, nervously willing Colin not to be here but then again wanting to see him to have all her suspicions squashed. She blinked as the disco lights dazzled her eyes, blinding her for a moment. She realized that she was reminded of being a teenager again, entering a nightclub, nervously wondering if the boy she had her eye on would be there. She looked over at her mum. How had it got to this? Dragging her mum, at sixty-two, to a Spanish bar dressed in a leopard-print jumpsuit? Nancy, on the other hand, looked right at home. She sat confidently upright, appearing to survey the room as though she were sitting on a throne rather than a mobility scooter.

'So what have we here?' a voice boomed over the sound system. 'I think we have some celebrities in the room. I'd like to welcome what looks like – well, I think it could be . . . do we actually have the Spice Girls here at the Flaming Flamingo?'

The opening bars of 'Wannabee' instantly struck up and what felt like the eyes of the entire bar turned to stare at them. So much for being incognito, thought Shelley. She prayed that Colin wasn't here yet so they could get this excruciating introduction over with.

'Big round of applause please, ladies and gentlemen,' continued the DJ, turning his spotlights towards them and nearly blinding them. 'Come on up, ladies. You look like you are on a special night out. Up you come. There are free bottles of champagne on offer every hour for the best dressed, and to be quite honest I'm not seeing anyone better dressed than you guys at this very moment.'

'No,' hissed Shelley. 'We cannot go up there. Everyone will see us.'

'I think they already have,' said Becca, looking around her and giving everyone a little wave. 'Come on, we can't just walk off, that would be worse. Let's go get our free champagne.'

Becca strode off towards the DJ's booth, quickly followed by Nancy on her scooter, with Chloe catching a lift on the back, waving to the now cheering crowd. This left Shelley, Peggy and Rosalind stranded on the edge of the dance floor, contemplating the horror of being thrust even further into the limelight.

'Why does going out with my mother always end in some kind of drama?' said Rosalind, shaking her head. 'Come on, let's get it over with,' she sighed, and followed the other three across the dance floor.

'So, you look like a really interesting bunch,' said the DJ, thrusting a microphone in Chloe's face as Shelley reached them. 'What's your name and where do you come from?'

'I'm Baby Spice, of course, from London,' said Chloe into the microphone, grinning.

'Ah ha,' laughed the DJ. 'Of course you are. Now would you introduce us to your fellow band-mates.'

Chloe turned to her mum and said, 'Well this is my very competitive mother, aka Sporty Spice. Say hello, Mother.'

'Hello,' said Rosalind through gritted teeth.

'And this is my terrifying great-aunt,' continued Chloe, pointing at a scowling Peggy.

'She looks like a very Scary Spice,' nodded the DJ.

'She totally is,' agreed Chloe. 'Then my nan is Ginger Spice. She's actually the best singer out of all of us, so really should be Sporty, but in true Ginger style she insisted on wearing the best outfit so there she is.'

'Loving the transport,' said the DJ.

'And Becca is also Ginger Spice because – well, she insisted, and seems like she enjoys getting her way.'

Shelley couldn't help but stifle a laugh. Chloe really had got the measure of everyone.

'And there at the back is my cousin-ish, Shelley. We are all here for her hen weekend and she's Posh because she's marrying someone who is minted.'

Jesus Christ, thought Shelley, frantically looking round. Could Chloe make a worse public statement than that? If Colin was in the crowd she would die.

'Hi Posh,' said the DJ, waving at her to step forward. 'Come on up here. Let's have a word with Posh-bride Spice.' He shoved the microphone in her face, forcing her to speak.

'I'm not posh,' she said. 'He's not that rich really,' she continued, feeling all flustered.

Peggy leaned forward and grabbed the microphone. 'She's not marrying him for his money,' she shouted at the device. 'She's not like that.'

Shelley didn't know whether to be chuffed with the compliment or absolutely mortified that her mum had chosen to say it in front of a room full of people.

'There is absolutely nothing wrong with marrying for money,' said the DJ. 'Has your fiancé got a sister?' He bellowed with laughter at his own joke. Shelley looked at Becca pleadingly. They needed to get off this stage and fast. Luckily Chloe stepped in, grabbing the microphone back.

'You said something about free champagne?' she asked.

The DJ nodded. 'Well, I think a hen party dressed as the Spice Girls does deserve some free bubbly, don't you?'

Thank goodness for that, thought Shelley. We can go and blend in now.

'But I think we deserve a little tune first, hey?' he continued. 'We can't let the Spice Girls leave without a song, can we? Ginger Nan, how about it? Granddaughter Spice reckons you have the best voice, so which song is it going to be? I assume you know the back catalogue?'

'Of course,' said Nancy looking mightily offended. 'I'm not that old. I do an excellent version of "Say You'll Be There", I'll have you know.'

'Really?' replied the DJ, his eyes wide.

Nooooooo, Shelley screamed inside.

'Well let's have it then, shall we,' said the DJ. 'The mikes are all set up on the stage here for our karaoke challenge later this evening, so off you go ladies. Really looking forward to this. Ladies and Gentlemen. I give you, the Spice Girls.'

It took a few moments for them to get themselves organized. Nancy had to park up her scooter for a start, and climb off it without flashing her knickers to the entire audience. And then she had to make sure everyone knew what they were doing so they could give the best performance possible.

'Right,' she said. 'I'll do lead vocals. You all back me up, okay?'

'I cannot believe we are doing this,' said Shelley, almost in tears. 'We were supposed to slip in here quietly, spy on my fiancé and disappear, and instead we're on stage about to sing in front of loads of people and make total fools of ourselves.'

'Come on,' said Nancy, putting her arm around her niece. 'It won't take a minute and it is supposed to be your hen weekend, after all. We are supposed to have *some* fun.'

Shelley would not call this fun. Shelley would call this torture. She pulled her veil over to cover her face again in the hope that she could pretend it wasn't happening and the crowd wouldn't be able to see her blushes.

They all shuffled around the two mikes as the familiar bars struck up. Nancy was beaming, so comfortable to be on stage, and loving the expectant looks of a larger-than-usual audience. Chloe also looked like she was having fun, already swigging from the open bottle of champagne.

Shelley found herself scanning the room again, peering through her veil. Still no sign of Colin. Normally she could spot him in a room instantly, seeing as she was tall and he was taller.

The first lines of 'Say You'll Be There' blasted through the speakers. Suddenly Shelley had a vision of the iconic, desert-based video with Posh dressed in a shiny PVC catsuit. She looked along the line at her fellow bandmates and suddenly felt the Girl Power flow through her. This was her gang, this was her crew, and here they were up on stage about to belt out a classic

Spice Girls song on her hen night. This was something to be embraced, this was something to enjoy. Colin was nowhere in sight and so she might as well go for it. She grabbed the bottle of champagne from Chloe, took a swig and prepared to sing her heart out.

They were only halfway through the first verse, and already most of the club had turned to watch and were swaying along. Nancy, as always, surprised everyone with her powerful voice and knowledge of popular lyrics, and was quite a sight dominating the stage in her Union Jack kaftan. Shelley glanced at Becca, who grinned back at her as she strangled the tune.

Shelley looked back out at the audience; seeing so many people having fun made her swell with pride. They were doing this. They were entertaining everyone. Singing one of her favourite songs. And actually, she had to admit it felt pretty good.

And then she saw them.

Colin and Neil were standing right at the back, having just walked in. Her heart leapt into her throat and she struggled to concentrate on her singing. She watched, transfixed, as Colin shouted something into Neil's ear. He nodded and then headed towards the bar, whilst Colin scanned the room, barely taking any notice of what was happening on the small stage on the other side of the room.

She couldn't quite believe it. There was Colin, her Colin. He was dressed in a deep blue shirt, which was her particular favourite. She'd bought it for him. It wasn't an expensive brand or anything, but it really suited him and it matched the colour of his eyes. She felt her heart leap a little. Shelley studied him closely, now only murmuring the words into the microphone. It was a very odd thing to observe someone you knew so well when they have no idea that you are there. I guess you always wonder if what you see is the whole person. Or if they present only a side of their personality. Do they play a role with you that they may not play with anyone else? Shelley was very aware that she played roles depending on whom she was with. Dutiful daughter, fun-loving friend, sensible teacher. She did it automatically, but occasionally she caught herself going overboard to pretend to be what she felt those closest to her needed, rather than just sitting back and being herself. Agreeing to go out for one more drink with Becca, when really all she wanted was to go home. Pretending to ignore her mother's put downs when all she wanted to do was scream at her and ask her to just occasionally try to boost her daughter's self-esteem. Attempting a level of sophistication that was beyond anything that came naturally to her in order to fit in with Colin's friends and family. He never asked it of her. Not once. But somehow, she felt she should at least try.

She stared at Colin. Did he look how he usually did when he was with her? What would she ask him, she thought, if she were a stranger to him?

So, you are getting married. Tell me about your fiancée. Is she the one? The one you have always been waiting for, or did you just run out of time? Did you just settle for a nice sensible girl?

She's a teacher, you say. Daughter of a dairyman. How do you think she is going to fit into your fancy lifestyle?

209

Will you be Colin with her? Who is the real Colin?

A thousand and one questions ran through her mind as she stared at him, dimly aware that the others were starting the final verse. Loads of questions she would really like the answer to, she realized. Before she got married preferably. Why did she not know the answers to these questions? Was it like this for all brides? Were there always unanswered questions? Was it always a leap of faith? Could you ever really be totally sure? Had she just been waiting for something to go wrong? It was, after all, too good to be true. Her bagging the most eligible man around.

She watched as he suddenly left his spot and headed right towards her. She felt her heart pound in her chest. She didn't want Colin to see her like this. Ironically dressed as Posh Spice, taking the mickey out of his wealthy background and making a fool of herself in front of a bar full of people, with two geriatrics beside her dressed in inappropriate clothes. She glanced over at Becca, panicking, and saw that Becca had also spotted Colin and had her gaze fixed on him as he continued to stride towards the stage.

Just as Shelley thought that her heart was about to pound out of her mouth, Colin stopped a few feet in front of them and tapped a girl on the shoulder. She was petite, with dark hair, and had olive skin that was wrapped in a skintight sequined dress. She was absolutely stunning.

Shelley stopped singing about promises to be there as she watched the woman spin round, grin broadly, and throw her arms around Colin and the deep blue shirt she had bought him. Shelley was sure she could feel her heart stopping. Sweat trickled down her back. They hugged for a long time. Too long. She watched them draw apart and saw a look in Colin's eye. One she didn't recognize.

She suddenly felt extremely faint, as if she was going to collapse there and then. She looked over at her band mates for help. The last line was fading, and they were all looking at Colin wrapped around another woman. Clearly Becca had pointed him out and now they couldn't take their eyes off him. She looked at Becca and shouted, 'Get me out of here.'

Becca nodded and took control. She grabbed Shelley's hand and hustled everyone off stage as the DJ asked for a round of applause for the incredible Spice Girls tribute band that he was convinced would be back again tomorrow night . . . if everyone clapped loudly enough.

Nancy remounted the mobility scooter and carved a path through the crowd, the rest of them following behind her. 'Coming through,' she shouted, whilst beeping her horn and flashing her lights. 'Out of the way. Yes, you with the enormous arse. Out of my way.'

Slowly the crowd parted whilst Shelley kept her head down at the back, desperate to get out of there as soon as possible and for Colin not to recognize her. It was only when they got to the exit that Shelley felt the need to turn back and take one last look to check what she had seen. Was it a greeting to an old friend, or was it more? Was he still hugging her?

She turned back, but by now the crowd had shifted

again and she couldn't see Colin or the mystery woman at all.

'Shelley,' she heard from beside her. 'Is that you?'

She turned to see Neil clutching two pints.

'Erm yeah,' she managed to say. 'Hi Neil, sorry, but I need to catch the others up, we were just leaving.'

'No way!' said Neil. 'What a shame. Have you seen Colin?'

'No!' said Shelley. 'God no, not seen him. Not at all. Please don't tell him I was here. Don't want him to think I'm stalking him or anything, you know.' She laughed a nervous laugh.

Neil looked back at her quizzically and shrugged. 'If you like,' he said. 'You look amazing by the way – that's quite a dress.'

Shelley swallowed. 'I look like an idiot,' she replied. 'They made me do it. We're all dressed as the Spice Girls and they made me dress as Posh Spice because . . . well, Colin's posh. Please don't tell him. Promise me you won't tell him.'

Neil laughed. 'Not if you don't want me to, but I think he would feel like a very lucky man if he saw you like this.'

But he didn't see me, thought Shelley. He only had eyes for someone else.

'It was you,' exclaimed Neil, 'you were up on stage, weren't you? I was watching from the bar. You were all brilliant.'

'Yeah, well, it is a hen night, after all. You have to make a fool of yourself somewhere.'

'Not at all,' said Neil. 'You were all great.'

'Speaking of which, I'd better go and find the rest of them,' said Shelley. 'They'll think I've got lost. You know my mum will be really panicking, thinking I've been kidnapped or something.'

'Sure. Well, it was nice to see you,' said Neil. 'Really glad you are having a good time.'

'Thanks,' said Shelley. If only he knew. 'Not a word to Colin?'

'My lips are sealed,' replied Neil. 'Look after yourself.'

'Thanks,' she replied, and turned and fled.

Chapter 28

They were all waiting outside on the wide pathway when Shelley finally emerged from the bar.

'Are you all right?' Becca asked, running towards her. 'I looked round and you were gone.'

Shelley nodded. 'I'm fine,' she said. 'I err, just got caught in the crowd.'

'Let's get out of here, shall we?' said Peggy.

'Good idea,' said Nancy, spinning her scooter around. 'Why don't we go and find something to eat? I'm starving. Follow me, everyone.'

Becca watched as Nancy revved up her scooter and zoomed off towards the middle of town, leaving the rest of them to trail behind in her wake. How could she be thinking about food right now? They'd only just eaten. Although Becca realized that she perhaps needed some serious carbs to soak up the alcohol.

The rest of them began to walk away from the Flaming Flamingo, all curiously silent. Becca ran over in her mind the vision of Colin greeting the mystery woman. She hadn't liked what she had seen and she wondered how Shelley had viewed it. Not well, she thought as she observed her friend's head hung low beside her.

They emerged into what looked like the town square and spotted Nancy parked outside a McDonald's.

'Why have we stopped here?' demanded Rosalind, when they reached her.

'I think we all deserve a Big Mac,' announced Nancy, parking her scooter up and beginning to get off.

'Are you serious?' declared Rosalind with her hands on her hips.

'What a brilliant idea,' said Becca and Chloe.

'A Big Mac? Here? In Andelica?' exclaimed Rosalind.

'I fancy a Big Mac,' said Nancy. 'With super-sized fries and a chocolate milkshake.'

Rosalind looked as if she was about to explode. 'But we have only just eaten. Have you any idea how bad that is for you?' she said. 'No wonder you are struggling to walk if you are eating Big Macs every day.'

'Not every day!' protested Nancy. 'Maybe once or twice a week.'

'*Mum*, how could you?' said Rosalind, in a tone that made it sound like her mother had gambled all her money away.

'She only wants a Big Mac, Mum,' said Chloe. 'She's not murdered anyone.'

'She's as good as murdering herself,' said Rosalind. 'If she's eating like this all the time. Can't you talk some sense into her, Auntie Peggy?'

Peggy opened her mouth to start to speak but was interrupted.

215

'Who the hell do you think you are?' screamed Chloe at her mum. 'You can't talk to Nan like that. She can do what the hell she likes.'

'It's all right, Chloe love,' said Nancy, putting a hand on her arm. 'I can handle your mother.'

Chloe turned to stare at her and shook her head.

'But what gives her the right to tell us all what to do, Nan? She does it all the time. Like she's getting it all right. Like she's living life perfectly. What gives her the right to tell you how to live when she and Dad aren't even sleeping in the same bed? When they are barely even talking to each other. When Dad can't bear to be in the same house as his wife so he's apparently *always* out on constituency business, which seems to involve wining and dining several women on the council who fawn over him just because he's some poxy MP.'

'Chloe!' exclaimed Rosalind. 'Don't talk about your father like that. He's an MP, for goodness' sake. You should be very proud of him.'

'I don't see him enough to be proud of him because you have driven him out of the house because you are so sodding miserable. Just like you did with Oscar. He's not coming back from uni for the summer, by the way. He's got a job in the Co-op in Exeter. He'd rather stay there and work in the corner shop than come home and see you.'

'That's not true,' shouted Rosalind. 'He's got exams coming up. He wanted to stay and revise.'

'He told me there was no way he was coming home just so you could rope him in to bullying me into going to university,' stated Chloe.

216

'I am *not* bullying you,' retorted Rosalind.

'You are. You are just a tired old woman who has so many regrets about her own life she doesn't know what to do with them, so she's determined to ruin everyone else's life around her. Now that's what I call being a really great mother. Thanks a lot, Mum.'

Chloe turned and fled back down the road towards the harbour.

Rosalind gasped and her entire face crumpled into tears.

'Wait!' she shouted.

'Let her go,' said Nancy, putting her hand on her arm. 'I think you both need to calm down, don't you?'

Rosalind glanced round at Shelley, Becca and Peggy staring at her. She looked shattered. No one knew what to say.

Eventually Nancy put her arm around her daughter. 'You know what you need?' she said to a still tearful Rosalind.

Rosalind shook her head.

'A Big Mac,' said Nancy. 'Honestly, it will make you feel better.'

'I'll go,' said Becca, practically running into McDonald's and not even stopping to get anyone's order.

No one said anything for a while as they perched on the steps of a stone monument that stood in the centre of the square, chewing on fried food. Becca bit into her Big Mac and sighed, instantly feeling slightly more sober.

'I'm sorry, Shelley,' said Rosalind eventually. 'I feel like, well, we are ruining your special weekend.'

Shelley shrugged. 'It's not very special, is it really?' she muttered. 'Not when . . . not when it looks like my fiancé is . . . well, not who I thought he was.'

'I'd forgotten about Colin for a moment,' admitted Nancy.

'I didn't mean to upstage you with my dramas,' said Rosalind.

'It's fine,' said Shelley, staring at the ground.

'So you might as well all know,' said Rosalind, taking a deep breath. 'Robert has taken a lease on a flat near Westminster. It helps when they have late-night voting, apparently.'

'But you only live forty-five minutes from Westminster,' said Nancy.

'That's what I said,' replied Rosalind.

'What did he say?' asked Nancy.

'To stop fretting. Loads of ministers do it. Makes life easier, he said.'

'Ministers who live a long way away?'

Rosalind shrugged.

'And was Chloe right? Are you sleeping in separate rooms?' asked Nancy.

Rosalind nodded. 'He got a cough last Christmas so moved out. He's never moved back in.'

'Bad cough then,' said Shelley.

'Must be,' muttered Rosalind, burying her head in her hands.

They sat munching their burgers in silence.

Unusually Becca didn't know what to say. She looked at Shelley, who was making no eye contact with anyone, just rota-feeding herself French fries. She'd not said

218

much since they'd left the club as her dilemma had been overshadowed by Rosalind and Chloe's monumental bust-up. What must she be thinking, thought Becca. The evidence was pretty damning. They had seen Shelley's fiancé with his arms round another woman. Fact. Now there might be a perfectly good explanation, but it was not a scenario that any imminent bride wants to see. Especially on her hen weekend. Well, actually at any time.

And then there was Rosalind facing some real home truths, with Chloe having run off to goodness knows where. Quite where they went from here, on this fun-packed occasion, was anyone's guess. It could almost make Becca wish she were at home. But not quite. No, actually not at all. She'd still rather be dressed as Ginger Spice eating a McDonald's, surrounded by misery, rather than at home. A fact that did nothing to make her feel any better about herself.

'Sorry I called you a bad mother for leaving your babies,' Rosalind suddenly said to Becca. 'You must be sitting there feeling pretty smug after that terrible display with my daughter.'

Becca swallowed. If only she knew, she thought. She nodded her acceptance of the apology and put her head down and began to rota-feed French fries just like Shelley. She no longer wanted to have eye contact with anyone either. She wasn't a good mother, Becca was sure of that. She was the worst kind of mother. Rosalind's problem was that she cared too much, whereas Becca's problem was that she didn't care enough. She wanted her old life back. Before kids.

When she was a successful human being. Not the miserable failure that she was now.

It didn't take long for everyone to be staring at the bottom of a French fries carton, desperately hoping for there to be just one more chip. The evening had been an absolute disaster. Nothing had gone right. Shelley had observed her fiancé sucking up to some strange woman, and Rosalind and Chloe had had a relationship-defining argument. One they might never come back from. Not the usual happy, devil-may-care celebrations of the first night of a hen weekend.

'I think we should just go home, don't you?' said Shelley, looking mournfully around her. No one had dared ask her about how she was feeling having seen Colin cosying up to the glamorous, petite brunette. It all seemed too raw and likely to spark yet another show of emotion, and perhaps they had had enough of that tonight.

'I think that's a very good idea,' said Peggy. 'I think everyone needs to just calm down and have a good night's sleep and everything will seem better in the morning.'

Becca stared back at Peggy, not convinced at all she was right.

Chapter 29

'This is very strange bread,' said Peggy, holding it up to the light and peering at it. She looked over at Nancy, who was on her hands and knees peering into the fridge. Peggy worried how she was going to get herself up again. She really needed to have a talk with her sister about her weight. She looked so unhealthy. What on earth would their mother have said, who'd never had an ounce of fat on her?

They'd both been up for hours. Well, it felt like it. Peggy had joined Nancy in the kitchen for breakfast at about 9 a.m. She was showered and fully dressed as she sat across from Nancy, who was still in her shapeless nightdress. Rosalind had appeared at one point in walking gear and declared she was taking herself off on a hike whilst everyone was still in bed. She'd left with a bottle of water and an orange, having not mentioned the events of the previous evening. Not that Peggy and Nancy had discussed it either. Peggy had fielded questions about life back in Derbyshire, as Nancy asked about the village and the various inhabitants who were still there from their childhood. Peggy had answered politely but begrudgingly. She found it hard to be generous in the sharing of news of their home village when Nancy had been the one to up sticks and desert it all those years ago. Nancy didn't have much right to her memories there, Peggy felt. She'd left them behind a long time ago.

When conversation had run out, Nancy had thankfully suggested they put a picnic together for a trip to the beach. Peggy had been relieved. She wasn't really one for small talk and sitting around. She liked to be busy and useful. And putting a meal together was one of her specialties. Albeit putting a picnic together in a foreign country with this weird bread was proving challenging.

'It's the only sliced I can get,' replied Nancy. 'They don't really do sliced bread here. Thomas likes it toasted. But finding a toaster was quite difficult when we first arrived.'

'They don't eat toast?' asked Peggy.

'Not really. But then they don't in America either. Toast, it turns out, is very British.'

'Gordon lived on toast when he was alive,' said Peggy, as she tried to butter the bread. 'Don't know what he would have done without toast and Golden Shred marmalade. He never could have lived in a foreign country that didn't have toast and Golden Shred marmalade.'

'Lucky he didn't then,' said Nancy.

Peggy turned her attention to the weird-looking ham that Nancy had handed her to put in the sandwiches.

'Gordon always liked breaded ham,' said Peggy. 'Always asked where the funny yellow stuff was if I couldn't get hold of it. Breaded ham, real butter and English mustard. Not French. He couldn't abide French mustard.'

'Mmm,' muttered Nancy.

'I once forgot the mustard,' she continued. 'He walked all the way back from the farm with his lunch box and asked, "What happened to the mustard?" I said I must have just forgot. I was breast-feeding Shelley at the time. So I told him to get the mustard out and put it on himself. He made his own sandwiches from that day on.'

'Right,' said Nancy, grabbing a bag of tomatoes and handing them to Peggy.

'I have to say the tomatoes taste better here, though,' said Peggy. 'Must be the sunshine. Not as good as Gordon's straight out of the greenhouse, of course. You don't get tomatoes like that nowadays, do you? In the summer, Gordon would just pick one straight off the vine on his way to work and he had his own salt pot in his lunch box and he'd eat it like an apple – with a bit of salt. Loved his tomatoes, did Gordon.'

'How's Ray?' asked Nancy.

'What?' said Peggy, not really hearing her.

'How's Ray, I said.'

'Oh, he's fine. He's Ray. Filling his garden with rubbish and wanting to fill mine as well.'

Nancy nodded. 'He sounds like fun. Shelley was telling me about the butcher's slice in his boot. Just hilarious.'

'I mean, who has a butcher's slice in his boot?' said Peggy.

'Exactly,' replied Nancy. 'He sounds like such a character.'

'You don't have to live next door to him.'

'Sounds like a great neighbour to me. He looks out for you, right? Talks to you? Does all those jobs you can't do. Didn't you tell me he'd cleared your drain for you?'

'Only because he'd just bought some draining rods at a house clearance.'

'But still, eh Peggy. He doesn't have to, does he? It's good of him.'

Peggy said nothing. Nancy didn't understand. She hated relying on Ray to do all the jobs around the house that Gordon would have done. Nancy still had her husband to do all that stuff. She had no idea how useful husbands were. You soon realized, once they were gone.

'I'm just glad you've got someone looking after you,' said Nancy.

Peggy bristled. Her sister had absolved any right to be worried about her, the day she left home after Dorothy had died. She wasn't worried about her little sister then and she had no right to be worried about her now. This ham really wasn't the right type of ham to have in sandwiches. It was thin and dry. What was Nancy thinking? And really, they should be boiling some eggs up. She could really do with an egg sandwich.

'Shall we make some egg sandwiches?' she asked Nancy.

'We can, but they don't sell salad cream here, so we can't make them like Mum used to make them. We could use mayonnaise, though.'

'No salad cream?' said Peggy.

'Another thing that turns out to be British,' said Nancy.

'You should have said,' said Peggy. 'I could have brought some with me.'

'It's not a problem. We don't really miss it.'

Peggy shook her head. Gordon could never have had a salad without salad cream. If there was no salad cream, they just would not have salad. End of story. What was a salad without salad cream?

Peggy heard a scuffle behind her. But it was only Nancy trying to get herself up from the floor. It wasn't a pretty sight, and by the time she had hauled herself onto a chair, she was bright red and pouring with sweat. Peggy really needed to have a serious word with her. She drew her breath ready to speak out, but Nancy beat her to it.

'So, are you going to have a chat with Shelley today?' she asked.

Peggy looked at her, startled. 'What about?' she asked.

'Well, about last night?'

'What about last night?'

'About the fact that a woman had her arms around Colin.'

Peggy blinked back at her. She really didn't know what she expected her to say. She had her own opinion on what she saw, sure. But it wasn't her opinion that mattered. It was Shelley's. *She* had to decide what she saw and whether she thought it was acceptable to her. She knew that Gordon would never have got himself in that position. But that was Gordon. They didn't make men like Gordon any more. Men seemed to play by totally different rules these days, so maybe it was all okay. In any case, she had no right to interfere. Shelley didn't need her mother sticking her oar in.

'She doesn't need me sticking my oar in,' said Peggy, turning back to butter more bread.

'Really?' said Nancy. 'Are you sure? She looked pretty confused to me last night. She might need someone to talk to about it.'

Peggy stiffened. This was so like her sister. Always knew best and yet in Peggy's opinion was not the best mother by any stretch of the imagination.

'She'll work it out,' said Peggy, reaching for a chopping board and knife to slice the tomatoes.

She could hear Nancy sigh behind her.

'But you don't think she should marry him. You said as much when I picked you up from the airport, and last night, well, if that doesn't set off alarm bells, I don't know what does.'

Peggy slammed the knife down and turned around. 'And what about Rosalind?' she demanded. 'You going to sit her down and tell her what to do about her sham of a marriage, are you? You've been there for her, have you, these past eighteen months, whilst he's been sleeping in another bedroom and renting another flat?'

Nancy looked back at her, startled.

'No. Nowhere in sight. And yet you have the audacity to tell me that I need to be more involved in my daughter's love life. Don't tell me how to be a mother to a daughter, and I won't tell you.'

Peggy turned back round and managed to massacre a tomato. She heard Nancy strain to get up.

'I'll put the kettle on,' Nancy said as she shuffled over to the other side of the kitchen.

Peggy bit her lip. Conversation over. Time for a cup of tea. Or what excuse for tea Nancy kept in her villa. She really should have told her to bring some PG Tips over.

They moved around in silence, Nancy making tea, Peggy making yet more sandwiches until Becca walked in, bleary eyed.

'Morning or afternoon or whatever,' she said, plonking herself down at the table. 'I'm praying you are making tea.'

'Sure am,' said Nancy. 'Fancy some toast too?'

'Definitely,' replied Becca. 'My stomach is crying out for it.'

'Would you put some toast in please, Peggy?' asked Nancy.

'Certainly,' replied Peggy curtly, popping two slices in before washing her hands. She turned to sit at the table just as Nancy placed two steaming mugs down.

'So killer night last night, eh ladies?' said Becca. 'What's the verdict? Is he in or out?'

Peggy glanced at Nancy but said nothing.

'Well, that's up to Shelley, isn't it?' said Nancy carefully, looking at Peggy the whole time.

'Mmm, yeah, yeah,' said Becca, nodding. 'I guess. Tricky though. I mean, technically all we saw was him

227

putting his arms around a girl. Not a crime, right? But then there is the text and what on earth that means, and where has it come from? I mean, they are all little red flags, aren't they? I guess what she really needs is either a good blast of wind to blow them all away, or one enormous red flag just to make it all crystal clear.'

'Not sure you ever get the enormous red flag,' mused Nancy. 'I mean, the obvious one. The one you simply cannot miss or ignore. You only ever get the small ones that could mean anything depending on how you look at them. That's what makes these situations so hard.'

'The flags are too small,' said Becca.

'Exactly,' agreed Nancy.

'We just need to let Shelley work it out,' said Peggy, glaring at Nancy.

'Yes, yes, I totally agree,' said Nancy, looking down.

'Work it out?' exclaimed Becca. 'Have you met your daughter? She's so insecure when it comes to relationships. Work this one out?' Becca shook her head.

'Well, what do you suggest?' asked Peggy. 'Tell her to dump him? Do you really want to have that responsibility? Do you really think you should tell her what to do? Is it your decision?' pressed Peggy.

'Well no,' said Becca.

'That's agreed then,' said Peggy. 'We say nothing. Let her make her own mind up.'

'All right, Peggy. If you say so,' said Becca. She took a gulp of her tea. 'So do we just carry on as normal then? Proceed as planned? Go all out to make sure Shelley has a good time and enjoys her hen party, come what may?'

'Yes,' said Peggy, nodding her head. 'I think that is for the best.'

'It would appear so,' sighed Nancy. 'Actually, we were just packing a picnic to go to the beach. Thought it would do us all good to get some fresh air.'

'Picnic, great,' nodded Becca.

'Ham sandwiches,' said Peggy. 'Well, it's that weird bread and ham and they don't have salad cream here, apparently, but the tomatoes are nice.'

'Oh right,' said Becca. 'We could always just get something at the beach?'

'No, there will be plenty, said Peggy. 'No need to buy expensive food at the beach. Oh, and we could take a flask. Do you have a flask, Nancy?'

'Not much need for flasks here, Peggy.'

'No, guess not. Well, we should at least take some water with us,' said Peggy.

'Is there a bar at the beach?' asked Becca.

'Oh yes,' replied Nancy. 'Don't panic, it's your typical Spanish holiday beach. All mod cons. You name it.'

Becca's eyes lit up. 'Then I have just the idea to really give us all some much-needed fresh air and take Shelley's mind off last night. Time to get everybody up.'

Chapter 30

'A banana boat!' said Shelley. 'No way. Not doing it.'

'A banana boat,' shrieked Chloe. 'Yes!'

'What's a banana boat?' asked Rosalind and Peggy.

'I'll sink it,' said Nancy.

It was some two hours later, and Shelley was staring at Becca, who was excitedly standing in front of them on the beach.

The first Shelley had heard of the plan to go to the beach had been when Becca had thundered into the bedroom and announced they were going out now and she needed to get up. The truth was that she'd already lain there for a good half-hour, wide awake, the events of the previous evening scrolling through her brain. The disappointment at the eyelashes comment and seeing Colin greet a strange woman with such delight. Watching her fiancé when he had no clue that she was there had been cruelly fascinating and deeply unsettling.

After they had left McDonald's, no one had said a word about seeing Colin. Maybe distracted by Rosalind and Chloe's major fallout, they had all pretty much ignored Shelley and trooped off to bed the minute they got back to the villa. What were they all thinking? Christ, what a loser. Colin is already straying and Shelley's not even got him up the aisle yet? Or no biggie. Colin was just being nice to an old friend?

'Come on, Shelley,' said Becca, bending over and shouting in her ear. 'We have hen party duties to attend to. There is fun to be had and you are still in bed. Your mum has already made substandard ham and cheese sandwiches, apparently to take to the beach. Can you imagine? What a sight we will be. You in your bride-to-be tiara and veil on the beach eating a butty. You've got ten minutes, then we are out the door.'

Better get up then, thought Shelley. She dragged herself out of bed and into the shower, then emerged into the kitchen to be greeted by Nancy and Peggy having a row over chairs.

'You can hire a chair at the beach,' Nancy was saying.

'Why would we do that when we can take our own?'

'It's a fifteen-minute walk.'

'Can't we put them on your scooter thing?'

'No. No one does that. There are chairs there, waiting to be hired. It's really easy.'

'What a waste of money.'

'They're pretty cheap.'

'But when you have perfectly good chairs and then pay to hire them, it makes no sense to me.'

'You bending over backwards to make life as difficult as possible for yourself makes no sense to me, either, but I'm not having a go at you. I will pay for your chair. Don't worry about it. You see, it is just how it's done.'

Peggy gave a big sigh. Shelley could tell she wasn't satisfied with the situation. However, she did seem to feel more passionately about the beach-chair situation than about how her only daughter was. Shelley had said good morning and asked how her mother was, to which she had replied with a terse, 'Fine.' Shelley waited for her mother to enquire after her own well-being but nothing came. In fact, no one asked how she was feeling, just busied themselves with preparing for the beach as if nothing at all had happened the night before.

And now she found herself standing on the sand, contemplating wrapping her legs around a large inflatable banana in the name of having a successful hen party.

'So, Nancy, Peggy, you are excused,' announced Becca. 'No offence, but we don't need any trips to A&E with geriatrics, so you can stay here and mind our stuff.'

Peggy looked like the least relaxed person ever on the Spanish beach. As naked flesh a-plenty bobbed around her, she sat bolt upright in her chair in a polyester frock, American tan tights and sandals still firmly on her feet, the seam of the tights peeping out of the end of her open-toe sandal. Nancy, however, was fully chilled in yet another flowing kaftan, bare feet and large floppy hat shading her face from the sun. Peggy sported a small straw hat and a very shiny face from excessive lotion application.

'Very wise,' replied Nancy. 'I would sink a banana like a torpedoed battleship, I fear. Never to be seen again.'

'But what does it do exactly?' asked Peggy.

232

'They drag it behind a speedboat and you hold on for dear life,' said Chloe, beaming at the thought of it. 'Just wicked.'

'I don't see the point in it,' said Rosalind.

Shelley looked over at her cousin. She and Chloe had not spoken a word to each other so far. It was casting a frosty tone over the whole day and, quite frankly, Shelley could do without it.

'Come on, Rosalind,' said Shelley. 'If I'm doing it, you are. Do you remember when Dad used to make us a slide in the garden with straw bales and plastic sheeting? We had a great time. You loved it.'

'Oh, you did so,' added Peggy. 'The screaming and the laughing that used to come from that garden. You should have heard them, Nancy.'

'I was twelve years old,' said Rosalind.

'So – you are only allowed to have fun at twelve years old, are you?' said Becca.

'Mum doesn't know how to have fun,' said Chloe.

Shelley watched Rosalind's face fall. Shelley could vividly remember Rosalind squealing with delight when her brother used to turn the hose on her in the back garden. She'd be the one running and jumping into the home-made paddling pool, trying to make the biggest splash out of everyone. She had a pink and white spotted swimsuit with a white frill fringing it. Shelley remembered it well because she longed to wear it herself, and thankfully received it as a hand-me-down some years later. She could see Rosalind now, twirling in her pretty swimsuit and spinning her arms round, trying to soak everything in sight. It was the most carefree, joyful, spirited thing you could imagine. And now here stood Rosalind, more than thirty years later, in a black one-piece swimsuit with cargo shorts still on, her daughter accusing her of not having the faintest idea of how to have fun. And in fact looking like she had no idea how to have fun. What had happened to her? Did that happen to everyone? Did the fun get sucked out of you the older you got? Or was it getting married? Or having kids? Was that what rendered you devoid of fun?

'Come on, Rosalind,' said Shelley. 'Let's go relive our youth. I think we both could do with a good scream, don't you? Bet I can scream louder than you!'

Rosalind cracked a small smile. 'You always could,' she said. 'But then Adam was the best screamer.'

'My brother was such a baby,' agreed Shelley.

Shelley wasn't feeling quite so fun-filled when the guy who hired out the banana boats told her she had no choice but to sit in the middle because of her size. Great. Talk about humiliation.

'Never mind, Shell,' said Becca. 'That's the safest place. Less likely to fall off.'

'Can I go on the back?' asked Chloe. 'Got to be the best fun on the back. Most likely to get flung off, I reckon.'

'Would you like to go on the front?' Becca asked Rosalind. 'That's really safe.'

Rosalind stared back at Becca. Then glanced at Shelley.

'No, I'll go near the back,' she said. 'Might as well get the full experience if I'm going to do it.'

'Does that mean I have to go on the front then?' said Becca. 'Boring!'

'Just shut up and get on the front,' said Shelley.

'Everyone all right back there?' shouted Becca when they were all mounted on the banana, waiting to go.

'Yes!' they all chorused.

'This is more like it hey,' she said. 'Now this is what I call a hen party.'

Shelley was trying to forget it was her hen party. She was trying to just have a good time, in the hope it would settle her mind. Maybe a shot of adrenaline was exactly what she needed to get her out of this funk she was in. Yes – this was perfect. A trip on a banana boat and all would become clear.

Fun was always the best medicine.

Shelley had never been more terrified in her life. At one point she was aware she was holding on for dear life, eyes tightly shut, praying. Praying to whom, she had absolutely no idea; she was no great believer since her dad had gone out for a paper and never come back. Despite her parents' regular church-going, she could no longer believe in something that was cruel enough to take her father. So she did the usual thing that non-believers do, and asked in her head if God – if there was one – wouldn't mind letting her believe briefly, and save her life, given that she had been put in mortal danger on this banana boat. And if he did spare her she would be eternally grateful and would believe in God the Father and the Holy Ghost until the end of her days.

As she said her prayers through gritted teeth, she could hear the other three screaming in delight. Loudest of all being Rosalind. She sounded just how Shelley remembered her in their back garden in Derbyshire.

Screaming with absolute joy. It was such a good sound to hear after so many years.

Not soon enough, Shelley felt the banana start to slow down, and she stopped being swung this way and that like a rag doll. Her heartbeat started to gradually abate, and she dared open her eyes as she saw the shore approach and the banana boat slowly ground to a halt. Shelley didn't think she would be able to let go. The thought of having to get herself from the banana to the small wooden pier was almost as terrifying as the ride itself.

Becca turned round and grinned at her.

'Shall we do it again?' she shouted.

'No,' said Shelley, releasing her grip and making a move to get off the banana boat as quickly as she could. There was only one thing worse than getting off and that was staying on.

'I'll do it again,' she heard Chloe shout from behind her. 'As many times as you like.'

The man was now helping haul Shelley to land, making it look as though she weighed a ton. Unnecessary, thought Shelley.

'There needs to be at least three of you,' said the man. 'It's too light otherwise.'

'You'll stay on, won't you, Mum?' said Chloe. 'Go on, Mum, don't be a spoilsport.'

Shelley looked over to Rosalind who, to her surprise, looked as though she had just had an orgasm. She had the biggest grin on her face.

'Okay then,' she said. 'Just once more, mind.'

'Hooray,' cheered Becca and Chloe, like two little kids.

'Come on, Shelley,' said Rosalind. 'Get back on with us.'

Shelley smiled back at her. 'No, it's fine,' she said. 'You always were a lot braver than me. You go and enjoy it again. I'll go and have a sit-down with Mum and Auntie Nancy.'

'Are we off then, ladies?' said the man. 'We can go faster this time if you like.'

'Yes,' screamed Chloe. 'Go as fast as you like.'

Shelley turned away to make her way back up the beach, trying to stop her legs from wobbling. She couldn't wait to fall onto a sun lounger. She found her mother sitting bolt upright, watching the world go by, whilst Nancy was sparked out flat. Perhaps asleep.

'I'm back,' she declared as she approached.

'Was it fun?' asked Nancy, immediately pulling herself up.

'About as much as having teeth pulled,' said Shelley. 'But the others enjoyed it so much they've gone for another go. Rosalind seemed to be loving it.'

'Oh great,' said Nancy. 'That girl so needs to chill. Right. I'm going to just go for a little paddle. I like to dip my toes in.'

'Shall I come with you?' asked Shelley.

'No, no, you stay here with your mother, I'll be fine.' She hauled herself up and wandered down towards the seafront.

'Auntie Nancy doesn't strike me as the paddling kind,' said Shelley, settling herself on a sun lounger next to her mother.

'No,' replied Peggy, letting out a big sigh.

'Have you two fallen out or something?' asked Shelley.

'No . . . well, not really. As usual we see things very differently. Nothing new there.'

'Oh, like what?'

'She thinks I should be sitting down and talking to you about last night.'

'Oh,' said Shelley. 'What about last night?'

'Well, I guess about what happened in the bar place, of course.'

'Oh,' said Shelley again.

'Stop saying oh.'

'Sorry.'

Shelley didn't know what to say if she couldn't say oh.

'She thinks I should be giving you an opinion, and I think I should keep my nose out of it. That it's up to you. I don't want to interfere.'

'Oh,' said Shelley.

'I told you to stop saying oh,' said Peggy.

'Sorry,' replied Shelley.

They sat in silence again.

'What your Auntie Nancy doesn't understand is that I never got to be independent, you see, not like you. I never got to make my own decisions.'

'Because of your generation, do you mean?' asked Shelley.

Peggy looked at her daughter sharply. 'No,' she said. 'Because of Nancy.'

'Nancy? You don't mean that.'

'I do,' said Peggy.

'No you don't,' replied Shelley.

'I do,' said Peggy, firmly.

'But why?' asked Shelley.

Peggy looked at Shelley for a long time without saying anything.

'Just tell me, Mum,' urged Shelley. 'Please,' she begged.

Peggy gave a long deep sigh and looked up into the distance.

'Well, if you must know, it was all to do with Dorothy,' she said eventually.

'Dorothy? Your sister – the one who died when you were young?'

'Yes,' nodded Peggy. 'Because you see, when Dorothy died, Nancy left home. Just like that. Gone. And she left me with all the responsibility. I had to look after Mum and Dad. She left me to do that on my own. I was ten, Shelley. Ten years old and I was making meals and making tea for endless visitors, and desperately trying to make Mum and Dad happy again.' She swallowed.

'I'm so sorry, Mum,' said Shelley, amazed that she had never heard this before.

'Then I had to stay, you see. Stay in Mapperton.'

'What do you mean? Why did you have to stay? Who told you that you had to stay?'

'Mum and Dad lost Dorothy and then they lost Nancy. I couldn't leave them too.'

Shelley sat back, stunned. She couldn't quite take in what she was hearing. Then she realized she had a question she had to ask. 'Is that why you married Dad?' she asked. 'Because he lived in Mapperton?'

Peggy looked at her. 'It just made sense,' she said.

Shelley stared at her mother. 'But . . . but you loved him, didn't you?' she asked, not really sure if she wanted to hear the answer.

Peggy swallowed and her eyes clouded. 'Maybe not at the beginning,' she said. 'But I soon did,' she added quickly, when she saw the look of horror on Shelley's face. 'When you came along, that's when I knew I'd fallen for him. He was such an amazing father. I mean, I always knew he adored me, but to see him with you as a baby, well it would melt any woman's heart strings.'

Shelley had no idea what to say to this revelation. So many questions were running through her head.

'Your father pursued me like a true gentleman,' explained Peggy. 'Took me to dances, bought me flowers, was so kind and thoughtful. My parents absolutely adored him, and I loved having someone truly take care of me. It was such a relief from having taken care of my parents for so long. And I wasn't expecting a proposal, but he went to so much trouble. Took me to the Coppice. Very fancy it was. It was way too expensive and I knew he couldn't really afford it, but he got on one knee after we'd eaten peach melba. He'd bought the ring already.' Peggy looked down at the single ruby that she still wore, mounted on a very thin ring of gold that had worn down over the years.

'And you said yes?' asked Shelley.

'I did,' said Peggy. She screwed her face up, as though thinking carefully. 'It just made sense,' she said eventually. 'I knew he would look after me and it meant I could stay near Mum and Dad.'

'That's why you said yes?'

'It had a lot to do with it,' said Peggy. 'I knew they really wanted me to marry Gordon. Now, I was lucky. Like I said, I did fall for your father. Perhaps somehow

I knew I would when I said yes but, even so, I do firmly believe that when it comes to marriage, you really need to make the decision on your own, you shouldn't allow yourself to be influenced by anyone else's opinion. It's what you think, and that's all that matters.'

Shelley nodded, her head still spinning, certain there were still things to ask but unsure of what they were.

'Oh look, they're heading back,' said Peggy, nodding towards the waterfront, putting a stop to any further questions.

Shelley turned to see Becca running towards her, waving her hands around and splashing her with sea spray, grinning from ear to ear.

'That was so good,' gasped Chloe, coming up behind her. 'Much better the second time, Shelley. He went much faster and flung us all over the place. I fell off twice. So did Becca. Mum was the only one who managed to hang on.'

'Well, you know,' smiled Rosalind, sauntering up. 'There was no way that banana was going to beat me.'

'The bloke driving the boat really tried to fling her off big time at the end, but she kept on,' said Becca. 'It was like watching a master of the banana boat. Are you sure you've never been on one before, Rosalind? Are you actually a secret banana-boat champion?'

'No,' laughed Rosalind. 'Never before and probably never again.'

'Oh Mum,' said Chloe. 'We have to do it again tomorrow.'

'No, that's enough fun for me,' said Rosalind sitting down.

'Mum, you can never have too much fun,' said Chloe.

Rosalind looked up at her daughter. 'Fun doesn't pay the bills,' she said. 'Fun doesn't get you a fulfilling career,' she added. 'Fun is fine in the short term, but fun doesn't bring long-term happiness.'

'Wow,' said Chloe, shaking her head. 'You really could take the fun out of anything, couldn't you?' She shook her head and strutted back down to the waterfront.

'What did you say that for?' challenged Becca.

'What do you mean?' asked Rosalind.

Shelley tried to give Becca a warning look. She could tell she was about to shoot her mouth off.

'You had her respect there for five minutes,' said Becca. 'Couldn't you see? She admired you. She thought you were cool and then you ruined it. With all that bollocks about fun not being important.' Becca shook her head. 'Fun is probably *the* most important thing. Actually, not probably, *definitely*. Fun *is* the most important thing.'

'In its place,' said Rosalind tersely.

'Well, you have firmly put it back in its place now,' said Becca, sitting down on a lounger with a thump. 'And I thought we were actually finally getting close to enjoying this weekend.'

Fortunately, Nancy returned and, on recognizing the frosty atmosphere, suggested that perhaps it was siesta time. Rosalind and Peggy quickly agreed.

'We really should have gone indoors at midday,' said Rosalind.

'But we would have only been out for five minutes if we had gone in then,' snapped Becca.

'Well, if some people had got up earlier, we could have enjoyed the morning sun and then we wouldn't have had that problem, would we?' said Rosalind.

'Do you fancy a walk down the promenade?' said Shelley to Becca, trying to keep the peace. 'I don't feel like going back just yet. We could have a look in some of the gift shops.'

'Definitely,' said Becca, turning to Shelley with a grateful look on her face. 'A change of scene is required.' Suddenly a smile spread across her face. 'Especially if it's a scene that happens to be near Andy's bar.'

Chapter 31

It didn't take them long to buy the obligatory seaside tat that was somehow essential for any trip. An 'I LOVE ANDELICA' fridge magnet was soon acquired, to be put in a bag and never seen again. Becca bought two kids' T-shirts bearing the slogan, 'My mum went to Spain and all I got was this lousy T-shirt', which she thought was hilarious; she said she couldn't wait to see her mother-in-law's face when she saw them.

Forty minutes later, they were sitting outside Andy's bar, cocktail in hand, watching the world go by . . . again.

'You don't really hate being married, do you?' asked Shelley after she'd drunk half her drink.

'Is that what I said last night?' asked Becca, looking horrified.

'Well kind of,' replied Shelley. 'Although you didn't blame Jason. You blamed marriage.'

Becca looked deep into her glass. 'I'm sorry, I shouldn't have said that. I don't hate being married at all. I just hate being so bad at it. You know me. I ace everything,' she said with a wry smile.

'I know,' said Shelley. 'It's why I hate you so much.'

'Cheers,' replied Becca. 'I'm just not good at the wifey stuff and the mumsy stuff, you know. Every other role I have ever played in my life I have been good at – but this . . . I'm shit at it, Shelley. I never wanted to be a homemaker. I never wanted to be a chef. I never wanted to be a cleaner. Jason doesn't expect any of that from me, but I kind of expect it from myself. And the understanding of what the hell two babies want – jeez Louise – I feel like I've landed on another planet and I've no idea what the language is.'

Shelley didn't say anything, just looked worried.

'But I think you will be so much better at it than me,' said Becca. 'Honestly. You're going to be a great wife and a great mum.'

'With Colin?' asked Shelley, raising her eyebrows.

Becca didn't say anything for a moment. 'Still having doubts?' she asked eventually.

'Well, yes.'

'Your mum told me not to give you any advice.'

'Yes. She's never liked you,' replied Shelley with a smile.

'Your mum is right, though, that really no one can tell you what to do. You know in your heart of hearts how you feel, and you are the only person you should listen to.'

Shelley nodded as two cocktails miraculously appeared in front of them on the table. Shelley looked up, expecting to see the lovely Andy, but there stood a very handsome-looking boy next to his not-so-handsome sidekick.

'May we join you, ladies?' said the good-looking one, staring at Becca's cleavage.

Becca glanced over at Shelley before she shrugged and nodded.

Shelley gave an inward sigh, as ghosts of many previous nights in the dim and distant past with Becca rattled through her brain. She knew exactly how this one was going to go. The good-looking one would introduce his not-so-good-looking mate to Shelley, and then turn to Becca and ignore them both as he tried to chat Becca up. Shelley would be left making stilted conversation with the most socially awkward man on the planet. After about half an hour, Becca would lean over and say that 'Ricky' had invited them to go to a nightclub, and could they go because she really fancied 'Ricky'. They would go to said nightclub, and Shelley and ugly best mate would stand on the side of the dance floor in silence as they watched 'Ricky' and Becca practically undress each other as they slow-danced to Lionel Richie. If it was a really bad night, the ugly best mate would ask her to dance and because she's kind/desperate she would agree, at which point their dramatic differences in height would become most noticeable as he strained on tiptoe to try and snog her to the strains of 'Through the Barricades' by Spandau Ballet.

The truly terrible nights were the ones that ended up in a taxi back to someone's house, with Shelley and ugly best friend forced to watch at close quarters while Becca and 'Ricky' ate each other on the back seat.

'I'm Dicky,' said the good-looking one with a grin.

He might have been good-looking but he had terrible dress sense. He was in a shell suit with a heavy gold chain around his neck. 'Don't ask me why they call me Dicky, bit of an in-joke.' He winked at Becca.

'Is it short for Dickhead?' asked Becca. Shelley nearly spat her cocktail out.

After a moment's surprise, Dicky began to fake laugh. 'Ha, ha, hilarious,' he said. 'We've got a live one here, hey Damian. This is Damian, by the way. He's pretty shy. You know, silent but deadly!' Dicky winked again.

'Like a fart,' said Becca.

'Ha ha,' said Dicky. 'You're really funny. I like you. I like a woman with banter. We are going to get along very well indeed. I can tell.'

Becca glanced across at Shelley and raised her eyebrows.

'So, what are you two lovely ladies doing in a place like this then?' asked Dicky.

'Hen party,' replied Becca.

'Winner!' declared Dicky. 'Didn't I say, Damo? Them two birds look like they are on a hen party and they are up for some big-time fun.'

Damo grunted and nodded.

'And guess what?' Dicky asked Shelley.

'Err,' replied Shelley, feeling herself blush for some ridiculous reason. 'I don't know, what?' she asked.

'Damo loves a tall woman, don't you Damo? He's got no problem with the tallness. He likes it tall. That's what you said, wasn't it Damo?'

Damo grunted again.

'Save me,' Shelley mouthed at Becca.

247

'Actually,' said Becca, 'sorry Damo, but Shelley is the bride-to-be. It's her hen party.'

'Oh right,' said Dicky, looking shocked.

Shelley stared at him.

'You wouldn't have thought I would have been the one getting married?' challenged Shelley.

'No, err, I just can only imagine your bloke must be a really big dude and well I don't want to upset no one. Damo just thought you looked like two women up for some fun, that's all.' Shelley noticed that he looked at the cocktails regretfully.

'What was your game plan?' demanded Becca.

'What?' said Dicky looking startled.

'What was your game plan on the plane?' she asked. 'Was it go older? Did someone tell you to go older, they're more desperate? Been round the block a few times, is that what your mates said? Maybe they will be able to teach you a thing or two. Is that what you thought? Did you spot Shelley and me and think: They're on their own, bit older, let's have a pop at them. Easy target, they will be, and the minute they learn my name is Dicky . . . well, they will be like putty in our hands. Is that what you said? And it's happy hour. So two for one cocktails, boys. Looks great buying us a drink, but actually it's cost you nothing. Cheers, boys, we'll enjoy these cocktails, now fuck off.'

Dicky stared at her for a moment and then said, 'I told Damo you'd be too old and stuck up, but he insisted.' He got up and walked off.

'Sorry,' muttered Damian and shuffled away.

Becca turned to Shelley and laughed. 'That showed them,' she said.

'Yeah,' said Shelley giving her a half-smile. She gulped her drink gladly. Dicky and Damian had just reminded her how much she hated being single, and how much she never wanted to be out on the dating game and exposed to men like that ever again.

Chapter 32

And so to night two of a hen weekend. When everyone is really too tired. When everyone would really like to be home, tucked up in bed, but when everyone knows they somehow have to summon up the energy to do it all over again, and try to force a good time out of a night destined to be doomed.

They'd all dragged themselves out of beds or off sun loungers, had showers, splashed cold water over their faces, and were gathering at the kitchen table before heading out to a restaurant in the town square that specialized in paella. Chloe was the last to walk in, dressed in a thigh-skimming leather skirt, a leather bra, a mesh top and black clumpy ankle boots.

'Tommy has texted me and said I can go and meet them at Andy's bar tonight. So I'm going there,' she announced.

'No you are not!' said Rosalind, standing up. 'You are here for Shelley's hen party. You can't just stand her up.'

'Really, it's okay,' said Shelley. 'It was good of her to come out with us last night, so if she doesn't want to tonight, that's fine by me.'

'Well it's not fine by me,' said Rosalind.

'You heard her,' said Chloe. 'Shelley says it's fine.'

'But, but . . . it's not right, and you are certainly not going anywhere looking like that.'

Chloe did a spin and turned to face her mother. 'You can talk,' she replied. 'No one should be seen dead wearing what you are wearing. I've seen dead daffodils look more attractive.'

'And you look like something out of the living dead,' retorted Rosalind. 'Can't you make a bit more effort? Try and look pretty at least?'

'Pretty? Pretty? You are going out for a nice meal in khaki shorts and a polo shirt!'

'Hey, just calm down the pair of you,' said Nancy.

'No, Mum,' said Rosalind, turning on Nancy. 'I will not calm down. You have no idea how depressing it is seeing her going out looking so . . . so . . . well, cheap.'

'I do *not* look cheap,' said Chloe. 'Just because it isn't what you would choose for me to wear, it doesn't mean it's cheap.'

'You would look a whole lot better if I chose what you wore,' announced Rosalind.

'And so would you,' retorted Chloe.

'Good,' said Nancy. 'So that's settled then.'

'What is?' asked Rosalind, turning on her mother.

'You dress each other and make each other look better,' replied Nancy.

251

'What!' they both exclaimed.

Nancy turned to Rosalind. 'You both say you can make each other look better, so why don't you? Then you can send Chloe out to meet her new friends, safe in the knowledge she is looking her best, and you – Chloe – can show your mother how to make more of her amazing figure and beautiful face.'

They both blinked back at her.

'No!' said Chloe. 'Absolutely not.'

'Come on, Chloe,' said Nancy. 'The thing is, I know that you both just want each other to look nice. And well, quite frankly, if you don't do it, then I think Shelley might change her mind and insist that you come out with us tonight, Chloe.' Nancy winked at Shelley.

'Yeah, I guess I could change my mind,' said Shelley, nodding.

'You can borrow some of my clothes if you want?' suggested Becca. 'I've brought way too many. You might find something you like.'

Chloe stared back at them all in frustration then shrugged her shoulders. 'At least no one knows me here, that's something. Come on then, let's get this over with. I need to be at the bar in forty minutes.'

'I need eyeliner on,' Chloe said firmly, as soon as she sat down on the bed in their room.

Rosalind was standing over her, holding out some cleansing wipes.

'Why?'

'Because I do.'

'But you wear so much. It makes you look so grim.'

252

'That's how I want to look.'

'Grim?'

'Yes.'

'Well, if you're not taking any off, then I'm not putting any on.'

'But you should,' said Chloe.

'Why?'

'I think it would suit you.'

'And I think less would suit you,' said Rosalind. 'So do we have a deal?'

Chloe sulkily took the wipe from Rosalind and dragged it around her eyes.

Rosalind watched mesmerized as the dark black lines disappeared and Chloe, her daughter, re-emerged. The version of her daughter she hadn't seen in at least a year. There she was, back in front of her, without the war paint she had adopted since she'd started sixth-form college. The daughter who had shone in her GCSEs, getting just short of the same grades as her brother. But then no one was going to beat Oscar. He was an exceptional child. A's all the way. Chloe was only just behind him and, as Rosalind had told her many times, if only she would work as hard as Oscar, then maybe she would get the outstanding grades that he did.

But she didn't, did she? She just seemed to get to sixth form and stop. Opting for college rather than staying on at school, it was as though she changed overnight. A thousand times more interested in going out and staying out, night after night, rather than hitting the books. Rosalind feared she'd lost Chloe for ever but, watching her take her make-up off, she could see a tiny glimpse of the old Chloe return.

'You look lovely,' said Rosalind, when she had finished and dumped the damp, black-stained wipe in her mother's hand. Chloe didn't comment. She got up and walked across the room.

'Come on then,' she said. 'My turn. Let's get you in some decent gear for a change. I reckon you and Becca must be the same size. Let's see what she's got.'

'I'm not sure I'm comfortable going through someone else's things,' said Rosalind, trailing after her into the room that Shelley and Becca were sharing.

'They said they didn't mind,' Chloe reminded her. 'Try this on,' she said, holding out a short dress that had been hung on the front of a wardrobe door. It was a shirt-style dress in white, with daisies printed on it. It had a nipped-in waist and the skirt flared out. It was a classic daytime dress for when the sun shone.

'Too girly,' said Rosalind, shaking her head.

'Put it on,' said Chloe, shaking the coat hanger.

Rosalind reluctantly took the dress into the bathroom next door and took off her khaki shorts and polo shirt. The dress slipped easily over her head and fitted pretty well, if a shade too loosely at the waist. It was so light she could barely feel it as it skimmed way above her knees. She walked straight out to show Chloe, without even looking at herself in the mirror.

'It's not me,' she declared. 'I can't carry this off.'

Chloe turned around from where she was going through some other dresses hanging up.

'That's the one,' she said. 'Those legs, Mum, were

made for that dress. You could do with a bit of fake tan, if I'm honest, but that is the dress.'

'What's so great about my legs?' asked Rosalind.

'Have you seen yourself? Have you even looked in a mirror in the last decade?'

'I try to avoid it.'

Chloe stared back at her. 'Follow me,' she said, storming past her and heading back into their room. 'Sit on the end of the bed,' she instructed, 'and close your eyes.'

Rosalind perched and watched fearfully as Chloe gathered up tubes and brushes and pencils from the top of a chest of drawers and dumped them on the bed.

'Close your eyes,' demanded Chloe.

She shut them abruptly, concerned as to what she might find when she opened them.

There was absolute silence whilst Chloe set to work, tugging gently at eyebrows and skin on various parts of her face. Rosalind felt the gentle waft of brushes and the cool smear of creams and finally the dreaded drag of pencil around the edges of her eye. She envisaged looking like Chloe, with her signature thick lines but around Rosalind's own wrinkled eyes. A witch came to mind, or perhaps – at best – a panda.

Then Chloe pulled out the elasticated bobble that Rosalind had used to tie her hair back, brushing it out before adding a little hairspray here and there and warning her mum to keep her eyes closed.

'Done,' said Chloe eventually. Rosalind remained seated on the end of the bed, blinking and feeling the strange tingle of make-up on her face. Chloe left the room, saying over her shoulder, 'I'll be in the living room when you have decided what monstrosity I have to wear. But don't even try to make me wear a fleece. Or anything in your wardrobe, for that matter.'

Rosalind had no idea what to dress her daughter in. She was so pleased to see her without her customary thick black eyeliner: just that seemed enough.

Rosalind stood up and caught sight of herself in the long mirror on the wardrobe. In actual fact, she thought someone else had entered the room. Over in the corner stood a slim woman. Actually someone who looked like a woman. Not at all like Rosalind. She walked towards the mirror and gasped slightly at what she saw. It was an image she wanted to look at. That hadn't happened for a long time. She felt confused. She wasn't supposed to care. For so long she had convinced herself not to care about her appearance. It was probably not since school, if she thought about it, that she had taken any trouble over it. She had probably been similar to Chloe's age. In her teens, when all you wanted was to look the right way, attractive yet cool. The sad fact of the matter was that some succeeded and some didn't. It was a defining time. Some managed it with what they were born with, good bone structure and a natural slimness; some managed it with money and good shopping choices, and others managed it with sheer force of personality, somehow exuding a confidence and a cool that came from somewhere within. However, many, including Rosalind, failed, turning up to key events in inappropriate clothes, badly applied make-up, and without the personality to carry it off. Being a teenager was a pretty binary affair, when you thought about it. You either succeeded or you failed. Rosalind had failed, lacking everything (money, sense of style, personality) that could have seen her in the winners' enclosure.

And so of course she developed coping mechanisms as she emerged out of her teens. 'Looks don't matter', 'Fashion is shallow', 'Intelligence is everything'. This had done a lot to restore her self-esteem at the time but, as she looked in the mirror, she felt a glow come over her that was like rain after an intense drought. For the first time in a very long time, she liked what she saw, and it made her emotional to think she had spent so many years looking in the mirror and disliking her own reflection.

She stared again at the silky dress that stopped above her knees, then back up at her face which Chloe had gently enhanced with just a touch of blusher, a deep gold eye shadow, a thin stroke of eyeliner and a sprinkling of mascara over her long lashes. She smiled. Two years of wearing braces at thirteen years old still showing dividends. She thought she might cry, she was so confused. This wasn't supposed to make her feel so good. Remember: 'Looks don't matter', 'Fashion is shallow' and 'Intelligence is everything.'

She walked out of the room to go and find her daughter. She didn't know what to say to her. She was so used to being cross and condemning all Chloe's actions that this had thrown her a curveball. Chloe had done something that had made her feel good and not at all what she expected. How to handle that, when all she wanted to do day and night was to scream at her for throwing away all the chances in life that she was being offered. Why was being the mother of a daughter so damn difficult?

Chloe was in the living room, sitting on the couch. Still make-up free, but sitting in her mesh top and short leather skirt.

Rosalind swallowed. Chloe looked up defiantly.

'You'd better get going, hadn't you?' said Rosalind.

'What hideous concoction are you going to make me wear?' asked Chloe.

Rosalind blinked. 'Why don't you go as you are?' she said. 'You look great.'

Chloe stared back at her, startled. 'Right,' she said slowly, as though she couldn't believe her ears. 'See you later,' she said over her shoulder as she ran out of the door.

Chapter 33

They had literally just walked through the door of her villa when Nancy's mobile phone rang. It was just after 10.30 p.m.. The five of them had been out for a very civilized meal. The paella had been delicious, the red wine had gone down a treat and everyone had had a lovely time.

For all her wanting to go wild, Becca realized she had really enjoyed herself. Nancy had spent most of the night asking her about her job and she had come alive, explaining the intricacies of the financial markets she dealt with. It was such a joy to be asked about something she was confident in and knew inside out, rather than the usual stream of questions about being the mother of twins, a subject on which she was a complete novice. Becca was also pleased to see Shelley relaxed and enjoying reminiscing with Rosalind and Peggy about summers together in Derbyshire. It had felt like a successful night, albeit not one Becca would have imagined enjoying quite so much. There was an air of contentment in the group as they walked through the door of the villa. That was until Nancy's phone rang.

'That's weird,' said Nancy, picking up her mobile phone. 'Hope it's not your Uncle Thomas. He should be out enjoying himself at the moment.' She fished her phone out of her bag, screwed her face up as she looked at the caller ID, then pressed the call answer button.

'Hi Andy,' she said. 'Shouldn't you be at work?'

She then proceeded to nod and furrow her brow a lot until she said, 'Let me just write down the address, hang on a minute.' She mouthed, 'Chloe' at everyone, then grabbed a pen and paper and wrote something down.

'What's happened?' said Rosalind immediately when Nancy put the phone down.

Nancy lowered herself into a chair and took Rosalind's hand. 'Now try and keep calm,' was the first thing she said, which sent Rosalind into near hyperventilation.

'What! What! Tell me . . . tell me now,' she demanded.

'That was Andy. Chloe has been down there with those two guys who were chatting her up.'

'I knew they were trouble,' shrieked Rosalind, getting up out of her chair. 'What have they done with her, where is she?'

'So, they had a few too many drinks and Andy said he had a word with her, told her to slow down a bit because he was worried she was getting really drunk and she was on her own and all that.'

'Oh my God, oh my God,' cried Rosalind, clutching her head and rocking. 'This is my worst nightmare.'

'So anyway, these boys took offence at Andy trying to look after Chloe and Chloe accused him of being just like her mother and said they were going to take her somewhere else. Andy tried to tell her not to go but, well, you know what she's like, she wouldn't listen. So she left with them and Andy is worried that she was just a bit too drunk to look after herself, so he rang me.'

'And does he know where they were heading?' asked Becca.

'They were going to a foam party at Unity, which apparently is a club down near the harbour.'

'Right, I'm going to get her,' said Rosalind, already pulling on her shoes. 'I knew this would happen!'

'Hang on a minute, love,' said Nancy, putting her hand on Rosalind's arm. 'Do you think you are the right person to go?'

'But I have to go,' said Rosalind. 'Make sure she's all right. Of course I'm going.'

'I'll go with her,' said Becca, getting up. 'Better if there are more of us.'

'Me too,' said Shelley. 'Auntie Nancy's right. And I do feel responsible.'

'Why should you feel responsible?' asked Rosalind.

'Because it's my fault that you are all here, isn't it?'

'Well, I'm coming too then,' said Nancy.

'No, Mum,' said Rosalind. 'Seriously. You must be tired. You just go to bed.'

'I am not tired,' roared Nancy. 'You cannot write me off just like that. In any case, I'm the only one who knows where they are going, so if you want to spend half the night wandering round the back streets, then so be it.'

261

'Well let's go then,' said Rosalind. 'You lead the way, Mum. And you will be taking your mobility scooter, won't you?'

'Ahh, suits you now, doesn't it? Coming, Peggy?' asked Nancy.

Peggy looked up stricken, confused. Clearly, she thought she had a pass on this one.

'You going to stay here like some old lady, are you?' asked Nancy. 'I've got eight years on you and I'm off out to a nightclub at ten thirty at night.'

'Wow,' said Becca. 'Things I never thought I'd hear this weekend.'

It took about fifteen minutes to find the dingy door that apparently led to foam party heaven. Nancy made a couple of wrong turns, inciting Rosalind's wrath in her desperation to make sure Chloe was okay. Eventually they found the door, but they also found a queue.

'Do you think she might be in the queue?' said Peggy hopefully.

'I'll run down it and check,' said Shelley. 'You stay here.'

The rest of them stood near the top of the line, attracting some unwanted attention.

'Oi Granny,' shouted someone from the crowd. 'That scooter foam-proof?' His friends around him collapsed in laughter.

'Is your head bullet-proof?' Nancy shouted back. 'It had better be or you could be in trouble.'

'Nancy!' said Peggy. 'You can't say things like that.'

'I think you will find I can say whatever I want,' replied Nancy.

'Can't see her,' said Shelley, running back towards them. 'She must be inside.'

'We can't queue,' said Rosalind. 'We need to get in now.' She stepped forward and strode straight up to the bouncer guarding the door.

'My daughter is in there drunk with two strange men,' she declared.

'Who isn't?' replied the bouncer.

'This is serious,' she continued. 'We need to get her out of there. She might come to some harm if we don't. Come on. Do you have a daughter? I'm asking you as a parent. Please let me go in and see if she is okay.'

The bouncer looked her up and down.

'All right, you can go in,' he said. 'But straight out, okay? No hanging around and enjoying yourself or else I'll have these lot on my back.'

'We need to accompany her,' said Becca, stepping forward. 'She can't go in alone.'

'And why is that?' asked the bouncer.

'It's complicated,' replied Becca.

'We all need to be there,' said Nancy. 'Because well, let's just say Chloe might not listen to her mother, so she needs us as back-up.'

'And you are?'

'Nan and great-auntie,' replied Nancy, pointing at herself and Peggy. 'And third cousin or something similar,' she continued, pointing at Shelley. 'And this is the third cousin's best friend,' she concluded, pointing at Becca.

The bouncer surveyed them all.

'We won't cause any trouble,' pleaded Becca. 'We only want to make sure Chloe is safe on your premises. You wouldn't want anything bad to happen, would you?'

The bouncer looked at them, exasperated.

'You need to be super-quick and that thing has to stay outside,' he said, pointing at the mobility scooter.

'Yes!' said Becca, doing a fist-pump. 'Thank you,' she said politely as they all filed past.

They walked into the vast open space, which was packed with sweaty bodies writhing around in foam, whilst the lights danced around them and the music thumped a heavy beat in the background.

'This looks amazing,' said Becca in awe. 'After we've found Chloe,' she said to Shelley, 'can we stay, please? Have one dance, at least.'

'I really don't understand,' said Peggy. 'Why do people do this? It must ruin their clothes.'

'Can anyone see Chloe?' urged Rosalind. 'Anyone? God, we are never going to find her in here. There are far too many people. What are we going to do?'

'I think we'll have to split up,' said Shelley.

'No!' said Peggy. 'No way. You are not leaving me alone in here. This is no place for someone like me.'

'What are you afraid of, Peggy?' asked Becca. 'That you are going to get sudded to death?'

'Is that her?' said Shelley, pointing over their heads towards the stage.

'Where?' gasped Rosalind, jumping up and down on the spot. 'Where? I can't see.'

'Up there on the end of the stage. Yes, I think it's her and those two guys from the bar. Must be her.'

Rosalind and Becca jumped up to see but couldn't get a better look.

'Does she look okay?' asked Rosalind.

'She's a bit unsteady on her feet but she's intact,' replied Shelley.

'Right, let's go get her,' said Rosalind. 'Come on.'

She stepped forward to start ploughing through the throng of dancers. Becca followed.

'Don't leave me,' said Peggy, grabbing Shelley's hand.

'Coming through,' announced Nancy, barging past them. She pushed ahead, using her body to part the revellers and the swathes of foam gathering around them.

Becca looked back up at Shelley.

'I just want to say this is so cool,' she said. 'Now we know Chloe is okay, obviously. I have always wanted to go to a foam party.'

The music changed to Whitney Houston belting out, 'I Wanna Dance with Somebody'.

'Tune,' shouted Becca, twirling round, chuckling to herself, laughing at the joy and jollity around her. Talk about being transported to another place. The white clouds of foam floated around her, making her feel as free and as happy as if she were a small child. She started to giggle and she couldn't stop. She wanted to feel like this for ever.

265

'Come on,' said Shelley, pulling her out of her reverie. 'We need to get to Chloe.'

Bloody hell, thought Becca. Why did everyone need to be so responsible?

Becca looked ahead and could see that Rosalind had just about reached the edge of the stage and was climbing the steps. Chloe was totally oblivious that her relatives were on the warpath. She had her eyes closed and unfortunately was currently writhing against one of the two men that they had met at the restaurant. Becca hoped very much that Nancy and Peggy weren't watching.

Then it all kind of went into slow motion as the rest of the party joined them on stage.

Rosalind had clearly seen what was happening and stalked on to the stage and started flailing her arms towards the man Chloe was entwined with. He turned round in surprise at the attack and in doing so stumbled to the ground, causing those in proximity to gasp and rush to his aid. Including Chloe. Becca watched as she bent to see if he was all right, struggling somewhat to keep her balance.

'What are you doing?' yelled Chloe at Rosalind, trying to get herself up but struggling.

'What am I doing?' she yelled back at her daughter. 'What are you doing? You can't just go off with strangers like that. It's not safe.'

'Go away, Mother,' said Chloe. 'I know exactly what I am doing. I'm showing you that I'm a grown-up and what you think is of no concern to me whatsoever.'

'But you are making an idiot of yourself and putting yourself in danger.'

'Like I said,' said Chloe, putting her face up close to Rosalind's. 'Fuck off, Mother.'

The man had managed to get himself up from the floor and lurched towards Chloe, clearly very drunk. Rosalind sprang forward and pushed him away from her daughter, causing him to topple backwards and fall to the ground yet again.

'Mum!' screamed Chloe.

Rosalind was breathing very heavily. She stared down at the man who was now rubbing his elbow. Two men dressed in dark suits appeared out of nowhere and one of them placed a firm hand on her shoulder.

'Enough of that,' he said. 'You need to come with me. We don't tolerate that sort of behaviour in here.'

'I was protecting my daughter!' said Rosalind, shrugging his hand off her arm.

He turned to look at Chloe.

'I have absolutely no idea who she is,' said Chloe. 'She hit my boyfriend. Twice!'

'This way, madam,' said the man, gently pulling at Rosalind's arm.

'I shall do no such thing,' said Rosalind. 'I was protecting my daughter.'

'She attacked him for no apparent reason,' raged Chloe.

'I was just trying to get him off you,' protested Rosalind.

'Why don't you let me deal with this?' said Nancy, stepping forward.

'And who are you?' asked the man.

'Her mother and her nan,' said Nancy, pointing at Rosalind and Chloe.

'Proper family outing, is it?' said the man. 'Are you sure you should be out after dark?' he asked.

'That is my mother you are talking about,' said Rosalind, turning on him. 'There is absolutely no reason to be rude.' She made the fatal mistake of jabbing him in the shoulder.

'Right, you are out of here, lady. We have eyewitnesses that you attacked a man twice and now you are threatening me. Now you must leave.'

'You are throwing me out of this place?' said Rosalind in disgust. 'You can't throw me out.'

'I think you'll find I can.'

'I'm not going anywhere without my daughter,' said Rosalind, crossing her arms.

'Like I said, I have no idea who this woman is,' said Chloe.

'Please leave now,' said the bouncer. 'I will not ask you again.'

'Make me,' said Rosalind.

'You leave me with no choice than to forcibly remove you and call the police to charge you with attacking one of our guests. Now, for the last time, will you leave?'

'*Not* without my daughter,' said Rosalind, angrily.

'Right, that's it,' said the man in the suit. He grabbed Rosalind's arm and pulled it behind her back.

Rosalind's face crumpled.

'Are you sure this is necessary?' said Nancy to the man restraining Rosalind.

'She was warned,' he replied. 'And, like I said, we do not tolerate this sort of behaviour.' He pulled Rosalind away, who was still looking defiant.

'This is not what was supposed to happen,' said Nancy, looking for once a bit ruffled at the sight of her daughter getting dragged away. Then she took a deep breath and appeared to gather herself. 'Right, Becca,' she said pointing at her. 'I need you to sort out Chloe. Stay here and sort her out, okay?'

'What?' said Becca. 'Why me? I'm not her mother! And in any case, I'm no good at that sort of thing. I can't sort her out.'

Nancy paused, looking at her. 'Oh, I think you can,' she said. 'Just trust your instincts and get on with it.' Nancy turned and grabbed Peggy's arm. 'Peggy and I will go and bail my daughter out of jail,' she told Becca. 'Words I never thought I'd say. Especially this weekend. But there you have it. See you back at base.'

Chapter 34

'Didn't realize I was coming here to be your relatives' babysitter,' mumbled Becca, looking mournfully at the throng enjoying the music and the foam out on the dance floor.

'Auntie Nancy clearly thinks you're up to the job,' replied Shelley. 'I note she didn't ask me.'

'I've no idea why she asked me. What do I know about rebellious teenager girls?'

'Because you were one?'

'No I wasn't.'

'It was always your idea to get the bus into Derby and go drinking when our parents thought we were going to Young Farmers'.'

Becca grinned. 'My mum was always confused that I took such an interest in farming at fifteen years old.'

'My dad was really proud. Never had the heart to tell him we never went to the meetings, just to the pub afterwards.'

'What am I supposed to do with that?' asked Becca, nodding over at Chloe, who was now draped all over the guy who had been attacked by Rosalind.

Shelley sighed. 'Say to her what you'd have liked to hear at that age, I guess.'

'Suppose I could give it a try,' said Becca. She went and tapped Chloe on her shoulder and shouted in her ear. 'There are some really hot guys on the main dance floor – you coming?' she said.

Chloe stared at her.

'Okay,' she said, dropping the man in her arms and following Becca like a sheep, down the steps and into the middle of the dance floor.

Of course it was a big-tune moment. As soon as the three of them hit the middle, 'Free' by Ultra Nate struck up. They jumped and twirled and threw their arms in the air. They joined hands and spun around and around, the euphoria of dancing in the foam totally blowing their minds. It was a moment. A great moment. The best moment so far. One that for a brief spell allowed them to ignore the issues that were currently clouding the weekend. That one of their party was on their way to the police station, a mother and daughter were at total loggerheads and, last but not least, the future bride was not quite sure whether she even wanted to get married any more.

The weekend really was a total success so far.

They danced to a few more tunes, Becca revelling in finally enjoying herself, and secretly hoping they were going to wear Chloe out and sober her up.

It was after Cher had finished warbling 'Believe' that Chloe declared she was ditching Becca and Shelley and was going to go and find Tommy and Jay.

271

'No, you are not,' declared Becca, when they finally caught up with her at the edge of the dancefloor.

Chloe looked back at her, startled. 'Who made you my mother?' she asked, still swaying slightly.

Becca glanced over at Shelley. Shelley shrugged. As far as she was concerned, Nancy had put Becca in charge of Chloe and not her.

'I'm not trying to be your mother,' retorted Becca, 'but don't you think we have some pressing issues to sort out?'

'Now you really sound like my mother,' shouted back Chloe. 'Are you about to give me a lecture on my A-levels and going to university and all that shit?'

'Just for one minute, can you just think of someone other than yourself?' replied Becca. 'I really couldn't give a damn if you screw up your life by giving up on your future.'

'Oh,' replied Chloe, looking confused.

'What I do care about is this young lady standing here,' she said, pointing at Shelley. 'Your third cousin, who needs our support at this moment. But rather than focusing on her, all we are doing is running around after you and clearing up your mess.'

Shelley sighed. She really didn't need this kind of attention. She was much happier with everyone focused on Chloe.

'You're right,' said Chloe. 'Sorry, cous.' She draped her arm heavily around Shelley's shoulders. 'So when are you dumping that shit-for-brains fiancé of yours?'

Shelley looked imploringly over at Becca. She really didn't want to deal with this now. And especially not with her drunken third cousin, or whatever she was.

'Poor you,' continued Chloe, throwing her arms around Shelley. 'I'm so sorry. This is so awful. What *are* you going to do?'

Shelley looked over Chloe's shoulder and mouthed 'help' to Becca.

'Actually, it's a great question,' said Becca. 'What *are* you going to do?'

Becca really wasn't helping now, was she? Hadn't she said it was none of her business?

'I don't know, do I?' said Shelley, trying to untangle herself from the spaghetti arms of Chloe. 'I've no idea what to do next.'

'You have some foam on your chin,' pointed out Becca.

'Great,' said Shelley, wiping it away.

'What is your gut telling you to do?' asked Becca.

'Now that's a great question,' said Chloe. 'She's quite smart, I reckon,' she continued, pointing at Becca. 'So what does your gut tell you, Shelley?'

Shelley looked back at them both, bewildered, then tried asking her gut the question. What should she do? Her gut immediately replied with a screaming 'ditch him' whilst her head almost simultaneously screamed 'Don't ditch him, you idiot – he can give you everything you want. And what has he done wrong? – nothing. He put his arms around another woman. That's it. You can't ditch your fiancé for that, can you? And as for the text . . . well, Colin's explanation was more than feasible. It was one of his mates having a laugh – must have been.'

'So?' said Chloe and Becca expectantly.

'I don't know,' she confessed. 'My gut says ditch him

273

but my head says he's not actually done anything wrong. All he did was put his arms around another woman. I can't ditch him just for that.'

'And the dodgy text?' pointed out Chloe.

'You think I should call it off?' asked Shelley.

'Absolutely,' replied Chloe. 'One hundred per cent.'

'You?' she asked Becca.

'Mmmmm,' said Becca, rocking her head from side to side. 'Not sure. It's a tricky one.'

'It's not tricky at all,' exclaimed Chloe. 'It's bullshit. Come on, Shelley. Wake up. You smell a weasel and there are no sparks without fire. That's a saying, right?'

'Not really,' said Becca.

'Just ditch him and move on,' said Chloe.

'It's all right for you to say that,' protested Shelley. 'You're young – you've got all the time in the world to find the right person. Look at me; I'm already past it. Time is running out. I haven't got time to *not* get married. I have to get married. Do you understand?'

Chloe screwed her eyes up at Shelley. Then said an emphatic, 'No.'

'If I don't get married, I can kiss goodbye to a family. That's it. I'll never find another man in time to have kids. Never. It took years to find Colin. I can't go through all that again. I just can't.'

'What do you want a family for anyway?' asked Chloe. 'Families are nothing but trouble. I give you Mum and me as Exhibit A.'

Shelley blinked at her. 'Because I want to be a family again,' she said emphatically. 'It's never been the same since Dad died.' She tried hard to blink back the tears.

'I can't bear the thought of not having what I had when I was young.'

'Oh Shell,' said Chloe, falling on Shelley for the second time. 'Oh Becca,' she continued, pulling Becca into the hug. 'You'll be such an amazing mum, Shell,' she said. 'Won't she, Becca? Like the best.'

'She will,' said Becca, trying to fight back the tears. 'I have absolutely no doubt about that.'

'It would be awful for you not to be a mum,' said Chloe. 'There are so many shit ones out there who don't give a damn.' Chloe took a deep breath and took a step back from the pair. 'Go,' she said, pointing into the distance. 'Go get what you want. Go fight for it. Go sort out whatever state it is in – if it is in a state – but just go and do something about it. It's pointless asking us two what we think. Go find Colin and sort it out.'

'What, *again*?' asked Shelley.

'Yes again! And don't come back until you have sorted it. This is no way for a hen to be feeling on her hen party. Go talk to the bastard.'

Shelley looked over at Becca. She nodded. Chloe in her youth was right. Turns out drunk Chloe was the wisest person in the room.

'But where will I find him? He could be anywhere.'

'Have you still got his room key?' asked Becca. 'Why don't you just go and wait for him in his room? If he's not there now, he'll come back eventually.'

'Brilliant!' said Chloe, slapping Becca on the back. 'Just brilliant. The old "wait in the hotel room" trick.'

'Do you think?' asked Shelley.

They both nodded.

'We'll come with you,' said Becca.

'*No*,' said Shelley. 'My problems have ruined enough of this weekend so far. You two stay here. Do some more dancing. Try and have some fun.'

'Yes!' said Chloe, twirling round. 'Let's *do* it.'

'If you are sure?' asked Becca, looking concerned.

'I'm sure,' said Shelley, hugging them both. 'Don't wait up,' she added, and she was gone.

Becca thought she must have been dancing like a zombie. She had no idea what time it was anymore.

The first half-hour after Shelley left had actually been quite good. The DJ had gone into Eighties mode and Becca had boogied her way through some classic Wham and Duran Duran and even some vintage Tina Turner. 'What's Love Got to Do with It' had gone down an absolute storm.

But now she was feeling her age as the music got slightly more obscure and the familiarity could no longer keep her buoyant. Becca was just wondering whether now would be a safe time to suggest that they go home, when Chloe leaned over and said, 'I could murder a McDonald's now.'

Becca could have kissed her. McDonald's was an excellent exit strategy. Even if it was for the second night running. She certainly wasn't going to say no.

And so, about twenty minutes later, Becca found herself sitting in the square outside the McDonald's once again, this time surrounded by drunks, whilst Chloe chewed her way through a Quarter Pounder and Becca had some restorative Chicken McNuggets.

Chloe didn't say a lot as she chewed. She'd sobered up quite a bit, given they had spent the best part of an hour dancing. Becca was starting to feel that she had her objective in sight. To get Chloe home safely.

Becca looked at her. She reminded her so much of herself at that age. At eighteen, Becca had thought she knew everything. No one could tell her what to do. She was going to do what she wanted. Fortunately, she had had the reverse experience to Chloe. Because she was a bit full of herself, her dad had told her that it was a pipe dream to think she could ever get into university. She wasn't their ideal candidate, he said, and she would never put the graft in. So of course she had totally rebelled against that, worked really hard and got herself a place. Her act of rebellion had been to get into univeristy, whereas Chloe's was to not do so. Becca hadn't realized at the time that her father was way smarter than her and, when she got her place, his reaction was to put his arm around her and say, 'I knew you would', which had left her somewhat deflated and feeling a little conned. Eventually she saw that he was just a very clever man and had the utmost faith in his daughter and knew exactly how to manage a feisty eighteen-year-old woman.

Rosalind clearly wasn't so smart. Her constant pushing had sent Chloe in the wrong direction. So sad, because the person it would ultimately hurt the most was Chloe.

What a waste, thought Becca.

'What are you going to do then?' she asked.

'What?'

'When you go back home. What do you want to do?'

'Sleep.'

'No, I mean home, home. Not tonight. What are you thinking?'

Chloe shrugged. 'Not sure.' She smiled. 'I'll get a job in a fast-food restaurant until I figure it out.'

'Right,' said Becca. 'Good plan. But I guess that means you are stuck at home for a while – you know, whilst you are working it out.'

Chloe shrugged again.

'That's going to be fun with just you and your mum, hey? Especially if your dad has virtually moved out. Lots of great mother–daughter bonding?'

Chloe looked up at Becca but said nothing.

'Plenty of time to really patch things up. Just the two of you. It will make all the difference.'

Chloe still said nothing.

'And of course, what will be even better is that all your mates will have gone to university, so won't be around. So you will really need your mum for company, because everyone else will have gone and you'll be left on your own.'

Becca polished off her last nugget. 'Funny, isn't it? What's really weird about your whole situation is that actually your mum gets exactly what she wants.'

'What do you mean?'

'She gets to keep you at home.' Becca shrugged. 'With her where she can keep an eye on you. Where you can keep her company. Bet she's not thought of that. Bet she's not worked out that, actually, you not

278

going to college could be the best thing that has ever happened to her. Especially if your dad is on the brink of leaving, which is what it sounds like. She won't be alone, will she?'

Becca looked Chloe straight in the eye. 'I bet if I pointed all this out to her then she'd get off your back totally about jacking in your exams. She'd see it for what it really means. That she gets to keep you for that little bit longer. Just whilst you work out what to do, of course. She'll have to expect that you'll fly the nest someday, but better to work it out whilst you're under her roof, living with her, earning minimum wage in some fast-food joint, rather than at college, living it up with people your age, learning stuff whilst trying to sort out what you want to do with your life. I can see that you have totally chosen the better option. Figuring out what to do with your life while at home with your mum sounds far more appealing than doing it at university. Good on you.' Becca slapped Chloe on the back and stood up.

'Now, shall we go back to the villa and see if your nan has managed to break your mum out of jail for hitting a man who dared show some interest in you?'

Chloe got up in a daze and meekly followed Becca on the long walk back to Nancy's villa.

Chapter 35

The foyer of Colin's hotel was relatively quiet as Shelley tiptoed through, heart beating hard in her chest. It had sounded like such a good idea when she left the club, but on the walk to the hotel, she'd got increasingly nervous about what she was going to find and what she was going to say. What if the woman from the Flaming Flamingo was in his room with him? Then what? At least she would know. That would certainly be a big red flag and solve her dilemma.

She knocked gently on the door. No answer. She got the key card out of her wallet where she had put it two days ago and swiped it through the reader. She heard the lock mechanism click open. Here we go, she thought.

She walked into the darkness. A crack in the curtains cast a sliver of moonlight across the bed. She thought she could see a body-sized lump. Just the one, she thought with a sigh of relief. She put her hand down and shook the lump.

'Hello,' she whispered. 'It's me, wake up. We need to talk.'

The lump groaned.

She shook again. 'Wake up! It's me. Wake up!'

The lump groaned again.

'What? What's happening?' The lump raised himself up and looked up and screamed.

'*Ahhhhhhhhhh*,' he gasped, pulling the bed covers up around him. 'Get out! Get out, whoever you are, get out!'

Shelley also screamed because it wasn't Colin.

'*Ahhhhhhhhh*,' she gasped, leaping up. 'Who are you and what have you done with Colin? Where is he? What have you done with him?'

At that point, the unidentified lump reached over to put on the light at the side of the bed, temporarily blinding them.

'Neil!' gasped Shelley, blinking. 'What are you doing here? Isn't this Colin's room?'

'Shelley!' gasped Neil. 'What are *you* doing here? It's err, it's err . . . two in the morning!' He was clasping the bedcovers up around his chest, displaying his bare arms, which Shelley found somewhat distracting. She looked up at the ceiling quickly.

'I . . . I . . .' she stuttered. She hadn't been prepared for this. 'I thought I'd drop in. That's all. What are *you* doing here?'

'Colin's gone back to a friend's place. He said I could crash in his room because, well, there are a couple in the room next to me keeping me awake all night having sex!'

'Oh,' said Shelley, feeling herself blush whilst still looking at the ceiling.

'Why are you looking at the ceiling?' asked Neil.

She glanced back down at him but had to look away quickly. 'Because, because . . . have you got any clothes on?'

'No.'

'That's why I'm looking at the ceiling.'

'Shall I put some clothes on?'

'Yes!'

'Can I trust you to keep looking at the ceiling whilst I get out of bed?'

'No!' squealed Shelley, aware that she was totally embarrassing herself.

'I didn't think you were that kind of girl,' said Neil.

'I'm not,' she shrieked, 'but you can't get out of bed with no clothes on whilst I'm in the room.'

'But you told me to put clothes on?'

'I know I did. Look, I'll go into the bathroom whilst you put your clothes on.'

Shelley proceeded to feel her way around the room with her eyes firmly fixed on the ceiling, until she got to where she thought the bathroom door was. She was very aware that she looked absolutely ridiculous. She reached for the door handle behind her back and tugged down. Nothing seemed to happen.

'Are you aware that you are currently trying to get into the closet?' pointed out Neil.

'Oh no!' she screeched, looking behind her. She shielded her eyes as she made a dash for the bathroom door across the room. She had never been more mortified.

She slammed the door behind her, breathing deeply. Her heart was pounding. This was not good. She wished she had just gone home with Becca and Chloe. What was she doing here? And what was she supposed to do now? She felt like she had never been more embarrassed, and she had done a lot of embarrassing things in her life.

She sank down to the floor and put her head in her hands. Was this nightmare of a hen weekend ever going to end?

Neil knocked on the door and she scrambled up. She took a deep breath and opened it. Neil was now respectably in shorts and a T-shirt. What a relief.

'I've put the kettle on,' he said. 'You look a bit shocked. Why don't you have a cup of tea and then I'll walk you back to where you are staying.'

'No! You don't need to do that. I'll just go. Just let me go. I'm so sorry to wake you up. Christ, what a mess.'

'Sit down,' said Neil. 'Please. Come on. You've had a shock. Just have a cup of tea, won't you?'

Shelley looked at him and decided that he was probably right. She wondered if there were any of those shortbreads you often get in hotel rooms. She could murder a biscuit.

'I bet you could murder a biscuit,' said Neil. 'Here. Have a try of these, they're really good.'

Shelley took them gratefully, but she was trembling slightly and her hands were sweating, so she just couldn't undo the plastic packaging. She really wanted a biscuit, but it was like trying to break into Fort Knox! There was no other option but to use her teeth. Always attractive. She was of course mid-plastic-biting when Neil turned round and presented her with a mug of tea.

'You aren't supposed to eat the wrapping,' he said with a grin.

She extracted the packet from her mouth and took the tea. She'd maybe have another go in a minute when he wasn't looking. He sat on the bed opposite her. He smiled and took a sip of his tea then shook his head. 'Should have brought some British teabags,' he said.

'Mmm,' she muttered back, taking a sip. He wasn't wrong. 'And some milk from Tesco's,' she added, as she detected the tang of UHT milk swamping the flavour.

'You know milk comes from cows, right?' he said with a grin.

'Of course. My dad was a dairyman. Cows practically brought me up.' Jesus, why did she say that?

'I didn't know he was a dairyman,' he said. 'I knew he'd died, of course. Sorry about that, by the way. Must be tough.'

'It was a long time ago.'

'Yeah, sure. But a dairyman. How cool. I've been thinking of adding some dairy cows to the smallholding, but the set-up costs are too high. Would love to have some cows, though. I help out the farmer next to me sometimes if he's desperate. But he has to be really desperate because I'm not very good at it. He pretty much only lets me herd them in and clear up the muck.'

Shelley nodded. 'It's harder than it looks. I used to go and help Dad sometimes and he was so fast and efficient and I was just all fingers and thumbs. I made the cows nervous – I swear they knew I was a novice. The looks they gave me. But Dad . . . they looked at him differently. Like they knew him.'

'You must miss him,' asked Neil. 'Especially at the moment. What with getting married.'

Shelley stared at the carpet feeling her eyes go prickly. She'd got used to her dad not being around over the years. Sure, she missed him, but the solid ache that she first experienced had dissipated. Time had healed to an extent, and she no longer felt like collapsing at the mention of his name. She could talk about him with a smile on her face, choosing to rejoice in the happy times rather than mourn his loss. But she suddenly felt that ache now. Deep down in her chest. What she would do for her father to put his arms around her and make her feel all right.

'Sorry,' said Neil, interrupting her thoughts. 'I didn't mean to make you feel sad. He sounds like he was a great man. I wish I could have met him.'

Shelley blinked and looked up at Neil.

What a lovely thing to say.

She didn't think anyone had ever said that to her before. Ever. A swell of emotions caught her off guard. How nice it was that someone was interested enough in her to want to have met her dad. Or that they thought her dad was interesting enough to have wanted to have met him. Or just the simple release of someone asking about your father and being interested enough to want to know about him. She looked up at Neil, confused. She hardly knew him, and yet he somehow seemed to know all the right things to say to her.

'Shelley?' he said suddenly, his expression changing.

'Yes,' she replied.

He looked at her and then said, 'Nothing.'

The room was deafeningly silent, and Shelley suddenly felt a desire to get away. She needed to be on her own.

'Look,' she said, putting her mug down and getting up. 'If you see Colin . . . where is he again?'

'Oh err, we bumped into some old business colleagues and he went back to their place. I'd had enough, long day.'

Shelley stared at him. Willing him to say more.

'Well, tell Colin I called in,' she said when Neil didn't continue.

'I'm sure he'll be sorry to have missed you,' said Neil.

'Hope so,' said Shelley.

'You sure I can't walk you home? It's really late.'

'No. I'm fine. The walk will do me good.'

'I wasn't going to carry you.'

'No,' Shelley laughed. 'No, I know you weren't. I just would enjoy the space, that's all.'

'Sure,' said Neil. 'Not long to go now?'

'Till what?'

'Until you're married.'

'Oh yeah. Of course. You never been married, Neil?' she found herself asking.

'Me?' he said, looking up. 'No,' he said quickly. 'No, not yet.'

'Why not, if I may ask?'

'Oh wow – great question. Because I'm the ugly one of the family and no one will have me.' He smiled to show he was joking.

'No, really?' asked Shelley. 'I'd like to know.'

He stared at her intently. Then shrugged. 'Because I've not found the right fit, I guess. Not yet. Maybe I'm just a fussy bugger, I don't know. But I haven't met anyone yet whom I want to *live* with – like, share my life with. All the relationships I've had seemed to have involved compromise on both sides. Maybe I have a romantic view of marriage, but I don't think it should feel like a compromise. It should feel like whoever you are going to marry is going to add to your life, not take away from it. And that's on both sides. I don't want to compromise someone else's life either, which can prove a challenge when you live in the middle of the Scottish Highlands where the most sociable thing around are the sheep.'

Shelley nodded.

Compromise. That word which was so often associated with marriage. Deemed to be part and parcel. Deemed to be the secret to happiness and contentment. Neil clearly didn't agree. Sounded like he thought a marriage should be about everyone getting everything they wanted. No compromises.

'Do you think you'll ever get married?' she asked him.

He shrugged.

'Who knows? I don't spend my time thinking about it. If it happens, it happens. I prefer to focus on making sure that I'm doing what makes me happy, and if I happen to find someone to share that with then great, but if I don't, I don't. At least whatever happens I'll have made sure I was happy. Relying on someone else for happiness strikes me as a risky place to be. Way too much pressure.'

She nodded.

'Colin's very lucky to have found you. You know that, don't you?' said Neil.

Shelley stared back at him.

'I'm very lucky to have found him,' she replied.

'That's not what I said. He's lucky to have you, and don't ever forget that.'

'Okay,' she nodded. 'I'll try. Thank you,' she added.

'You're welcome,' he said.

'Better go,' she said, turning for the door.

'Take care,' was the last thing she heard him say as she closed the door softly behind her.

Chapter 36

Peggy had never been in a police station before. Particularly not a Spanish one in the middle of the night. She was so tired she could barely keep upright. So tired that she had been forced to hitch a lift on the back of her sister's mobility scooter. So tired that it was with relief rather than humiliation when she stepped onto the back plate.

Peggy watched as Nancy strode up to the desk and blurted out a flow of Spanish, pointing intermittently at the mobility scooter parked outside and putting her arm around Peggy's shoulders. She was pretty convinced that Nancy was telling them that she was very angry that they had arrested the forty-five-year-old daughter of a disabled pensioner, whose sister – standing next to her – was suffering with some kind of dementia. Peggy shrugged off her arm and went to find a seat. Typical of Nancy to use theatrics to try and wheedle her way out of a situation. Peggy didn't want to be any part of it.

The surly police officer did not say a word as Nancy

released her tirade. He merely tapped his fingers on the desktop and then pointed at the bench where Peggy was sitting and ordered her to wait.

They had sat there for at least fifteen minutes in silence.

'I suppose you think this is all my own doing?' said Nancy eventually.

Peggy was too tired to argue. 'I do actually,' she replied.

Nancy turned to her sharply. 'I can never do anything right in your eyes, can I?'

Peggy shook her head and looked away. She wasn't one for confrontation. Especially at this time of night. But Nancy was not going to let it lie.

'I never have, have I?' she continued. 'As far back as I can remember. What did I ever do to make you so cross with me all the time?'

Peggy couldn't speak. Shocked by her sister's sudden outburst. Shocked that, after all these years, Nancy was finally asking her what was wrong between them.

'Is it because you think I'm a terrible mother?' demanded Nancy. 'Is that what it is? Because I didn't do it like you did it. I didn't stay at home to look after my family. I tried, Peggy, really I tried, but I just couldn't. It wasn't me. I needed something for me. I *needed* the theatre.'

Peggy felt a swell of emotion rise up inside her. For a moment she thought she couldn't breathe. This wasn't to do with what she thought of Nancy's parenting skills. Why would she think that? Although she did have a pretty low opinion of Nancy as a mother. No, it was much deeper than that. Much, much deeper. She knew she had to respond. She swallowed. 'You left me,' she whispered. 'I lost Dorothy and then I lost you.'

'What?' said Nancy, looking confused. 'Why are you talking about Dorothy?'

Peggy concentrated on her breathing so she could talk. 'Your *need* for the theatre as you call it,' she said steadily. 'It wasn't just Rosalind who suffered, it was me as well, and Mum and Dad.'

'I . . . I don't understand,' said Nancy. Deep furrows had emerged across her forehead.

'When Dorothy died and you left for the theatre, have you any idea what it was like, being left at home with Mum and Dad, whilst they fell apart? I was ten, Nancy. And you left me to deal with them on my own.'

Tears were pouring down her cheeks now and Nancy was staring at her in shock.

Eventually Nancy reached out and touched her arm. 'I had no idea,' she said.

Peggy turned to her, utterly amazed. 'How can you not have realized what you were leaving me with?'

'I don't know what to say,' replied Nancy, shaking her head. 'I was so young. I . . . I just couldn't deal with what was happening. I had to run away. I know that must seem selfish, of course it was, but I was eighteen, Peggy. Same age as Chloe is now. I knew that if I stayed I would have fallen apart. I would have been no use to anyone.'

Peggy looked at her in silence. When she thought about Chloe, it hit her for the first time what a difficult age Nancy had been to be experiencing such loss.

Being eighteen was a time of such confusion and turmoil. Still really a child but expected to behave like an adult.

'I'm so sorry,' said Nancy, taking both Peggy's hands in hers. Tears were streaming down her face now. 'Please forgive me. I realize that it's a lot to ask after all this time but do you think you can at least try? I've been so looking forward to you coming out here and to be honest I was really hoping it would somehow make us closer. So please, will you forgive me? All I want is for us to enjoy the rest of our time together.'

Peggy blinked back at Nancy. 'What do you mean, rest of our time together?'

'Nothing . . . nothing . . .' said a flustered Nancy. 'I just meant that we both have to face up to the fact that we are both getting on a bit and so I don't want to waste what time we have left with you continuing to be upset with me. I want to make it up to you. I really do. Tell me what I can do, sis? Please, I'm begging you.'

Peggy was struggling to comprehend what was going on. Nancy looked desperate. This was so out of character for her.

'Is there something you're not telling me?' asked Peggy.

'No nothing,' said Nancy, shaking her head. 'I just can't believe I've never asked you before. We've wasted so much time.' She paused to wipe the tears from her eyes. 'I've already lost one sister. I want to enjoy my time with the other one. Please forgive me, Peggy.

292

I really am so, so sorry. I just want the chance to be a good sister. And I really want to create some happy times with you rather than this constant tension.'

Suddenly an image of Dorothy reared up in Peggy's mind. They were both clinging to a rope swing that hung from an old oak tree in their parents' garden. They were screaming with joy as Nancy pushed them higher and higher. It was such a happy time. Maybe the last happy time she remembered with her sisters.

'I wonder what Dorothy would be like now?' Peggy said, biting her lip. 'I wonder how things would have been if she hadn't died.'

Nancy said nothing for a while. Then she smiled as though a memory had passed through her mind too.

'Remember how she used to make us play doctors and nurses all the time? She'd make me go to sleep in the middle of the afternoon because she said that is what patients did in the afternoons,' said Nancy

'She never let me be a doctor or a nurse,' said Peggy.

'Me neither,' sighed Nancy. 'She was the ringleader really, wasn't she?'

'Yes, looking back, she was,' agreed Peggy. 'We lost our ringleader.'

'We lost our sister,' sighed Nancy.

'We lost our sister,' repeated Peggy, squeezing Nancy's hand. She squeezed it back and laid her head on her shoulder.

They must have both fallen asleep. Peggy woke with a start to see a bedraggled-looking Rosalind standing in front of them, next to a female police officer.

'Are you responsible for this woman?' asked the police officer, in English.

'Yes, we both are,' said Peggy. 'I'm her auntie and this is her mother.'

'I need you to sign some documents and then you can go,' said the lady, handing a clipboard to Peggy.

'Nancy!' said Peggy. 'Wake up. We can go home. Look, here's Rosalind. You need to sign these.'

Nancy stirred and then leapt up at the sight of her daughter and flung her arms around her. 'Oh Rosalind,' she said. 'Are you okay?'

Rosalind nodded. 'I'm fine,' she said.

'Sign these,' said the police officer. 'You are lucky the man your daughter hit will not press charges.'

'Bet he's too embarrassed to admit he got beaten up by a middle-aged woman,' said Nancy, putting her arm around her daughter and leading her out of the police station.

'I can't get two of you on the scooter,' said Nancy as they gathered on the pavement. 'Shall we call a taxi?'

'Where's Chloe?' asked Rosalind.

'We left her at the club with Becca and Shelley,' said Nancy, 'who had strict instructions to take care of her.'

Rosalind nodded slowly.

'They'll look after her, love,' said Peggy. 'I know they will.'

Peggy and Nancy exchanged glances. Rosalind looked in shock.

'I was so angry with her,' she said, tears welling in the corners of her eyes.

'I know,' said Nancy. 'She said some terrible things.

But she is eighteen. She's selfish. She didn't mean any of it. None of us have a clue at eighteen.'

'We have no idea at any age, do we?' said Rosalind. 'Really?'

Nancy smiled and put her arm around her daughter. 'Not a clue,' she said. 'Not a clue.'

Chapter 37

Nancy was cooking breakfast for Chloe and Becca when Rosalind emerged the following morning. It was midday and everyone had had a lie-in. Becca was huddled in a corner, her nose deep in a magazine, her eyes protected from the painful light with dark shades. Chloe sat at the table, still in pyjamas, looking bleary eyed, in stark contrast to her mother who had showered and had on a well-pressed pair of canvas walking shorts, her customary polo shirt and socks and walking shoes. The only sign of the previous night was a very tidy bandage on her hand.

'Good God, Mother!' cried Chloe. 'I feel like shit and you look like you could run a marathon. Clearly beating up men half your age suits you.'

Rosalind was about to tell her not to swear, then bit her lip.

'Sit down,' said Nancy. 'I'm just doing bacon butties.'

'I'll just have a yoghurt,' said Rosalind.

Chloe tutted her judgement on her mother's breakfast choice. It was going to be a long and difficult day, thought Rosalind. She slid into a chair and reached forward for a jug of orange juice. Was it all right to have orange juice, or was her teenage daughter going to criticize that as well? She gulped it down, suddenly aware of how thirsty she was. She put the empty glass down and dared look at her daughter. Her skin was grey, she had massive bags under her eyes, and her hair was matted from the effects of the foam party the night before. It wasn't a good look. She really needed a shower. That would make her feel so much better.

'Shouldn't you have a shower?' ventured Rosalind.

'And shouldn't you not hit people?' said Chloe, glaring at her.

Rosalind shrank back in her chair.

'I'm sorry,' she said, as Nancy slapped plates laden with bread and bacon in front of them.

'What for?' asked Chloe. 'Hitting some poor innocent bloke who had done nothing wrong?'

Rosalind wanted to argue that she thought the man was far from innocent. That he was treating her daughter like a piece of meat when she was too drunk to defend herself and there was no excuse for that, but she wasn't sure how her defence would land this morning. Wasn't sure if Chloe would listen.

'I'm just sorry,' she shrugged.

Chloe said nothing, just reached for the brown sauce and slathered it over her bacon.

Nancy sat down between them with a cup of tea.

'We've been having a chat this morning,' began Nancy.

'Nan has come up with a brilliant idea,' said Chloe, suddenly perking up.

'Not me,' said Nancy. 'You really. I've just filled in the gaps.'

'I'm going to stay here for the summer,' said Chloe.

'What!' said Rosalind, staring at them both.

'Now that is not the conversation we had,' Nancy scolded Chloe. 'Tell your mum what you said to me this morning.'

Chloe looked sideways at her mum then stared at her fingers. 'I said I think I want to go to university after all.'

'What!' said Rosalind. 'How? You dropped out!'

'I can,' said Chloe. 'Brendan did.'

'Who is Brendan?' asked Rosalind.

'Someone who works for me,' interrupted Becca, peering over her sunglasses from the corner of the room. 'He came onto our graduate recruitment scheme last year. He flunked his A-levels due to personal reasons, but retook them in the November. Passed, went to uni, and now he works for me. He's the best graduate we've got.'

Rosalind turned to Chloe. 'So having walked out on A-levels last month, you now want to take them.' Rosalind knew she shouldn't be sceptical but she couldn't help it. Her daughter was so frustrating. 'Why the change of mind?'

'Oh Mum, does it matter?' Chloe sighed. 'I fucked up, okay? I realized that actually I don't have to drop out to work out what I want to do with my life. I can go to uni and work out what to do with my life.'

'I would have thought that was obvious,' Rosalind said as gently as she could.

'No!' said Chloe. 'Not at all. Particularly when your mother doesn't present going to college as a choice but as a demand. I felt like I was being led to slaughter, not to a window of opportunity.'

Rosalind was struggling to understand what was going on. Her face must have said it all.

'And Becca pointed out that I could either retake and go to college, or spend the next three years living at home whilst you and Dad try to work out how to split up!'

Rosalind gasped and stared at Becca.

'You're welcome,' said Becca, nodding.

'Nan thinks that Andy might give me a job as well, Mum, whilst I'm here. How good would that be?' said Chloe.

'It's just an idea,' said Nancy to Rosalind. 'I could do with some help around the house and it would be lovely to spend some time with Chloe and . . . and it might help you and Robert. You could go away together, take a proper holiday with him whilst he's on recess.'

'Please, Mum,' said Chloe. 'It helps everyone. It's genius.'

Rosalind looked at her mother and her daughter then back to her mother.

'I suppose it does,' muttered Rosalind, still struggling to catch up.

Nancy reached forward and took her daughter's hand. She looked as though she was about to say something, but was interrupted by the arrival of Peggy, with whom Chloe was desperate to share her news.

'I'm not going home!' declared Chloe with glee.

'What do you mean?' asked Peggy.

'Nana said I can stay here for the summer,' she gasped.

'*If* you go back and retake your A-levels in the autumn,' pointed out Nancy.

Peggy looked at Nancy. Nancy smiled back. 'It's a win-win,' she declared. 'I get a free housemaid and spend time with my granddaughter, and Rosalind gets some quality time with Robert.'

'Sounds like you have it all sewn up, Nancy,' said Peggy, furrowing her brow. 'Almost like you had it all planned?'

Nancy was saved from replying by a knock at the door.

'I'll get it,' said Chloe, leaping up.

'Now Rosalind,' said Nancy, ignoring Peggy's question and turning to her daughter the minute Chloe was out of the room. 'I think you need to thank Becca. Chloe wants to go to university, and it's really all down to her. She was the one who talked to her last night and changed her thinking.'

Rosalind knew her mum was right. Becca had managed to convince her daughter of something that she had failed to. It was so utterly exasperating, but nonetheless she couldn't deny the outcome was good.

'Thank you,' she whispered to Becca.

'You're welcome,' said Becca again.

'You did really good,' said Nancy to Becca. 'You convinced a teenager to change her mind. Now tell me that you have no parenting skills and are a failure as a mother.' She took a large bite of her butty and then proceeded to talk with her mouth full. 'Because I know that's what you think. It's what we all think by and large. Now for goodness' sake, stop moaning about being a mum and just enjoy it.' She wiped a smear of butter from the corner of her mouth with the back of her hand.

Becca stared at her for a long time, speechless. 'I will,' she said eventually. 'You're a wise old bird, aren't you?'

'Oi, less of the old, you,' said Nancy with a grin.

Peggy and Rosalind watched open-mouthed as Becca got up and put her arms around Nancy.

'Thank you,' said Becca. 'You've somehow managed to make me feel better about everything.'

'It's nothing,' said Nancy with a shrug.

'You are lucky to have Nancy as a mother,' Becca told Rosalind.

Rosalind wasn't convinced, and was about to point out that being Nancy's daughter was no bed of roses, when Chloe walked in with Colin in tow holding a very large bunch of flowers.

'Colin!' said Peggy. 'What are you doing here?'

'Colin,' said Nancy, getting to her feet. 'I'm Nancy. The tragically overweight but fun auntie. We meet at last. Do come in and sit down.'

'I've just had to explain to Colin that I knew who he was because Shelley showed us his photograph, didn't she?' announced Chloe, looking pink in the face. Clearly, she had forgotten to hide the fact that they had already spied on him in the Flaming Flamingo.

'Yes, yes,' said Nancy. 'We can't stop her getting her photo of you out,' she added. 'Gets it out all the time.'

Chloe nodded emphatically. 'All the time.'

'I'm Shelley's cousin,' said Rosalind, offering her hand to Colin. 'Rosalind. And Chloe's mother.'

'But I thought Chloe was Shell's cousin,' said Colin, looking confused.

'Third cousin,' said Chloe. 'But she isn't. We're not sure, you see. Just leave it at "we are related".'

'Right,' said Colin, sitting down. Clearly not expecting to be surrounded by Shelley's entourage.

'Are they for Shelley?' Peggy asked, indicating the flowers.

'Well actually I brought them for Nancy,' said Colin. 'Didn't think Shelley would be able to take them on the plane.'

'My,' said Nancy. 'It's a very long time since a young man brought me flowers. They are gorgeous. Thank you.'

'Bigger than the bunch you brought me when you came to inform me you were engaged,' stated Peggy.

'I . . . I . . . Shelley bought those actually,' stuttered Colin. 'She said you wouldn't want anything over the top.'

'Did she now.'

'Whereas I'm over the top all the way,' grinned Nancy. 'You can over the top me, any time you like.'

Colin looked nervously around him.

'So,' said Becca, folding her arms over her pyjamas. 'To what do we owe the pleasure?'

'Well, I wanted to see Shelley. Make sure she got home okay last night. She is home, isn't she?' He swallowed.

'Snoring like a baby as we speak,' said Becca.

'Good, good.'

'So did you see her last night?' asked Becca. 'Last I saw of her, she was coming to see you on the way home from the nightclub.'

'Well, yes and no. Well, you see, we met some friends and ended up going back to their villa, but my brother Neil wanted to go home and he borrowed my room key and well, Shelley ended up waking him up in the middle of the night.'

Everyone was silent as they took in this piece of information.

'You must have stayed out late,' said Peggy. 'It's not like we got back early. We only left the foam party at – what? – well after midnight.'

'You went to a foam party?' asked Colin, aghast.

'Yes,' said Nancy and Peggy rather proudly, and without offering any explanation.

'And who were these friends?' asked Becca, her eyebrows raised.

Colin looked at her, startled. 'They are just people that my dad has a joint venture with out here. We've known the family a very long time.'

Becca nodded. 'Any other questions?' she asked the group.

'Is there something going on?' asked Colin. 'I just wanted to check if Shelley's all right. That Neil didn't terrify her too much last night.'

'And the text?' asked Chloe.

Colin went white. 'She told you about that?'

Chloe nodded.

'I . . . I . . . I told her. It was a mate of mine winding her up.'

No one said anything.

'I'm sorry, Colin,' said Nancy. 'You understand we are very protective of Shelley. It did upset her.'

'I'm sure it did. I realize how it looks. Which is why I'm here to tell her that she has absolutely nothing to worry about. And I can't wait until we are finally married and can, well, just get on with it.'

'Neither can I,' said Shelley, appearing at the door. 'Are they for me?' she asked, pointing at the flowers.

'Actually I brought them for your Auntie Nancy. Didn't think you'd be able to take them on the plane.'

'Wow, that's so kind. Isn't it, Auntie Nancy?'

'Indeed it is,' she agreed.

'Sorry I didn't see you last night,' he said, getting up to hug her. 'Neil told me first thing. Must have given you a real fright seeing him. I think I just missed you. He said you had only just gone when I came in.'

'Probably a good job you weren't there,' said Shelley. 'I looked horrendous, did Neil tell you?'

'No, he did say you fell into the bathroom, though?'

Shelley looked around, blushing. 'I mistook the cupboard for the bathroom and it was all very embarrassing.' She turned bright red.

'Would you like a bacon sandwich?' Nancy asked Colin. 'We're all just tucking in. We've not been up long, as you can imagine.'

'Err well, I'm supposed to be meeting my parents for lunch so I'd better not,' he muttered.

'Nonsense,' said Nancy, pulling out a chair and

indicating he sit down again. 'A growing lad like you can always make room for a bacon butty.'

'He's forty-two, Auntie Nancy,' said Shelley.

'I know, I know, but I'll bet he could do with an energy boost after last night; after all, he was out very late. Now, red or brown sauce?' asked Nancy.

'Err, red, please,' said Colin, sitting down looking a little nervous.

'So did you have a good time last night then?' asked Shelley.

'Well, err, we went to a couple of bars, all pretty tame, but then we bumped into some associates and they invited us back to their villa. So, you know, it lasted longer than expected.'

'And you say you've known these associates a long time?' pressed Nancy, glancing sideways at Shelley.

'Well, they were part of a consortium we were in that built the Sun Valley development down the coast. I've not seen them for ages so it was great to catch up. They have a beautiful villa up in Calsetti, overlooking the sea. Perhaps I could take you there next time we come back?' Colin said to Shelley.

'And what are the demographics of these associates?' asked Chloe.

Colin stared back at her, looking confused.

'I'm doing geography A-level,' she explained. 'This type of information interests me. If you could tell me the location of this development, I would be keen to take a look.'

Colin furrowed his brow. 'Well, the main people I dealt with were the two brothers who run the company,

Juan and Miguel. Juan's wife, Adelina, was particularly kind to me, and would always invite me over for a meal whenever I was here.'

'Age?' asked Chloe.

'Err well, I don't know – sixties, I guess.'

'Kids then?'

'Yes,' replied Colin.

'What type?' demanded Chloe.

Colin looked around uncomfortably.

'This must be really helping with that coursework you were telling me about,' said Becca to Chloe.

'Exactly,' said Chloe. 'Very useful input. So, what type of kids?'

'Err, two. Both in their thirties, I guess.'

'I asked what type?'

'One of each.'

The room went quiet.

'Will they be joining us tonight?' asked Nancy. 'They sound pretty close to your family.'

'No,' he said. 'I won't be seeing them again now.' He bit into his bacon butty. Everyone watched as he chewed.

'Mum and Dad are really looking forward to meeting you all,' he added, after he had finished his mouthful.

'And we can't wait to meet them,' said Nancy. 'I'm picking Thomas up from the airport this afternoon. He's extremely proud to be performing his first duty as father of the bride.' Nancy smiled at Shelley.

'I'm sure he is,' nodded Colin, putting his half-eaten butty down. He swallowed, then went to get up. 'Right, well, I'd better head off,' he said. 'I only meant to pop in. Thanks for the butty. And I'll see you all later.'

'I'll walk you out,' said Shelley, getting up and ushering Colin out before closing the door behind her.

Nancy, Peggy, Rosalind, Chloe and Becca looked at each other across the crumb-strewn table.

'Guilty,' declared Chloe.

No one else said anything.

'Red sauce on a bacon butty? How could he?' she added. 'Never trust a man who puts red sauce on a bacon butty. Besides which, he looked shifty.'

'Being shifty is no proof,' said Rosalind.

'You agree he looked shifty, though?' said Chloe.

'He looked uncomfortable. Awkward. But then he was surrounded by Shelley's nearest and dearest, giving him the third degree. That's enough to make anyone uncomfortable. I think we need to give him the benefit of the doubt.'

'He's never the most relaxed of people in company,' said Becca. 'From what I've seen.'

'He's scared of me,' said Peggy proudly.

'It's got to be up to Shelley, hasn't it?' said Nancy. 'I think we have done all we can, really. We've spied on him and interrogated him. In plain sight of her. I'm not sure what else we can do, really. She's got to make her own mind up.'

'I think she already has,' said Chloe, nodding out through the window at the pool where Shelley was involved in a full snogathon with her fiancé. 'That looks like a couple about to get married to me.'

'Or a couple desperate to make sure they do get married,' muttered Becca.

Chapter 38

Peggy had spent rather a restless night going over the evening's events. Particularly the conversation she had had with Nancy at the police station. It had been surprising, to say the least. Not only had she finally got her long-held angst out about how Nancy had dealt with the death of their sister, but she had also received an unashamed apology. Something that she realized she had longed to hear for a very long time. But there was something just not sitting right regarding Nancy's reaction to Peggy's outburst. She kept going over and over it in her head. Nancy had never really shown any interest in spending time with her sister. In fact, Peggy had been gobsmacked to be invited on this trip at all. There was more to all this than met the eye, she was sure.

Peggy had begged Nancy to let her stop in the villa whilst she went to the airport to pick up Thomas. She really needed a nap before they went out that night. But Nancy wasn't having any of it; practically dragged her to the car, telling her quite bluntly that she could sleep when she was dead!

Peggy wound the window down to let the air rush past her face in the hope that would keep her awake. Her mind was distracted by the line of birds perched on the wire over the road, then the small child skipping along a pavement. She had to admit that something felt a little unblocked. The sun shone brighter; the sea looked bluer. She looked across at her sister and realized – for the first time in a very long time – that she didn't feel entirely alone. They hadn't directly discussed the conversation between them the night before, but the constant tension that had surrounded them for so many years had somewhat relaxed. And it felt really good.

They stood under the arrivals board, looking for Thomas's flight in from Portugal. Peggy found it first. 'We are half an hour early!' she exclaimed. 'I could have had a nap before we came out.'

'Must have got my times mixed up,' said Nancy, not looking at the board but casting her eye around the arrivals hall. She had gone a bit pale and was breathing heavily, observed Peggy. She really needed to have a chat with her about her weight and her health before she left. She was going to make herself really ill if she wasn't careful.

'Peggy!' she suddenly heard a shout from across the vast hall. 'Peggy! Is that you?'

She looked up and couldn't believe her eyes. Barging across the tiles from the arrivals gate, pushing a trolley piled high with a random assortment of cases, was . . . Ray.

She felt her jaw drop. They were here to meet Thomas, not her neighbour who should be tidying his garden up back in Derbyshire.

Peggy glanced over at Nancy, who was grinning from ear to ear.

Ray abandoned his trolley a good ten feet in front of Peggy, then ran the rest of the way and wrapped his arms around her.

Peggy stood stiff and awkward.

'I'm so excited to be here,' he gushed. 'And you must be Nancy,' he said, unwrapping Peggy and wrapping Nancy, who returned the gesture warmly. 'So lovely to meet you at last.' He turned back to Peggy, grinning. 'What a marvellous sister you have,' he said. 'Tracking me down and asking me to come along as a surprise. It's been a nightmare keeping it a secret from you, Peggy. A nightmare. I was expecting you to guess any minute. You're usually sharp like that, but I'm so glad I managed to keep it as a surprise – your face!' He doubled up in laughter, which gave Peggy a chance to give Nancy a hard stare. What on earth was she up to, inviting Ray along? It didn't make any sense whatsoever.

Nancy grinned inanely back at Peggy, and gave her an extremely inappropriate thumbs up. Peggy shook her head.

'Why don't you take Ray over to the café for a coffee and a catch-up whilst I go and try and find out what's happened to Thomas's flight. Off you go. I won't be long.'

Peggy was left looking like a fish out of water, gaping whilst Ray retrieved his trolley and confidently strode over to the café. He got his wallet out of his pocket.

310

'Coffee, Peggy?' he asked.

'Err yes,' she said. 'I guess. I'll get some euros out.'

'No need,' he said. 'I've already got some. As well as some dollars, just in case.'

'Dollars?'

'Frank down the road had a few spare. I said I was coming to Spain so he gave them to me. Always pays to have dollars when you are travelling,' he said.

'I still can't quite believe you are here,' said Peggy. 'I don't really understand.'

'Good surprise, I hope. I have to say I was very pleased and surprised to get Nancy's letter.'

'Amazing,' agreed Peggy, still extremely confused. 'She wrote to you? What did she say exactly?' she asked.

'Well, she asked me to ring her. Sent me her number, so I did. She wanted to know if you were all right. Asked me to keep an eye on you, you know, as she can't do it herself. Said I was to call her if I was worried at all.'

'Did she? When did she do this?'

'About six months ago. Maybe. Yes, must have been. Was about the time that Shelley got engaged, because she wanted to know if Shelley was okay too?'

This was really confusing.

'She's been ringing me every Sunday night to see if you are okay,' said Ray. 'She told me not to tell you. Told me that you'd be cross if you thought she was checking up on you. But she wanted to know how you were. That's all. She was worried that she wouldn't find out if anything was wrong.'

Peggy was speechless.

'Did she not say anything? Perhaps I shouldn't have told you.' Ray suddenly looked bothered, which didn't suit his sunny demeanour at all.

'Here he is,' said Nancy, hobbling towards their table with Thomas.

'Hello Peggy,' said Thomas, putting his arms around Peggy. He was a big stocky bear of a man, with a big personality, who liked to be at the centre of everything.

'And you must be Ray,' he grinned, sticking his hand out and pumping Ray's hand up and down.

'So happy to be here,' said Ray, 'and before you ask, I've brought you those tools you asked about the other week. I had some in my shed that must have been there a decade. I cleaned them up with some oil and they are as good as new, look.' He unzipped a holdall to reveal a collection of screwdrivers, a chisel and a wood planer.

'You bought those on the plane?' said Peggy.

'Very hard to get hold of these items here,' Thomas told her. 'Ray is a godsend, I'm telling you.'

'He most certainly is,' said Nancy. 'Now, shall we go? Peggy needs some beauty sleep before tonight's proceedings, and we need to get Ray settled into Dora's.'

'Dora's?' said Peggy.

'Yes,' said Nancy. 'She lives next door. He's staying in her spare room. She's really looking forward to it. I'm sure she'll make you most welcome, Ray.'

'Well it's very good of her. I've brought her some clothes pegs and a washing line. Always useful,' said Ray.

Nancy suppressed a grin. 'She'll be over the moon, Ray.'

'And I hear you have had a very lively time already,' said Thomas to Peggy. 'Been leading them all astray, have you?'

Peggy raised her eyebrows. 'Not me, Thomas.'

'Foam party, I hear?' he added.

'Foam party?' said Ray. 'Now, I think I have a foam machine somewhere. Or perhaps it's a dry-ice machine? I did a clear-out of a nightclub in Mansfield a few years back. Just got rid of the last few cocktail glasses, but I'm pretty sure there's still some box thing in the shed. Tell you what, we should get it out when we get back, Peggy. Have ourselves a little foam party in the garden. I bet Pippa and Mike next door would be up for it.'

'You,' said Nancy to Ray, grinning, 'are perfect. Now let's get back so we can get ready for this fancy dinner tonight.'

'I bought a tux,' said Ray. 'Well, I found one in my wardrobe. No idea where that came from. I did buy the entire contents of a wardrobe from a theatre that was closing down once, so it might have been from there. Anyway, I brought the tux – just in case, you know. Didn't want to let you down, Peggy. Not in front of those posh in-laws.'

'You,' said Nancy, 'could never let anyone down. Shall we go?'

'God yes,' said Thomas. 'Looking forward to seeing the daughter and the granddaughter and their explanations of the shenanigans last night. Sounds like I should have stayed here rather than go golfing. Our only excitement was Pete upending his golf buggy in a bunker and having to be dug out.'

'Tell me how much golf buggies are worth,' said Ray to Thomas. 'A chap called me last week. He'd got a fleet of about ten he wanted to offload.'

'I think I need a word with you,' said Peggy to Nancy as they left the building.

'I just thought you might want some extra moral support tonight, that's all,' said Nancy.

'But what's with getting him to spy on me?'

'Oh, he told you, did he?' said Nancy. 'Well, it's not like you are going to tell me if you are in trouble, is it? I needed an inside job.'

'But why now?' asked Peggy. 'What's going on, Nancy?'

'Nothing,' replied Nancy. 'You can't have a go at me for trying to look after you at long last, can you? It's clearly overdue.'

Peggy shook her head, not convinced at all.

Chapter 39

They called it pre-dinner drinks. Peggy wasn't sure that Andy's bar was posh enough to host pre-dinner drinks, but Nancy had insisted that they all needed a little low-level Dutch courage before they joined the Gifford family in the fancy hotel restaurant.

When Peggy thought about pre-dinner drinks, she didn't have in her mind somewhere with a TV playing sport above the bar, or with a line of men with bellies hanging over their shorts lined up in front of it. Still, there they were, looking somewhat different to when they had last been in this direction, dressed up as the Spice Girls. But as Peggy glanced around the group, she had to admit they were still a somewhat bizarre-looking crowd.

Becca had arrived in a very pretty strapless maxidress, teamed with high heels and immaculate make-up and hair. Shelley was sporting a flowing lemon yellow mid-calf-length dress with flat shoes so she didn't tower over the rest of the group. Chloe had offered to do her hair and make-up, and had been rather heavy handed on the eyeliner, which Shelley claimed she liked but Peggy suspected her daughter was just being polite. Added to her look was an air of nervousness. She'd already downed one drink, which was not like her. The subject of Colin had been a no-go area all day; Shelley had made it abundantly clear – by the show of affection by the pool that morning – that she intended to go ahead with the wedding. Hence no-one had broached the subject at all.

Nancy had gone all-out evening gown/kaftan. The long black coverall was bedecked with sequins and gold thread. She was a one-woman Bedouin tent. Thomas had joined Ray and dug out his tuxedo, and looked like the perfect master of ceremonies, his big jolly face beaming at everyone. Peggy had to admit they both looked very smart albeit, she suspected, completely overdressed. She had gone safe – well, relatively. She was in a blue M&S special with a touch of sparkle on the sleeve that she had worn to Frank and Sue's ruby wedding party last year in the village hall. Rosalind's only nod to formality was long trousers rather than her customary shorts and a blouse rather than a shirt. The clean, efficient look was rather disturbed by the bandage she still had wrapped around her right hand. It was a good job she didn't have a black eye, thought Peggy, or goodness knows what Mr and Mrs Gifford would have made of her. And finally Chloe. If Chloe had been her daughter, she would have made her change. She wore a black holey net thing over a neon yellow bikini top and jeans shorts. Her eyes were circled in jet black, and her lipstick was what could only be described as grey. Ray had only been introduced to Chloe as they left the villa and very politely said, 'What a pretty daughter you have,' to Rosalind. Rosalind, rather impolitely Peggy thought, had just harrumphed and walked off.

Peggy was now bristling over Nancy inviting Ray over without asking her, all the goodwill brought about by their honest conversation the night before, brushed aside. She had had the rest of the day to get over the shock, and the more she thought about it, the more she didn't understand why Nancy had done it, and the more she thought it really was a step too far. It was all very well that Nancy claimed she wanted to be more of a caring sister, but to invite Ray, her highly irritating neighbour, who had apparently been spying on her for the last six months? What on earth was she thinking? Peggy tolerated Ray. He was very well meaning, but his untidiness drove her mad. What she would do to be allowed to get stuck into his front garden, clear it all out and take it to a car-boot sale. Just being tidy, that would improve their relationship no end, thought Peggy, not dragging him out here and pretending they were close. No, Nancy was meddling and she wasn't at all happy about it.

'Peggy,' Ray shouted across the table from where he was sitting next to Nancy. 'You never told me your sister used to be a singer,' he said.

Peggy looked at Nancy. Not taken her long to get her past life back to centre stage again, she thought.

'Well, it was a long time ago,' said Peggy.

'Oh Nancy, give us a song again,' sighed Becca. 'I loved it on Friday when you sang.'

'You sang here Friday?' asked Thomas.

Nancy nodded, grinning.

'What did you sing?'

'"Girls Just Wanna Have Fun",' replied Nancy.

Thomas paused and swallowed. If Peggy wasn't mistaken, a tear leapt to his eye. He reached over and hugged his wife. Peggy felt her heartstrings pull. No one had looked at her like that in a very long time. Suddenly she wished with all her heart that Gordon was there.

'Sing with me,' said Nancy to Thomas.

'Oh you must,' said Ray. 'Come on guys, let's hear it. A song from the pros. I wasn't expecting this, Peggy, were you?'

Peggy shook her head. She wasn't sure if she could watch. Her anger at Nancy inviting Ray and her sudden jealousy about her sister's very alive relationship might just eat her up.

'Come on then, if you insist,' said Thomas, the smile back on his face.

'Shall we do "the one"?' he said, making speech marks with his fingers.

'Let's do it,' said Nancy.

Peggy watched as they held hands, making their way to the mini stage at the back of the bar. Thomas beckoned to Andy to come over and set it up. Peggy wanted to put her hands over her ears and close her eyes, but of course she couldn't. She braced herself as Nancy and Thomas picked up the microphones and took their positions.

And yet again it was an unexpected song choice that blared out over the speakers. Thomas and Nancy showed their true indie pop song colours, strutting it large, singing 'Wonderwall' by Oasis.

'Your auntie is epic,' Peggy heard Becca say to Shelley, making her bristle even more. 'How old is she again?'

'I don't know,' replied Shelley. 'Older than Mum.'

'Really!' replied Becca. 'I wouldn't have thought that.'

'Yeah, quite a bit older, I think. I think she turned seventy last year.'

'Wow,' said Becca. 'Tell you what, I would like to be just like her when I'm seventy. Living in the sunshine, singing pop songs on karaoke. Now that's what I call growing old in style! Please don't let me get boring, Shelley. Shoot me rather than let me bore myself to death when I am old.'

Peggy caught Becca's eye just as she said this. 'I don't mean you, Peggy,' she said. 'You are not boring.'

Peggy didn't reply, just turned back in time to see her sister do a pirouette under Thomas's arm and then bow as the song came to an end.

'Bravo,' shouted Ray, getting to his feet. He wolf-whistled, which about blasted Peggy's eardrums out. Becca, Shelley and Chloe also got to their feet, clapping and cheering. Peggy and Rosalind remained seated, casting glances at each other in the joint acknowledgement that they had been in the shadow of Nancy's limelight far too often.

'Fancy a song?' Ray asked Peggy across the table. 'It's a very long time since I have sung in public, but

I can hold a note. Well, I used to on the football terraces, anyway – how about it, Peggy?'

Peggy couldn't believe what she was hearing. No one had ever asked her such a ludicrous question in her life.

'No,' she said quite simply. 'And I think it is probably time we were going. We don't want to have to say to the Giffords that we were late because we got caught up singing karaoke in a bar on our way, do we?'

'Don't we?' said Nancy arriving back at the table. 'I think that quite possibly would be a tremendous reason to be late . . . But you are right. I'm starving. Now where did I park my scooter?'

Chapter 40

Shelley hung at the back of the entourage making its way along the harbour front towards Colin's hotel. She couldn't help but notice what a strange-looking crowd they were. With its mixture of tuxedos, blue polyester, diamanté kaftans and neon bikini tops, you would have no idea what linked this motley crew together. No idea at all. It was then that Shelley realized that it was her. These were her representatives as they went to meet her fiancé's family. That nuclear family of mum, dad and two children. Here she was with her miserable mum, her slightly eccentric auntie, her larger-than-life uncle, her boring cousin, her rebellious 'third cousin', her outrageous best friend, oh and her kleptomaniac, hoarder-extraordinaire mother's neighbour. Shelley thought back to the family New Year's Eve party she attended where she and Colin got engaged. Everyone was very civilized, with the usual family structure in evidence. You would be hard pressed to work out what linked this random crowd in a month of Sundays.

She couldn't help feeling nervous about the evening

ahead, even though Colin had been at great pains to reassure her that morning. He'd been so lovely. He'd said he was gutted to have missed her last night and talked openly about the family friends he had ended up spending the night with. Said how good it was to see them. Laughed about how overly affectionate they were and said he couldn't wait to bring her back and introduce her on a later trip. It had all strengthened her resolve to think that she was just being insecure and silly. That there was a perfectly reasonable explanation for everything that had occurred that weekend and she needed to brush it all off. None of it was down to the fact that she wasn't good enough for him, that he'd inevitably ditch her for someone else because she clearly wasn't in his league.

After all, Neil had said Colin was lucky to have her.

So she was worthy. Of course she was. She shouldn't read too much into the text and how things had looked in the Flaming Flamingo and assume that Colin was bound to be easily distracted by somebody better than her.

He'd chosen her.

And that was that.

She couldn't help but feel butterflies in her stomach, however, as they walked down the sweeping drive to the hotel. It wasn't helped when Nancy drew up and asked for her scooter to be put in valet parking. The porter didn't turn a hair, but Shelley could see him giving his mate on the desk a smirk as he handed the keys over after Thomas had given him a rundown on how to drive it.

They arrived in the reception area in a clatter of heels and cloud of department-store perfume and aftershave.

'Very nice,' said Ray. 'Cost a bob to stay here, I reckon.'

'Still can't believe Shelley is going to be rich,' mumbled Chloe.

'Shhh,' said Shelley and Rosalind.

'No remarks on money or status tonight,' warned Rosalind. 'Don't embarrass Shelley, will you?'

Chloe saluted Shelley and she felt her heart sink. The chances of Chloe keeping her gob shut were practically nil.

'So where is this terrace restaurant then?' said Becca. 'Shall I ask at reception?'

'Yes please,' nodded Shelley.

'We are meeting someone at the terrace restaurant,' Shelley heard her say. 'Could you tell us where to go?'

'Is this the engagement party?' asked the lady in a strong Spanish accent.

Becca shouted across reception. 'Would we call this an engagement party?'

'I'm not sure. Bit late for an engagement party, isn't it?' said Thomas, striding over to the desk to help Becca. 'Look, I'm the future bride's uncle, although I'll be standing in as her father on the day as Shelley's poor dad Gordon passed away some years ago. Now I am here to meet the father of the groom for the first time, a Jim Gifford . . .'

'Mr Gifford,' nodded the receptionist enthusiastically. 'Of course. Of course. Much apologies. We have been expecting you. Please come with me.'

The receptionist came out from behind the desk and guided them across the lobby and out round the pool to a terrace laid out with dining tables. At the far end sat Jim, Joan, Colin and Neil. Shelley felt a very hard lump form in her throat.

Jim was the first to catch sight of Shelley's gang making their way towards them. He leapt up out of his chair, revealing his relaxed-looking pale green linen shirt and chino-style trousers. Joan followed him, dressed in a cream dress that would give Shelley the heebie-jeebies to wear. It was so clean looking. She had never worn anything that pristine, she was sure. They waited at the top of the steps ready to greet their guests.

'Welcome,' said Jim, as though he owned the place. Perhaps he did, thought Shelley fleetingly. It really wouldn't surprise her. 'Peggy,' he said, stepping forward to greet her first, much to Shelley's relief. 'You look lovely. The sunshine clearly suits you.'

'We've only been here three days and I seem to have spent most of my time indoors,' returned Peggy, accepting a kiss on both cheeks from Jim and Joan, something Shelley knew her mother could not abide. 'This is my brother-in-law Thomas,' said Peggy, dipping out of the way, 'and my sister Nancy.'

'Delighted to finally meet you,' said Jim, pumping Thomas's hand.

'Likewise,' beamed Thomas. 'So glad we could make this happen before the wedding. Here, say hello, Nancy.'

Nancy stepped forward and gave Jim and Joan a full-on hug. 'Now,' she said, 'before I forget, the lovely lad on valet duty has parked my mobility scooter in your parking bay in the basement, he says. Now is that okay?'

'Bet you've never been asked that before, Dad,' laughed Neil.

'Of course, not a problem,' said Jim, looking bemused.

'Excellent,' replied Nancy. 'Apologies that I had to bring it, but I will never get back up that hill without it.'

'Don't mention it, really,' said Jim.

'Now, you must be Colin,' said Thomas, pushing his hand at Neil.

'No!' said Shelley, pointing at her fiancé. 'This is Colin.'

'Very pleased to meet you,' Colin said, shaking Thomas's hand. 'I'm sure you wish your niece was marrying the younger, better-looking one, but sorry, you are stuck with me.'

Thomas laughed a little too hard whilst pumping Colin's arm.

'So have you all met my daughter and granddaughter?' he asked.

'Just me,' nodded Colin. 'Rosalind, Chloe, this is my mum and dad, Jim and Joan, and my baby brother Neil.'

Rosalind was the first to step forward but forgot that her shaking hand was wrapped in a bandage. She offered it, then whipped it away.

'Oh dear,' said Joan, looking genuinely concerned. 'Have you hurt yourself? You didn't go on one of those banana boats, did you? They're terribly dangerous.'

'Yes I did actually,' said Rosalind. 'But that is not how I got my injury.'

'She got into a fight,' said Chloe. Of course she did.

'No need to go into detail,' said Rosalind, shaking her head.

'Wow,' declared Neil, looking her up and down. 'Who with?'

'As I said, no need to go into detail,' said Rosalind.

'She punched a man in a nightclub last night trying to protect her daughter,' explained Nancy.

'Mum!' wailed Rosalind.

'Chloe would have told them,' shrugged Nancy. 'But in a worse way. I was trying to paint you in a good light.'

'Nan had to bail her out of prison,' added Chloe.

'See,' said Nancy to her daughter. 'I was trying to get in there before your daughter.'

'Prison,' said Jim, trying to hide the shock in his voice.

'She hit him quite hard,' stated Chloe.

Shelley could feel her heart pounding. This conversation needed to end now.

'Shall we sit down?' she shrilled.

'They had no right to arrest me for protecting my own daughter,' declared Rosalind.

'They weren't doing anything,' Chloe told a shocked-looking Jim and Joan. 'Just sort of that sexy dancing thing, you know. When you grind behind somebody.'

'I'm Ray, by the way,' said Ray stepping forward. 'Peggy's neighbour. A late addition, I'm afraid. Hope that's okay?'

'Who?' asked Joan, looking at Peggy for an explanation. 'Is this . . . are you . . . no one said?'

'I didn't know he was joining us,' said Peggy. 'My sister invited him. Did she not let you know?'

'I left a message at reception to ask if it was all right,' said Nancy. 'I'm so sorry, did you not get it?'

Joan shook her head, clearly not used to spontaneous guests and how to deal with them.

'It's fine!' said Ray, backing away. 'Fine, no problem. I'll go back to the villa. I don't want to intrude—'

'Oh goodness, no,' said Jim. 'You must stay. After all, you are all dressed up. I'll get the maître d' to set an extra place, no problem at all. Of course, any special friend of Peggy's is more than welcome.'

'He's my neighbour,' said Peggy. 'Nothing more.'

'Well that's so kind,' said Ray. 'On an interesting side note, I worked for you many moons ago,' he said to Jim, who gave him a look of surprise. 'I've been a bricky, you see, and a plumber actually, so when you first started up, I did some work for you. Travelling all over the country for work, I was, and as soon as Peggy said your name, I knew I remembered it. I helped you with a housing development in Bristol. Must have been in the Sixties. Cash in hand, like. Under the radar, as it were. That's how it was then.' Ray gave Jim a knowing wink.

'Well, that was a long time ago,' Jim said quickly. 'Don't do anything like that nowadays, of course. Not on the scale we are operating on.'

'No, of course,' said Ray. 'Of course. But I like to think me taking those jobs helped set you on your way, you know. Helped you make sense of it at the time, as it were. I'm always very proud to read of your success in the papers, knowing I had a tiny part to do with it.' Ray gave a massive grin. Shelley could tell he was totally genuine, but she wasn't sure that Jim would see it that way.

'Can't wait to hear some stories about Dad when he was younger,' said Neil, winking at a delighted Ray.

'I'm Becca by the way,' said Becca, stepping forward. 'Seeing as no one has introduced me.'

'God, I'm sorry, Becca,' said Colin. 'This is Shelley's best friend,' he announced to his family.

'And I'm Neil,' said Neil. 'The other "also-ran" at this shindig. I've heard a lot about you, Becca, from Shelley and Colin. I'm hoping you're going to help me out on the day, telling me who all Shelley's friends and relatives are.'

'Yes, of course,' said Becca. 'I think I'll be able to hide a few of them up my skirt, given how big my bridesmaid dress is.'

'No it is not!' said Shelley. 'In any case, I let you pick. You can't complain about it now. That's totally not fair.'

'All right, keep your hair on,' said Becca grinning.

'Now, you all must be hungry,' said Jim. 'I know I am. You come with me, Becca,' he said, holding his arm out for her. 'I think you should sit next to me, don't you, and you can tell me all about growing up with Shelley.'

Shelley watched Becca happily follow Jim. Chloe held back to whisper in Shelley's ear.

'So far so good?' she said.

'What do you mean?' asked Shelley.

'Well, clearly they don't recognize us from the other night. Colin and Neil, I mean.'

Shelley gave Chloe a blank look.

'Spice Girls? The Flaming Flamingo?'

'Bloody hell, I'd forgotten all about that,' said Shelley, glancing nervously over at Neil and Colin. She'd not told them she'd bumped into Neil on the way out, and it would seem that Neil hadn't blown their cover either. 'Let's try not to let the cat out of the bag now, eh,' said Shelley.

'If you say so, cous',' said Chloe. 'If you say so. My lips are sealed.'

As she sat herself down Shelley allowed herself to relax ever so slightly. Jim and Thomas were already deep in conversation about some pub they used to drink in when they were young. Peggy was looking a little tight-lipped, but Nancy was doing her best to include her in a conversation with Joan and Rosalind. Neil was keeping Becca, Ray and Chloe exceptionally well entertained, to the point where Shelley was almost jealous at the gales of laughter that kept coming from their end of the table.

'This is all right, isn't it?' said Colin, sitting next to her. 'I was a bit nervous, but everyone is getting on just fine.'

Shelley nodded. She looked over at him and noticed he was biting his nails.

'I was worried because . . . well, your family are full of such characters, I wasn't sure how it was going to work,' he said.

Shelley nodded thoughtfully, looking at the polished attire of Jim and Joan afforded by wealth, contrasted with the incongruous tuxes and diamanté kaftans on her side of the table. 'We do come from very different backgrounds,' she said.

'It's going to be an interesting wedding,' said Colin.

'It sure is,' nodded Shelley.

'And I wouldn't want it any other way,' said Colin, leaning forward to kiss her. She kissed him back, really hoping he meant it.

It wasn't long before the coffees were being poured and Jim was demanding after-dinner mints be handed round by the waitress.

'These people have come all the way from England,' he boomed. 'Of course they need after-dinner mints.'

'So have you, Dad,' said Neil.

'I know, but I come here so often I'm practically native. We really should buy a villa here, you know,' he said to his wife. 'Don't you think?'

'But we already have one in the South of France. I'm not sure we need two in southern Europe,' replied Joan.

Shelley watched Becca nearly spit out her coffee at the outrageousness of the statement. Peggy shook her head in wonder.

'Fair enough,' said Jim. 'She's often right,' Jim told Thomas. 'Well, sometimes.' He gave him a wink. 'So is it time for the champagne, darling?' Jim asked Joan. 'I think it's time to have a little toast, don't you?'

'Agreed,' nodded Joan.

330

And as if by magic, champagne glasses appeared and were speedily filled with fizzing pale liquid.

Jim got to his feet in the manner of a man who was used to getting to his feet at important occasions and being listened to. No one needed to be told to be quiet; they all just looked up expectantly, somehow knowing that important words were about to be said by this clearly important man.

'Well, if anyone asks, I have to say that I can thoroughly recommend a weekend like this before one's children's wedding,' he said, looking round. 'A gathering of the two families in a delightful setting to share excellent food and wine. What more could anyone ask?'

Everyone nodded in agreement.

'It has been an absolute honour to host Shelley and Peggy, along with their nearest and dearest, and I have no doubt that by doing this, the wedding will be the marvellous occasion that we all expect it to be. I'd like to pay respects to your father, Shelley, his absence being the reason why we are here. We are sorry that he will not be presiding over events; however, having now had the chance to meet Thomas, then I know he will be a worthy stand-in. Family values are so important to us, and it is a pleasure, Shelley, to meet so many of your extended family tonight, and we look forward to meeting them again at the wedding.' He paused to pick up his glass. 'So, without further ado, if you would all raise a glass then I would like to propose a toast. To family.'

'To family!' Everyone cheered and clinked glasses happily. Shelley looked at Jim gratefully. He had summed it all up wonderfully, and made her random family feel so welcome. Perhaps everything was going to be all right. Perhaps her thinking she wasn't going to fit in was only in her mind. This was all so perfect that it was clearly meant to be. She reached over and took Colin's hand and gave it a squeeze, smiling at him through a quality wine and champagne haze.

Uncle Thomas coughed and got to his feet. He was still in his dickie bow and cummerbund and jacket. He must be so hot, thought Shelley, as he wiped his forehead.

'I feel I really should respond on behalf of Shelley and all her family and friends seated here tonight. We must all just say thank you for such splendid hospitality. You have been such generous hosts, and have created a highly memorable evening, one which we will all remember and cherish for many years to come.'

'Can I just say how much I appreciate you fitting me in last minute,' interrupted Ray. 'I can't believe I'm here, to be honest.'

'Quiet, Ray,' shushed Peggy. 'Let Thomas finish.'

'Sorry, sorry,' said Ray. 'Just wanted to—'

Peggy put her finger on her lips and shushed him. 'Carry on, Thomas.'

'We are all very grateful, including Ray,' said Thomas with a smile. 'I know you visit here a lot, but to take time out to get to know us is very impressive and we all truly appreciate it.'

'Definitely,' nodded Shelley vigorously.

'Now, whilst I'm here, I must also pay tribute to my wife, Nancy, who masterminded the occasion on our side of the fence, as it were. Persuading Peggy to come over, and getting Rosalind and Chloe here, as well as

332

of course Becca and Ray. It was no easy task, and she really put a lot of time and effort in.'

Shelley stole a glance at Peggy, who was scowling, no doubt upset to be upstaged by her sister.

'It has meant a great deal to Nancy, more than you could ever know, to get you all here together.'

Peggy audibly harrumphed.

'Especially when she's not feeling one hundred per cent.'

'Thomas!' said Nancy sternly. 'I think you've said enough.'

'If she lost a bit of weight then she might feel better,' muttered Peggy under her breath.

'Excuse me?' asked Thomas.

'Leave it!' warned Nancy.

'A mobility scooter, Thomas?' said Peggy, raising her eyebrows. 'Can't be right, can it?'

The whole table went quiet.

'Funny story,' chipped in Colin. 'I saw a woman in a nightclub the other night on a mobility scooter. Did you see her, Neil? She was there with a whole crowd dressed as the Spice Girls, I seem to remember. Funny that. Not met anyone with a mobility scooter before, and now I've met two in two days.'

Shelley looked down at her lap. She didn't dare catch anyone's eye. It was about to all fall apart, wasn't it? All fall apart, because of being spotted with a mobility scooter.

There was a long pause.

'It was you, wasn't it?' said Colin, as Shelley felt his hand withdraw from hers. She looked up. He was pointing at Nancy. 'You were on the scooter the other night. You had a similar dress thingy on, but made out of Union Jacks.'

'It's called a kaftan,' said Peggy.

'Yes, it was you,' he continued, shaking his head. 'So who were the rest of the Spice Girls up on stage then?' he asked, looking round. He looked very confused, a deep furrow appearing on his forehead.

No one said anything.

'What on earth are you talking about?' asked Joan. 'I don't understand.'

'We were in the Flaming Flamingo,' explained Colin, 'and people sometimes go there in fancy dress, you know, like on stag parties and hen parties . . .'

He stopped mid-sentence.

'It was you,' he said, looking directly at Shelley. 'All of you.' He turned to look at Rosalind and Chloe and Becca, who were all looking into their laps. 'You were all there. On the stage. Singing some silly song.'

'I didn't want to do it,' piped up Peggy. 'She made me,' she said, pointing at Nancy.

'Yes, it was us, you've got it,' said Nancy, holding her hands up in mock surrender. 'I organized the costumes. It was just a bit of fun. As you say, we were on a hen party after all, so we had to dress up.'

'I was right next to the stage,' said Colin, turning to Shelley. 'Did you not see me?'

Colin had gone white. Shelley thought she might be sick. She tried to speak but no words would come out.

'It was all Nancy's idea,' insisted Peggy. 'I thought it was wrong from the start.'

'I was trying to help,' protested Nancy. 'You know I was.'

'Really,' said Peggy. 'And this is helping, is it?' she said, gesturing around the table. The Giffords looked confused and awkward. Shelley's side just looked awkward.

'Would someone please just tell me what is going on?' asked Joan. 'Colin? Shelley?'

'I'm not really sure, to be honest,' said Colin, looking at Shelley, still deathly pale.

'Sounds like a harmless bit of dressing up,' said Jim, laughing. 'That clearly some of you enjoyed, but not so much you, hey Peggy. May I ask which Spice Girl you were?'

'Scary Spice,' replied Peggy.

'Right, right,' nodded Jim. 'Of course you were. Okay, so shall we just let Thomas continue with his speech, then we can have another toast and I can get some more champagne ordered.'

'You're right, I didn't enjoy it,' stated Peggy, looking very agitated. 'It was a stupid waste of time that has probably caused more harm than good,' she said, looking pointedly at her sister.

'Well, at least I tried to do something. Help in some way rather than sticking my head in the sand,' said Nancy, looking furtively at Shelley.

Shelley wished everyone would just shut up, especially her mother. She had no idea what had got into her.

'It's called not interfering,' continued Peggy. 'It's called keeping your nose out of other people's business. Not like you. Sticking it in here, there and everywhere

335

this weekend. I don't know what's got into you, trying to fix everything. Not to mention inviting Ray here without asking me. What on earth are you up to, Nancy?'

Nancy sat with her mouth open, unusually quiet.

'I'll tell you what she's up to,' said Thomas.

'No!' said Nancy. 'Really. No!' Tears started to roll down her cheeks.

Thomas put his arms around her, then took his handkerchief out and wiped away the tears. 'It's time,' he said, and turned to face everyone.

'She's not been interfering,' said Thomas. 'Far from it.'

Nancy had her head in her hands.

Shelley was suddenly aware of something else going on here. She'd been so wrapped up in her own problems, but something else was definitely up. Her mother was clearly really upset about something and so was Nancy by the look of it.

Thomas gave a big sigh and rubbed his forehead, clearly struggling with what to say.

'Thank you,' he finally said to Jim and Joan. 'Thank you for providing the excuse for Nancy to invite her sister, her daughter, her granddaughter and her niece over here. It has come just at the right time. I told Nancy just to invite you all,' he said, turning to face his family, 'but she didn't think you would come and she really wanted a chance . . . well, to make sure you were all going to be all right.' He swallowed and looked down.

'What do you mean?' Peggy asked.

'Look, guys,' said Nancy, pulling herself up out of her chair. She took a deep breath. 'I don't want anyone to panic. I'm going to be fine. Honestly. But I've had a little health scare.'

'What kind of health scare?' said Rosalind, immediately standing up.

'Sit down, Rosalind,' replied Nancy. 'It's complicated. But I should be fine. They've spotted it and I'm being treated, so let's not get overexcited.'

'But what is it?' asked Rosalind. 'You have to tell us what it is.'

'I told you it would be like this,' said Nancy, looking at her husband. 'So they've found a heart murmur? That's why I'm on the mobility scooter. They are going to operate and it all should be fine, *but* it gave us quite a scare and so I guess I wanted to just touch base with you all and make sure, if the worst happens, that you are all okay.'

'What do you mean "if the worst happens"?' asked Chloe quietly.

'I'm going to be fine,' repeated Nancy 'but there is always a risk with major surgery and someone my age so . . . so you see I'm just making sure. But more than likely I will be back to terrorize the lot of you as soon as I'm done.'

Everyone stared back at her.

'I'll be back,' she repeated firmly.

'She'll be back,' said Thomas, putting his hand over hers. 'She has to be.'

'Why didn't you tell us?' said Rosalind, tears beginning to roll down her face.

'Because you'd react like this,' said Nancy. 'Because I didn't want to worry you and because I don't want to stop living just because I've got this hanging over me. In fact, it's made me want to live more. Made me realize how precious every moment is, which is why it's been so amazing to have you all here and why I've been trying and probably failing to make sure that all of you make the most of every moment too. That you are all doing whatever you need to do to be happy, regardless of what other people may think. God, I didn't mean this to turn into a lecture,' she said, shaking her head, breathing far too fast. She paused, looking down at the table, before raising her head again.

'Now, I know what you are thinking, particularly you, Peggy,' she continued. 'You're thinking I have always done what makes me happy, and sometimes that has meant that others have suffered because of it. And it's meant that perhaps I've not always been the best sister and certainly not the best mother.' She paused to give a regretful smile to Rosalind and Peggy. 'It can make you very unpopular, doing what you want to do rather than what others might want you to. But I have concluded, and I have to say it has totally been reinforced this weekend, that if we all made decisions based on what makes us happy, then actually it's best for everyone, because it forces others to make decisions based on what makes them happiest too. Makes everyone take responsibility for their own happiness. That has to be right, doesn't it?' said Nancy, sitting down suddenly. 'Lecture over. I didn't mean it to come to this. But there you have it. You know it all now. Yes, I've had a bit of a hidden agenda this weekend, and perhaps I have failed miserably, but I had to try. Maybe I should have just been direct. Rosalind,' she said, turning to her daughter. 'Leave Chloe to work out her own life, because at the moment all that makes Chloe happy is rebelling against you! So, ignore her and then she'll have to find whatever it is that really makes her happy. And you, Rosalind, need to get off your backside and do something for yourself. Go train to be a teacher, go volunteer, become an MP, I don't know what it is, but stop relying on your kids and your husband to make you happy. Go work it out yourself.'

Rosalind sat staring at her mother, not saying a word. Nancy turned to her granddaughter.

'Chloe, stop focusing on your mother's anger at your decisions as a victory and enjoy your intelligence and wit and work out what you want to do with it.'

'Can I still stay here for the summer?' asked Chloe.

'That would make me very happy,' smiled Nancy.

'And Peggy,' she said, turning to her sister. 'Gordon has been gone ten years. I know you will never forget him, but being constantly maudlin is doing nothing to honour his name. Start living, Peggy. Now. You didn't die. Your husband did. Please start living again. Ray's going to help aren't you, Ray? I've booked you a cruise back to the UK, leaving tomorrow.'

'What!' shrieked Peggy.

Ray gave Nancy a thumbs up. 'Never been on a cruise,' he said. 'All you can eat buffets. Everywhere. You and I, Peggy, are going to have a ball.'

Peggy's mouth was agape; she was staring at her sister in shock.

'Don't worry, separate cabins,' said Nancy. 'You are both good people, now just go and enjoy yourselves.'

'Now Becca, I hadn't expected to need to sort you out, but it turned out that I did, given your constant whinging when you arrived.'

Becca was silently nodding. 'It's why you told me to look after Chloe, wasn't it?' she said. 'You wanted to show me that I could be a good mum; I just needed to do it my way.'

'You are a very smart lady,' said Nancy, nodding. 'I knew you'd get it. Now get on with it and *stop* whinging.'

Becca looked close to tears. 'You have changed my life,' she muttered.

'Rubbish,' said Nancy. 'I think you would have worked it out eventually.'

'What about me?' asked Shelley.

Nancy shook her head.

'Same message as for everyone else, Shelley. Just to make yourself happy. You just need to believe in who you are because you are amazing. Trust in your own feelings and when you see it, grab it.'

Shelley nodded, feeling tears prickle her eyes. Colin leaned over and took her hand. She swallowed and turned to him.

'I can't marry you,' she said quietly.

'What!' exclaimed Colin. 'What are you talking about?'

Joan and Jim gasped.

'I just can't,' said Shelley. 'I'm so sorry,' she said. 'The whole time Auntie Nancy has been speaking, all I have been thinking about is that we will not make each other happy.'

'What do you mean?' he exclaimed.

She looked at him for a moment, struggling for the words to come. 'Turns out,' she said, 'I think we've both settled.'

'No,' said Colin, 'that's not true.'

'I think it is,' she replied. 'I didn't think I had. I mean, look at you. As everyone kept telling me, I'd somehow landed my very own Prince Charming. How could marrying you be "settling"? I thought I was punching well above my weight. But then, well, I realized that you never made me feel like you were lucky to have me. Not once.'

Colin stared back at her, saying nothing.

'Other people did, but not you.' Shelley looked down at her hands and swallowed, then looked up again and cleared her throat.

'And I did see you, Colin. In the Flaming Flamingo, with that girl. Now I don't know who she is. I guess she's one of your close family friends and all that, but it doesn't really matter who she is, to be honest, because you looked like you felt lucky to be even in the same room as her. And you've never looked at me like that.'

'But . . . but . . . she is just a family friend,' whimpered Colin.

'I know,' replied Shelley. 'But you have never looked at me in that way. And I guess I don't want to spend the rest of my life wishing that you did.'

341

Colin didn't say anything, clearly too shocked to speak.

'I want to be with someone who thinks they are the luckiest man in the room to have me. Not someone who perhaps compromised because they thought I was the best they could get at the time.'

Colin still said nothing. Didn't even protest.

'Are you serious?' Jim piped up. 'I'm confused here. Are you calling off the wedding?' he demanded.

'Yes,' said Shelley, turning towards him. 'I'm so sorry. I'll pay you back for whatever you have spent. Might take me a while but I'll do it. I just know in my heart of hearts it's the wrong thing to do, and I can't quite believe I'm saying it but I am.'

'Is there someone else?' asked Colin quietly.

'What?' asked Shelley.

'Is there someone else?'

Shelley could feel herself go bright red. There wasn't. Not really. But someone else had cast a different light over her and Colin's relationship, that was all. Helped to make her realize she was with the wrong guy after all.

How did she explain that?

'No,' she said, trying to keep her voice even. 'No, there isn't. But I now think I know the type of person it would be. I've seen a glimpse of what happiness could look like so . . . maybe I'll find it someday, but for now it's about not screwing up mine or your life, Colin.'

Just at that moment the waiter arrived with fresh champagne for the next toast.

Thomas put his hand on the waiter's arm and nodded for him to leave. 'Maybe we should go now,' he said. 'Would you do me the honour of letting me pay the

342

bill, Jim, seeing as this evening hasn't quite turned out as planned?'

Jim was still in a daze. He silently shook his head and got up and walked off, quickly followed by Joan.

'I'm really so sorry,' said Shelley to Colin. Colin looked at her then got up and followed his parents.

Neil remained.

'Well, I guess that's that then,' he said.

'I'm so sorry,' said Shelley again.

'They'll be fine, eventually,' he said, nodding towards where the rest of the family had gone. 'They need to get over the shock but they'll survive. And they'll realize one day that your honesty probably saved them an expensive divorce in a few years' time!'

'Oh, I never wanted any money!' protested Shelley.

'I know you didn't,' smiled Neil. 'Which is probably why it's the right decision.'

Shelley nodded, fighting back the tears.

'Well,' said Neil, standing up. 'I'd better go and see how everyone is my side. And well, I'm just sorry that I won't get to see you all again, it would have been such a fun wedding with you lot.'

He paused and turned to Nancy.

'Best of luck with the op. Make sure you let me know that you have come through all right, won't you?'

'Of course,' said Nancy. 'Thank you.'

'So, bye then,' he said. 'It's been great knowing you. Even if it has been for too short a time.' He glanced at Shelley and left.

Shelley wondered why it felt harder saying goodbye to Neil than it did to Colin.

343

Chapter 41

Half an hour later they were all sitting around the table at Andy's bar, staring into drinks, not knowing what to say.

'Well, quite a hen weekend,' said Chloe. 'Never would have dreamed that's how they roll.'

'A hen weekend that ends with the wedding being called off,' said Becca. 'That's good for your very first one.'

'Epic,' replied Chloe. 'And one that gets me a summer in Spain!'

'All hen parties are going to be a massive disappointment from now on,' added Becca. 'I reckon that this is the best one I've ever been on. Maybe that's what hen parties should be. A true test of whether the bride really should get married.'

'Oh don't,' said Shelley. 'I still feel sick.'

'I'm proud of you,' said Rosalind.

'What?' replied Shelley, looking up.

'Well, you had – on paper – the perfect marriage lined up, yet you had the guts to walk away knowing it wasn't right. That's so brave. Most women would have snapped the hand off a man like Colin. And then to announce it at a dinner hosted by his parents. Well. I'm very much in awe of my cousin right now. You are quite an inspiration.'

'I still can't believe I did that,' said Shelley, covering her face with her hands. 'Normally . . . well, normally I would spend weeks fretting and then do nothing about it. But I just had to. I couldn't wait. I had to make a decision.'

'I'm proud of you too,' said Nancy. 'I never intended for you to come here and call off your wedding, but I did intend for you to come here and make sure you were doing everything you could to be happy.' She looked nervously over at Peggy, who so far had been exceptionally quiet. 'Are you okay, Peggy?' asked Nancy.

She nodded. 'I'm proud of you too,' she said to Shelley. 'You deserve so much more. I'm so glad you realized that.'

Shelley looked at her mother in shock. 'Did you just say that you were proud of me?'

'Of course I'm proud of you. Always have been.'

'It's really good to hear you say it,' said Shelley, tearfully.

'Well, it seems like I should have been saying a lot of things recently,' she said turning to Nancy. 'You've made me realize I've been wallowing in self-pity for far too long. Blaming other people for being unhappy. Gordon dying, you leaving, Shelley living in London and not getting married, Ray having a tip outside his door. I've had it all wrong. You were right. I have to take responsibility. Work out what makes me happy.'

Nancy reached over and took her sister's hand.

'Do you know what I'm going to do when I get home?' said Peggy.

'What?' asked Nancy.

'I'm going to help Ray clear out all his junk and we are going to spend the next few weekends at car-boot sales.'

'Both of us?' asked Ray.

'Both of us,' nodded Peggy.

'Wow,' he said. 'I love a car-boot sale. The bargains you can get.'

'You will be *selling* and not buying,' added Peggy with a grin. 'Might let you start buying again when you've cleared the lawn.'

'Agreed,' he said, shaking her hand. 'I know exactly which ones we will go to. We'll do a tour. Different one each weekend, although we might go to Glossop a couple of times because they have the best bacon butty van.'

'I'll make us some bacon butties to take with us,' said Peggy.

Ray looked as if he was about to burst into tears.

'You'll make me a bacon butty?' he asked incredulously. She nodded.

'This is the best weekend ever,' he grinned.

'And we'll be back here often,' added Peggy to Nancy. 'If you'll have us?'

'I'd like that very much,' said Nancy.

'Well, it's not quite of the quality that we were drinking earlier,' said Thomas, approaching the table with a tray holding a champagne bucket and several glasses, 'but it somehow feels appropriate that we sort of should be celebrating.'

Ray leapt up to help him hand out the glasses.

'Celebrating what?' asked Chloe. 'Shelley is no longer marrying the millionaire, the future of Mum and Dad's marriage is anyone's guess, all Auntie Peggy has to look forward to is the grand tour of car-boot sales this summer, and Nan is about to have major surgery. Sure, sounds like we have loads to celebrate.'

'Or to put it another way,' said Nancy, 'we are all taking control and making changes to make us happier people.'

'Cheers to that,' said Peggy, holding her glass up highest of everyone.

'Cheers,' they all chimed.

'Now I've taken the liberty of asking Andy to line up our song,' said Thomas to Nancy.

'Our other song?' asked Nancy.

Thomas nodded.

'Do you really want to sing that now?' she asked, looking slightly pained.

'I absolutely do,' he replied, getting up and offering his hand. 'Would you join me on the stage once again?' he asked Nancy.

The rest of the group whooped and catcalled as they made their way to the makeshift stage and got themselves organized.

This is going to kill me, thought Peggy, as the very familiar opening bars struck up. Thomas and Nancy's voices intertwined effortlessly, despite the fact the song was not a duet. But it was as they built to the chorus that Peggy felt herself grip her hands tightly round the arms of the plastic chair.

They sang out the chorus of LeAnn Rimes's slam-dunk heart-stopping, cry-fest-inducing classic, 'How Do I Live' and Peggy didn't dare look at anyone else. She swallowed and swallowed, trying to fight back the tears. She didn't need her memories of Gordon flooding back now.

She glanced up at Thomas and Nancy to see them struggling to hold back the tears too. In fact, when she looked round at the rest of the group, they were all looking pretty churned up. Shelley kept wiping her eyes. Becca was biting down hard on her lip; Rosalind was staring at her hands with a very glazed expression on her face. Only Ray looked calm. As she looked over at him, he caught her eye and smiled. He noticed the tears welling in her eyes and reached across and put his hand over hers.

'I know,' he said before he turned back to watch Nancy and Thomas.

Peggy let him leave his hand there.

There was a standing ovation when they had finished. From the entire bar. They'd nailed it. Packing the emotion in in spades. Rosalind stepped forward and hugged them both in a display of affection never before offered. When they had all settled down, Rosalind piped up: 'Do you know what I really want to do now?'

'What, Mother?' sighed Chloe.

'Go back to that foam party place. It really looked like fun, and I don't think I made the most of it last night.'

'Are you serious?' said Chloe.

Rosalind nodded.

'Is this really my mother talking?' asked Chloe, incredulous.

'It really is. Your nan was right. Time to start living.'

'Yes!' said Chloe, getting up. 'Okay then, let's go! Yeah – let's do it.'

'Aren't you banned?' asked Peggy.

'Oh yeah,' said Rosalind, sitting down. 'Damn it.'

'No probs,' said Chloe. 'We are going to give you a makeover. Even more so than last night. No one will recognize you. I promise.'

'But I don't really—'

'Come on, Mum,' said Chloe, dragging her out of her chair. 'Let's do this. Let's have the night we should have had last night. Let's have a proper hen party night, only without it being a hen party because no one is getting married anymore, thank goodness. Come on. Shelley, Becca? You coming?'

'Absolutely,' said Becca, leaping up. 'I have just the dress for you, Rosalind. You'll look amazing.'

'Okay,' said Rosalind. 'You're right. Let's do this.'

'Us oldies will stay here,' I think,' said Nancy. 'Far too much excitement for one day.'

Peggy nodded. 'Go have fun. Early night for me.'

'I am so excited!' declared Becca. 'Let's go!'

Chapter 42

'Man! I Feel Like a Woman' by Shania Twain was the tune that got them all rocking on the dance floor. All four of them lined up and danced their hearts out.

'Let's go, girl,' winked Chloe to her mum, and they all stormed the stage, euphoric. A proper girls' night. Dancing like an entire nightclub is watching. Now it felt like a real hen party.

Chapter 43

Shelley was asleep on a lounger by the pool the next day when Neil turned up. She'd seen no one all morning. The foam party gang had stayed out until 2 a.m., when Chloe had been the first to cave and admit she needed to go home to bed. Shelley was grateful that she had an excuse to leave too, as she was on her knees, as was Becca, but it was Rosalind who they couldn't persuade to go back to the villa.

'I'm staying out,' she said. 'I'll be okay – don't worry. I just need some space.'

Knowing that she had some handy scrapping skills with which to defend herself, if need be, they left her to it – looking like the happiest dancer on the planet.

Shelley felt a shadow fall over her before she opened her eyes. As soon as she recognized it was Neil, she sat up rapidly, sending her magazine flying.

'Sorry,' she spluttered. 'Wasn't expecting to see anyone.'

'It's fine,' he said, sitting down on the paving slabs. 'Please don't get up. I've been sent over to see if you are all okay. Well, actually I suggested that we should check you are all okay, and I think the rest of the family thought perhaps I would be the best person to send.'

'How are they all?' asked Shelley. 'How's Colin?'

'So-so. Ego bruised more than anything. So he'll get over that.'

'I really am sorry, you know,' added Shelley. 'I feel terrible about it.'

'I know,' replied Neil. 'Listen, I need to tell you something. Just in case it changes anything at all.' He suddenly looked serious. Pained, in fact.

'Is everything okay?' asked Shelley.

'Well, I did a stupid thing. Well, it was stupid, but I had the best of intentions and I don't know why I did it but I thought I should do it and well . . . and I need to tell you what I did.'

'Okay,' said Shelley, no clue what he was talking about.

'I sent you the text.'

'What!' said Shelley. 'What, as some kind of sick joke? Did you think that was funny?'

'No, it wasn't as a joke. I promise you. I just . . . well, I just saw how Colin was with Adriana . . .'

'That was Adriana!' exclaimed Shelley.

'Well yes,' said Neil. 'Has Colin mentioned her before?'

'Not Colin, actually. But your dad did when we got engaged. Said Colin had asked a woman called Adriana to marry him years ago and she turned him down. I . . . I just didn't put two and two together. Wow,' she said, trying to process this new information.

'I'm sorry,' said Neil. 'Perhaps I shouldn't have told you that.'

'No, you absolutely should have,' said Shelley. 'I just can't believe I didn't guess.'

'Well, I asked him if he still had feelings for her,' continued Neil, 'and he denied it but . . . I know my brother. I've seen him look like that before and I just thought you deserved better. I tried to get him to be honest with you, but he just kept denying it – he wasn't being honest with himself. So I sent the text. I sent it in the hope you would challenge him and then he would come clean. Either way. That he'd either fight for you or realize he still had feelings for Adriana. I don't know what I was thinking, to be honest, but I knew you had to talk, and it was the only way I could think of making you. Honestly.'

'Wow,' said Shelley. 'I never expected it to be you.'

'I felt you should know it was me,' he said. 'So you can hate me or blame me or whatever, or if I took it a step too far then you can go and tell Colin it was all my fault. Do whatever you need to do.'

'You've not told Colin.'

He looked away, not able to meet her eye. 'No. But you can. If you want to. Then you can both blame me and put the wedding back on, if that's what you think you want to do.'

Shelley didn't hesitate. She shook her head.

'You did us a favour,' she said. 'You really did. Even more so now I know it was Adriana. You saved me from soon being a divorced woman. Because that is exactly what would have happened.'

Neil nodded thoughtfully. 'I'm so sorry it turned out this way,' he said.

Shelley shrugged. 'I'm somehow not surprised but I do feel relieved. I'm kind of overwhelmed with relief, in fact.'

Neil sighed. 'Thanks for telling me that. I've had a few sleepless nights, I can tell you.'

'I feel terrible about the cost of the wedding, though,' said Shelley. 'I will pay for anything that your dad is out of pocket on. I meant what I said last night. It might take a while, but I will pay it all back.'

'Oh, I had an idea about that actually. So they should be able to cancel some of it, but I suggested to Dad that he turn it into a big charity fundraiser. You know – sell tickets and have an auction or something in the marquee. Great PR for the firm and makes Dad look good – so all is not lost.'

Shelley nodded. 'That is a good idea, but your dad will still be out of pocket somewhere. I need to make that right.'

'My dad has very big pockets – he'll barely notice. If he does a fundraiser, he can write a load of it off against tax. He wouldn't accept your money anyway – you know that, don't you?'

Shelley sighed. 'Well, that's really good of him.'

'He never begrudged paying for the wedding, you know,' said Neil. 'He really liked you.'

'Really. I bet he doesn't now.'

'He'll come round. But he knows you are genuine. He gets that. He was really hoping that Colin would marry someone like you, not the airheads he typically goes for.'

'Well, that's up to Colin, now isn't it?'

'And what about you?' asked Neil. 'What will you do now?'

Shelley shrugged. 'Back to the job I love. Back to the kids. Rebuild again. It's all right. I've done it many times before. Oh, watch out, Mother is looming.'

Peggy approached them holding a mug of coffee.

'Hello Neil,' she said, looking puzzled. 'When did you arrive?'

'Just now,' he said, scrambling up. 'I was sent to see how everyone is.'

'Well, that is very kind in the circumstances, isn't it Shelley?'

'Amazingly kind,' agreed Shelley.

'Can I get you a drink, Neil?' asked Peggy.

'No, no, I'd better go back. I promised Colin I'd go sailing with him this afternoon – take his mind off it.'

'Thanks for coming over,' said Shelley. 'I really do appreciate it.'

'No problem. Goodbye then.'

'Goodbye,' said Shelley.

'Bye,' said Peggy.

They both watched him disappear past the end of the pool.

'Shame he's Colin's brother,' said Peggy, picking up the magazine and starting to flick through it. 'I could see you two together.'

Chapter 44

'She's not there,' said Chloe, running into the kitchen. 'Looks like she didn't come home!'

'What do you mean?' said Nancy. 'She must be there.'

'Her bed has not been slept in,' said Chloe.

'Why did you not notice before?' asked Nancy. 'We have to leave to take her to the airport in half an hour.'

'I don't know,' replied Chloe. 'I don't normally check whether my mother is in bed or not.'

'One day,' said Nancy through gritted teeth, 'you will spend your life worrying about whether your daughter is safe in bed or not.'

They were interrupted by an almighty roar outside the kitchen window. Nancy and Chloe looked out to see what on earth was happening. A large black motorcycle had just turned up and halted outside the villa.

'Who the hell is that?' asked Nancy. 'They'll wake all the neighbours. Don't they realize it's a Sunday?'

The person on the back threw their leg over and dismounted before reaching up to pull off their helmet.

The lady, as it turned out, shook out her hair to reveal Rosalind with a massive grin on her face.

'What the . . . ?' began Chloe, still staring out of the window.

'No swearing in this house,' said Nancy.

'Sorry Nan, but I mean, is that really my mother?'

'Looks like it.'

'She's stayed out all night?'

'Looks like it.'

They watched as she handed the helmet back to the rider, who looped it over the handle bar, turned their bike around and accelerated away. Rosalind stood and waved until they disappeared at the end of the road.

'I must be seeing things,' said Chloe.

'Oh hi,' said Rosalind breezily as she walked in. 'Sorry if I worried you,' with a look that said she wasn't sorry in the slightest.

'Well your daughter has only just noticed you hadn't come back. Where have you been?' asked Nancy.

'Oh, I just got dancing with this crowd and then we ended up going to a bar and it was late so I slept on their sofa, that's all.' Rosalind whistled as she went to put the kettle on.

Chloe and Nancy exchanged looks.

'And who was that man who brought you home?' asked Chloe, aghast. 'You would kill me if I did that – stayed out all night then let a strange man bring me home on his bike. What were you thinking, Mother?'

Rosalind paused and laughed.

'It wasn't a bloke. It was Bridget. She lives here but used to live in Wandsworth. Anyway, best go and pack. We need to leave for the airport soon, hey?'

Rosalind disappeared, leaving Chloe and Nancy open-mouthed.

'Guess she really took you seriously last night,' said Chloe.

Chapter 45

Present day

'Mum!' came the shout from behind the door.

Shelley, Peggy, Rosalind, Becca and Chloe all looked at each other and smiled.

'Are you ready? Dad says to get a move on. He's waited nearly eighteen years and he can't wait any longer.'

Shelley laughed.

Gemma burst in wearing a cream trouser suit, looking immaculate for her seventeen years. She had chosen to support her father today as best woman rather than just be another bridesmaid, seeing as her mother had insisted on so many.

'We were just reminiscing,' said Shelley. 'We're coming now.'

'What about?' asked Gemma. 'And why now? Come on, there is a desperate man down there.'

'We were remembering a very special weekend twenty years ago,' said Peggy. 'And what a difference it made to all of us. Well, we wouldn't have you otherwise, for a start,' she said, stepping forward and embracing her beloved granddaughter.

'I'd be divorced, I reckon,' said Becca. 'A single mum, can you imagine! I would have murdered one of the boys for sure.'

Gemma gasped, 'Not Toby!' she said.

Shelley smiled at Becca. Gemma had a bit of a crush on Toby.

'I'd be homeless probably,' said Chloe. 'Jesus, I was a nightmare way back then. Do you remember? I'd dropped out of college! What was I thinking?'

'And now look at you, Mrs Professor,' said Rosalind, smirking at her daughter.

'Yeah, no thanks to you!' said Chloe. 'Mind you, you were a bigger train wreck than me,' said Chloe to her mother. 'Total basket case.'

'You still seem kind of crazy to me,' said Gemma, giving her a sideways glance.

Rosalind laughed. 'I was different crazy then. Miserable crazy. The worst kind.'

'If only Auntie Nancy was here to see us all,' said Shelley. 'I reckon she'd be very proud.'

'She nearly made it,' said Rosalind with a sigh. 'She lasted – what – another ten years after her heart op.'

'I'm so glad she lasted long enough to meet her namesake,' said Peggy, grinning at Chloe. 'She loved that you called your eldest Nancy, Chloe.'

'She's a proper Nancy too,' grinned back Chloe. 'Busy telling us all what to do. She already is taking after her great-grandma.'

'And she lasted long enough to attend all the other weddings we've had,' said Shelley. 'Chloe and Daniel, Rosalind and Valerie and Peggy and Ray.'

'Oh yes, she made sure she was centre stage for all those weddings,' said Peggy. 'Still, I really think she would have liked to have been at this one.'

'I know,' said Shelley. 'And I wish she was here. Because I know I wouldn't be getting married feeling this happy if it wasn't for her.'

'If it wasn't for her, you'd have married Colin,' said Chloe bluntly.

'My God, can you imagine?' said Peggy, shaking her head.

'Not Uncle Colin?' asked Gemma, screwing her face up in confusion.

Shelley turned to her daughter and gasped. 'Oh God,' she said. 'We . . . I . . . yes . . . well yes, but I can explain . . .'

'You were going to marry Uncle Colin?' said Gemma, shaking her head. 'But he's been divorced twice!'

'Yes, I know,' flustered Shelley. 'Look, it was a long time ago and we always thought it wasn't worth telling you and it was just complicated and—'

'So you were engaged to Uncle Colin before you got together with Dad?'

'Yes, well yes. This really is the wrong time to be doing this, but yes, I was engaged to your Uncle Colin – nearly twenty years ago – and this weekend we were talking about my hen party and I realized – well, Nancy made me realize . . . well, she made us all realize a lot of things and so I called it off and I didn't intend to see your father ever again. But well, Grandpa Ray invited him to meet the dairy farmer that Dad used to work for because he wanted to learn how to milk, and Grandma invited me up to stay the same weekend without telling me that Neil, your dad, was going to be there. And well, we kind of got it together and then it all snowballed and we kept it really quiet for a while because of Uncle Colin, but eventually we had to come clean because we wanted to be together and we wanted you – we both wanted to have a baby and so we did; and well, we felt we couldn't get married – not then. Not since I'd not married Colin, so we agreed not to get married. For Colin's sake.'

'Uncle Colin is rubbish at weddings,' agreed Gemma.

'Totally,' said Shelley.

Gemma thought for a moment.

'It's taken you nearly twenty years after that weekend to get married?' asked Gemma.

Shelley nodded. 'It was quite a weekend.'

'I think we'd better get going then, hadn't we?' said Gemma. 'Dad looks like he's about to explode.'

'I do,' she said emphatically about twenty minutes later. Peggy, Chloe and Rosalind cheered. Shelley glanced over at them. Peggy was sitting on the front row with Ray, their hands clenched firmly together. Ray gave her a little wave and held his wife's hand aloft in victory. He looked almost as happy as he had done on their wedding day some ten years ago. Their tour of Derbyshire car-boot sales proved to be a cleansing and bonding experience until, whenever Shelley visited, she noticed that Ray's boots seemed to be permanently in the hallway and his garden was permanently tidy. And

362

Peggy was smiling for quite a lot of the time. Their wedding had been a small affair in Andelica, hosted by Nancy and Thomas, of course. Very different to Peggy's first wedding. Warm, for a start.

And then there was Rosalind sitting next to Peggy. Tears in her eyes. Valerie, her wife, handing her a tissue. What an amazing wedding theirs had been. In a field, and almost no men apart from Thomas, Ray and Neil. They stuck together like glue, half afraid of the abundance of female joy around them. And, of course, Chloe's wedding in her Cambridge chapel. Rosalind bursting with joy and happiness at where her daughter had ended up in life since the day she started ignoring her.

And now here Shelley was, finally at her own wedding day, standing in front of Neil. The man she had loved for a very long time.

'I do,' said Neil loudly when he was asked the crucial question.

Jim and Joan cheered. Colin didn't. Colin was too busy stroking the hand of the twenty-something girl he had brought along as his plus one.

A few hours later, Shelley got up and did a speech. She'd waited a long time for her wedding, and she wasn't going to miss the chance to say what she wanted. A hush fell around the marquee as she cleared her throat.

'I first met my husband nearly twenty years ago at a wedding reception,' she said. 'It was at a very fancy place and, as I was in my late thirties, I couldn't have been more jealous of the young bride walking down the aisle. But as I look around now, I know I have got married to exactly the right man in exactly the right place at exactly the right time.'

Everyone cheered and clapped. Shelley patiently waited for quiet.

'Here we are, in a marquee on the farm where my dad used to work,' she continued. 'My dad would have thought this was amazing as he could give me away, have his dinner and then still have time for milking!'

Everyone laughed. Most of all Peggy.

'My husband's dream has always been to own a dairy farm,' continued Shelley. 'So, when this farm became available, it made his dream come true to buy it. And now this is our home, it made perfect sense to get married here and now. The most perfect wedding day. No compromises.' She glanced over at Neil who beamed back at her. 'To the perfect day,' she said and raised her glass.

Acknowledgements

I'd like to start by thanking my distractors for doing their absolute best to not distract me too much during the writing of this book. This novel was written and edited during the Covid-19 pandemic and so my usual empty house/office was inundated by children home-schooling and husband home-working. Challenging for all of us to achieve anything, we kept each other sane whilst driving each other mad! I wouldn't want to be cooped up with anyone else, so thank you Bruce, Tom, Sally and of course, Connie the dog, for being there (sometimes literally standing right next to me) as I wrote.

Thanks must also go to Kate Bradley and the rest of the team at HarperCollins for cheering me on through this creation. You have been great, Kate, at pushing me on and having faith in this book throughout. I've never needed it more.

Madeleine Milburn and Hannah Todd, of the Madeleine Milburn Agency, I know you have my back, which I so appreciate. Thank you for your continued support.

These past couple of years, many more people have experienced the highs and lows of working from home. For me it has highlighted the incredible value of our

So here is my idiots guide to being a hen that will set you on the right track for a successful send-off, whatever you mean to the bride-to-be.

BEST FRIEND/CHIEF BRIDESMAID:
STAY SOBER

I know – dull as hell but you are the MC, the negotiator, the nurse, the queuer, the tour guide, the tissue provider. Do not be confused. Your job is *not* to have a good time. Your job is to somehow navigate the treacherous path of herding a random group of women safely through a night out and make sure that your best mate can say at the end 'I had the best night ever'. This might be the hardest night of your life and I am not joking. You cannot do this drunk. You will fail.

What to wear: A utility belt - there is no end to the equipment that could be called upon.

Key accessory: Slippers for the bride to walk home in. Guaranteed to make her night.

MOTHER OF THE BRIDE:
KEEP YOUR OPINIONS TO YOURSELF

Your daughter's hen party is not the time to be saying that you preferred her last boyfriend. Or that you have never liked any of her friends. Or to have a stand-up row with your daughter's future mother-in-law about the table plan at the wedding. Your only opinion is that you are very proud and that you think your daughter has chosen wisely to marry a man twice her age. With this in mind I strongly advise that you also stay sober. If you get drunk, not only are you more likely to share some honest opinions but you also run into the danger of stealing the limelight from your daughter. You become the person everyone talks about. 'How was the hen night?' 'Great. Cassie's Mum got absolutely hammered.' Do you really want that? No one wants you to have had the best time. It just shows everyone else up. Just be a mum.

What to wear: Flat shoes – it's unlikely you'll get to sit down – they don't do that in pubs anymore!

Key accessory: A mother-of-the-bride sash so no one thinks you are just some sad old lady come out on her own.

OLDEST FRIENDS FROM WAY BACK: TELL LOTS OF HUMILIATING STORIES ABOUT THE BRIDE

You arguably have the best role on a hen party. You've stuck together through thick and thin. Your friendship is bulletproof so this is your chance to throw in the grenades and reminisce via the brides most embarrassing moments. Show her new friends that you go way deeper. Stake your claim. Show them that they may think they are close to the bride, but they will never share the closeness of watching her pee in a paddling pool at five years old.

What to wear: Penis deely boppers. Go as low as possible, because you can.

Key accessory: Phone with hideous old pictures of the bride-to-be scanned in.

WORK COLLEAGUES:
FORGET EVERYTHING YOU SEE AND HEAR

We all have a work persona. We all present ourselves in a peculiar way in our job. Even at work bashes there is still a line we draw keeping our true selves just behind it. But a poor hen is stripped bare on a hen night surrounded by family and her life choices. The temptation is to judge her by those she mixes with out of work. But for you more than anyone: what happens on a hen party, stays on a hen party. Wipe your memory and move on. If need be get very, very drunk so you forget everything.

What to wear: Beer goggles

Key accessory: Hip flask

GROOM'S MOTHER/SISTER:
STAY AT HOME

However much you love your future daughter-in-law, seeing her with her head down a toilet, throwing up or asking a strange man to hand over his underpants is not a visual you want to hold in your head. Especially as you watch your precious son commit his life to someone who you last saw spank a naked butler's backside. Make your excuses, steer clear and enjoy the ignorance.

What to wear: A dressing gown

Key accessory: Netflix

SINGLE FRIENDS:
PULL

Nothing captures male attention more that a hen party. So make the most of it. There is never an easier occasion to approach a man at a bar than if you are on a hen night. Get in with the chief bridesmaid beforehand and make sure there are challenges which require you to approach men on behalf of the bride. If they are not interested, you can just walk away. Zero embarrassment. You were doing it for the bride-to-be. If they do show some positive signals then chat away, throw some positive signals back and if it means you get left behind by the rest of the party, so be it. The bride-to-be has got her man, she wouldn't deny you chatting up your potential future husband, would she?

What to wear: Your phone number on a placard round your neck

Key accessory: A wedding invite with a plus one – yet to be allocated.

If you want more hilarious fiction from Tracy Bloom, pick up her feel-good read *The Wife Who Got a Life*, available now.

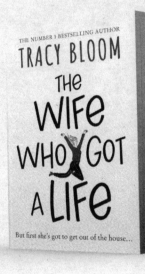